**Queen & Country**



This is a work of fiction. All of the characters, organisations, and events portrayed in this novel are either products of the author's imagination or are used fictitiously.

Print ISBN: 979-8-9916638-0-9

Cover design by 100 Covers

Editor: Janet F Williams www.janetfwilliams.com and www.gooddaymedia.com

## Acknowledgements

I'm grateful to the following beta readers: D A Hartman, Teresa Purkis, Wayne Berman and Todd C Ramsay.

I'm especially grateful to Todd C Ramsay, my writing partner, for his companionship through this journey and for his wisdom and encouragement.

My thanks also to Karin Kallmaker for some valuable coaching on the beginning of the novel and to The Stallion Springs Writer's Group, led by Kathleen Kline, for helping me get started.

To Eunice, my wife and Encourager in Chief. If it weren't for you, I would never have started, let alone finished, any of my novels. I love you.

## Dedication

This work is dedicated to the many hundreds of women wrongly discharged from the British Army.

## LGBT Veterans' Independent Review Report

Findings from the LGBT Veteran's Independent Review Report, conducted in 2022 and made available to the public in 2023, resulted in Prime Minister Rishi Sunak apologising to all veterans who had served and been mistreated between 1967 and 2014.

The report is thorough in its research and recommendations and is available at https://www.gov.uk/government/publications/lgbt-veterans-independent-review. It documents many of the atrocities committed against LGBTQ veterans. Some of them deny belief and are horrific to read.

The report made numerous recommendations, including restoring medals and pensions. While the intention is good, many personnel records have been destroyed, and some veterans are so scarred by what they endured that they may not come forward to collect what is rightfully theirs.

## Chapter 1

*September 1970. Harold Hill, Essex, England.*

After school, Jo changed into her jeans and T-shirt to meet Terry in their usual haunt, known locally as 'The Field'. She and Terry had met there every day during the summer holidays, during which they had built themselves a den underneath an old May Tree. Now that school had restarted, their time was limited to the evenings. The warm summer sun would set just past seven in the autumn. The two teenagers would meet every evening in their make-believe house until the weather changed and the skies darkened for the winter.

Jo jogged through the patch of wilderness. The golden knee-length grass swished against her jeans as she navigated the narrow winding track to the river. Deep, brown water flowed in the brook that divided Farmer Elkins' land from the council estate. The river flooded in winter, saving the field from being built upon. Next to the river was an ancient oak tree, over which a rope had been slung so the local teenagers could swing over the water and back again. The boys dared each other to swing across the river and land on the farm. Legend had it that if Elkins caught you, he would give you a good hiding. Nobody ever dared to stop for one second on the other bank.

As Jo approached the brook, she heard the boys yelling and cheering. She wrinkled her nose as she neared the farm. The acrid smell of cow dung told her the cattle had been pastured across the water. She slowed to a walk to admire the graceful swifts and swallows, diving and feeding on the insects the cow pats attracted.

She looked around for Terry as she got to their makeshift home. A long branch swept from its crown to the ground, forming a front door, hiding what was inside. Jo pulled it back, carefully avoiding the thorns, and saw Terry huddled on the edge of the square they had dug out to create a sunken floor. They built it after Terry confessed to Jo that she never wanted to go home again she wanted to live with Jo.

Jo knew her best friend wore the same clothes every day, that she only had one pair of jeans and a jumper, and that her father, Mr White, was bad-tempered. And she wanted to protect Terry as much as she could, so she came up with the idea of making a pretend home in the tree's drooping branches, hollowing out a sunken floor decorated with pebbles imitating a Roman mosaic, just as they had learned in history that year. Jo filled it with love; her mother gave them food, and they retreated there as often as possible, so Terry didn't have to be with her family until teatime.

'Hello. Mum gave me sarnies and an apple for you.' Jo proffered a plastic box, then leant her lanky frame against the tree trunk.

'Thanks, Jo.' Terry got up and placed the box into a nook they had carved into the tree. 'I'll eat it later. Let's go and play on the rope swing!'

Jo and Terry sauntered towards the group of boys they shared a class with. This year, at the age of thirteen, their voices were beginning to break, and instead of welcoming both girls to the rope swing as they had done in previous years, Jo and Terry met with some resistance to their presence.

Jo kept her distance as Terry negotiated with a tall boy before he handed the rope to her as the rest of his gang sniggered insults. Jo longed to show them how brave she was and how far she could swing over the river. Farmer Elkins did not scare her, but her mother did, and she had forbidden Jo from using the rope swing. So, she contented herself with admiring her best friend's athleticism. Jo knew that Terry's prowess and command of the rope swing impressed the boys as much as it did her, and maybe they were all just a bit jealous of Terry's skills.

'You gotta land both feet on the other side. Right. You promised. Then we'll let you have another go.' The boy commanded.

Terry, though scrawny, had the promise of muscles that Jo would never have. She grasped the rope as high as she could reach. Jo moved nearer, running a hand through her short, fair hair.

'Terry, be careful. Don't do what they say!' Jo warned, 'Remember Elkins!'

Terry grinned confidently, shaking her brown fringe from her eyes before taking a few steps back until she could barely hang onto it. Then she sprinted towards the brook, taking her bottom hand off and placing it higher above her other as she flew out over the water.

'Feet on the bank, Terry,' The tall boy shouted.

Terry dropped onto the farmland, struggling to keep the rope as it jerked out of her hand. Jo ran towards the boys, who captured it.

The boys gleefully danced silly jigs because they had Terry captive on the other side. The tall boy mocked Terry in a voice cracking with adolescent uncertainty for failing to keep hold of her lifeline.

Incensed, Jo strode to Terry's tormenter, who was a head taller. She demanded the rope. He laughed at her. Jo clenched her fists, assuming the boxer's stance her father had coached her in so she could defend herself. Today, she needed to call upon those skills for real. Moving lightly on her feet, she advanced toward him while he mocked her as she dodged and weaved before delivering her best uppercut to the boy's chin. Her punch landed solidly, surprising to both Jo and the boy. He hit the ground like a fallen tree. Jo stood over him, trying to shake off the pain in her hand while ensuring he didn't get up. Jo realised this was the moment she could rescue Terry, and she grabbed the rope, throwing it across the water with all her might. As she gave it flight, the boys wrestled her to the ground. Jo wriggled underneath a pile of boys to free herself from their blows, kicks and strangleholds.

Terry caught the lifeline and swept back to aid Jo, who was struggling to free herself from the bottom of a heap of boys, fists lying and legs kicking.

Terry pulled the boys off one at a time from the melee using their trouser waistbands. It was an effective strategy, rendering the fighter useless while he writhed on the floor, clutching his crotch. Finally, after eliminating three of the lads, Jo sat astride the leader's chest. He knew what was coming. He had already tasted his blood. Jo glared at him. She was tempted to punch him again and was preparing to give him the whacking of his life when she realised Terry had despatched the others, who were red-faced and lying on the ground, cradling their groins.

'Blimey Terry, that was fast.'

Terry laughed. 'Boys and their balls! Easy targets when you know how. Leave him be, Jo. He's had enough. Come on, let's go!'

Together, they strolled to their den, pretending nonchalance. Once inside, Terry opened the plastic box to get a sandwich and sat on the edge of the floor. 'Whoa, that was close!' Terry, buoyed up by adrenaline, tucked into the jam sandwiches. 'Want one?'

'Nah. My hand hurts, and I'll have a few black 'n' blues tomorrow. You okay? Anyway, Mum's got Shepherd's pie for me. She'll keep it warm in the oven until I get back. You eat them all.' Jo sat down.

Terry smiled and then sniffed. 'Thank your Mum for me. I doubt Dad'll let me have any tea tonight, especially if he knows I've been down here with the boys.'

'Why? I thought he was okay with you being here.'

'He says now I'm thirteen, I've got to start being more ladylike, and I shouldn't play with boys.'

'So, he doesn't know you're here?' Jo's voice quavered with concern.

'Nope! If he finds out, he'll belt me, good and proper.'

Jo knew Mr White's reputation and was concerned at Terry's matter-of-fact tone. 'My dad says your dad's a heathen. Needs a taste of his own medicine. And he's a good mind to give it 'im.'

'What's a heeven?'

'Dunno, but it's bad. My mum told him to stop.' Jo got up, her mind recoiled at the thought of Mr White and his belt.

Terry finished her sandwich and tucked into her apple, handing Jo the sandwich box. 'Thanks. What time is it?' She carried on munching.

'Dunno. I left ours at five, so I'm guessing six?'

Terry sprung from her perch. She popped the rest of the apple into the pocket of her cardigan. 'I gotta go. Tea's at six. Bloody hell. Dad'll give me a larruping if I ain't home in time.'

'I thought you said you weren't getting any tea?'

'Doesn't matter. I still have to be home in time for it.' Terry sprinted down the narrow lane leading to her home. Jo was out of breath by the time she caught up with her.

'Want me to come with you?'

'Nah, best not.'

Panting, Jo stopped running to watch her friend sprint up the road through the garden gate and stop at the front door. Anxious to remain hidden, she inched towards Terry's house using the unkempt privet hedge for cover. She stopped at the gate, worried about what Mr White might do.

Terry's mum opened the front door, a scraggy, grey-haired woman in a homemade flowery pinny. Jo breathed a sigh of relief as Terry stood on the doorstep and conversed with her mother. When Terry attempted to step inside, a beefy man in a string vest and brown trousers with braces dangling around his hips confronted her, then shoved her backwards off the step.

Jo heard the crack of Terry's skull on the cement and ran to her friend. 'You all right, Terry?'

Terry sat up and rubbed her head. She looked in horror at the blood smeared over her fingers and palm. Jo spun around to face Mr White, her hands on her hips, legs astride.

'You can't do that, Mr White. That ain't fair. I kept her. You should punish me, not her.'

'Get out of it! You hoighty-toighty little shit. It's none of your effin business. Now fuck off.' Mr White curled his fist and gesticulated for Jo to leave. Mrs White shrank back into the house. Terry got to her feet, staggering a few steps. Jo pulled her friend's arm over her shoulder to steady her.

'Can I come in, Dad?'

'Get in yer bed. Go on, where the rubbish goes.'

Terry shuffled to the dustbin, pleading with her father for clemency.

'Get in the bin. I'm not gonna say it twice. Don't make me take my belt to you.'

Jo watched, mesmerised by the brutality on display. Her natural instinct was to rescue her friend, but her instincts also told her what she was witnessing was something to fear.

Terry reluctantly took off the lid. A feeling of powerlessness swept over Jo, followed by anger.

'Put the lid on!' Mr White's face was livid with power. He turned to Jo. 'And you! 'Aven't I told you to fuck off already?'

Jo chewed her bottom lip as she watched her friend crumple and disappear inside the metal container, pulling the lid over her head. Outrage mixed with fear swirled in her brain. Before running to Terry's side, she sized up Mr White's porky frame fuelled by drink.

'Get out, Terry. Get out!' Jo tore the lid off the dustbin.

Terry stood up, trying to grab the dustbin lid back from Jo.

'I gotta Jo. I don't want the belt. He'll give me the buckle end.'

'No, he won't!' Jo threw the lid to the ground before turning to shout at Mr White. 'She's coming home with me. So, you fuck off.' Jo dragged Terry out of the bin.

'Run!' Jo shouted, keeping her eyes on Mr White. 'Run!'

The pair ran for the safety of the Clark's house.

Puffing hard, Jo pushed open the kitchen door. Terry fell up the back step and pushed Jo onto the floor. The two girls landed in a heap, breathless from their escape.

'What's all this, Josephine Clark?' Sylvia Clark demanded, rising from the kitchen table.

'Terry's dad.' Jo gulped air. 'Made her get in a dustbin.' She got up, brushing herself down. 'That ain't right!' Though she was indignant at Terry's treatment, she was glad to be home with her parents, who never beat her or made her sleep anywhere but her own bed.

Jo watched her parents exchange anxious glances. Her father got up from the table and pulled out a chair for Terry.

'We can't be 'aving that now, can we? Terry, you'll eat with us. Alright, Mother?' Jo heard her father's Yorkshire accent thicken as it always did when he was emotional. She knew then everything would be all right.

Her mother smiled at Jo before reaching into a cupboard for two plates and placing them on the table with the Shepherd's pie. 'Terry, help yourself, love.'

Terry looked to Jo for permission. Jo knew what was left was her dinner and a second helping for her father. Grateful for his generosity, she gave him a fulsome smile before cutting the remainder of the pie in two.

'Come on, Terry love, dig in. God knows you could do with fattening up. It's bed at eight—right, Jo?' her mother commanded.

'Can Terry stay the night?'

'I was just going to make up the spare room for Linda. That way, you can be together. Would you like that, Terry?'

Terry nodded. A contented smile spread across her face.

'I'd like her to stay every night.' Jo got up and cuddled into her father's broad shoulders.

'Would you now?' Her father pulled her in tighter. 'Terry can stay as long as she likes, can't she, Mother? That's if your dad doesn't mind.'

'Me, Dad, don't care.' Terry shrugged.

'No, I don't suppose he does.' Jo saw her father's disapproval in the slow shake of his head.

Her mother leaned her slender but shapely body against the sink. 'You'll need to talk to the White's, Brian. We don't want the authorities involved.'

'I know. I'll chat to White.' Her father hugged her tighter. 'It'll be all right, lass. I'll make sure of it. Don't you worry, now.'

Later in the evening, after they had bathed, Terry, in borrowed pyjamas, sat on one of the twin beds in Jo and her sister Linda's room. Jo sat beside her, wrapping a protective arm around her best friend.

‘Thanks for rescuing me, Jo. I hope your dad speaks to my dad, and I don’t have to go back.’

‘Me too. I’ll always be there for you, Terry, no matter what.’

‘Same for me, Jo. Always, no matter what.’ Terry clumsily pecked Jo’s cheek. Jo felt Terry’s soft lips upon her face and a somersault in her stomach that was both surprising and pleasant. Jo thought if she’d been a cat, she would have purred.

## Chapter 2

Friday 13 April 1984. 12 Company Women's Royal Army Corps, Mill Hill, London.

Jo and Terry worked at a local greengrocer after they left school at sixteen. Their relationship had blossomed from a peck on the cheek to lovers with Terry taking the lead on nearly everything. Terry decided they should join the Army because they were bored with serving fruit and vegetables. At the Army recruiter's office, Jo was excited about the opportunities. She realised that joining the Army meant Terry could escape her past and they could become independent women—they would rely on no man. Jo persuaded Terry of the financial benefits while Terry fantasised about the promise to travel the world. Ironically, they were both based in London, less than forty miles from Jo's family home.

This morning, as she had done every morning for the last four weeks, she met Terry at the gym around seven to run the Army's Basic Fitness Test course before she started her shift at eight-thirty as a Postal and Courier Operator. It was the only way the lovers could legitimately spend time together every day, and they cherished the twenty or so minutes they spent running together. She jogged through the barracks, grateful the forecasted April showers had not begun. The moment she opened the doors to the gym shared by the men from the Royal Engineers and the women of the WRAC, Deep Heat liniment and what she thought to be foetid jockstraps abused her nostrils. She rapped on the open door labelled Female PTI three times.

'Good morning, Sarn't White.' Jo stood to attention, grinning. 'Corporal Clark reporting for a run, Sergeant White.'

Terry played along with the charade. 'Corporal Clark! You are a professional soldier! Act like one!' She pointed to a poster on the wall of a man in combat kit running with his rifle and read the caption. "Are you fit to fight! Be alert!" She turned to face Jo, stifling a giggle. 'Are you a Lert?'

'Yes, sergeant!' Jo snapped out her reply, hamming her respect for Terry's senior rank.

'Then let's be 'aving you!' Terry laughed as she barked the jocular hurry-up used by senior ranks to their subordinates and occasionally to errant junior officers.

Terry retrieved a stopwatch from her desk drawer, and the pair jogged to a start line outside. Jo gently barged Terry's muscular upper arm with her shoulder, causing her to fall off balance. Terry responded by starting her stopwatch the moment she took off, leaving Jo behind before shouting 'go'. She looked over her shoulder and shouted to Jo. 'Did you say you'd beat me? I don't think so!'

Jo quickly caught up with Terry.

'What took you so long, Corporal?'

'I was admiring your pert backside in those tight blue tracksuit trousers, Sarn't.'

'Shame you're not as fast as you are, cheeky!'

'Seriously, Terry, I don't know how I will get through my day without seeing you in your sexy PTI kit.'

Terry, smiling, slapped Jo's upper arm. 'Shut up, you plonker!'

Their footfall pounded the pavement in a steady rhythm, ensuring they would make the allotted time with a minute or two to spare.

'Is it today—the big heist?' Terry joked, controlling her breathing.

'Yeah. Can't wait for it to be over. It's been hard pretending to be someone I'm not for four weeks.' Her attachment to the Special Investigations Branch meant she had to be undercover, posing as a Postal and Courier Operator. Today, they planned to make arrests based on the intel she had gleaned—surely, she would be promoted after this tough assignment—she had proved herself–hadn't she? 'I'm going to miss you badly. But maybe it's for the best. People might gossip, seeing us together all the time. Neither of us can afford that.'

'I'll miss you too, popping in and out of the gym. But I know what you mean. Max asked me if we were a couple.'

'Shit! What did you say?' Jo felt the heat of lies and fear flash through her body. They had too much to lose if gossip outed them. After ten years of service, they would qualify for a decent pension, but if they were dishonourably discharged, they would never receive it. And, with no references, they would likely be unemployed for a long time.

'I changed the subject.'

'Brilliant!' Jo picked up her pace. 'Come on, short arse, keep up.'

Terry sped up to keep up with Jo's long legs.

'I might be a short arse, but at least I'm not a Monkey.' Terry teased.

'Ohh, below the belt. You know that's not nice.' Jo laughed and wagged a finger at Terry for using the derogatory nickname for the Military Police. 'I can't help that Army selection thought I would make an excellent policewoman. Someone's got to do it. Might as well be me.'

'But no one likes the RMP. And the SIB are hated. That's got to hurt,' reasoned Terry.

'Can't all be running and jumping and throwing things for a living. Someone's got to keep the rules.'

'True. But if you get SIB, you could end up investigating—well, you know.'

Jo mentally ducked. She didn't ever want to think about that. Nothing good ever came from a Witch Hunt, just misery and sadness, and she didn't want to play any part in the dishonourable discharge of a sister soldier just for being a lesbian. She increased her speed to distract herself from dwelling on the matter.

'Any news on your promotion?' Terry lengthened her stride.

'Don't know. Sore point. I'm sure I've done everything right. I mean, we joined up at the same time. I have similar annual reports to you. By rights, I should be a sergeant too by now.' Jo took a deep breath.

'Ah! But have you?' Terry teased. 'I mean, if you're not promoted, are you on par with me?'

Jo almost stopped in her tracks. Then she noticed the cheeky grin on Terry's lips that prompted her to sprint the last quarter of a mile before stopping at the gym's entrance. Terry finished a few paces behind.

'Told you I'd beat you!'

'I let you. You being the junior rank and all that.'

'Shut up!' Jo laughed between gasps for fresh breath. They stood in the cool, cloudy spring air that promised an April shower, their hands on their hips bent over at the waist, drawing oxygen into their lungs, their heads almost touching. A tender smile passed between them. They wanted more but also knew they could be observed. Not touching was tantalising.

Terry began to stretch out. 'You know, I can't wait for you to be promoted. The more money we earn, the quicker we can buy our own house. Then, we'll be free to do what we like at the weekends, and nobody will know about us.'

'I know. It's got to be soon, Terry. It's got to be.' Jo walked off the lactic acid building in her legs.

Terry patted Jo's shoulder and looked around to check if anyone might have seen them before whispering in Jo's ear. 'I need to kiss you.' The want in Terry's voice was unmistakable.

'I know. Me too. It'll be Easter soon. We can make up for it then.'

'It's been harder having you around every day and not being able to touch you. It was easier when you weren't here because I didn't have to second-guess everything, I did in case someone was watching. I've not told a soul you're my girlfriend. I bet when everyone finds out you're not a Postie, they'll not be happy.'

'Probably. But Lizzie Lowe really helped me. She showed me how to sort and fly the letters into the pigeonholes. I never thought I'd be convincing enough as a postie when I first saw the huge sack of letters dropped at my sorting frame, but with her coaching and showing me the ropes, I'm not half-bad.'

'Talking of which—how's Lizzie doing? Especially after, you know what.'

'The suicide attempt?'

'Yeah'

'Mostly okay.'

'Do you know why she… you know… did it?'

'I tried asking her, but she wouldn't tell me. She said it was best left. Though… when I'm not around, Dee Quade always seems to be right near her. Something's off. Just don't know what.'

'What? Jo Clark, aka Hercule Poirot, doesn't know.' Terry mocked.

Jo grinned before adding a serious note. 'No. But Quade always seems to have Lizzie running errands, and when she's not doing that, it's weird; she's like right next to her. I mean, like stuck to her. I thought, at first, they might be friends.'

'Are they?'

'Lizzie denied it. Said Quade was not what she seemed, and it was best to stay on the right side of her or steer clear of her altogether. Though, she probably wouldn't tell me if they were friends, as she knows I'm an MP.'

'True. But you need to take care of her. You know Lizzie, she's not… well, mentally strong—fragile like.'

'It's hard, Terry. I need to keep a low profile while I'm on this job. But yesterday, Lizzie sorted Quade's letters for her while she sat and drank coffee.

So, I went over and told the lazy bastard to sort her own out, and I just stood there and stared at her until she let Lizzie go. She actually caved easily, which was a bit of a relief. Not sure what else I could've done.'

Terry stretched her hamstrings and continued her musings. 'You know Quade doesn't seem to have any real friends.' She added quizzically. 'More like lackeys, you know, henchman type of thing.'

'Henchman?'

'Yeah, don't think she ever gets her hands dirty.'

'Quade's weird. Talking of weird.' Jo paused for effect. 'A certain Corporal Max Dart tells everyone she's going to be a PTI, and, of course, the sun shines out of your backside, as far as she is concerned.'

'Of course, it does. I can't help it if I'm good-looking and talented,' Terry, smiling, walked towards the gym.

'In your dreams, darlin',' Jo said, following Terry to her office.

'You found me attractive.'

'Yeah, well, you had a moment. Don't milk it.' Jo joked. 'What've you got on today?'

'Oh, the usual. Lots of running. Got Major Marwood for another session on her BFT.'

'Again?'

'Virtually every day at the moment. She's not making much progress. She's just not cut out for running. Her feet flap.'

'Flap?'

'Drives me nuts. Every step, it's like a flapping sound, like she's flat-footed. You know, like a duck might make on land.'

Jo cocked her head to one side, giving the suggestion some consideration. 'Don't think ducks make a sound on land, do they?'

'God Jo! Use your imagination. No, wait, you can't coz you're a Red Cap. You only do facts. At first, I thought her trainers were too large for her. But they're not. And she's boring to run with—no sense of humour, just patronising silence, and she thinks I don't notice. She's clever, I know that, but she could push through the pain.'

'She's probably concentrating?'

'Blimey, you always think of the strangest reasons for things. I swear you're not normal.'

Jo grinned as she lowered her voice. 'Ah, but you love me anyway.'

Terry raised her eyes and eyebrows and opened her office door before waving Jo away. 'See you later. Good luck with the heist!

An hour later, adrenaline pumped through Jo's veins. Today, she needed to prove she was worthy of promotion to Sergeant. After five years in the Royal Military Police, with postings in Aldershot and Northern Ireland, and now the London Provost Company, she knew she was ready. Standing in front of the full-length mirror hung on the wall at the entrance to the Block, she inspected her uniform, starting as she had been taught during basic training, with her shoes working up to her beret. Her black leather drill shoes were bulled to a patent leather shine from heel to toe, and the shoelaces tied so the bows were equal on both sides of the knot. Next, she checked her tie was straight and all her buttons fastened. Finally, she put on a green beret with the Women's Royal Army Corps cap badge, tucking her short blonde hair under the front band. She had taken great pains to shrink and shape the beret to make it look like she had worn it for years, not weeks.

Jo was satisfied with her appearance—she was the perfect picture of a woman in uniform. Her tall, athletic frame meant she wore the heavy, lovat green greatcoat well. Though it was not cold, it would likely rain today; regulations required her to wear it to work. Her shapely legs attracted wolf-whistles from the Sappers as she marched to her morning shift in The Postal and Courier Depot.

In your dreams, lads.

Jo opened the double doors to the brightly lit cavernous former munitions depot, where The Army's post office was rarely quiet as hundreds of men and women ensured Ministry of Defence missives were delivered and the crucial letters that kept soldiers' morale high reached the intended recipients all around the globe. BBC Radio One's Breakfast Show played in the background. The metal tips on the heels of Jo's drill shoes on the polished concrete floor announced her arrival for her shift. The depot was humming despite the shift changeovers. She hung her hat and coat on the pegs provided and walked to her station, comprised of a line of wooden frames, to begin her shift under her section commander Corporal Beth Pugh, who was late.

'Morning, Jo,' Eve deftly launched the first letter of her shift into her sorting frame.

'Morning. How was the 'Do' last night?'

'Oh, the usual. Dee got smashed—she's a social hand grenade, that one!' Eve shot another envelope into a larger pigeonhole.

'She had a few bevvies then?'

'A few? More like a brewery.'

Chuckling, Jo picked up a pile of letters from a wheeled canvas container and began sorting them.

'What did she get up to?' Jo asked as she tossed the first letter of the morning.

'The usual. Tried kissing everyone in sight. Forcing girls to dance with her, especially Lizzie.'

Jo groaned as she considered what, if anything, she should do to help her friend.

As 'Girls Just Wanna Have Fun' played on the radio, Corporal Beth Pugh and two other soldiers joined them and began sorting mail. Jo noted the targets were all present and that Pugh was wearing lightweight trousers, which the senior officers of the WRAC considered inappropriate for women to wear if they were to maintain their feminity.

'What's with the kit, Beth?' Eve probed.

'Too bloody cold for a skirt. Anyway, I prefer lightweights and the men's woolly pulley—keep me warm in this icebox.'

Eve nodded but seemed determined to have her say. 'Well, you'd better make sure Major Marwood doesn't see you. You know the OC likes us to wear our barrack dress skirts. She won't be best pleased.'

'Because it's not feminine,' all of them except Jo chorused.

Pugh muttered curses. She picked up another bunch of letters and began sorting them, dispensing each with a simple flick of her wrist that sent hundreds of letters into large pigeonholes for Garrisons and smaller ones for units and battalions.

After two letters, she paused. 'Oh, lookee here! A love letter!' Pugh held the letter to her nose. 'Perfume! And look at all 'em hearts all over it.' Pugh looked closer at the envelope. 'Going to a Woman Lance Corporal. My guess is she is one of us.' Pugh waved the letter triumphantly. 'On your way! May you make her heart flutter!' She shot the billet-doux into a large pigeonhole marked Catterick Garrison.

'Shush, Beth! You'll get us into trouble!' Eve turned around to check they hadn't been overheard.

Jo observed Pugh inspect another envelope before turning her back to Jo and signalling Eve to cover her. Patiently, Jo waited to observe Pugh slide the envelope into the leg pocket of her lightweight trousers.

'Bloody hell! Why didn't anyone tell me I had a pocket undone?' exclaimed Pugh, fastening the button.

'Didn't notice,' Jo lied. 'Sorry.' She looked at the large clock on the depot wall and noted the time: 08:10 hours. She re-checked the entry doors and the whereabouts of Eve and Pugh's three other accomplices.

Good, they're nearby. Should make it easy.

Raised voices in another section of the depot temporarily halted productivity. Jo's heart sank as she looked across the depot to Corporal Quade's section. Lizzie was scurrying, her head bent low to the pile of mailbags that had just been dropped at the edge of Quade's section.

'Go and get that bag now!' Quade strode toward Lizzie before stretching herself to her full height to tower over her. Then she bent and whispered in Lizzie's ear before stabbing a finger into her chest. 'Go on, you fucking tease. You might as well make use of the air you're wasting.'

Lizzie looked at the large bag that Quade had pointed at. She crouched beside it and began whimpering, an eerie sound echoing in the depot's chasm.

'And for fucks sake, shut up whingeing,' Quade said, the disgust evident in both her tone and volume.

Jo scanned the room to see if anyone might go and rescue Lizzie. No one moved. Jo surmised they were either intimidated or wanted no part of the bullying. Jo sighed. She was desperate to protect Lizzie, but any minute now, her colleagues would enter the depot and expect her to be ready to facilitate arrests. Now, she was seriously torn. She owed Lizzie big time, but she didn't dare fuck up the operation. Not after all the hard work that had gone into it. They would never ask her again. Her promotion would be in the balance, and her permanent assignment to the SIB would be put on hold.

Her eyes flicked between the doors, the clock and Lizzie.

Jo heard Lizzie whimper again, and she couldn't bear it any longer. Her natural instinct to protect her friend kicked in. She left her station, jogging through the other sections until she reached Quade's sorting area.

'It's alright, Lizzie.' Jo bent down and lifted the heavy bag.

Lizzie glanced at Quade as if asking for permission.

'No, Jo. Don't want you to get in any trouble. I can handle the bag.'

'Trouble?' Jo said. 'I promise I won't. But I can't say as much for her.' She sneered in Quade's direction. 'What's going on, Lizzie?'

'Nothing.'

Jo knew her friend had lied.

'She has a thing for me, and don't I know it.' Lizzie faked a chuckle.

Quade swaggered menacingly towards them—a snarl curling her lips. 'Talking about me?'

Jo and Lizzie ignored the question and carried the bag toward Quade's station.

Quade followed them. 'Better me than you, Clark.' She focussed on Lizzie. 'Come on, shit fer brains. Get that bag sorted. I want it done by the time I've finished my cuppa.' Quade sat down and picked up her mug, sniggering at Jo and Lizzie. 'Of course, if you were nice to me, I'd have someone sort the bag for you. So, you could sit here right next to me.' Quade patted a vacant seat next to her.

Jo saw Lizzie wince at the invitation and wondered whether there had been more to Eve's report of Quade forcing girls to dance with her.

Quade rosed and moved nearer to Jo and Lizzie.

'You're weird, Dee. Sort the fucking bag yourself.' Jo stepped into Quade's space, stretching her spine to look intently into Quade's face. 'Word to the wise, mate. I would shut the fuck up if you don't want anyone investigating you for being queer.' Jo was pissed but knew she couldn't give herself away. There was she and Terry and hundreds like them watching everything they said or did, and here was Quade behaving stupidly, inviting trouble! If Quade was investigated and discharged, Jo was sure she would take Lizzie down with her. She needed to protect Lizzie from the likes of Quade, who thought she was untouchable and played with fire. 'Listen, if I find out, you made Lizzie sort those letters or you made her do anything against her will, you'd better watch out.'

'Why? What're you gonna do, Clark? Oh, I'm scared.' Quade mocked Jo, pretending to flinch. She turned to look at Jo, her disgust lasering the policewoman's face, before straightening up. Quade smiled with menace and purpose, closing the gap between them.

Jo stood her ground. Her jaw squared with determination. No good deed goes unpunished, and her intervention took longer than she had thought. Now, the situation was on the verge of escalating. Not what she needed. Jo looked at the clock. 'Why don't you shut the fuck up! Just do your job. You're pathetic the way you have everyone do your work.'

‘Careful, Clark, you might regret you said that. Might she, girls?’ Quade’s entourage gathered behind her. ‘Lizzie’s not interested in you.’

And I’m not interested in her. You arsehole. Jo’s impatience was growing along with her dilemma. She couldn’t let Quade think she was rattled, yet she had to be ready to execute the arrest of four women she had been shadowing in her section. She leaned in to whisper in Quade’s ear. ‘You’ll save for another day. I’ve got work to do.’

Quade grinned. ‘I can hardly wait.’

‘Piss off, Quade!’ Jo wanted to teach Quade a lesson, right there, right on that spot in front of her—what was it Terry called them? Henchman, that was it, right in front of her henchman. But she had a job to do. Too bad it wasn’t arresting Quade for being a bastard.

She bit her tongue, returned to her frame, and sorted the letters in her bag. At 08:30 hours, Sergeant Major Carol Hart arrived wearing a grey civvy skirt suit and a navy raincoat. Jo always thought she looked like a stately galleon in full sail, not someone who rough seas could roil easily. The strike of her two-inch patent leather heels on concrete demanded respect from her subordinates and set a purposeful tone. Her coat collar was stylishly turned up, and the belt buckled at her back rather than the front. She knocked on the Officer Commanding depot’s office door and entered without permission before closing it.

Jo continued to watch her quarry as she sorted the letters in front of her.

Pugh sidled up to Jo. ‘What’s occurring?’

‘Dunno.’

‘Who’s the bird bothering the OC?’

‘Dunno.’

‘Hmm. Maybe it’s his bit on the side. Bet wifey doesn’t know.’ Pugh beckoned her accomplices over. Jo was not invited. ‘The OC’s got a bit on the side.’

The group cackled. Jo ignored them, watching Pugh slyly slip another envelope up her woolly pulley.

‘My guess,’ Pugh addressed her co-conspirators. ‘His missus isn’t giving him any. You should have a go, Eve. You like ’em old.’

The group joshed Eve. She simpered at their sexual innuendos.

The joking and teasing abruptly stopped as three men, wearing suits of varying shades of grey with beige trench-style raincoats casually unbuttoned, burst through the double doors and into the sorting area and headed straight for Pugh's section.

'Uh oh, I spy SIB. Heads down, girls.' Pugh whispered to her workgroup. 'Looks like they're on the hunt again.'

Throughout the depot, letters flew at warp speed into boxes. Jo knew that every single woman would be straining their ears in the silence, scared the SIB had begun a witch-hunt.

Pugh and her four accomplices lowered their heads as the men approached.

A chunky man in his late thirties with a light brown comb-over stopped in front of Pugh. 'Stay where you are. Corporal Pugh, I'm Staff Sergeant Armstrong, Special Investigations Bureau.' He took out a leather wallet adorned with the golden cap badge of the Royal Military Police and flipped it open at his ID and warrant card.

'So, you are Staff.' Pugh's sarcasm was rich yet polite.

Jo stood and faced Pugh, irritated by the suspect's insolence. 'Give me the letter you stuffed up your woolly pulley. And the one in your lightweights' pocket.'

Pugh sighed and failed to respond.

'No?' asked Armstrong. 'Right, stand still, Corporal Pugh. Corporal Clark! Search her!'

Jo patted Pugh down, starting with her shoulders. She pulled one letter from under Pugh's jumper. She found the others where she had observed Pugh stashed them before handing them to Armstrong.

'Corporal Pugh, I'm arresting you for mail theft. You three— stay where you are. My colleagues will place you under arrest for aiding and abetting,' said Armstrong. He expertly turned Pugh around as he spoke and cuffed her hands behind her back while delivering the Right to Silence.

'Is that it?' Pugh replied, looking around at her accomplices with a sly and satisfied smile.

The two other detectives cuffed two of the women. Only Eve remained un-cuffed, and sensing an opportunity, she bolted for the exit as best she could in the confines of her knee-length A-line skirt. Jo sprinted after her, diving to bring her down. They hit the cold, solid and unforgiving floor. Jo's bottom jaw jolted into her top one. But determined to succeed and with adrenaline driving her actions and masking the pain in her jaw, she wrestled and slithered on the ground until she had Eve face down on the cement. Her skirt seams strained and groaned before tearing. Confident she had her suspect under control, Jo, with her skirt torn and no longer holding her back, sat astride her suspect as Hart walked into the sorting area.

'Anyone got any cuffs spare?' asked Jo.

Hart took out a pair from her coat pocket. 'Here you are, Corporal Clark, use mine. Don't get 'em dirty, mind. I'll want 'em back in good order.'

Jo cuffed Eve, who lay beneath her, panting and swearing before dragging her to her feet. The commotion encouraged some Postal and Courier Operators to rubberneck the kerfuffle. Most of the shift, some one hundred women, stayed at their station, though productivity slowed.

Quade swaggered towards Jo. 'Well, well, what do we have here? A Monkey or, wait a minute, no, you're Shit In Bulk!' Quade raised her voice, cocking her head to one side as she slid her hands into her lightweight trouser pockets and glared at Jo.

The four detectives watched. One released his charge to his colleague but maintained his distance. Jo confidently left Eve near the detectives to stand square in front of her accuser.

'Shut up, Quade. If you know what's good for you—you'll wind your neck in.'

'Now we know what you meant earlier.' Quade casually leaned her lanky frame against the counter and muttered, 'Fucking Monkey,' under her breath.

Jo moved towards the exit. 'Come on, let's get them in the van. I don't want to listen to any more of her shit.'

'The thing is,' Quade pointed aggressively at Jo. 'You posed as one of us.' She turned to her workmates. 'We took you under our wing, didn't we?'

Jo hovered uneasily while Quade verbally gathered her bravado and her supporters. It was true she had deceived them, but it was her job. Someone had to stop thieves from stealing what rightfully belonged to honest soldiers posted away from their loved ones. That was her duty, and she was proud of it—proud of keeping the rules when others didn't, proud of maintaining good order and military discipline.

'And all the time, you were spying on us. We won't make that mistake again, will we, girls?' Quade worked her gang. 'Well, I guess we should count ourselves lucky, eh, girls? Obviously, you won't be working here tomorrow. You're the fucking worst of the worst, Clark!' Quade turned away in disgust. 'Come on, let's get back to work before they start a witch-hunt.'

Jo's feet shifted without her permission. Despite the cool air in the vast depot, she was feeling uncomfortably warm. The four SIB detectives exchanged questioning glances with her. She shrugged.

Hart spoke. 'Get them into the van, lads. Let's not be having any more altercations.'

Jo and her colleagues marched the prisoners through the back doors of the depot to a van parked on a perimeter road before helping them into the van. Each sat next to a detective. Jo shut the rear doors. From experience, Jo knew the journey to Rochester Row would be silent and uncomfortable for her former co-workers.

Armstrong took the driver's seat in the van. He leaned out of the window. 'You coming, Jo? Or are you going in the gaffer's comfy car?'

'She's coming with me in my comfy car, Staff,' Hart replied, imitating Staff's sarcastic tone. 'And I'll see you all back at Rochester Row later. And don't forget to write your reports before you leave tonight. I want them in my tray first thing.'

## Chapter 4

Jo had arranged to meet Sergeant Major Hart at the roadway behind the accommodation. Elated at her successful arrest, she was still running on adrenaline. It was gratifying to go on a job, but it was better to be among real friends who knew who you were or mostly who you were. And soon, she would be with Terry—it was about the only benefit of being posted forty miles from home. She smiled as her stomach flipped, and a pleasure briefly thrilled her body.

The walk to the Block was short. She pushed open the glass door without looking and was about to sprint up the stairs. A pair of feet brushed her face, startling her. She jumped backwards before looking up. It was Lizzie! She must have slipped out during the commotion of the arrests.

'No, Lizzie! No!'

Jo shouted for help before lifting Lizzie's body, hoping it would somehow loosen the noose around Lizzie's neck. She scanned the area for something to climb up on. Nothing. She gently let Lizzie hang down again. Jo stumbled up the stairs to where Lizzie had tied the makeshift rope to the bannister. She tried to unravel the knot at the railing, quickly reasoning she would need to cut the tights that formed the ligature. She looked down at Lizzie's blond head, lolling to one side and saw that her tongue was hanging out of her mouth. She searched her handbag for her Swiss Army knife. Her fingers worked faster than her brain, and she struggled to pull the blade from its sheath, achieving success seconds later. She knelt to cut the pantyhose at the tautest point. Lizzie had tied a slipknot, which had tightened as she leapt from the first floor to the ground—no mistakes this time. The knot, combined with Lizzie's weight, had almost melded the nylon together.

As Jo slashed wildly, she screamed again for assistance. Where is everybody? Why, Lizzie? That shit Quade, did she make you do this?

She wept in frustration as she continued to hack at the rope, grimacing with the effort and her fears for her friend. Out of the corner of her eye, she saw a young woman run towards her, then wheeled around to run to the telephone on the landing.

'Quick, Lowe's hanged herself. First floor in the Block.' The woman yelled into the phone before returning to Jo.

'Go outside, now!' Commanded Jo. 'There's a Sarn't Major in a black

Cortina. Get her in here, fast!'

Jo continued to work to free Lizzie. The material that typically tore at a splinter on a chair or desk was holding firm. Moments later, Hart burst through the door and held up Lizzie's body to ease the strain on the nylon noose, finally giving way to Jo's efforts. Hart, staggering under Lizzie's dead weight, managed to hold the body upright until Jo joined her, and together, they laid Lizzie on her back.

'She's not breathing!' exclaimed Jo before retching.

Hart checked for an elusive pulse at Lizzie's wrist, then her neck, where the ligature had left its mark. Two Civilian ambulance men burst through the doors. 'It's alright, we'll take it from here. What's her name?'

Jo and Hart got up from the floor, grateful the professionals had arrived.

'Lizzie…Lizzie Lowe,' Jo's voice faltered.

Jo heard the Junior Ranks' Accommodation door open and watched with indignation as Quade, surrounded by her henchmen, came to gawp.

One ambulance man searched for a pulse, then tried again with a stethoscope. He stood up as a high-pitched noise emanated from Lizzie. The small crowd murmured their collective fears. The man shook his head.

Hart pulled Jo into her ample bosom. Grateful for the comfort, Jo buried her face and wept shoulder-wracking sobs.

'Sorry, Jo. I know you had come to know her.'

'Not that, ma'am, she's a friend. She protected me while I was undercover. And I…I failed her.' Jo sobbed a kind of deep animal coughing sound. A few moments later, embarrassed she had let her emotions betray her professionalism, Jo withdrew from Hart. The shame of showing her feelings prevented her from making eye contact with her boss.

'Do we have any ID?' asked one of the men.

Max, Terry's admirer, pushed through the onlookers. 'Lance Corporal Dart, ma'am. Here's her ID card. I got it from her handbag in her bedspace.'

Hart examined it before thanking Max.

The medics placed Lizzie on a stretcher. 'We'll take her to Edgeware General.'

'Should I go with her?' Jo asked Hart.

'No. I need you to complete a report.'

'But she'll be all alone.' Jo felt a flush of heat course through her body as she worked to arrest the tears, threatening to breech all her attempts at remaining professional.

Hart shook her head. 'Nothing you can do for her now, Jo.' Hart turned to the women standing in the hallway. 'Okay, listen up. You need to leave.'

'What's happening?' Quade asked.

'They're taking her to hospital. They'll take care of her there. Now, everyone, go back to work or your rooms. We'll be cordoning this area off.'

The group moved away, some chatting their conjectures. Jo caught sight of Quade wiping a tear from her eye. Jo scoffed her disgust at Quade, silently blaming her for Lizzie's actions. Jo was about to confront Quade when Hart blocked her path.

'Don't do anything stupid, Corporal Clark.'

Embarrassed, Jo avoided Hart's eye, her voice broken with emotion. 'If only…'

'No, if onlys Jo. You did everything you could. Suicide is always tough.' Hart shook her head. 'And remember, it's not about you. Right?'

Jo nodded numbly. 'I'm going to buy a bigger knife. It took me ages to cut her down.' She struggled to remain detached and professional, and one outburst was enough—she was a soldier and a policewoman. She was not supposed to have emotions and certainly not supposed to cry, but her tears defied her attempt at self-control.

'Come on.' Hart wrapped a protective arm around Jo's shoulder. I'll ask Miss Gordon to invite you into the Mess for a stiffener.'

□

## Chapter 5

Terry surveyed the mess in the store cupboard. It would take a bit of tidying up, but she didn't have time because spring was a busy time of year with inter-unit sports competitions, which meant she spent time holding hockey, netball, and swimming practices. After team selection, they would attend the various tournaments in Aldershot, 'The Home of The British Army,' where the women loved competing. As one of the larger units, they usually came away with a team trophy or a medal each. And, of course, every soldier had to complete the annual Basic Fitness Test (BFT), whatever their rank, and after that, the ongoing remedial work with the stragglers. When would she get it all done? The rain didn't help, especially as the men always got first dibs on the gym. She sighed.

Max tapped on the storeroom door before blurting, 'Sarn't! Lizzie Lowe committed suicide!'

'What?'

Max struggled for breath, gulping air. 'Honest, Sarn't, I saw it all! Corporal Clark isn't a postie. She's a Monkey! An' she arrested Beth Pugh and her gang and then cut Lizzie Lowe down from the bannister. I saw it all!'

'What? Hang on, Max.' Terry guided Max to her office and closed the door. 'Sit down. You say Lizzie's dead.'

Max nodded seriously.

Terry thought for a moment. 'This isn't good for any of us.'

'Why's that?'

'Because there'll be an investigation by the SIB. And you never know what that will lead to.'

Max sat silently for a moment. 'Not sure what to do with meself Sarn't. I'm all out of sorts now.'

Terry's mind leapt from one thought to another. First, the SIB and the possibility of a witch-hunt. Then, to Jo, would she be involved, and how would she handle dealing with this terrible kind of police work? And finally, how could she help Max? Poor Max, so young and naive yet desperate to impress her.

'Want to lend me a hand?'

'Yes, sarn't.'

'Could you tidy the storeroom for me?'

Max jumped out of her seat and headed out of the office, shutting the door behind her.

Terry relieved to be alone, allowed her tears to brim and fall, dabbing at them with her handkerchief. How was Jo going to deal with this? This was supposed to be her big day when she made arrests and impressed her SIB colleagues. She wanted to be with Jo, but how could she without attracting unwanted attention and suspicion? They needed to be together to process Lizzie's suicide. She didn't even know where Jo was. Perhaps she had to leave without saying a final goodbye. Maybe she was still on campus. No, she wouldn't go without saying goodbye, not after this. Terry decided to stay at her desk in the claustrophobic room, smelling of liniment and sweaty socks.

Jo knocked lightly on the door before entering and closing it behind her.

'Jo!' Terry, relieved, jumped up and hugged her lover. Then, self-consciously, she released her almost immediately, fearing being caught and opening herself to suspicion. And, yet, wouldn't a friend comfort another in such circumstances?

Jo's tears dropped on the tile floor. She worked them into the stone with her foot.

Terry motioned for Jo to sit on the other side of her desk as she took her chair. 'What happened?' Terry asked in a quiet voice. 'Max said you made some arrests. Did that go well? And that Lizzie committed suicide. Is that true? Do you know why Lizzie did it?'

'No.' Jo's shoulders heaved with her sobs. 'Terry, I didn't even know she'd left the depot. She was there one minute and gone the next.' Jo struggled to breathe and cry at the same time. 'I witnessed Dee Quade being shitty to her before I made the arrests. After that, I went to the Block.'

Terry nodded, encouragement. All the while, she could feel Jo's pain in the pit of her stomach. It had always been that way. Whatever Jo felt, Terry could feel it too. 'And then what?'

'I opened the door, and there she was!' Jo wailed.

Terry reached out and placed her hand on top of Jo's. 'It's okay. You don't have to tell me anymore if you don't want to.'

'I can't bear it, Terry. I let Lizzie down. She took care of me and helped me be a convincing Postie and when she needed me. I wasn't there for her.'

'You couldn't have known Jo.' Terry pleaded.

Jo stood, the action seeming to stem her tears. 'No, you don't get it, do you? I'm a policewoman. I rescue people. I don't let them die on my watch. I failed Terry. I failed her!'

Terry got up and walked around the desk until she faced Jo. She gazed into Jo's watery blue-grey eyes and stroked her blonde fringe to one side to better read her lover's mind. She touched her forehead briefly onto Jo's. 'We need to go home.'

Jo nodded.

'Mum' n' Dad won't be expecting us, but they won't mind. Not when you tell them what's happened.'

'Sarn't Major is waiting for me. I have to go. I'll see you at home tonight.'

Terry went to kiss Jo. Jo shrunk back. 'Best not.' Jo looked around the closed room. 'We don't know who is watching or listening. Tonight.

## Chapter 6

*The Clark Family Home, Harold Hill, Essex.*

Jo drove on autopilot to the sanctity of the Clark home. She knew her parents loved her and were proud of her achievements, but she could not be open about the most important thing—who she loved. What she feared most was losing the love of her parents and her family, something she cherished as much as she did Terry.

All her actions at work and home were guided by one principle– to make them proud. That meant not disappointing or bringing them distress or shame. Because she was gay, this meant she second-guessed herself in almost everything she said or did. Had Lizzie done that too? Had that been a factor in Lizzie's suicide? Is that why she had taken such irrevocable action? Lizzie shared with Jo that she was an only child her parents doted on. Jo didn't know if Lizzie was gay or straight. It hadn't mattered until now. Did it matter? These thoughts and questions spun like a carousel during her journey.

She parked outside her home—her real home. She smiled because this was the safest place in the world for her, where she could share all her anguish and grief with Terry. Jo retrieved her bag from the car and walked up the driveway.

The back door was unlocked, and she slid unnoticed into an empty kitchen, dropping her bag near the doorway before slumping into one of the four chairs at the kitchen table. She looked around her sanctuary, tearing up at the thought that Mr and Mrs Lowe would never see their beloved daughter again. It induced melancholic thoughts of how her parents might react if they received similar news, prompting more tears, accompanied by ragged breathing.

'Jo!' Her mother bustled through the kitchen door. 'Whatever is it?' Sylvia placed a hand on her daughter's shoulder. 'Come on, now. Can't be that bad.' Sylvia soothed.

'Oh, Mum. It's Lizzie.' Jo continued in broken sentences to share the story of Lizzie's suicide, omitting the possibility that Quade wanted Lizzie to be her girlfriend and, when she had refused, resorted to coercing Lizzie into a relationship. A plan that failed to deliver on its objective and went spectacularly wrong, leaving Lizzie dead and Jo full of regrets that she would never ever rectify.

'Mum, she was just hanging there. There was nothing I could do. I'm supposed to be able to help people, rescue them, keep them safe.'

Sylvia lifted Jo's chin. 'You didn't kill Lizzie, darlin'. Lizzie chose to end her life.' In a sterner tone, she continued. 'And, if you ever, ever, get that desperate, my girl, you call me or your dad, and you come home. There's nothing that we can't handle as a family. Nothing! Do you hear me?'

Jo nodded, though the tears kept coming.

'Right, I'll put the kettle on, and we'll say no more about it.' Sylvia busied herself making a pot of tea.

Terry opened the back door, dropping her weekend bag beside Jo's.

'Oh good, I could murder a cuppa. Been a hell of a week.'

'So, I heard,' Sylvia said.

'Did you tell her about Lizzie?' Terry asked.

'Yes, she did,' Sylvia turned off the tap. 'Very sorry, business. I can't imagine what her poor parents are going through.' Sylvia tutted, shaking her head as she put the makings for tea on the table.

'Well, your dad and I weren't expecting you this weekend, with it being Easter next week. But now I understand why the surprise visit.' Sylvia chatted as she poured tea for them all. 'We'll have fish n chips tonight from the chippy. Terry, can you pick it up? You girls going with your Dad to the pub? You know he likes to show you off to his mates.'

'Don't think so, Mum,' Jo said. 'Doesn't feel right.'

'Won't bring her back, Jo,' Sylvia chided.

Jo knew that. Why did everyone keep saying that? She, of all people, knew Lizzie was dead. Wasn't it she who had been with Lizzie the moment she had died? Now, Lizzie had left her with a mess and stuff that she didn't know how to handle. She needed to do something more than cry. She felt powerless and useless, something she couldn't bear.

Brian entered the kitchen, adding his briefcase to the parade of bags at the back door. His smile grew broader when he saw his daughters. 'Hello, girls. I wasn't expecting you until next weekend!' His relish at seeing Jo and Terry filled his voice. 'So, what do we owe the privilege?' He collected a mug from a cabinet and poured himself a cuppa before settling at the kitchen table.

Sylvia shook her head slowly at her husband and mouthed. 'Don't ask.'

Brian sipped thoughtfully. A prolonged silence followed, broken by Jo.

'I had to cut a woman down, Dad.' She placed her empty mug on the table.

Brian looked askance at Jo and then at his wife.

'She committed suicide.' Jo battled with her brimming emotions. Her throat tightened as if she could not bear to speak of the pain that was tearing her apart. She shared the episode that had left her unable to think of anything else, unable to function, unable to feel anything except grief tinged with anger and frustration.

'Well, Lass.' Brian's northern accent thickened with his concern. 'I'm not sure I understand what drove her to it. But should you ever feel that bad…'

'I know, Dad,' Jo interrupted. 'Mum said.'

'Yes, well.' Brian cleared his throat of his emotions before adding. 'Same goes for you, Terry.'

Terry nodded. 'Let's unpack, Jo, then we can go for fish' n' chips.' Terry led Jo upstairs to their shared childhood bedroom. She closed the door and took the taller woman into her arms.

Jo nestled her face in Terry's shoulder and cried, holding onto Terry's short and muscular frame lest she collapse under the strain. Terry caressed Jo's back and nuzzled her hair, uttering soothing words of love and support. After some time, when the jumble of emotions left Jo for that moment, she lifted her head.

'I'm alright now.' Jo sat on the bed with Terry by her side. 'I can't get the picture of Lizzie hanging there out of my mind.' She gesticulated. 'Right there in front of me. I tried; I really did.' She shook her head, twisting her fingers into knots until her exertions turned her hands red to white and back again.

Terry took one hand and kissed it, looking deep into Jo's eyes so that she could determine the depth of Jo's sadness.

'What made her do it? Do you know? Was there a note? Terry asked.

'No note. Not that I know of, anyway. Might be. Maybe we'll find out later. I'm pretty sure it's Quade's fault.' Jo chewed her lip. 'One of the girls said Quade had made a nuisance of herself with Lizzie at the Camden Palace.'

'No!'

'Yep.' Jo shook her head with disgust. 'Can't believe it. Lizzie didn't want anything to do with her. So, for the life of me, I can't think why, she decided to make Lizzie's life a misery.'

'Told you she had henchman.'

'I know. But I didn't expect this.'

'Don't suppose Quade did either.'

'Well, it doesn't matter what she expected—it's what she got, what Lizzie got! Now What? I'll bet there'll be repercussions—nothing good.' Jo's eyes darkened. 'Whatever way it goes, I swear to God, I'm going to make Quade pay.'

'Steady Jo. Don't do anything stupid.'

Jo leapt off the bed. 'Stupid! What do you take me for!' Jo stood legs astride, arms crossed over her chest.

'Jo, calm down. You know, when you get riled, you can be a bit wild.'

'Wild? Of course, I am. I'm fucking mad! I tell you, Quade is at the root of this.' Jo, fists balled, paced the room.

'Sit down, Jo. Let's talk about this.'

'No! I'll sit down when I want to sit down.' Jo stopped before turning to face Terry. 'Fuck it! Let's go and get the fish 'n' chips.' Jo defeated, wrenched open the bedroom door. 'You coming?'

## Chapter 7

Terry followed Jo down the stairs and into the kitchen.

'Are you going to the chippy?' asked Sylvia in a voice that suggested a false light-heartedness. 'Cod and chips for four, then.' She handed Terry a ten-pound note.

'I'll drive.' Terry grabbed her car keys, concerned that Jo was in no fit state to drive.

Terry started the car while stealing a sly look at Jo. She felt Jo's anger, pain and sadness, and she knew that when Jo entered this dark place it was hard to get her back to herself. Terry knew she needed to leave Jo space to process her feelings, but she also learned not to leave her lover to stew too long.

Five minutes later, parked in the marked space outside the chippy, she got out, leaving Jo in the car. Standing in the queue to order, she considered how to help Jo. She knew Jo was not the biggest of thinkers—she was more inclined to action and that often got her into trouble. She collected her order and paid the shopkeeper before returning with four paper-wrapped packages of fish and chips, which she handed to Jo.

'I got us an extra bag of chips so we could eat them on the way home.' Terry chippered. 'Open it! I'm starving.'

'You're always Hank Marvin,' Jo chuckled as she waved a chip sprinkled with salt and vinegar in front of Terry's nose. 'Smell that. Salt 'n' vinegar! Now that's a proper chip.' She popped it into Terry's mouth.

Terry grinned as she chewed. 'Nice. You having one?'

Jo shoved a few chips into her mouth and, without fully digesting them, spoke. 'I'm sorry I'm not cross at you. I'm cross at Quade. I'm so angry I could almost burst.'

'I know.' Terry comforted. At last, Jo was healing. 'It's understandable. I'm mad too and sad. But I didn't cut her down. I didn't see her. It's got to eat away at you. But please don't do anything stupid. Promise me.'

Jo didn't respond, choosing to eat another chip.

'Promise me!' Terry urged.

'Promise. And I promised Lizzie I would avenge her death.' She popped another chip in Terry's mouth before taking one for herself.

'Careful, Jo.' Terry chewed and swallowed as fast as she could. 'Have you been asked to investigate?'

'No. But...'

'Stick to the rules, Jo. Don't be muddying waters.'

'You saying I shouldn't care?'

'No, I'm…'

'Because I do! It fucking hurts! It hurts because she protected me, and I didn't…' Jo's voice dropped to a whisper, her chin almost on her chest. 'Do the same for her.'

Terry took her hand off the steering wheel and placed it on Jo's thigh. For a moment, she took her eyes off the road and looked at her lover's face; it was full of despair and grief.

'I'm not saying you shouldn't. Jus' saying you need to be careful. Don't go letting your emotions run you. That's all. You know how you are. You don't think, you just act.'

'Sorted your Dad out, though, didn't it?'

Terry heard the tiredness in Jo's voice. 'You don't know how often I've wondered how you managed to get me out of there without him coming after us. Now I realise… he never genuinely cared. And you are impetuous, and there's no stopping you when you got a mind to it. And, one day, it will land you into trouble.' Terry withdrew her hand and accelerated towards home. 'So…jus' sayin''

Jo gave Terry another chip before stuffing one in her own mouth. 'Not in trouble yet,' sniggered Jo.

'Don't be cocky. Pride 'n' fall and all that.' Terry's disapproving tone persuaded Jo to leave the matter be.

Minutes later, her mother unwrapped fish 'n' chips and placed them on warmed plates. Everyone shuffled their chair closer to the kitchen table, and the family enjoyed their ritual Friday night feast.

'Coming to the pub?' Brian got up from the table.

'No, Dad. Not in the mood,' Jo said.

'Don't blame yer lass. Did I tell you both I'm going to build a fishpond?'

'Yes, Dad.' Jo and Terry chorused their boredom.

'Good! So, you'll be up for a bit of pond digging this weekend?' Brian suggested enthusiastically.

Jo and Terry groaned.

'Take your mind off things.'

'More like cheap labour!' Terry laughed.

Brian tousled Terry's hair. 'Up sharp, mind. Tomorrow, we start digging!' Brian's smile matched the glee in his voice as he collected his coat from the rack next to the back door and left for the pub. 'Laters.'

## Chapter 8

*Monday 16 April. London Provost Company, Rochester Row, London.*

Although Jo had enjoyed her mother's cooking and being with Terry, her back was sore from digging and carting the soil to the dump. The project was a lot bigger than her father had let on, and in some ways, she was glad to be back at her day job, though most of her 'To Do List' was tedious paperwork.

Jo made her way around the edge of the parade ground, which doubled as a car park. The impressive facade of the Edwardian building belied the worn and outdated decor inside. She opened one of the wooden double doors, noticing her fingerprints spoil the cold, shiny brass doorplate. Her heart always sank when she entered because the offices were painted with standard-issue magnolia. She guessed it was supposed to be inoffensive, but as it was on the wall of every Army building, it had undoubtedly bred her contempt for the colour. Wooden desks, placed in blocks of two commissioned during World War II, once varnished deep brown, were now unpleasantly stressed to a nondescript grey colour. A typewriter, wooden admin trays and a beige square buttoned dial phone adorned each desk.

Jo placed her army-issue handbag next to her chair and slumped down on it. She had spotted the Charge Sheet and report she had hurriedly typed on Friday back in her In-Tray. Paper clipped to the report was a memo from the unit's Officer Commanding, Major Relish, requesting that she retype it.

'Fuck.' Jo sighed and began inserting a new charge sheet into the typewriter—always tricky for Jo.

She saw Sergeant Major Hart leave the OC's office and approach her. She feigned interest in the report.

Hart stopped at Jo's desk. 'OC wants you.'

'Me?' Jo stood up.

'Yes, you.'

'Yes, ma'am.

'Good luck. You're gonna need it.' Hart appeared grim.

Shit! Now what? Jo put on her scarlet red beret and smoothed down the left side, accentuating the Women's Royal Army Corps cap badge before checking her tie and skirt seams were straight. Her heart beat faster as she knocked on the Major's door. Her mind raced through all the reasons why he wanted to see her. Had someone seen her with Terry? Had she fucked up on the operation? She didn't think she had. Maybe it had to do with Lizzie? Yes, probably to do with Lizzie.

'Enter.' Major Relish commanded.

Jo opened the door and marched in, saluting before closing the door behind her.

'You asked to see me, sir.'

A thin man about forty years old sat behind a single desk in his large and sparsely furnished office. A portrait of Queen Elizabeth the Second, aged about twenty-five, hung on the wall behind him.

'Well, Corporal Clark, congratulations on your work last week.'

'Thank you, sir.'

Relish cleared his throat and avoided eye contact. 'And I'm sorry you had to deal with the death of your friend. It's never easy.' After a short pause, he looked up and smiled warmly. 'But I've good news. I've been instructed to promote you to the rank of Sergeant. Congratulations, Sarn't Clark. You've earned it. And Manning and Records has agreed to you joining the SIB permanently.' He vigorously shook her hand.

'Thank you, sir.' Jo grinned as she took the three stripes he offered with her left hand before stepping back and saluting. She couldn't wait to tell Terry. The pay raise would go a long way to buying their house. But she still needed to know if she was a candidate for the Close Protection Unit. She quite fancied looking after royalty and the like.

'Sir, is there any news on my transfer to CPU?'

Relish's lips twitched. 'Sergeant Clark, as much as I'm impressed by your ambition to be a member of The Close Protection Unit, I only promoted you...' He checked his watch and chuckled. 'Sixty seconds ago.'

'I know, sir, but I put in for the transfer ages ago.'

'Well, Sarn't, I'd leave it for a while if I were you. And maybe you'll prefer the SIB in the long run. You've a lot to offer us, and we you. Anyway, all that vetting is tiresome and intrusive. I'm sure you value your privacy. On top of that, they will talk to everyone about everything you do, your family and friends, even your sex life—and you don't want that now, do you? Stay with us. We'll take care of you. Don't worry, Sarn't, I'm sure you'll be promoted again soon. Now, is that all?'

Jo took the hint, stepped back, saluted, turned to her right and marched out of his office. Hart called out from her office as Jo returned to her desk in the Main Office.

'Sarn't Clark, get yourself in here.'

'Yes, ma'am!'

Hart rose from her chair, smiling. 'Congratulations, Jo. Take this afternoon off to move into the Senior Ranks' Mess.'

Smiling, Jo shook Hart's hand. 'Thanks, Sarn't Major.'

'Not sure why you're so happy—it's drinks all round tonight.'

Jo's grin broadened. 'Yes, ma'am!'

A few minutes later, Jo packed a couple of suitcases and carried them from the Junior Ranks Accommodation to the Sergeants' Mess. The Messing Sergeant opened the door for her.

'Welcome, Jo. I've allocated you room nine. Let me know if anything needs fixing. Dinner is at six. Dress rules are in your room on your desk. See you later.'

Jo struggled up the staircase and along the first-floor corridor. Almost at the end, she found room nine on the right. Pushing the door open with her elbow, she put her suitcases down and surveyed the room. It was larger than her corporal's accommodation, but not by much. It was still just as functional with a washbasin next to the single-door wardrobe. A window looked out onto the parade square. Jo hung her clothes and placed Knick-knacks around the room, with a photograph of her parents on the bedside locker. Then she returned to the Block to collect the rest of her things.

At six o'clock, ten senior ranks who lived in and Staff Sergeant Armstrong stood expectantly at the bar, cheering her arrival.

'Get 'em in, Jo,' ordered Armstrong. 'You're lucky it's not the whole Mess. You're going to get away lightly.' He took his pint of beer and drank it swiftly, not hesitating to order a second.

Her colleagues jostled her as she ordered drinks on her tab. Half an hour later, the gong sounded for dinner. Hart led Jo in, followed by the other members.

'Bit different from the cookhouse.' Hart winked. 'You'll soon get used to it. Just don't get on the mess staff's bad side.'

The two women sat together at one of the long polished wooden tables, where places had been set. Jo touched a knife in the array of cutlery in front of her, unsure what to use first.

'Work from the outside in,' Hart suggested.' Oh, and call me Carol when you're in the Mess.'

'Thanks. Didn't know that.'

Mess stewards served three courses, and Jo negotiated the banter and cutlery with equal aplomb. After dinner, everyone reverted to the bar.

'Jo, you don't owe any more drinks. Though they will tell you otherwise.' Hart chuckled. 'And you don't have to stay longer than you want.' Carol collected a drink before joining another Warrant Officer at a table in a corner.

Armstrong sidled up to Jo. 'Are you up for a bit of fun and games?'

'Of course.'

Armstrong explained the drinking game rules to Jo while the others joined two small tables, putting chairs along each side. Then Armstrong divided the ensemble into two teams, which sat on opposite sides of the table. The Barman put four pints in front of each team.

The Barman yelled, 'Go!'

The first person in each team began drinking. When he finished his beer, the next person started theirs. The race became frantic, the raucous cheering and cursing louder. One drinker poured most of his glass over his head and suit. The moment the glass was empty, his teammate began drinking his pint. Now, Jo had a chance of sinking the winning pint, chugging it down as fast as she could and out of the corner of her eyes, she noticed her opponent was catching up fast. She had drunk about two-thirds before making a hasty decision, pouring the remainder over her head. Her team cheered, and Armstrong held Jo's arm in triumph.

'Well done, Jo! Good call.'

Jo attempted to squeeze the liquid out of her hair.

Armstrong slapped her on the back. 'Let's go again. Get 'em in, Jo.'

She examined her jacket and skirt and considered her options. 'Thanks, chaps, but I'm going to pass.'

Drenched from head to foot, Jo walked out of the Anteroom to the derision of her fellow senior ranks.

Ignoring them, she pushed on the brass door plate to leave and caught Hart's approving smile. Jo collected a purse containing ten and fifty pence pieces from her room before going to the public telephone box at the front of the Mess. A glass door to the call box gave the illusion of privacy, but Jo knew better. She knew her calls to Terry might be monitored, depending on the authorities' resources and suspicions.

She dialled the number of the public call box situated in 12 Company's Senior Ranks' Mess. When the pips sounded, she slotted two ten-pence pieces into the box.

'Miss Gordon speaking. Who do you want to speak to?'

Jo surprised the Regimental Sergeant Major had answered, stammered Terry's name.

'I got it!' Exclaimed Jo to Terry when she picked up the receiver.

'Congratulations! How's your room?'

'Not that different, really. Had to buy a round of beers and played the usual beer games.'

'Ugh. I hate that.'

'Me too.'

A lull in the conversation ensued—the possibility the call might be recorded jostled with thoughts of danger, passion and love. Danger always won out, so they waited, listening to each other's breath, imagining a dialogue that declared their feelings.

The pips sounded again.

'Shall I put in another?' Jo asked.

'No, don't waste your ten p pieces. We'll see…'

The pips interrupted again, and Jo replaced the phone on the cradle.

## Chapter 9

*Monday 16 April. 12 Company WRAC, Inglis Barracks, London.*

At 08:15 hours, Major Marwood prepared to leave her Army flat for her office. Looking in the hall mirror, she centred her forage cap, admiring the newly acquired gold braid, denoting a Field Officer, around its peak. She loved calling it scrambled eggs. It made her chuckle. How long, she wondered, would it be before she would be promoted to Acting Lieutenant Colonel? She was looking forward to selection for Staff College, and after that slog, she would be in line for promotion.

However, one matter was standing in her way—her fitness. She had failed her Basic Fitness Test in January, retaken it at the beginning of February, and failed again. She had more time to complete the one-and-a-half mile BFT at age forty, but she was still forty-five seconds outside the allotted time.

Marwood buttoned up her great coat per regulations, donned her gloves and headed for the office. Though preoccupied with a difficult decision, she walked smartly along the pathway from the female officer's mess to her office in the Company headquarters, returning the salutes of the women who passed her. Her mind oscillated between Private Lowe's suicide and whether she should call in the Special Investigations Branch to investigate the rumours that surrounded the cause of the soldier's death and that of her future attendance at Staff College critical to gaining promotion to full colonel. Maybe she would even make Brigadier.

Shuddering, she felt the burden of a decision that was hers to make. Should she call in the SIB? No one liked the SIB. And no one wanted to acknowledge the existence of lesbians in one's unit. Yes, you knew they were there, but….

She had discussed the matter with her Second in command, Captain Trueman. She disliked the popular officer but knew that in a crisis, the Regimental Sergeant Major and Captain Trueman were her best-sounding boards. Both of her advisers had recommended the matter be formally investigated because rumours flying around the unit suggested lesbians had played a part in Pte Lowe's untimely death.

Letitia Marwood had never experienced a witch-hunt. She'd heard about them. She knew it didn't look good for one's career if, as the Officer Commanding, you had to call in the SIB. It was a universally accepted fact that most senior ranks were gay and that one turned a blind eye to such matters if the Women's Royal Army Corps was to function efficiently, providing support to the larger Army.

She entered her office and hung her coat and hat on the stand. Standing in front of a frameless mirror on the back wall of her office, Marwood absent-mindedly checked that her blond bun was still tidy and that her green eyeshadow and brown mascara had not smudged. As she did so, she pondered further, gathering her mental strength to make the call. Rules are rules! Officers like her obeyed and upheld them for the good order and military discipline of their troops. Indeed, in this dilemma, the SIB was probably the lesser of the two evils. What she was about to do was for the good of her unit—it was her duty to her Queen and Country to protect her soldiers—wasn't it? Of course it was! She nodded her resolve to the figure in the mirror.

Marwood sat down at her desk and automatically reached for the ever-present pack of Benson and Hedges before lighting a cigarette and inhaling. Lipstick-red lips pursed and blew out a plume of smoke as she considered RSM Gordon, then Sergeant White. Yes, they were probably both lesbian—it was par for the course. However, the RSM cautioned her that calling in the SIB would have a swift and debilitating impact on company morale.

Marwood took comfort in the fact the RSM had done all she could to find out who had pushed Pte Lowe to the brink—but it was only hearsay. She contemplated the fact that the Bible explicitly forbade homosexuality. Her officer training insisted religion was an absolute necessity for an officer to function in a conflict so one can bury one's troops and still be able to carry on fighting. Ergo, she was protecting the troops under her command by upholding ancient religious beliefs and Ministry of Defence policy.

Sergeant Treacher knocked on her door and brought in the first of many cups of coffee.

'Morning, Sarn't. Close the door on your way out and see I'm not disturbed.'

Marwood waited until she was alone. Boosted by nicotine and caffeine, she dialled the Deputy Director, London District, Colonel Cato-West.

The Directors assistant patched her through.

'Good morning, ma'am,' Marwood hesitated, waiting for the usual reply—there wasn't one. Discouraged, she carried on. 'I don't know whether you have read the report, ma'am?'

'I have Letitia. Difficult reading. Always very sad when one learns of suicide. Looks like we can't protect our women. It'll put parents off, you know.'

'I know, ma'am.'

'Now, Letitia, am I given to understand you wish to have the SIB investigate?'

'I was hoping you might advise me, ma'am.'

'Have you discussed this with your RSM and Two I C?'

'Yes, ma'am.'

'And?'

'They think we need to find the ringleader and get rid of her.'

'So, there is a ring?'

'Those are the rumours.'

'Well, we don't need the press getting wind of that. Suicide is bad enough, but a lesbian ring—The Sunday People will have a field day.' Cato-West scoffed.

'No, ma'am.'

'You have my permission. But do not, and I repeat, do not let the press get hold of this. And make sure it counts, Letitia. Remember, the Director takes a dim view of this kind of thing, especially if it gets in the press or fails to achieve its objective. Keep me posted, Letitia.'

'Yes, ma'am.'

'Very well. Goodbye and good luck.'

Marwood didn't get to reply. She replaced the handset and exhaled tobacco smoke. She had her orders, yet she was fearful and somewhat reluctant to carry them out.

Where's your backbone, Letitia? Marwood sat up straighter and finished her coffee. She dialled The London Provost Company.

'Major Relish, Letitia Marwood, OC Twelve Company here. I have permission to engage your team to investigate an alleged lesbian ring.'

**Chapter 10**

*Day One of the investigation*

Jo, still on a high from being promoted to Sergeant, would have skipped from the Mess to the office if Standing Orders permitted. Instead, she walked swiftly, with purpose. She could hear the London traffic despite the barrack's high walls. And after last night's heavy drinking to celebrate her promotion, she was glad to breathe in the fresh air, such as it was.

As she entered the office, a strong smell of coffee permeated the air. Glancing around the room, she saw her colleagues sitting on their desks rather than at them. Each policeman nursed his hangover with a mug of coffee. The conversation was minimal and muted.

She settled at her desk, curious that no one was working. 'What's happening?'

'Wait out. The Sarn't Major is with the OC,' Staff Sergeant Armstrong replied. 'Something's up.'

'Lezzers again, probably,' Sergeant Nick Acorn added.

'Probably.' Armstrong sipped his coffee. 'Hope it's not too far away. The missus is getting fidgety with me being away 'n' all that.'

'Ahh! Who'd have thought your missus would've missed you?' Nick mocked.

'Shut up, Acorn. You don't even have a missus.'

'Me? Nah! I like to play the field.'

The senior ranks laughed.

'There you are, Jo. Have Nick here. He's free and not too fussy.' Armstrong sniggered.

'No, thanks, Staff, I'm fussier than Nick.'

The male sergeants chuckled in unison.

Nick grinned. 'Let me know when you're ready, Jo, and I'll show you a good time.' He followed up his offer with a wink.

'You into necrophilia, then?' Jo shot back.

Cackles of laughter filled the room.

'Listen up!' Sergeant Major Hart commanded as she walked into the office. The banter abruptly stopped as she sat on the corner of the nearest desk. 'There is a situation at Mill Hill.'

All the men leaned forward. Jo bit her lip and sat as still as her nerves would allow. Fuck! What now?

'We've been asked to investigate a lesbian ring at Twelve Company. The ringleader is presumed to be a Corporal Quade.'

Jo's stomach roiled. Nausea palpitated in her stomach. Her chest heaved with her anxiety. She looked around, hoping she hadn't given herself away and nobody noticed her reaction to the news. She watched the men guffaw and nudge each other in the ribs without comprehending the situation. All she could think about was Terry and how they had to stay out of this mess. She calmed her thoughts and tuned back in.

Hart had been briefing the team and paused to check her notebook. 'The OC a Major er…Marwood has called us in to investigate. As you know, there was a suicide in that particular unit last week. The intel is that Corporal Quade….'

'Quade the queer!' Nick yelled.

'Enough!' Hart impatiently waited for silence. 'We will RV in one hour at the guardroom. Staff, strut your stuff. Hart left the office.

Armstrong called the team together. As Jo listened to his instructions, she felt her body temperature rise as she focused on how to alert Terry. If things went badly, they could end up on the wrong end of this investigation. Some time ago, they agreed to a coded message to alert each other. The problem was how and how fast she would get it to her—speed was of the essence.

At the close of the briefing, Nick rubbed his hands together 'Great, we have a nice juicy lesbo witch-hunt, and we'll be busy for a week or two. Get your kit together, Jo. We'll be staying over.'

'Jo, with me,' Armstrong ordered.

Jo shrugged at Nick and followed Armstrong into a back office, where Susan, a civilian administrator, sat.

'Hello, Susan. This is Jo. Can you show her around your Queers' catalogue? She has an unbelievable system for tracking lesbians.' Armstrong left, shutting the door behind him.

Jo looked around the office cum storeroom. Eight grey steel filing cabinets, approximately four feet high, lined the walls. Six had drawers labelled with a portion of the alphabet.

'I don't remember seeing you before,' Susan acknowledged Jo.

'No, this is my first time investigating this sort of thing. Bloody hell, how many people are in here?' Jo silently judged Susan's fashion sense. As a civilian, Susan got to wear what she wanted—a green tweed skirt, a cream blouse and a camel-coloured cardigan today. Despite dressing like a forty-year-old, Susan was probably the same age as Jo.

'I've never counted. These over here are male homosexuals.' She waved her hand in the direction of the cabinets. 'The rest are female homosexuals—The Queen Alexandra nurses and the WRAC.'

'Female homosexuals?'

'Yes, that's what the Ministry of Defence likes to call them.'

'Weird. Why not lesbian?'

'Oh, I don't know. Not my place to question what the MOD wants. I just do my job.' She gave Jo a quizzical look before brightening. 'Come over here.' They walked to a desk with an index card filing system.

Jo opened a drawer. 'You filed all these?'

'No, some go back before my time. But I've done a lot. More in recent years.'

'Must take some organising?' Jo covered her disgust with an ultra-matter-of-fact tone that seemed to encourage Susan.

'Yes. Taken me years to organise it so we can get the information out easily. You should've seen what I inherited.' Susan tutted and rolled her eyes.

'I had no idea.' Jo turned away before Susan could see her emotions boiling beneath her professional facade. What a waste of time and taxpayers' money and for what exactly?

'Yeah, not many people do. We have everything we've ever confiscated in these four.' She paused to point to a set of specific cabinets. 'Photos, letters, cards and the like.'

'What's in the boxes on the shelves?'

Susan chuckled. 'The men call them the toys!'

'Toys?'

'Dildos, that kind of thing.' Susan blushed, though she tried valiantly to be nonchalant. 'Actually, I've never looked in there—the men do that cataloguing. Doesn't bear thinking about, really. Honestly, lesbians are seriously depraved. Right, let's focus on the Index Cards.' Susan redirected Jo's attention. 'This holds every name that has come up in our investigations. Whether guilty or not.'

'Guilty? Can't be guilty because it's not a crime anymore.' Jo's hands curled into fists, fists that she would never use to fight the injustice she felt.

She stared at the secretive steel silos, concealing documentation on friends, kindred spirits and sister soldiers. A blast of heat coursed through her body she recognised as uncontrolled anger. She took a deep breath.

Susan spluttered. 'No. But yes. Well, yes, because they get kicked out.'

'Yeah, but there's no court-martial, is there?' Jo's nails dug into the palms of her hands—anger edged into her voice.

'There is for the men.'

'But not for the women.' Jo corrected.

'Oh, I don't know about Military Law and things—that's for you to sort out.' Susan shook her head. 'I keep my head down and do my job.'

'So, you said.' The irritation in Jo's tone was obvious.

'So,' Susan smiled nervously, opening a drawer and pulling out a card. 'If you have a name, you go to this system first.'

'Right, this one is a Corporal Smollett. Dated June last year. Someone tipped us off she'd been having an affair with a private. Likely a revenge tip.'

'A revenge tip?'

'Well, let's see.' Susan went to a grey cabinet with the drawer labelled DA-EA and rifled through the files. 'Yes. Here she is. The tipster was one Private Dobbs. She left the Army after giving us the name.'

'Left? Not discharged?'

Susan turned the card over. 'Yeah, Dishonourable Discharge. Army Act nineteen fifty-five, section sixty-six, Conducting oneself disgracefully - unnatural act. Private Dobbs informed us Corporal Smollet had a string of girlfriends. That's the problem, you see—they're so promiscuous. Amazing they don't catch AIDS or something. Corporal Smollet—yes, also discharged. Took us some time, judging by the date, but our lads got her in the end.' She slotted it back into the filing cabinet before shoving the drawer with a pelvic thrust.

'How long? To catch her, I mean?'

'Three years. Her file is over here.' She walked to a cabinet and opened the cabinet labelled SA-T, retrieving a blue folder. 'Let me see…. yes, three years, a bit of cat and mouse.'

'Cat and mouse?'

'Yeah, let her go back to her unit and surveillance on and off. She requested to change trade and was denied, and they made it difficult for her to be promoted. By putting the kybosh on her career, they hoped she would leave. Took a while, though, and she had to be pushed.' She popped the folder back in its place, turning to Jo and slamming the drawer shut with her backside. 'So, we have the index cards here for the initial search. If they have a file, it will be indicated on the card, and then the details will be held in their P file—Okay?'

'I think I understand,' Jo spoke with a note of sadness.

'Good. It's easy once you get the hang of it. Let me know if I can help.' Susan hummed the tune to 'Jesus Wants Me for a Sunbeam' as she ambled back to her desk, hidden behind the filing cabinets.

Jo was tempted to open the index card drawer marked CA-D. She touched the brass handle, feeling its smoothness with her forefinger, glancing to the corner of the room where Susan's desk was hidden. Jo withdrew her hand but committed to memory the location of the drawer, and the one marked WA-X. It was too risky to search now. More importantly, she had to tell Terry the SIB were about to turn 12 Company upside down in their search for 'perverted' women. She couldn't use the military phone here, Susan may hear, and in any case, the military exchange would log it. She decided she would phone on the way to Inglis Barracks.

Jo met the team as arranged and waited at the barrier.

'Right Jo, you're with me.' Hart pointed to the black Ford Cortina. 'We'll RV outside their Guardroom. Don't go beyond the barrier until we're all present.'

'Right you are, ma'am,' Armstrong tugged his non-existent forelock.

A convoy of two black Ford Escort Estates and a Cortina drove out of Rochester Row Barracks for North London.

'You're quiet, Jo.'

Jo chewed her lip.'Mmm.'

'Worried? I suspect you made a few friends while you were there.'

'Not really, ma'am. Maybe an enemy in Corporal Quade, just before I left.'

'Ah, yes, Quade. Not the sort of woman you'd go out on a limb for.'

Jo was anxious to change the subject and call Terry. She felt the sweat of her anxiety in her armpits despite her new antiperspirant.

'Ma'am, it's me Mum's birthday today, and I forgot it. I need to buy a card. Can we stop at a corner shop?'

'No probs. I'll stop at one near the barracks.'

Jo wanted a more immediate solution to her problem. She wanted Terry to know what was coming her way ASAP. Instead, she looked out the window at passers-by and motorcars—the world going about its business. At the same time, her mind worked on other options for communicating with Terry. What if someone else took the message? What if they worked out their code? No, they couldn't work out the code— could they?

An hour later, Hart pulled over at the bottom of Bittacy Hill, about a two-minute drive to the barracks, parking in a lay-by in front of a row of shops.

'Right, Jo, be quick! We must get there before word gets out.'

Jo jogged to the paper shop. While completing the purchase she didn't need, she calculated the risk of calling Terry from the phone box outside the shop. Risk or no risk, she must alert Terry. The shop bell jangled Jo's exit. She hesitated outside the door. Hart was watching her. Jo motioned she needed to make a call before stepping into the red phone box and onto an accumulation of weeks of newspapers. The stink of ammonia irritated her nostrils. She punched in an array of numbers and, when the pips sounded, jammed a ten-pence piece hard into the slot.

'Gymnasium, Lance Corporal Dart speaking, ma'am.'

Shit! Jo disguised her voice. 'Is Sarn't White available?'

'No, ma'am. I can take a message.'

Fuck! Fuck! Stay calm, Jo. 'We'd like her to play in the Southend Hockey tournament.' Having delivered the code words, she and Terry had previously agreed, Jo replaced the receiver. She sprinted to the car. 'Sorry. Thought I'd call me Mum. Made her day.'

Hart returned an enigmatic smile, started the engine, and drove to join the rest of the team outside the entrance to Inglis Barracks.

## Chapter 11

Terry, slightly damp from the rain shower that interrupted the last BFT, headed for her office to find a towel to dry her hair. She guessed she could run from John O'Groats to Land End in a week if she counted all the tests she ran. Still, it was good to have nearly all the unit pass their test. Her supervising warrant officer at district HQ would be pleased. She reflected on the women who marred her results, Private Cook and Major Marwood. Cook had an excuse because she had been in hospital with some kind of eating disorder. But Marwood, as an officer, should set a good example and just grind it out.

Max, breathless, intercepted her proffering a piece of paper.

'Everything all right, Max?'

'Someone phoned for you.'

'Yeah, who?' Terry opened her office door.

'Didn't say, But here's the message. Something about hockey.'

Terry rubbed her chin as she read the note. 'Come in the office and shut the door.' Terry stood in front of Max, placing her hands on the young woman's shoulders. 'Max, what I'm about to say to you now, I never said, Okay?'

Max frowned as she grasped the situation was serious.

'Go to your bed space and get rid of any letters from your girlfriends.'

Max opened her mouth to protest her innocence.

Terry held up a hand. 'Listen to me. Photos anything. Don't stop to talk to anyone. Tell no one. Don't ask me any questions. Just go. I'll see you later. And remember, I didn't tell you this. Now scarper. And remember, if you're asked any questions about anything or anyone.' Terry put a finger to her lips. 'Schtum. Got it?'

'Yes, Sarn't.'

Max left the office, sprinting to the women's accommodation, colloquially called The Block.

Terry left to jog across the parade square cum car park, past the main offices, to the Senior Ranks Mess. She ran two at a time up the stairs to her room, opened her bedroom door and shut it quietly. Her heart was beating fast, not from the effort of running but from the fear of being caught. She picked up the photo frame on her bedside locker and slid the latch back on the short end of the frame to remove the photograph of her and Jo at Brighton Pier from its beard—a picture of her chosen parents, before slipping it into her tracksuit trouser pocket. She refixed the latch on the frame and returned to the gym. As she approached, she saw Marwood standing in the doorway, hands on hips. She placed her hand over her tracksuit pocket as if to hide the evidence of her relationship better.

'Good morning, Sarn't White. You're late.'

'I know, sorry, ma'am, I needed to change my shirt. I went for a run with Captain Trueman earlier. She put in a nine-thirty. Fair wore me out.'

Terry watched the OC's face harden.

'Well, no danger of that with me. Right! Let's get on with it. I've got a busy day.'

'I'll get the stopwatch, ma'am.' Terry unlocked the drawer and was about to slip the photograph into the drawer when she felt the OC observing her. She hesitated momentarily and left the picture in the secrecy of her pocket.

'Right, ma'am. Let's walk to the starting point. Then listen for my....'

'Count down, and you will keep the pace.' Marwood's impatience was explicit.

Terry set a steady, fast walking pace. Because of her age, the OC had more time to complete the course and could easily complete it if she kept up with Terry. The route took them towards the Junior ranks accommodation before veering off to the depot. Terry encouraged the OC to keep up before noticing four men and two women in almost identical raincoats hurrying toward the accommodation block. Terry's attention wandered from Marwood to the group.

'What's caught your eye, Sarn't?'

'Lot of visitors.' Terry tried to sound curious but not concerned.

Marwood slowed to a stop. 'Sorry, Sarn't, I have to go.'

'Tomorrow, ma'am?'

'I'll keep you posted.' Marwood changed direction and headed back to the officer's mess.

Terry dashed to the gym. Checking no one was around, she went into the storeroom. Max had done an excellent job tidying it yesterday. Terry stood in front of the stack of navy hockey skirts and slid a hand into the pile near the bottom, assuring herself this was as safe a place as any. She retrieved the photo from her pocket and pushed it into the gap she had made. As she withdrew her hand, the skirts filled the space. Terry stood back to satisfy herself that nothing looked amiss before whispering a prayer.

## Chapter 12

Lance Corporal Maxine Dart, Max to her friends, sprinted across the grass quadrangle, ensuring she kept to the concrete pathway. Terry's words spun around in her head. She cursed herself for keeping the letters and pictures of her girlfriend. Now, she would have to destroy them without being seen and as fast as possible. How the fuck was she going to do that?

As she neared The Block, she noticed four men and two women in civilian clothes heading in her direction. Max wrenched open the door to the accommodation and bounded upstairs to her bed space. She opened the drawer of her bedside locker, grabbing an envelope containing letters and photographs before running into the laundry area with the intention of either hiding or disposing of the envelope. Panicking, she checked behind water pipes, then looked out the window before deciding that would be too risky. She spotted a plastic yellow cigarette lighter beside an empty but still dirty ashtray. She tried the lighter. It flickered. She tried it again, and it lit, sputtered, and extinguished.

Shit!

She looked around the kitchen area, but there was nothing she could use. She picked up the lighter again, shook it and sparked it into life. It stayed alight. Max exhaled her relief as she put the tiny flame to the corner of one letter and then another, dropping them as they caught fire into the sink one after the other and then the two photos. Hearing footsteps closing in on her, she mumbled for the paper to burn. A burly man in a raincoat, who she recognised from the depot theft as Staff Armstrong, pushed her aside to extinguish her sacrifice by turning on the taps, reducing the letters and photos to a brown mulch.

Realising Armstrong was focused on gathering evidence, Max took the opportunity to sprint into the corridor, dodging past two men and down the stairs. She judged she could make a run for it and reach the safety of the gym. Max's past life had furnished her with an inbuilt bias against authority, with one exception, Sergeant Terry White, and if she reached her, she knew she would be safe, so she ran until her feet were swept from under her as she was about to reach the exit. She had enough time to turn her face to the right before she hit the ground chin first. Her teeth jolted into her jaw, stunning her for a second before Armstrong roughly pulled her to her feet.

'Name, rank and number?' Armstrong demanded.

Max opened and closed her jaw to check it was still working before answering. 'W405189, Lance Corporal Dart.'

'Stay where you are, Corporal.' He retrieved his notebook from his raincoat pocket and made a note. Max shuffled her feet, anxious to be at the gym.

'Can I go now, Staff?'

'Go on, get out of here. But mark my words. You and I will be talking again.'

Max walked as carefree as she was able, considering her injuries—she tasted her blood, and her cheek throbbed. When she thought she was out of sight, she jogged the final stretch to the gym straight into Terry's office.

'Blimey Max, what's happened to you?'

'That SIB Staff Sarn't forced me to the ground.' Max's tears trickled down her face, and she sniffed. 'Bloody hurts.'

'Let me look at you.' Terry looked into Max's mouth and gently tilted her head to one side, examining the damage to her face. 'Max, go to the toilet and rinse your mouth out. When you come back, I'll fix your face.'

Terry opened the first aid box and rummaged through it, looking for something to help. Max limped back into the office, dabbing her face with toilet paper.

'I'm okay. Not sure there's much you can do with my face. It hurts like fuck, but the skin's not broken, and I've had worse.'

'Worse? Blimey. My Dad knocked me about as a kid, so I know how that can be.'

'I didn't have a dad.'

'Oh.' Terry looked at the floor.

'Yeah.' Max stood up straight with false bravado. 'Don't bovver me, and I ain't about to let this bastard grind me down.'

Terry glimpsed a look of fear on Max's baby face.

'What else happened at the Block?'

'Burnt the letters from Maggie and the photos, but I think Staff may have what's left of them. I hope they can't use it as evidence.'

'Who knows, sometimes they don't need actual evidence. Someone only has to mention your name and say they suspect you're a lesbian and….'

'And, what?' Max gasped.

'You never seen a witch-hunt before?'

'No, Sarn't. Is that what this is?'

'It is. It pisses me off. The SIB come barging into our lives. All we're doing is loving someone, and it's a crime because they're the same sex. It's shitty. But it gets worse. They turn women on other women. People who want revenge use the SIB to get even—some to get rivals out of the way, others to get a jammy posting. And some of our friends will break under the questioning.'

Max's eyes widened. 'How do they do that? What? Do they torture you or something?'

'Listen, Max, do yourself a favour, don't listen to rumours. Keep your mouth shut. Don't give any names. That way, you can live with yourself after this is all over. And don't, whatever you do, admit to anything. Say nothing. That way, they can't get you.'

'But what about the torture?'

'No torture, Max. They might leave you alone for hours on end. Might not let you have lunch. They'll try subtle ways of breaking you. But remember, anything is better than leaving the Army.' Terry put her forefinger to her lips. 'Schtum.'

## Chapter 13

Jo waited for Armstrong at the entrance to the block. Her apprehension wreaked havoc on her digestive system. A multitude of thoughts combined into a burgeoning paranoia that made her hot and sweaty. How can I search someone's possessions, a violation for anyone, especially when I'm guilty of the same thing? What if I find something? How will I deal with that? What if I can't? Shit! This is a nightmare.

Armstrong strutted towards Jo with a smug grin that Jo wanted to physically remove. 'Just had a runner. Got her details. Come on, Jo. You're with me,' Armstrong opened the door to the first four-man room on the ground-floor corridor. Two other Sergeants took the rooms on the other side. Nick and three others did the same thing on the first floor.

'Right Jo, we're looking for photos, letters, basically anything that might implicate them in the ring or a relationship. Check everything, and I mean everything.' He opened a photo frame, shaking the photo and backing to the floor, tossing the frame on a bed.

Jo looked at the bed in front of her—soft toys of every kind, colour, and size covered the entire single bed. Jo considered how long it took for the Private to get into bed and then make it again in the morning to meet the exacting standards of a Block Inspection. She didn't fancy putting them all in order after inspecting each one, so she left them alone, instead choosing to search the bedside locker, hoping it would reveal the necessary evidence.

'Staff, shouldn't the owners of the kit be here?' Jo asked, struggling with the situation. This was her worst nightmare, searching women's belongings just because they were gay. It was all so unfair and unnecessary, and she was part of the problem when she had only ever wanted to be someone who kept others safe.

'No, we've got permission to go in. Come on. Don't slack!' Armstrong stroked a wayward strand of dark blonde comb-over out of his eyes, opened the wardrobe and pulled out every piece of clothing before pulling the mattress off the bed and up-ending it onto the pile.

Jo opened the wardrobe door. She hesitated, conflicted between following orders and following her natural empathy for a fellow lesbian. Jo spotted two cardboard shoeboxes decorated with hearts and flowers cut from magazines pasted on the pale green sides. It nestled secretively in the far corner of the wardrobe. Sliding one towards her, Jo felt her heart beat faster. She carefully opened it as if a cobra would strike at any moment. Lifting the lid, she sighed with relief as it contained sports trophies. Jo picked one up and read the engraving: Inter unit hockey, 1981. She replaced the medal with the dozens of others and slotted it back into the bottom of the wardrobe. She reached for another.

'Find anything?' Armstrong's head bobbed out of the wardrobe he was searching.

'Not yet, Staff.'

'Well, put your back into it. We can't come up empty-handed. There's always something.' He began systematically pulling out drawers and emptying the contents on the floor. Staff opened another wardrobe door, rummaging in the bottom. He stood up, holding a single.

''Ere we go!' A sinister smugness in his voice spread to his face. "I Am What I Am'. Now, if that ain't a lesbian anthem, I don't know what is.' He read the nameplate above the bedhead and made a note in his pocketbook. 'Right, Private Thurgood, we're gonna have a little chat.'

Jo stopped searching. 'It's only a record, Staff. Put it back.'

'No, this is evidence, Jo. She's definitely a lezzer.' He rummaged through the rest of the wardrobe. 'Hang on! Hang on! What do we have here?' He threw a lovingly ironed Army-issue white shirt to the floor, piled on two barrack dress jumpers and a skirt, followed by a raincoat.

'Look at these.' Grinning, he held up a pair of Levis 501s with a button fly. 'Bet there's a pair of boxers in 'ere somewhere. There's always a pair of boxers!' He continued to rifle through the pile of clothes at the back of the wardrobe.

Jo stopped her search and waited for Armstrong to resurface.

'Nope. Nothing this time. But there'll be a pair somewhere in this block, or I'm a monkey's uncle.'

Jo searched another bedside locker, pulling open the single drawer. It stuck a little, so she gave it a gentle tug, giving her enough room to put her hand into the space left by the drawer. She ran her fingers along the sides and over the top frame. Here it is. She retrieved the envelope taped to the top. Opening the flap, she sifted through the photos. Two girls in one picture, the identical girls in another, smiling their happiness. In the background was Brighton Pier.

'Got something?'

'Not sure, Staff. Photos—a couple of women.' Jo slid the precious moments back into the envelope.

'Naked?' he smirked.

'No!' She laughed. 'Looks like Brighton.'

'Brighton! Well done. Keep looking. Pop them in the box by the door.'

Jo hesitated. She knew what her duty was. But it didn't feel good. Their search was interrupted by half a dozen uniformed women dashing through the Block entrance. Some ran upstairs, others into the other bedrooms on the ground floor.

'Come on, girls, the Shit In Bulk is here,' shouted one.

'You can't search my stuff without my permission,' stated another.

'Oh yes, I can. Your boss said I could.' Armstrong replied, fussing with his comb-over again.

'Who? The OC depot? He wouldn't! I know he wouldn't!'

'No, Major Marwood was kind enough to help us,' Armstrong said.

'Might've known,' she shouted to her friends. 'Major Marwood, the cow! She asked for this!'

A cacophony of chaos filled the air as doors banged, drawers shunted open and closed, and the catches of wardrobe door locks clicked, heralding the advent of trouble. Young women filled with fear and dread bailed from doorways, crying and screaming.

Jo took the opportunity to return the envelope to its hiding place as its owner walked into the room and stared at her. Jo froze. She had been caught red-handed, failing to do her job. Had she been seen? Would she be reported? Panic shook Jo's hands.

'What're you doing?' the female soldier whispered.

'Searching your stuff,' Jo tried to sound confident.

The young woman ran to the window and yelled, 'SIB! Quick! Tell everyone.'

Seconds later, women ran from every direction of the compass to the Junior Ranks Accommodation, some to their cars, before driving out of the barracks.

After two hours of the team rifling through clothing and personal possessions, Armstrong called his team together.

'Okay, the boss says we should put this,' he pointed to a large cardboard box. 'In the mothballed guardroom, we'll meet the Sarn't Major there. Nick, come with me, and we'll take a little look at the bins behind the Sergeant's Mess. I'm thinking we might find some interesting stuff in there.' Armstrong rubbed his hands together at the prospect of what he might find. 'Jo, you go with the others to the guardroom. I'll meet you there when I'm done.'

The four junior sergeants carried their haul to the reopened 12 Company guardroom, complete with cells. Jo and the other Sergeants lined up some tables down the centre of the room and displayed their plunder.

Moments later, Hart, accompanied by a short, wispy woman in her early forties with gold braid on her forage cap, tottering in black patent leather shoes, pushed open the Guardroom door. Behind her were three younger women, wearing the barrack dress with the officers' haute couture lovat green skirts.

Hart spoke. 'Ma'am, this is Staff Armstrong and the team. Staff, this is Major Marwood.'

'And what's this?' Marwood said, grinning and pointing to a bullwhip. 'Fascinating, I must say.' She smiled insidiously at Armstrong, who smirked.

Nick stepped forward. 'Belongs to one Corporal Minter, ma'am.'

'Well, that says everything, doesn't it?' Marwood addressed her posse of young officers.

'Actually, ma'am,' said Captain Trueman, the second in command. 'I think she uses it to train horses at Belmont Racing Stables. I gather she's a dab hand at it. Did you find other riding clothes? Jodhpurs? Boots? That sort of thing?' she asked Nick.

'Dunno, ma'am.' Nick shrugged. 'Might've. But they aren't suspicious. But the whip is!' He grinned.

Trueman turned away in disgust.

'Quite right, Sarn't,' Marwood walked towards the door. 'Quite right. Well, we'll be off. See you tomorrow. Oh, before I go, anything in the Sergeant's mess?'

'Nothing,' Armstrong replied. 'And it weren't for the lack of looking, were it, Nick?'

'Yeah. Nothing,' Nick backed up his immediate superior.

'I find that hard to believe.' Disgusted, Marwood pushed open the door to leave, with her officers following in her wake.

## Chapter 14

*Day Two*

At 08:30 hours precisely, Marwood sat at her desk in the office of the Officer Commanding. It was in the middle of the headquarters corridor, so the OC was at the centre of everything. She reached for the ever-present Benson and Hedges packet and lit a cigarette. She considered who in her unit might be lesbian and whose name would come up. People, especially women soldiers, always surprised her. Those she thought might be gay were often not. She could never quite work who was what. And it had never really bothered her until now.

She checked her diary before exhaling noisily. At nine, she would meet the Warrant Officer in charge of the investigation, who was also gay, no doubt, and probably a good friend of the RSM. She wouldn't let that get in the way of things—she needed to protect her reputation. No, she would supervise this awful business, not the Regimental Sergeant Major. Going against one's RSM wasn't usual, but she felt she could no longer trust RSM Gordon or Trueman—they got on too well. Maybe this would be the time to shake things up around here and get things back on track—her track. She scanned the diary page again.

'Oh, Gawd!' Marwood exclaimed.

'Something the matter, ma'am?' Sergeant Treacher knocked casually before entering and placing the first cup of coffee of the day on her boss's desk.

'No, just realised I've got PT with Sarn't White today. Don't suppose the rain will put her off.'

'No, ma'am, she'll have you running around the gym or something. Miss Hart is in with the RSM. Thought you might want to know.' Treacher bobbed her head out of the office doorway. 'Ah, she's on her way up now.'

'Is she now? Thank you, Sarn't.'

Hart and Treacher met in the doorway. Hart smiled at Treacher before politely tapping on the OC's door and entering.

'Come in, Miss Hart. Take a seat. What do you have for me?' Marwood stubbed out a cigarette.

Hart's nose wrinkled at the smell of stale and fresh tobacco mingling in the air she was about to breathe. An almost finished black coffee was next to the dirty ashtray, adding to the strong odour.

'Ma'am, first off, Private Lowe didn't leave a suicide note. So, we're still in the dark about why she did it. As for the other matter, here's the complete list of names.' Hart passed a slip of paper to the OC before closing the office door.

Marwood's narrow shoulders hunched over as she bent forward to study the list. She ran her finger down the paper. 'Hmm, some Ministry of Defence, the rest are Posties. Focus on MOD first. We can't afford any scandals. Bad enough as it is. No senior ranks. Are you sure about that?' She lit another cigarette, inhaling deeply before exhaling a blast of grey smoke.

'Ma'am?' Hart cocked her head to one side.

Marwood grimaced and took another drag on her cigarette. Well, how about White, for example? Or your girlfriend, RSM Gordon! Oh, never mind. You all bloody close ranks anyway. 'What's your plan?'

'Sergeants Clark and Acorn will conduct the interviews. Staff Armstrong heads the team, and I shall supervise. If we're not here, then you can get us at The London Provost Company. I expect to complete our investigation within a few weeks, maybe sooner.'

'Good. Morale is at an all-time low, and I need you to do your job and be gone. Nobody likes the RMP or the SIB around. But I need you to be thorough. I want them all gone. I don't care who or what their rank is. Oh, and I'd be obliged if you kept me informed and only me. I will inform the RSM and the two IC as necessary. The discharges will be done on the day you find them guilty. I'll have Sarn't Treacher parcel up Private Lowe's belongings and have her platoon officer take them to her parents.'

Treacher knocked on the door and entered, carrying a second cup of coffee. She placed it on the OC's desk and retrieved the previous one. 'Want one?' Treacher asked Hart, with a note of reluctance in her voice.

'No, she doesn't. She's not staying,' replied the OC. 'Let me introduce you, Sarn't Major Hart. This is the Orderly Room Sergeant, Sergeant Treacher. She'll be doing all the documentation.'

'Anything else, ma'am?' asked Treacher.

'No. Oh, yes, wait a minute. Anyone going shopping today?'

'I can go, ma'am. The usual, is it?'

'Yes, if you wouldn't mind, Sarn't.' Marwood reached into her handbag and unzipped her purse, handing Treacher five pounds.

'Right, you are, ma'am.' Treacher closed the door behind her.

'I think that's it, ma'am.' Hart left the OC's office and walked down the corridor to the RSM's office. She knocked and entered before shutting the door firmly behind her and resting her back on it. 'How do you work for such a bitch?'

Gordon looked up. 'I look forward to the weekend.' She grinned.

Hart smiled. 'Anyway, she's asked me not to keep you informed. And what's with the Orderly Sergeant? She's an odd one.'

'Hmm, well, between you and me, we can let the OC think she's in the know. But we know different. Jo Clark knows what she's doing?'

'Yeah. I'm heading back to Rochester Row. I'll see you at home on Friday unless I get called in.' She placed her hand on the door handle, hesitating for a second and turning for one more question. 'What do you know about Sergeant Treacher?'

'Ann? She's okay—bit of a gossip. Seems to know everything that goes on around here, sometimes before I do, which I don't like. Come to think of it, whenever I want to find her, she's never in her office but mysteriously manages to be back in her office within minutes. I know we're not a huge garrison, but there's something of Uriah Heep in her.' Gordon noticed the lack of recognition in her friend's face. 'You know, the greasy chap. A Dickens character. Always rubbing his hands.'

'Yeah.' Hart shrugged. 'Does she run the OC's errands all the time?'

'Are you being a policeman again or just nosy, Carol?'

Hart chuckled. 'Bit of both. Right, I'm on my way. I'll keep you posted. See you Friday night?'

Gordon smiled. 'Roger that.'

## Chapter 15

Jo waited in the headquarters corridor while Sergeant Treacher unlocked the large, unused room at the end. Jo stepped inside and shivered.

'Yeah, we don't heat this room. Budget cuts.'

'Don't you think this is weird, Ann?' Jo walked towards the back wall and studied the portrait of the Queen. 'The only painting you ever see on the walls of offices like these is a picture of Queen Elizabeth. She must be what? Twenty-five in this picture. She's the same age, wherever and whenever you look at her, despite the fact this is 1984.'

'It's not a painting. It's a photograph.'

Jo looked closer at the portrait on the bare wall. 'Hmm, you might be right. Tricky to tell. I think it's one of those touched-up ones.'

'Doesn't matter, really. We don't use this office except for meetings of the officers or senior ranks. And that's rare these days, especially under Major Marwood. She asked me to make sure you have everything you need. As you can see, the furniture is stacked over there. My office will supply you with tea and coffee. Also, stationery unless you've brought your own. And I'll be doing the discharge documentation, so we'll be working together. How many do you have?' Treacher reached down to turn on a radiator.

'That's confidential at the moment.' Jo watched Treacher bob up, her face hardening as she stood upright. It made her hooked nose appear sharper, more pointed. Jo, disconcerted, continued. 'We want to make sure the innocent are not tainted. I'm sure you'd feel the same if your name were on the list.'

'Of course. You can turn the other radiator on when you've moved the other chairs.'

Jo continued her placation. 'But as soon as I need your services, I'll let you know. I assume you know your way around The Army Act Section sixty-six and sixty-nine.'

'Should do, Jo. I've done fifteen years.' Treacher's pissed tone was unmistakable.

Jo felt the hair on her neck bristle with Treacher's patronising. What was it about this woman that made her think she was not to be trusted? Jo dragged a table to the centre of the room. Treacher watched Jo work for a moment or two, then left. Still shivering, Jo carried three chairs to the table, placing one with the back to the door and the others across the table. She moved the remaining stack of chairs and turned on the second radiator. She heard it tick into action. Sergeant Major Hart opened the door and walked in, followed by Staff Sergeant Armstrong and the rest of the team.

Hart delivered a pithy brief before walking to the doorway. 'Any problems, let me or Staff know. Let's wrap this up quickly and efficiently. The OC is anxious the unit gets back to normal ASAP. She's already informed me morale is at an all-time low, and she's not happy. So, Staff, let's start with the prime suspect, Quade.'

'Quade the queer.' Nick sniggered.

Hart paused in the open doorway, pulling the door almost closed before turning around to make eye contact with Nick, her jaw set square. 'No matter what you think, Sergeant Acorn, all the suspects are to be treated with respect. If I find your particular peccadilloes have been excited by your pornographic imagination, I will have you off the job—got it?' She turned her head to address Armstrong. 'I think you should lead the first couple of interviews. After that, you can decide how to play it. Keep me informed. Right, let's get it done.' Hart left the team to their allotted tasks, her heels clicking her departure along the tiled floor.

Armstrong sat down. 'Right Jo, you heard the Sarn't Major, Corporal Quade it is. Nick, have the Orderly Sarn't summon her. I'd like you to escort her. Nothing like a nice bit of drama to start the investigation off. Show 'em we mean business.'

Armstrong fiddled with the list of names. 'I'll start, Jo. When I leave a gap, you come in. I'll go in hard, and you can soften her up. You know it won't stay at ten—they'll all give us loads of names by the end. I shouldn't wonder if we could get excess of thirty. Could be here for weeks.'

An involuntary shudder shot through Jo. 'Aren't we supposed to wrap this up ASAP? And, doesn't your missus miss you and all that?'

'Yeah, but if we get the names, we can't stop! Got to keep going. We have to get the queers out.'

'Can't we just settle with the major culprits? Quade and her gang?'

'Of course, we want them, but we also want every single one out. That's the rules, Jo.'

Jo thought the rules set by men were outdated. 'Staff, have you ever done a gay male investigation?'

Staff Armstrong shuddered. 'Yep! I hate the fuckers. Brown hatters, all of 'em. Got a fair few chucked out. Don't belong in The Army. They're not real men, and they're a danger to young, impressionable soldiers like my lad.'

Jo considered whether Mark Armstrong was a proper man—her thoughts were inconclusive. She turned her attention to the ten names and their details. Who were these women? What was their trade? Would they be able to tell she was one of them? And would they do what Susan said and offer her name as a 'Revenge Tip' to get them off the hook? And what should she do with those names? Hide them? Report them? She could feel her armpits prick with her nervousness.

Nick knocked on the door and entered the room, marching Corporal Quade in at the double. 'Lef ri, lef ri. Halt!'

Jo sat back in her chair, her arms folded while she glared at Quade, who, in barrack dress with drill shoes and beret, swung her arms to Nick's commands before stamping one-two to the halt and standing to attention.

'Sit down, Corporal Quade,' Armstrong spoke calmly. 'You know why you're here?'

Quade sat, crossing her arms and cocking her head to one side as if to hear the questions better. Jo realised she had gritted her teeth and tried to relax her jaw. She could feel the tension coiling the muscles in her body; she would get Quade for bullying. She owed Lizzie, but she knew she was complicit in using the witch hunt in all its awfulness to get even. She didn't like it, but she had no choice.

Armstrong waited for an answer. Nick scraped a plastic chair across the floor and set it down to Jo's left before taking a seat.

'Right. Now. Corporal Quade, or should I call you Delia?' Armstrong patronised.

'Call me what you like, Staff. It won't make no difference.'

Jo shifted her weight to the front of her seat, resting her arms on the desk. She scrutinised Quade and didn't care if it made her adversary uneasy.

'Well, Corporal, er Delia,' Armstrong studied the woman before him with a short blond bob, Princess Di style. 'Do they call you Delia?'

'Nope.'

'Didn't think so. What do they call you?'

'Doesn't matter, Staff. You won't be using my nickname coz you're not a mate.'

Armstrong was immune to the insult. 'Right, Delia. Let's get down to business, then. I have here a photograph of you, and I believe a Private Campbell. Looks like you're more than mates here.'

'Yeah, what of it?'

'Well, she's obviously your girlfriend.'

'How so?'

'Well, look at the photo and tell me she isn't your girlfriend.' He held the photo up in front of her face and, using his forefinger, flicked the image of Campbell. 'This here is your girlfriend, isn't it?' He raised his voice.

Quade didn't shift her position. Jo saw the hatred and disgust in Quade's eyes.

'She isn't my girlfriend,' Quade spat between gritted teeth.

'But you're here, in Brighton, with your arm around this attractive girl. You are preying on her Corporal Quade. She is a nice, innocent young girl, and you've turned her.'

'So let me get this straight, Staff.' Quade eyeballed Armstrong. 'You think because I'm in Brighton and I have my arm around a woman's shoulders, I'm gay?'

He tossed the photograph onto the table. Jo looked at the smiling couple, the woman's long hair blowing in the Brighton breeze, the iconic Palace Pier in the background. It reminded her of the trip she and Terry had taken to the Long Branch lesbian club in Brighton. They'd stayed at a cheap bed-and-breakfast in Kemp Town, known locally as Camp Town, for obvious reasons. After breakfast, they had walked to the beach and got a stranger to photograph them with the pier in the background, posing with their arms around each other's shoulders, giddy with the freedom that Brighton encouraged. They had sent the photos away to be developed and had them delivered to the Clark's home to be sure they didn't fall into the wrong hands.

'And what about this one? I think this is a Private Madden with you—another Dirty Weekend? Again, in Brighton—you seem to like a DWE in Brighton.' Armstrong tossed the photo on top of the other one.

Quade scowled.

Like a magician, Armstrong spilling cards impossibly hidden from within his hand produced one photo after another while running a commentary on what he thought they represented.

Quade stared at the wall behind him, presumably studying the portrait of the twenty-five-year-old Queen Elizabeth the Second.

There was silence. Jo took her cue. Fuck! Now she had to play good cop to this piece of shit. She shuffled her chair nearer the desk and leaned forward.

'When were these photos taken?' Jo asked, struggling to find a tone that suggested empathy.

'None of your business, Sarn't. See, they promoted you. I won't congratulate you, though.'

'And I told you—you'd get your comeuppance. And here you are.'

Armstrong shot Jo a look to remind her to be nice.

Jo fidgeted in her chair, hoping to find a more comfy and open position. After settling, she adjusted her tone and adopted a more relaxed pose, leaning back in her chair. 'So, when were these photos taken?'

Quade gawped at Jo.

'Is there a reason, Corporal Quade, why you won't tell me?'

Quade looked through Jo.

Jo continued. 'It seems rather incriminating if you don't say anything. Like you have something to hide. Do you have something to hide?'

Quade held Jo's gaze telepathically, communicating what she thought of her interrogator.

Jo sat upright, clasped her hands in front of her, and leaned forward. 'Corporal Quade, we can keep you here as long as we like. At some point, you will tell us what we want to know.'

'I don't think you can.'

'Can what?'

'Keep me here as long as you like.' Quade leaned forward into Jo's space, enjoying a moment of victory, forcing Jo to lean back in her chair.

Armstrong interrupted. 'We call the shots, Quade, not you.'

'Yeah? Well, I've been here an hour now. It'll be lunch soon, and you can't starve me.'

Armstrong lounged in his chair, legs splayed open, clasping his hands behind his head. 'You think you're clever, don't you, Quade? Let's see how clever you really are. Stand up. Attention! Sit down!'

Quade followed the orders.

'See, Quade, I call the shots!' He leered.

Quade sat down, fuming at being bullied.

'Right, let's take a break and get some coffee.' Armstrong got up. Quade got up as well. 'No. Not you, Quade. You're staying put.'

The three Senior Ranks left Quade sitting in her chair, closing the door behind them.

'Let's find some coffee!' Armstrong said. 'Bet there's some girly in the Orderly Room who does that. Off you pop, Jo.'

Jo strolled to the Orderly Room. 'Anyone know where we can make coffee?'

'I'll do it, Sarn't. Follow me.' A bustling Private Dawson, as short as she was wide, showed Jo and her colleagues where they could make coffee.

'Better get more milk from the cookhouse, or we'll run out this afternoon.' Dawson sighed, leaving the group in a huddle.

'She'll crack. Mark my words. They all do in the end,' Armstrong rubbed his hands together. 'Okay, we need to rough her up a bit. Watch and learn.' He picked up a mug and slurped his coffee. 'I'll go hard on her. Jo, you be nice. Nick, toughen up, mate, okay?'

Nick nodded. The trio sipped in silence for a few seconds.

'How's your son doing now?' Jo asked Armstrong, attempting to warm up the atmosphere.

'Good, thanks. Yeah, at RAF Cosford, training PTIs.'

'Play Rugby like his dad?' Nick asked.

'No. More of an athlete. Sprinter. Right, let's get on with it.' Armstrong placed his mug on the tray.

Jo and Nick followed suit leaving the small room cum kitchen to walk the twenty paces to the interrogation room. Armstrong opened the door and immediately began his interrogation.

'Sit up, Quade, don't slouch,' Armstrong bellowed from the doorway.

Quade flinched, then recovered. 'I need water.'

'No, you don't. I'll tell you when you can have water. If you have water, you'll want to pee, and then we have to have Sarn't Clark here escort you and watch,' Armstrong snarled from behind her. 'Don't want that now, do yer?'

Quade chose not to respond.

'Oh, I get it! You're getting off on a woman watching you pee. Pervert!' he barracked.

Jo winced at the verbal abuse but sat in her seat. She shot a sly glance at Nick and wondered what he was thinking about Quade's treatment. He was motionless—they were both motionless, not just motionless but struggling not to show their unease at Armstrong's treatment of Quade.

A sneer appeared on Quade's lips.

'So, Delia! You like to lick girls' cunts, do you?' Armstrong threw a photograph down of Quade with an arm around another woman. 'Lick this one, did you? Did she taste all lovely like peaches and cream?' He rose from his seat and strolled around the room, his head tilted slightly upwards, his hands behind his back. Smirking, he added. 'Or did she smell like a piece of rotting fish? Taste of wee?' He walked to the back of her chair and bent so his head was the same level as the seated Quade. 'Tell me! Do you lick women's cunts?' He snarled.

Jo shivered involuntarily. She hated Quade for what she did to Lizzie, but this—wasn't this abuse? He was a senior rank, and therefore, he called the shots. But this? The C word always made her feel uncomfortable. The short word was so brutal in her head, and it seemed that men only used it when they wished to be derogatory towards women. The word hurt and demeaned women in her eyes, and she saw the same effect in Quade's. Jo was torn between jumping to Quade's defence and remonstrating with Armstrong's interrogation technique, though she knew Quade was equally capable of the same menacing behaviour. Armstrong sat down, relaxing into the chair, his legs splayed open as he leaned back with an ugly smile, expressing a smug self-satisfaction. He nodded at Jo.

'Tell me, Corporal Quade, have you been to Brighton?' Jo leaned forward.

'You know I have.'

'And have you stayed in a B and B or a hotel?'

'What's that got to do with things?'

'I'm merely trying to establish some context for your visit.' Jo waited for Quade to answer. 'So you went for the day, then?' Jo smiled encouragement. 'You know, if you don't answer our questions—simple questions, which you know the answer to, you could be sitting in that chair a long time.'

Quade didn't answer. The foursome sat silent, waiting for Quade to break. After five minutes, Armstrong got up.

'Answer the fucking question?' He picked up an unstacked chair. 'Did you stay in a hotel or B and B?' He threw the chair across the room. It hit the back wall and bounced off it, gouging the plaster.

Jo winced and checked to see how Quade was doing. Quade appeared visibly shaken but remained silent.

'Right!' said Armstrong. 'Lunch. See you at two. Quade, you're going nowhere until you answer our questions. And, just in case you think we won't notice, an MP will be outside the door. See you later. Cunt sucker!'

## Chapter 16

After lunch, Jo loitered in the coffee area. She needed time to think. Dawson bustled through the doorway, whistling, 'What's Love Got To Do With It.'

'Sorry, Sarn't didn't know you was going to be in here. All right, if I…' Dawson mimed, making coffee. Jo wanted to laugh but thought better of it.

'Hi, Private Dawson, please could you do one more?'

'No problem, Sarn't,' Dawson took another mug from the cupboard. 'Can I have a word, Sarn't?' Dawson closed the door. 'I need to be quick. I don't want to be caught telling like. It's Corporal Quade—she's a bully.'

'I know.'

'In the block, on bull night, she never does her chores. She gives them to everyone else.'

'What does she do then?'

'Dunno goes to the NAFFI or sits in the lounge and reads a magazine. But that's not it. One night, she wanted me to do the ablutions, her chore that week. I refused. Didn't go down well.' Dawson picked up the electric kettle when it clicked off and poured hot water onto the instant coffee in each mug. 'I didn't do what she wanted. When I got back to my bed space, everything had been emptied out of my wardrobe bedside locker, and my bed had been stripped and turned upside down.'

'Did Corporal Quade do it?'

'I didn't see her do it. Later, one of the girls told me she'd had the same thing happen to her. It's Corporal Quade's MO. Don't do as she says, and she gets revenge. No one likes her. And, if you go with her to a club and she dances with you…well, you better be ready—that's all.'

'Is that what happened to Lizzie?' Jo asked, desperation in her voice.

Dawson nodded.

Jo sighed. 'Why doesn't anyone bloody well tell us?'

'Because no one dobs anyone in—right? And what if you don't catch her? Then we're in trouble. Real trouble. Got to go now. Sarn't Treacher will give me an earful if they're cold.'

Jo picked up a mug off the tray and leaned against the wall, her anger building at Quade as her thoughts flitted through all the possible options for charging her.

'Hello Jo, all alone? Is there one for me?' Nick chose a mug from the selection available.

'Bit cramped in here.' Jo shifted to make room for Nick.

'Better than being in the Sappers' mess with Staff Armstrong, making out he's 'The Big I Am'.'

'Yeah?'

'He's telling some story about when he conducted a witch-hunt in Germany. All the gory details and him the hero, who plays it hard and gets results.'

'Exaggerated?'

'Yeah. Maybe….'

'I was shocked by the chair throwing and the C word.' Jo sipped her coffee.

'Yeah, me too. I've seen others go in hard, but…'

'Have I actually got to watch her wee?'

'Yeah. Happened on my last witch-hunt. The female sergeant I was with said it was gross and humiliating for both of them. But she didn't dare buck Staff.'

'He's a bully, Nick.'

'He is, but what can we do? He's senior to us, and I think, generally, he can do what he wants on this kind of assignment. The end justifies the means kind of thing.'

'It seems so personal. He wouldn't get away with this under the Geneva Convention.'

'I dunno. I saw some rough stuff in Northern Ireland.'

'Yeah, but not like this. It's verbal abuse.'

'But you have to ask them how they have sex. Otherwise, we can't discharge them. We need the proof!'

'But do we need to be so shitty? So explicit and nasty?'

'If we don't, Jo, they won't break. If they don't break and tell us, where does that leave us?'

'So, you condone the chair throwing?'

The door opened. Jo and Nick looked deep into their coffee mugs.

'Talking about me?' Armstrong asked. 'Get one in for me, Jo. Right Nick, with me. We're going to break the bitch.' The venom in Armstrong's voice was unrestrained.

Jo carried Armstrong's coffee to him, placing it on the desk between Quade and her interrogators. He took a large gulp. 'Ah, that's nice—a perfect end to a perfect lunch. Guess what I had for lunch, Delia?'

Quade eyed the coffee but said nothing.

'I had chicken supreme, followed by chocolate pudding and custard.' He patted his belly, all the while watching the effect of his words on his victim.

'Right, Sarn't Clark, take over while I drink this lovely coffee.' He sipped and smacked his lips.

'So, Corporal Quade, where we left off was whether you stayed at a hotel or a B and B in Brighton. Can you tell us where you stayed?'

'No, Sarn't. I need to go to the toilet.'

Jo swallowed. 'Can't it wait?'

'Not really.'

Armstrong interrupted. 'Make it wait! You'll go when we tell you and not before now answer the question.'

Quade crossed her legs tighter. The effort coloured her face.

'Okay, Jo, tell her we have her chequebook and all that goes with it. Including an entry for a certain B and B.' Armstrong pulled a black and yellow Midland Bank chequebook from the cardboard box and threw it on the table.

'What are you doing with my chequebook? That's mine and none of your business. It's private!' Quade tried swiping the chequebook from the table, but Armstrong was too quick. He held her hand tight over the evidence and breathed coffee and bad breath into her nostrils.

'It's evidence of your dirty and depraved weekend in Brighton. We know where you stayed. The fact you won't tell us tells me you have something to hide. And you're not very good at it.' He scoffed.

'I need the toilet!' screamed Quade.

'You'll go when I let you,' shouted Armstrong. 'Answer the question! Where did you go? For how long and who with?'

'Please, Sarn't Clark,' Quade pleaded.

'Let her go, Staff,' Jo said. 'We don't want to have to clear up after her.'

'We'd make her clear up her own piss. Go on, but watch her! Who knows what she'll get up to in there?'

Jo wanted to roll her eyes. Instead, she escorted Quade to the nearest toilet. Quade dashed in and went to shut the door. Jo shoved the door with her whole body, preventing Quade from locking it. 'Leave the door open!'

Quade, desperate to urinate, pulled down her knickers and sat on the toilet. 'Don't look, Sarn't. It's bad enough you escort me. I'm not going to do anything. Turn around.'

Jo knew she had to observe the suspect, but instinctively, she wanted to give Quade some privacy. Conflicted, she turned her back. 'You finished yet? Taking your time.'

'I haven't been since breakfast at eight this morning. It's been six hours—of course, it's long.'

Jo listened to the crisp rustle of the Izal toilet paper being torn off the roll and turned back to see Quade wipe herself. Disgusted, she turned away. Who had she become? Yes, she was doing her job, but did it need to be like this?

Quade and Jo returned to the interview room in silence, avoiding eye contact with each other and everyone in the room.

'Sit down, Quade.' Armstrong pointed to a chair he had moved into the middle of the room.

Quade sat, and he circled her like a vulture waiting on a future carcass.

'So, we've established you stayed in a B and B in Brighton. Now tell us who with.'

Quade folded her arms, her grey eyes, now almost black with anger, told him all he was ever going to know.

'No problem, in fact, that's rather good because.' Armstrong bent low again and whispered. 'It means me an' Sarn't Clark need to go down to Brighton to the Radclyffe Hotel and pay a visit to the proprietor, who no doubt will tell us everything we want to know.'

'Get to have your own dirty and depraved weekend with Sarn't Clark—nice!' Quade's sarcasm was clear.

Armstrong turned over the table between them. The metal and laminate crashed loudly against the Marley tile. Books, notepads, pens and pencils hit the floor, skittering to a resting place around the room. Jo flinched at the sound. Nick jumped out of his seat, ready to take evasive action. Quade stayed seated and appeared unimpressed by the display of mock anger and aggression.

'You done now, Staff?' Quade sneered.

Incensed, Armstrong leapt toward her, skating on pens and paper. Raging, he attempted to grab Quade by the throat. Nick stepped in front of him, guarding Quade.

'Think carefully, Staff,' Nick whispered. 'Don't want to give her the upper hand now.'

At that moment, Sergeant Major Hart knocked and entered. She stood and looked at the chaotic scene in front of her.

'Good afternoon. Looks like we're having fun and games.' She walked to Armstrong and spoke square into his face. 'What's going on?'

'Theatrics, ma'am,' he whispered before looking over Hart's shoulder and addressing Quade. 'I get bored when they're guilty and don't answer.'

'Well, Staff, you've got your own bit of drama. Get your stuff and report to Major Relish.'

'What about?' Armstrong seemed annoyed at the intrusion.

'He didn't say. Just said he needed to see you ASAP. Got a vehicle?'

'Yes, ma'am.'

'Off you pop, then. Don't keep the OC waiting.'

Armstrong pushed the long hair from his comb-over back in place, collected his jacket from the back of his chair, and tucked his shirt into the waistband that drooped below his stomach before leaving.

Jo and Nick looked at Hart.

'Right, where were you?' Hart asked.

'We need a break. Corporal Quade needs something to eat and drink,' Nick said.

'Right, run along, Corporal Quade. Be back tomorrow. At o nine hundred hours.' Hart paused until Quade had left the room. 'Someone tell me how we got to this mess?' Hart surveyed the room.

Jo began the verbal report. Nick augmented where appropriate.

'Hmm. Not a nice business. I don't like theatrics. Means you're weak on good questioning skills. So, no more of this kind of thing. Evidence and good questions. You do not need to throw things around. I'll be picking up Staff's role tomorrow.'

'What's happening, ma'am, with Staff?' Jo asked.

'I'm sure he'll tell you when he's ready. In the meantime, best tidy up. I'll go and tell the RSM what all the noise was about. Everyone heard it down the corridor. Miss Gordon was not pleased.'

## Chapter 17

*Day Three*

Jo sat at the interrogation table. She had gone to work early to think through her day and be fully prepared. She didn't want to disappoint her immediate boss, Sergeant Major Hart.

Nick walked through the door whistling. 'Morning Jo.'

'Morning. You're cheery.'

'Every reason to be. Staff isn't here. Now we have the Sarn't Major. But I'd prefer her any day to him.'

'What's going on with Staff? Do you know?' Jo doodled a heart on her notepad. She added a Cupid's arrow and was about to add her and Terry's initials when she caught herself and scribbled through the sketch.

'Dunno. Don't care. 'Spect, he'll be along later, throwing his weight around.'

'You didn't like the drama either?'

'No. I've seen the intimidation before. Sometimes, I wonder whether people give in and think—I don't want to be part of this kind of Army.' Nick sat down and looked at the list of names. 'Okay, let's take.… Lance Corporal Watson works in MOD. She's a security risk. Jo, you start. I'll be the bad cop. See if we can link her to Quade. If we can, then we might kill two birds with one stone.'

Jo called the orderly room to summon Watson. A few moments later, Watson knocked on the closed door and entered. She marched to the desk.

'Sit down, Corporal Watson,' said Jo. 'You may remove your hat.'

Jo noticed Watson's make-up—sufficient without being distracting. She observed the slim brunette check the status of the bun behind her head after she had removed her Forage cap and placed her gloves in the up-turned hat, resting it on her lap. She was pretty and the perfect female soldier for the poster job as the assistant to the Minister of Defence.

'Right, Corporal Watson. I think you know why you're here.' Jo paused to acknowledge Watson's nod.

'And in your case, it is particularly dangerous for you to continue to work for the MOD. You are a security risk. Aren't you?'

Watson licked her lips.

'Aren't you?' Jo raised her voice.

Watson focussed on her hat. 'Yes,' she whispered.

'Right.' The quick response took Jo aback. 'So, we need details. Who with and where and what did you do?'

'I'm not giving a name. You can discharge me. That's the end of it. I'm not dobbing anyone in. And that's final.'

Nick interrupted. 'Well, we need details.'

Jo looked askance at his intrusion.

'What did you do?' he pressed.

'What do you mean?' Watson's voice trembled.

'Did you kiss?'

Watson nodded without looking up from her hat.

'Tongues?'

Watson ignored his intrusion into her privacy.

'Did you fuck?' he asked matter-of-factly.

Watson's head jerked up, and her face coloured.

'Well? Did you? Did you put your fingers inside her and fuck her?'

A tear slipped down Watson's crimson cheeks. She hesitated before whispering, 'Yes.'

Nick leaned back in his chair, watching Watson disassemble. He sprang out of his chair and stood behind the broken young woman, towering over her. 'How many fingers?'

'Shut up!' Watson blurted. 'You're being crude. I've given you what you wanted. Now let me go!'

'Not yet. We have more questions for you. What about you and Corporal Quade? You fucked her too? She's the butch, and you the femme?'

Watson studied her hat, slipping the patent leather chin strap back and forth over the cap badge.

Nick stepped to her side, then bent low so his face was level with Watson's, before yelling, 'Enjoy your dirty weekend with Corporal Quade, did you?'

Watson flinched.

'You know she has a string of girlfriends? And she takes all of you to Brighton. I dunno probably the same bed. Fucking you all senseless before chucking you over.'

Watson shed no more tears, straightened her back, and jutted her chin.

'As I said, Sarn't, no names,' her voice firm and clear.

'You can go now, Corporal Watson. I'll make an appointment for you to make a statement,' Jo spoke gently, trying hard to hide her sympathy for the young soldier.

Watson stood, put on her hat and saluted before turning left and marching for the exit.

'You don't salute me!' shouted Nick. 'I'm not a fucking officer!'

Watson quietly closed the door behind her.

'There was no need for that, Nick,' Jo reprimanded. 'We got what we needed to discharge her. You don't have to humiliate her. She got confused.'

'I was trying to get her to incriminate Quade. And if you hadn't gone all soppy on me, I might've got a confession.'

'Don't think so, Nick. You pissed her off good and proper. Didn't you notice? Of course not. While you did your bloody Sweeney impersonations, she stopped crying and became passive-aggressive.'

'Passive-aggressive, was she? Very fancy!' He turned his attention away from Jo.

Jo closed her notebook. 'I'm going to the Sarn't's mess to eat my meal on my own, seeing as none of the Twelve Company Senior Ranks are talking to me. See you at two, Nick.'

## Chapter 18

At two o'clock, Jo returned to the interview room, dreading what the afternoon might hold for her. The thought of interviewing more women about their most private moments was overwhelming and threatening to derail her well-being. She opened the interrogation room door and glanced to the back wall where the Queen's portrait hung. She politely and silently addressed her monarch. Well, this is a fine thing, isn't it, ma'am? Jo refocused her attention on her job and her position at the table, surprised to see Sergeant Major Hart already seated; she jumped, realising that her actions had been observed.

'Just wondering what Her Majesty would think of all this.'

'I don't know. But I wouldn't think she's been too impressed so far. Take a seat, Jo. I have some intel from the RSM. The grapevine says that Corporal Quade and Private Lowe went to the Camden Palace on a lesbian night. Quade danced with Lowe. There was some intense discussion between them, and then Lowe stormed off. So, Corporal Quade was kind of publicly jilted—.'

'And therefore humiliated,' Jo surmised out loud.

'Yes. So, she got her friends to gang up on our victim to persuade her to continue her relationship with Quade. What I don't know, and no one seems to be able to tell us, is if Private Lowe was gay or not.'

'Dunno.' Jo shrugged before collecting her thoughts. 'People choose not to go out with people all the time. Don't matter whether you're straight or gay. But it doesn't end up with someone hanging themselves.'

'Sometimes, Jo, a rotten apple, is a rotten apple. Just the way it is. This, though, is shitty and deviant. We need that woman discharged. I know plenty of lesbians who have gone through their disappointments, but none like this. You keep it secret in the Army and let your best mates help you through it. You don't neglect your duty to the service or each other. I dunno, young people today.' Hart shook her head with despair.

'Mm. It's heavy going.' Jo paused. 'Can't wait for the weekend.'

'Me neither. I'm going to my cottage in Wales. How about you?'

'Mum 'n' Dad's. Probably digging Dad's pond again.'

'Be good to get your own place now that you've got a raise. Then you can do what you like.' Hart winked.

'That's the plan. Just need some money for all the costs.'

'Yeah, gets expensive. Right, let's focus. Nick should be here in a bit; when he gets here, I'll be off. See you after the long weekend. I want to beat the holiday traffic. The Severn Bridge can be murder. Just going to pop in and see the RSM before I leave.'

While Jo waited for Nick to join her, she looked at the list of names on the table and decided that Quade was the problem and that they should call her in for another interrogation.

'I know that look, Jo. What're you planning?' said Nick, walking towards the tables.

'We should do Quade again.'

'Why? She's a tough nut to crack. We'd be better focussing on lower-hanging fruit and maybe get her that way.'

'Because Nick, seeing as you fancy yourself as a member of the Spanish Inquisition...'

'No one expects the Spanish Inquisition!' Nick stood and flourished an imaginary hat. Jo giggled at his Monty Python reference.

'Seriously, if we can get her, we can end all this. The OC will love that we caught the main culprit. It would mean we don't have to chase down any more suspects. We can let them get on with their lives.'

'It makes sense—can't argue with that. It's just the how.' Nick rubbed his chin.

Hart walked through the open door. 'Sorry, Captain Trueman caught me on my way out. But looking at you two, you look like you've got a plan. Let me guess. You think if you can catch Corporal Quade, we can get out of here?'

'Something like that, ma'am. How did you know?' Jo was surprised.

Hart tapped her nose with her forefinger. 'Well, we've a slight problem.' Hart dragged another chair to the table. 'Typically, we don't allow suspects to be represented.'

'Can they be?' asked Jo.

'Yes, they can. They can have a unit representative.'

'What about a legal rep?'

'Well, that's tricky because it's not illegal, more a contravention of MOD policy, so they don't get to have one.'

'So, of course, we use good old section sixty-nine of The Army Act, nineteen fifty-five. The catch-all for anything not covered in the regs that we don't like or think is improper,' Jo responded sarcastically.

'Come on, Jo, what's the problem?'

'Well, all I know is that some good soldiers seem to get kicked out. And for what?'

'Them's the rules, and not only do we play by them, we enforce them. Remember that.'

'So, what's the spanner in the works, then?' Nick asked.

'It seems,' Hart paused. 'That Corporal Quade's father is a solicitor. And he's been looking up the regs. So, now she wants a unit rep with her to ensure you're not doing anything improper. And she has chosen Captain Trueman to do the job.'

'Bloody hell, that's a turn-up for the books,' Jo said.

'Uhuh, Captain Trueman, just put me in the picture, and she is genning up on the protocols. She's asked that we start again after the long weekend on Tuesday so she and Quade can properly prepare. I gather Quade is going home for the long weekend and will consult with her father—one more thing. Major Marwood is adamant this doesn't come back and bite us. So, we play it by the book—right?'

Jo nodded.

Nick took a step toward Hart. 'The OC does realise that Quade is probably the reason Private Lowe committed suicide and that she is now likely to get away with it?'

'Yes, we are all aware of the implications. My guess is that they will find another way to get her out. Probably around her work—something along those lines.'

'We could do surveillance, ma'am,' Jo said.

'We could. Not sure how that would go down with solicitor Daddy. It wouldn't be our decision. That's something for the higher-ups.'

'What do we do now?' Nick asked.

'Bring Tuesday's interviews forward to today. I think our best plan is to complete the interviews on the current list. Discharge those who incriminate themselves and leave it at that and get out of here as soon as.'

'What if they give us names?' Jo asked.

'Don't encourage them. Know what I mean?'

'Yes, ma'am.' The relief in Nick's voice was noticeable.

'As it's Good Friday tomorrow, can we finish early, ma'am?' Jo asked.

'Of course, and if I can bloody well get out of here without anyone stopping me, I might get a head start on the traffic. How many left on the list to interview?'

'Half a dozen, ma'am.'

'Do you have any good evidence on them?'

'Not really,' Nick said despondently.

'Okay, should be quick, then. I think we've all agreed it's time to get back to proper police work. So, the last interview for Corporal Quade is on Tuesday—next week. Make it the first one, and then we can be done. Right, I am heading for Wales!'

## Chapter 19

*The Clark home, Harold Hill, Essex.*

After lunch, Jo headed for the car park next to the parade square at Inglis Barracks, where she had left her car for a quick getaway. She was excited to be taking a much-needed Easter break. She would be home soon. No more witch-hunts or fear of discovery—it would all be simple. Her mother's home cooking, the pub with her dad, and sleeping in Terry's arms, a luxury she would treasure more than ever, given recent events.

On the familiar route out of London on the M11 and M25, it would be stop-and-go all the way, but every route would be like that on the eve of the long weekend. Two hours later, she parked outside 24 Dell Close. She turned off the engine and gazed at the post box red door. Smiling, she pulled her bag from the back seat, slung it over her shoulder, and strode up the pathway at the side of the house. Her mother opened the back door. Her excited smile embraced her eldest daughter.

'Hello, Jo. Put your bag down there, love. I've made you a ham sandwich. You'd best eat it quick.'

'Why?' Jo bit into the thickly buttered sliced white bread and processed tinned ham.

'I'm going to the hairdressers. I want me hair done nice for the holiday. And I thought you would probably have nothing to do so you can take me in that new car of yours. Save me a trip on the bus.'

Jo finished her sandwich. Her mother was right—she had nothing better to do but wait for Terry to come home. 'Okay. We leaving now?'

Her mother glanced at her watch. 'Yes, I don't want to be late. You know what Connie's like.' She checked her appearance in the mirror on the wall next to the back door. 'Thank god I'm going because I look a fright.'

Jo started the car, and her mother slid into the front passenger seat as she glanced up and down the street at the neighbours' windows.

'They'll all be watching, you know.'

'I know, Mum.'

'I want them to see what a success you are.'

Jo felt her mother's pride wash over her like aloe on a burn. It soothed, but she knew she was not quite the success her parents thought her to be.

'Yer sister will be there.'

'Linda? At the hairdressers?'

'Since she got married and had the baby, it's the only day she leaves the house. Pete's,' she paused. 'Well, you know.'

'A controlling and possessive bastard?'

'Jo, less of the swearing. That's one thing the Army taught you, and I don't like it.'

'And you don't like him either.'

'No, and neither does your father. But Linda likes him. And we get to see little Karl when Pete lets us.'

'What's he like?'

'Oh, bonny like his mother. He's only seven months—lots of wind and nappies.'

'Bet he looks like Winston Churchill—all babies do.'

'Jo!' The disapproval in her mother's voice never failed to curb Jo's tongue.

Jo pulled up outside Chez Maurice. The salon bell tinkled twice, first for her mother and then for her. Jo instinctively recoiled from the smell of ammonia from the perm lotion as she walked into the salon. She looked around. Nothing had changed in six years. The only sign that time had passed was the dilapidation of the furnishings. It never failed to surprise her that Maurice was never present, but what he lacked in presence, he made up for in decor. On one side of the shop were four pink dryer hoods. Two were currently occupied. Both ladies had their hair in curlers under a hairnet. Jo judged by the red cheeks of one lady that she had been under for a good while. Either that or she was reading the letters page of the tattered Cosmopolitan.

The hairdressing stands were wooden tables, divided in half by tall mirrors the width of the table so the station could seat two clients, one on either side. Clients sat on trendy art déco-style seats. The chrome frame held a black vinyl seat and back with pink piping. And to bring the entire ensemble together, Maurice had carefully painted or probably had someone do it—an accent wall of pink and black swirls. The salon and Maurice were still clearly in the seventies.

'Right, Mrs. Clark, would you like to come over?' Connie pulled out a chair.

Jo sat in the waiting area, watching Connie fuss around her mother. Connie was still single at forty-something, smoked like a trooper and drank black coffee whenever her fingers weren't busy with someone's hair. Sylvia sat with her back to Jo at Connie's station.

'The usual?' Connie asked as she lifted dark brown locks and ran them through her expert fingers.

'Yes, please, Connie, Luv.'

'Right over to the basin, then.' Connie lathered shampoo into Sylvia Clark's hair. 'So, Jo, how's Army life treating you?' Connie raised her voice above the hum of the hairdryers.

'Good, thanks.'

'Jo got promoted to Sergeant,' said her mother.

'Did you?' Connie asked incredulously.

'Yep. A week ago.'

'More money?' Connie inquired.

'Yeah, not much, but a little.'

'Need your hair done while you're here? I can fit you in while your sister's under. Talking of which, here she comes, your Linda.'

Her mother beamed. 'Both my lovely girls.'

Linda pushed open the door. The bell clanged her arrival. 'Didn't expect to see you here, Jo.'

'No? You sound disappointed.' Jo rose to hug her sister. 'How are you and the baby?'

Linda avoided the hug, choosing to sit two seats away from Jo. 'We're okay. The usual—up all hours. Course, Pete never does a thing. Mum helps from time to time when Pete lets her.'

Jo nodded twice. She looked at her sister's face—dark circles testified to the trials of motherhood. Her blonde hair was greasy and appeared thinner every time Jo saw her.

'Yeah, don't look at my hair. I hardly get time to myself. When I'm not seeing to Karl, it's Pete. I have to do his dinner and keep the house the way his mum likes it.'

Jo noted her pretty sister had become wan and worn.

'So, how's the Army then? No boyfriend, I see. I dunno–all them blokes, and you're still single.'

'How do you know I ain't got a boyfriend?'

'Because no bloke would be seen dead with a girl in jeans with a white line down the front of them. Do you really iron them jeans? And trainers? Really Jo. You look like a bloke.'

Jo blushed.

'Stop it, you two,' ordered their mother. Though prone with her head deep within the black plastic basin, she could command absolute obedience from her offspring.

'Have you got a fella, then Jo?' queried Connie. 'Must be loads of 'em for you to choose from.'

'No, Connie. And yes, there are lots of them. But most of them are scrotes. And yes, I know, Mum, that's not a nice thing to say. But it's true. Anyway, I just got into the Senior Ranks' Mess, so I might find better quality in there.'

'Bet most of them are married. Aren't they?' Linda asked.

'Some are, but not all.'

'Hang on, Linda luv. I'll just get Mrs Simmonds out from under the dryer. Then I'll roll your mum and then do you. Okay?' Connie bustled across the salon.

Linda nodded. 'Where's Terry? Thought you two were joined at the hip.'

'Still at work, I think. She'll be along later.'

'Right.'

Connie brought Sylvia back to her station, seating the red-cheeked Mrs Simmonds on the other side of the mirror.

'Anything interesting in that magazine, Mrs Simmonds?' Connie shouted. 'Something about sex, I'm sure!' Connie raised her eyes and eyebrows in mock surprise.

'An article on lesbians. I was reading about lesbians and the CND at Greenham. I think CND stands for Nuclear something.'

'Our Jo will know, won't you Jo?' said her mother, with unbridled pride.

Out of her mother's sight, Linda looked at Jo, screwed up her face, and mimicked her mother.

'Campaign for Nuclear Disarmament,' Jo announced.

'Oh yes. That's right—they're camping there. Just women, probably all lesbians and few who don't know whether they're Martha or Arthur. Ban the bomb and burn yer bra all in one,' Connie cackled.

'Have you finished with the magazine?' Sylvia put her arm around the mirror to Mrs Simmonds.

'Page twelve,' Mrs Simmonds advised, with a knowing nod.

'Plenty of lesbians in the Army, aren't there, Jo?' Linda stared eyeball to eyeball with Jo.

'Some.'

'You met any?' Connie asked.

'Jo's met loads, haven't you?' Linda pushed.

Jo was sure her cheeks would betray her pretence at nonchalance. 'You don't really notice them. Everyone works and plays hard. That's it, really.'

'Surely, you'd notice them, Jo. I mean, you notice everything, don't you?' Linda needled.

Jo considered how best to handle the conversation. She could change tack, but that would be obvious. 'Actually, I got called to a lesbian investigation this week.'

'Did you?' Connie moved around Mrs Simmonds nearer to Jo as she pulled out the rollers, focussing on Jo.

'Yeah. Nothing special.' Jo tried to sound casual and worldly.

'What're they like?' Connie chucked the last roller into a black tray on her trolley.

'All butch, I should imagine—short hair and men's suits. That's what I heard. They like to do the whole butch and femme thing,' Linda chimed in.

'You seem to know a lot about it, Linda. Well, Connie,' Jo sensed an opportunity to shift the attention away from her love life. 'Mostly, they're like you and me, except when they're interviewed. Then they're shit scared.'

'Language, Jo!' her mother chastised.

'Sorry, Mum. But they are.'

'Why's that?' Linda cocked her to one side.

'Because… well, because if they're found guilty, they're dishonourably discharged.'

'Is that a problem, then?' Connie asked.

'Would you employ someone who has been dishonourably discharged?' Jo shot back at Connie.

'Don't suppose I would unless I knew them. Anyway, it's a crime if they get caught having sex 'n' stuff.'

'Actually, it's not.'

'It's not?' Connie checked.

'No. It's not even a crime between two men over twenty-one. Hasn't been since 1967.'

'Bloody should be if you ask me because it's a sin according to the bible,' Linda stated.

Jo guffawed. 'A sin! The Bible! Since when did you last go to church? Oh yeah, for baby Karl's christening. But that's it! Anyway,' Jo adopted a more serious tone. 'It's my job to know the law.'

'So, what happens to them, then? When they get caught?' Connie teased out the last of Sylvia's curls.

'The Army discharges them under section sixty-nine or sixty-six of The Army Act, nineteen fifty-five. So, with no job, there's no money and nowhere to live. Life gets hard for them. If that happened to me, I'd be scared.'

'They could live with their parents,' Sylvia suggested.

'No, they can't, Mum. Because mostly their parents are ashamed of them and won't have them in their home.' Jo was matter of fact.

'Well, what happens to them, then?' Connie queried.

'Some commit suicide. Many drink or take drugs. Others take any job they can get and rent or doss where they can.'

For a beat, the salon was silent.

'Don't blame them, though,' Linda added brightly. 'It's embarrassing for the family, like, in it? I mean, who'd want someone back who brought shame on the family?'

'Love should always beat shame. And you, my girl, will learn that as a mother. It doesn't matter who or what your child is—they're yours. They didn't ask to stand by them, whatever happens.' Sylvia closed the magazine.

## Chapter 20

*Good Friday*

Terry had hardly slept during the night. Her fears for Jo ran deep. She was scared that Jo would give up on Quade, which would, in the long run, impact Jo's self-confidence, something she knew was essential to Jo.

'How are you feeling this morning?' Terry scrutinised Jo's face.

Jo turned away. 'I'm alright. Just had to talk about it to someone.'

'Someone Jo? I'm your partner.'

'I know.' Jo tried to smile. 'I didn't mean it like that.'

'Tell you what. I'll get you some paper. Got a pen?' Terry leapt out of bed and rummaged in her overnight bag.

'Bloody hell, Terry, what's got you all enthusiastic?'

'You have to bring Quade down, Jo. I'll bring you breakfast. What do you want? I'll tell Mum you're working on a case, and you're not to be disturbed.'

Jo smiled her surrender. 'Bacon sarnie. Red sauce, mind, and make sure it's plastic bread. Mum's gone posh. She's buying proper bread from the new bakery.'

Minutes later, Terry returned with Jo's rations and paper. 'Right, I'm leaving you to it. Me and Mum are going Tescos.'

Terry hurried down the stairs to take Sylvia to the shops.

'Tea, love?' Sylvia asked. 'I'm making yer Father one before I go, and I know you two never turn down a cuppa.'

'We got time?' Terry sat down.

'Think we have to make time.' Sylvia nodded at the kitchen door as it flew open.

Linda backed in through the kitchen door, pulling a pushchair in which baby Karl was crying. Brian got up to assist his younger daughter.

'Hello, lass, weren't expecting you this morning.'

'So, you're not pleased to see me either, then?'

Bewildered, Brian looked to his wife for support.

'Tea, love?' asked Sylvia.

Brian got Karl out of the pushchair and sat him on his knee, jiggling him up and down until he stopped crying and started giggling.

Linda took a sip of tea. 'Mind if I stay the weekend, Mum? Pete's on night shift. Plus, he's mad at Karl because he keeps crying and stops Pete from sleeping. And I can't stand the shouting anymore.'

Brian studied his daughter. He mouthed 'face' to his wife. Sylvia stroked Karl's hair while surreptitiously checking her daughter's visage.

'He hit you again, Linda?' Sylvia asked.

'No.' Linda turned away from her mother, taking Karl from her father before nuzzling into her son.

Brian picked up his mug and headed for the sanctuary of his garden shed.

Sylvia sat in the seat next to Linda. 'Listen, love, your face is bruised I can see it even under that heavy make-up you're wearing. And I won't believe any cock 'n' bull story of you walking into a door or a wall. You've lived in that house long enough to know exactly where all the doors and walls are now.' Sylvia paused, observing the anxiety on her daughter's face. 'Come home, love, where we can support you. You won't have to see him again.'

'No, Mum, it's temporary. He just needs some space, that's all. At least until he's off shift.'

'Terry and I are going to Tescos. Coming?' Sylvia asked.

'No, Mum. I think I'd better stay here. I don't need the gossip.'

'Hmm. Need baby food and nappies?'

'Please, Mum.'

'Come on then, Terry, let's use them strong arms of yours. God knows we're going to have a lot of shopping. Yer Father won't be pleased with the bill, that's for sure. And Linda, you take care now and top your dad's tea up when he needs it.' Sylvia tutted, discarding her pinny and hanging it on the hook beside the mirror before following Terry out of the back door.

Linda carried Karl and her mug of tea into the living room.

After Terry and Sylvia had left, Brian returned to the kitchen for a refill and for reinforcements. He left his mug on the drainer and went in search of his eldest daughter. He knocked politely on the bedroom door before entering.

'Hello, lass. Doing anything important?'

'Trying to figure out some questions for an interview, Dad.'

'Oh,' he nodded. 'The Post theft.'

'Oh, er, yeah, the theft.'

'Fancy helping your ole dad for a bit? It will be the talk of the street when I've finished. But I need a head start.' Brian walked out of the room. 'Come and help me?'

'All right, but I need to get back to this.'

The pair went into the back garden.

'I started it, but I've hit what I think is an old air raid shelter. See here,' Brian pointed. 'This is the floor, and these breeze blocks form the bottom of the walls. They must've just knocked down what they could and then buried it. I'm having one helluva time getting it up.'

'Didn't know there were houses here during the war,' said Jo.

'Oh yeah. Bob, next door, told me that when he was a kid, there was a big estate here, with farm buildings and a manor house. The army billeted soldiers here for a while. Guess it must've been for them. Anyway, I've been using this sledgehammer. I made some progress. Bob next door lent me a pickaxe. I reckon the two of us could get it done.'

'Dad, I don't think it's worth it. Can't we just put the pond liner on top? It would give it a nice firm bottom for all the water it will hold.'

Brian scratched his head. 'You must take after your mother. She has the brains in the family. That makes sense. How about we just knock down the bits of wall that are left?'

'Okay, let's get it done before Mum and Terry get back. I need to get back to my prep.'

The two chipped and hammered away at sections of the wall that were proud of the solid and unforgiving concrete base.

'Didn't know you had to bring work home in the Army. Didin't in my day,' Brian said.

No, this one is tricky, Dad. The villain thinks she's smarter than us. I'm thinking of ways to trap her.'

'Can't you just go undercover? Do surveillance like?'

'All about budget, Dad. We have to interview her and get a confession. The only way.'

'Seems complicated to me.' Brain scratched his head once more. 'But knowing my daughter, she'll come up with a way. I'm parched. Oh, and here's your mother, right on cue.' Brian ambled to help his wife and Terry with the shopping, taking two bags from his wife. 'Good job, you came home when you did, Mother. I'm fair knackered. My back is killing me.' He placed the shopping on the kitchen table and filled the kettle.

'Can't hack it, Dad,' teased Jo.

'None of your cheek, young lady!' Brian eased himself into a chair at the kitchen table, relishing the rest and the tea.

'That it for today, Dad?'

'Think so, lass. Think I might get in the bath for a bit of a soak. Got any of that nice bubble bath Sylv?'

'Come on,' Sylvia said. 'I'll run you a bath.'

Brian and Sylvia went upstairs to the bathroom. Jo and Terry sipped their tea. Linda, carrying Karl, joined them at the kitchen table.

'One in the pot for me?' Linda asked.

Terry poured a mug for Linda before asking Jo. 'How far've you got?'

'Not far. The bomb shelter put a spanner in the works. But I think we're past it now.'

'No, I meant planning for the interview.'

'Oh, that. I can't, Terry. Every time I think about it I feel sick. Come and look at the pond.'

'Coming, Linda?' Terry asked.

'Not interested. What's the point of the pond anyway, just for some silly goldfish? Can't see why you're all so excited.'

Jo shrugged at Terry before they wandered to the pond site.

'Hmm,' Terry said. 'I'll give you a hand tomorrow. And, Jo, you need to concentrate on getting Quade. She needs to go. And I think you are the only one who can do it. I think the others have accepted defeat.'

'What makes you think I'm not defeated?'

'Because, Jo, I'm right behind you and won't let you give in. That woman has to go for the good of every other soldier at twelve company. She's bad news all 'round.'

## Chapter 21

Jo and Terry sat at the kitchen table, waiting for dinner. It was a tighter fit than usual now that Linda was staying for Saturday night. Baby Karl was in his highchair beside Sylvia, who hummed as she served dinner, content her family was together. As she ate, she fed Karl, giving her daughter a break from motherhood. Meanwhile, Terry and Jo exchanged war stories with Brian.

'We're going to the pub after, Dad. Wanna come?' Jo smiled encouragement at her father.

'No. It's Saturday. You know I only go out on Fridays.'

'Come on, Dad—you don't have Terry and me home very often. Come with us.'

'No. Fridays is pub night. It's when I meet the boys. You girls go out. I'm staying in with yer mother and Linda.'

'I'll come with you,' Linda said.

'Best you stay home, lass. Keep me and yer mother company.'

Jo grabbed her coat from the row of hooks near the back door. Terry followed her, stepping out into the brisk evening air before shutting the door behind them.

'God, Dad's so stuck in his ways,' Jo sighed.

'I think he's protecting Linda.' Terry shrugged on her coat.

'Let's do the Royal Forest. I'm feeling flush since I got promoted. Let's go somewhere a bit classy, seeing as Dad ain't coming.' Jo opened the car door before driving to the Royal Forest Hotel in Epping.

'Saloon?' Jo suggested.

'Yeah, probably the only bar now it's been turned into one of them chain restaurant things.'

They strode in through the doors and straight to the bar.

'Find us a table while I get 'em in.'

Terry went in search of a suitable table for two and sat down. Jo joined her within minutes. They sat in companionable silence, sipping their beers and looking around at the clientele.

'It's more upmarket than I thought. Do they still have rooms here?' Terry said, admiring the decor.

'Think so,' Jo said. 'Always was posh. And it's nice not to have to worry who might see us.' Jo leaned back in her chair. 'And it's good to be out of the house. It's claustrophobic with Linda and Karl.'

'Yeah, but Mum loves it. She's in her element. I agree it's good to get out and away from the family. It's been a tad rough this week—I just needed a break. I hope Max gets selected for PTI soon because she's wearing me down with all her enthus—hang on.' Terry leaned forward, peering into the darkened centre of the room. 'Is that Pete?'

'Pete, who?'

'Pete, your brother-in-law, married to your sister! Pete!'

'What's he doing here? And who's that with him?'

'Dunno. But it doesn't look right.'

Jo leaned forward, hoping the few extra inches she gained would give her better sight of the situation. 'He better not be,' Jo muttered as she observed Pete lean sideways and kiss a strawberry blond on her lips. 'Did you see that?' Shocked, Jo exclaimed in a loud whisper.

'Yeah. Shut your mouth, Jo. You look gormless.'

'He bloody kissed her!'

Terry shuffled her chair closer to the table to speak directly into Jo's ear. 'Drink up—let's go.'

'No, I'm in no hurry. That's just confirmed everything I've always thought about him.'

Terry looked at the table, mixing the rings of condensation and beer with her finger. 'I know. Leave it.'

Jo got up.

'Where're you going?' Terry stood up and stopped Jo from moving.

'I'm going to confront him. Give over, Terry. My sister is at home with their baby, and he's here with his bit of fluff!'

'Sit down. You'll only make it worse.'

Jo sat down and glowered in Pete's direction. She watched him throw back his head with laughter, then kiss the strawberry blonde again. This time, his lust engendered a longer, more intense kiss.

'I'm going to the loo. Mine's a pint.' Jo headed for the Powder Room, hesitating in the doorway to see Terry go to the bar. Satisfied Terry couldn't see her, she strode through the archway and into the hotel's reception area.

'Can I help you?' The receptionist asked.

'I'm looking for a Peter—goes by the name of Pete Blake.'

The receptionist cocked her head to one side.

'Is he staying here?' Jo prompted.

'We don't normally give out those kinds of details about our guests.'

Jo pulled out her warrant card. 'Military Police. He's AWOL.'

The receptionist brought out a thick, leather-bound book. She opened it, flicking through the pages at speed, using a moistened fingertip to help turn them until she got to bookings for today. She ran the same finger down the list. 'We have a Mister Peter Blake. He is staying one night. Room twenty-one. It's a double room on the first floor.'

'Thank you. You've been most helpful.' Jo walked back into the saloon bar.

Terry was sitting at the table. She had already made in-roads on her second pint. 'Blimey, where've you been? You've been gone ages.'

'He's staying the night. And obviously not with my sister.' Jo tightened her lips into a straight line. 'I don't know what to do.' She thought for a moment. 'I should confront him. He's cheating on my sister!'

'Stay where you are, Jo.' Terry thrust out an arm, creating a barrier. 'This is not your battle. I'm fairly sure your sister knows, and if she wants us to do something about it, she'll ask. Now finish your drink.'

Jo sipped her beer. 'I can't. I hate him. Always have.'

'I know, and I do too. But it's not your battle.'

'Yeah, but Linda needs to know.'

'No. She doesn't. Believe me, if Pete finds out that we know,' Terry paused to consider her words. 'It'll be worse, that's all.'

'How can it be worse?'

'Trust me, Jo. I know about these things. I know about the heavy makeup my mum used to put on her face on a Saturday morning. I know about her hiding in the toilet while sobbing her heart out. I know the sound of a fist hitting bone. And how to scrub blood off the kitchen floor.' Terry sipped her pint, closing her eyes. She hunched her shoulders and hung her head over her beer glass.

Jo blanched. Torn between doing what she thought was the right thing, the thing she had always done and letting Pete have his way at the expense of her sister. She broke the tense silence. 'Either way, Linda gets hurt.'

'But there are two kinds of hurt, Jo. Physical, sometimes you can't recover from, and emotional.'

'Emotional! You mean he's driving her bloody mental? I can't let that happen. I can't,' Jo hissed.

'Jo, listen. You have to be there for her. Not do things for her. Your mum and dad know. They keep an eye on her—we must do the same. Just don't make it worse for her. She'll come round in her own time.'

'I got you out of trouble.' Jo was indignant.

Terry stared at Jo in disbelief. 'I was ready. I wanted help, but I didn't know who could help me. And I was thirteen. I couldn't make those kinds of decisions. But you did. And your mum and dad did. And I was and still am grateful.' Terry relaxed at the memory.

'So, why not now?'

'Because, oh Jo,' Terry shook her head, 'Linda may be handling it her way. She's an adult. She has to make her own decisions. Who knows, she might be waiting for her moment. Maybe she will be ready to leave Pete when baby Karl grows up.'

'What if she needs me to go and get her? I could—we could.'

'Believe me, Linda will tell us when she's ready. Until then, leave it alone. Now drink up—let's go home. I'm not enjoying watching you seethe over the bastard.'

'I'm not seething. I'm angry.'

Terry rolled her eyes and downed the rest of her pint.

## Chapter 22

*Easter Sunday*

Jo and Terry slipped into their usual places at the kitchen table the following morning. Linda encouraged Karl to eat his breakfast with little success despite playing 'trains' and 'down the hatch'. Brian came in from the garden carrying an enormous Easter Egg.

'Look, Karl! Look what Papa found in the garden—an Easter egg!'

Brian's smile was equalled by the marvel on his grandson's face. Brian popped the egg on the highchair table. Karl tried to rip off the cardboard packaging, but his pudgy hands lacked the strength to unwrap his gift. Frustrated, he began to cry, prompting Linda to do the same. Brian placed a protective arm around his daughter's shoulders and soothed her.

'It's okay, lass. We all get a bit down. Here, let me. Eat yer breakfast. I'll do his nibs,' Brian said. He had not lost his expertise in feeding reluctant babies and toddlers, so Karl finished his breakfast within minutes and sat playing with his spoon and eating pieces of chocolate egg. Meanwhile, Sylvia, with her pinny on, dished up a full English.

'You girls were out late last night. We heard you come in. And we heard you laughing and mucking about in your room. What was so funny? One too many?' Sylvia reproached Jo and Terry.

'Sorry, Mum,' Jo said. 'Won't happen again.'

Terry nodded her agreement.

'Where did you go last night?' Linda asked.

'Royal Forest,' Jo replied.

'That's a bit posh for you two, in it?'

'We thought we'd splash out a bit, you know, now I've got promoted.'

'Nice for some, eh Mother?' Brian's pride was evident in his smile and tone.

Sylvia nodded warily.

'See anyone I know?' Linda asked.

Jo hesitated to answer. Linda stared at her.

'No,' Terry interjected. 'Don't think so. We hardly know anyone around here, anyway.'

'Yeah, bit out of our local woods, really,' Jo added.

It was Sylvia's turn to study her eldest daughter. 'So, what's it like there? Now it's a chain.'

'Nice,' Jo said, not looking at her mother.

'Do a decent pint,' Terry added, trying to catch Jo's eye.

'Obviously, more than one pint by the amount of chatter and laughter coming out of your room last night,' Sylvia said.

Terry and Jo finished their breakfast without a word.

'Pete goes there sometimes. He goes there with his workmates. Says it's nice. He's stayed over a couple of times. You know, when he's too drunk to drive home.' Linda rolled her eyes. 'Usually comes home in a foul mood with a bunch of cheap garage flowers.'

'What?' Jo asked.

'Yeah, flowers and a bad temper. I never really understand why.' Linda took a bite of toast and ate it thoughtfully. 'You didn't happen to see Pete there?'

'Don't think so. Did you Jo?' Terry fidgeted in her chair.

'Erm, … I need to get back to planning that interview I've got next week.' Jo got up and pushed her chair under the table.

'Big deal, is it?' Brian asked, smiling at the change of subject.

'Yeah. You know, I said she thinks she's smarter than us. Well, turns out her dad's a Lord something or other and a Silk.'

'A Queen's Counsel and a Lord,' Brian marvelled. 'My daughter is interviewing nobility. How about that, Mother?' Brian paused and looked into his daughter's eyes. 'Now, why in heaven's name would she be stealing postal orders?'

Jo hesitated, wondering why her father was thinking about postal order theft. Then she remembered the white lie she had uttered days ago. 'Oh, yeah, I know. It's a puzzle.' Jo sighed. 'Still, that's why we must ask her the questions.'

Sylvia watched her daughter ascend the stairs.

'Linda, help Terry, will you love? And tidy up the kitchen. I need to do something. I'll be down soon.'

Brian watched his wife follow his oldest daughter.

'Right girls, I'll wash, and you two dry.' Brian grabbed a tea towel and whipped Terry's backside with it. 'And don't keep me waiting,' he grinned before chucking his grandson under the chin. 'Oohh, choccy chin!'

Jo settled on her bed with the paper and pen Terry had brought her the day before and began scribbling some possible questions she might ask. Now she had a determination that had been absent yesterday—if she couldn't get Pete, she would get Quade, or if she was lucky, both.

Sylvia knocked on the open bedroom door. 'Mind if I come in?'

Jo shifted to a sitting position, so her legs hung over the bed. She put the paper and pen beside her, waiting for her mother to speak.

'Jo, what happened the other night?' Sylvia sat next to her daughter.

'Nothing. Why?'

'You were crying, crying your heart out. Your father and I could hear it. It took everything I had to stop your father from going into your room. Now, what was it all about?'

'Oh, nothing, Mum. Nothing I can't handle.'

'But you'll tell Terry.' Sylvia's disappointment was not lost on Jo.

'Not that, Mum, just Terry and me—you know, being Army, we get certain things.'

'And your old mum is too stupid to know anything—is that it?'

'No!'

'So, what is it?' Sylvia demanded.

Jo panicked, her dilemma overwhelming her. She quickly weighed up which truth to tell, her sexuality and the problems it was causing with her career or Pete. Then she blabbed. 'Terry and I saw Pete with another woman last night.'

'And what's that got to do with the Army?'

'Nothing. Well, maybe—I used my military police warrant card to make some enquiries. Terry made me swear not to tell. She said it would only create more trouble.'

'Well, she's not wrong there. That's as maybe, but there's still something you're not telling me.'

Jo smiled at her mother, knowing her mother knew she had not told the entire truth about anything and everything.

Sylvia got up, tutting as she left the room.

Jo went back to planning her questions. Some minutes later, there was a commotion downstairs. She put aside her work and joined the family in the kitchen. As she opened the kitchen door, the occupants fell silent. 'Oh, you're here,' Jo was miffed.

'Nice way to greet your brother-in-law. Nice to see you, Jo. How's life treating you? Been to any nice pubs recently?'

'If I had, it would be none of your business.'

'Little bird tells me you were at the Royal Forest last night.'

Stunned, Jo wondered how Pete knew she and Terry had been in the pub.

'I can see by your look that you were. See anyone interesting?'

Sylvia bit her lip. Terry stared at Jo, warning her.

'No, just had a pint and left.'

'Ah, right.' Pete gave Jo a leery grin. 'Come on Linda, time to come home. Get your stuff. Hello, son.' Pete lifted Karl out of his highchair, rubbing his nose against Karl's. 'Come on, Linda. We ain't got all day. I'm on shift at ten and need my dinner before then.'

'Saw the answering machine you gave Mum and Dad. Nice one, Pete,' said Jo.

Pete gave Jo a crooked smile.

'Knock-off, was it?' Jo probed.

'Jo,' said Pete in a measured tone with a hint of malice. 'I'm a policeman. And you, of all people, should know we don't deal in stolen goods.'

'Course not,' Jo scoffed and muttered under her breath, 'But you'll bloody cheat on your wife.'

Linda, refusing to acknowledge the truth Jo had said out loud, hurriedly collected Karl's toys and his bag of nappies, picked up her overnight bag, and struggled to the car in Pete's wake. Brian stepped in, relieving his daughter of her heaviest load, and helped her to the car. Sylvia shut the door before leaning against it and sighed.

'What was that all about? I thought they had rowed,' Terry said.

'You never know with Pete. One minute he's as nice as pie, the next he's ….' Sylvia wrung her hands.

'A toe rag,' Jo said.

Sylvia went to the sink to fill the kettle. 'Tea?'

'Yeah, thanks, Mum,' Jo paused. 'Mum, I'm going back to barracks early. I need to prep for the interro…, erm, interview I've got on Tuesday. You know, the one with the Lord's daughter. I can't concentrate here with all the comings and goings.'

'Okay, but your father is going to be disappointed. We don't see much of you.'

'I might go as well,' Terry said. 'Anyway, cheer up, you'll see us next weekend for the May bank holiday,' Terry laughed. 'You'll want us to go back early then.'

## Chapter 23

*Easter Sunday Afternoon, Inglis Barracks, Mill Hill.*

Terry got in her car and drove away from 24 Dell Close, preoccupied with finding the photograph she had hastily hidden. Negotiating the arterial roads and the motorway on autopilot until she reached the barracks, Terry flashed her ID card to the soldier on duty and drove into the almost empty car park, choosing a spot close to the gym. She sent up a prayer and good thoughts to the universe and anyone listening that the photograph would remain undiscovered. After walking through the gym doors and into her office, she sat and waited to see if anyone had followed her. Five minutes later, she headed to the storeroom and began her search.

Terry estimated she had hidden the picture about three skirts from the bottom. She slid a hand in. Nothing. Next one up—not there either. Two down, then? Nope. She systematically pulled one skirt from the pile after another, tossing it to the floor. With each retrieval, her anxiety increased, despite applying the logic that if she put the photo there, it would still be there—somewhere, because only she knew she had put it there. She pulled the last one from the shelf—no photo. Fuck! Now what?

Terry turned around, looking at every shelf in the storeroom. She definitely put it in with the skirts—she remembered doing it. Keep calm. It's got to be here.

Methodically, she picked up a skirt from the floor, folded it, and placed it neatly back on the shelf. And another, and another, until every skirt had been replaced. Nothing.

A prickle of panic rose from her feet to her throat. Her breathing became ragged. She felt dizzy and sat down with her head bent low, waiting for the attack to pass. Thoughts whirled in a chaotic stream of consciousness. Who had the photo? What would they do with it? Would she and Jo be dishonourably discharged? Shame burned in her body.

She heard the gym entrance doors open and close, then the door to the storeroom open. Terry's stomach lurched. Was this it—the moment she would be arrested? She held her breath in fear of being discovered, and her mind reeled with the consequences of being discovered.

'You okay?'

Terry lifted her head.

Max smiled at her. 'It's okay, I destroyed it.'

'Destroyed what?'

'The photo of you and Sarn't Clark in Brighton.'

'How?'

'How did I know where it was? Or how did I destroy it?'

'Both. Anyway, why are you here? It's a holiday weekend.'

'I've got no home to go to. Been in care all my life. Or should I say uncare all my life. No money and nowhere to go, so I stay in the barracks. Was coming to the gym and saw your car. So, I guessed you'd come back for it.'

Terry exhaled noisily. 'Shit, Max, you scared me.' Terry tried to steady her breathing. 'What did you do with the photo?' In her head, she calculated how much evidence was out there against her and Jo and how it might be used against them.

'No worries. The photo is in little pieces all over the place as far as I could run. No one's going to find it. And, if they found one piece, they have to find the other forty-nine.'

'Forty-nine?'

'Well,' Max chuckled, 'I'm guessing forty-nine. Anyway, it's a lot of tiny pieces. I buried them in people's dustbins, street litter bins, the tube line, post boxes, that sort of thing.

'Bloody hell, Max, is there anywhere you didn't put it?'

'Wanted to do a good job Sarn't. Like you always say, right first time. You've looked after me. No one's done that, looked out for me, like. So I returned the favour.'

'No favour needed, Max. But how did you know?'

'I saw you go into the storeroom. I guessed you were checking up on my work. So I went in after. And I saw the bottom skirts were not too tidy, so I straightened up the pile. And the photo just came out. I thought it best if you didn't know. You know schtum—if you didn't know where it was, you couldn't tell anyone, and they wouldn't find it. No evidence, schtum—like.'

Terry got up from the floor. 'Thank you, Max.'

Max shrugged, 'No problem. I know you'd do it for me.'

Terry smiled and clapped Max on the back. 'Right, well, I've got to meet Jo back at the mess for dinner. See you tomorrow.'

Jo returned to 12 Company WRAC Senior Ranks' Mess instead of Rochester Row. That way, she could be with Terry and be early for the interview with Quade in the morning. After changing for dinner, she went downstairs and met Terry at the bar, talking to a mess stewardess. She had a pint waiting for Jo. Picking up their drinks, they found a table for two in the corner of the adjoining anteroom.

'Did you find the photo?' Jo asked.

'No. But…'

'What?' Jo's whispered tone broadcasted fear.

'If you let me finish…. Max took care of it.'

'How?'

'It's all 'round the town in the tiniest of bits, including the underground. Unless someone has a real jigsaw puzzle fetish, no one will be able to find them, let alone have all the pieces to put it together.' Terry sighed. 'We're in the clear.'

'I'll drink to that!' Jo raised her glass.

Terry looked up as the mess stewardess put the bar phone down before walking towards them.

'Excuse me, Sarn't Clark, a policeman is waiting for you in the mess stewards' office. Sarn't Cook says can you see the Copper now because she wants her office back ASAP.'

'What's his name?' Jo asked.

'PC Blake.'

Startled, Terry sprang out of her chair. 'I'll come with you. If Pete's here, it can't be good news.'

The two women walked swiftly to the mess office, knocking on the open door. Pete sat in the easy chair. Cook sat at her desk. It was clear that something more than polite conversation had passed between them.

'Jo, make it quick, will you? I've got dinner to serve in half an hour. Hi Terry. Hope you two have been behaving yourselves,' Cook winked.

Terry closed the door before perching on the edge of the desk. Jo sat at the desk.

'Hello, ladies.' Pete grinned with malice.

'How did you know we were here?' Jo asked.

'Because Jo…,' Pete watched Jo struggle to make her face appear neutral and confident. He laughed. 'Because I know you, Jo. I know that you can't lie. I know that you don't like me. I know that you're a dyke, and I know that you run away when there is conflict. So…,' he smirked with an unpleasant confidence. 'I knew you'd be here with Terry. And I know where this mess is because, as you know, I like a dalliance now and then. And, once upon a time, I dallied here when I was a young cadet. Ah, sweet memories.'

'Yeah, Jackanory, tell us another story. To what do we owe the honour? You're a long way from your manor.'

'Well, as it happens, they needed volunteers for a football match at Wembley. And as it isn't too far from you girls, I volunteered my services. Very convenient for me to pay you a little visit. I get to stay here for a local footie match tomorrow. So, two nights of freedom from the ball and chain, and I get to talk to you two lovely ladies.'

Pete's sarcasm and confidence irked Jo.

'Well, make it quick then. There's no point in hanging around where you're not wanted.' Jo wanted to smack Pete between his cocky eyes. Instead, she sat without moving a muscle on Cook's desk.

'On Saturday, I was out with some workmates down the Royal.'

'Funny-looking workmate,' Jo said.

'We were undercover.'

'Pete,' Jo sighed, 'You're uniform. You don't do plain clothes. Anyway, stop the blagging and get on with it.'

'Want to know how I know, you know, I was there?'

'Pete, do you think I really give a shit?'

'Oh, you do! And I'm sorry to say, you were sloppy, Jo. Very, very sloppy. That's the problem with you, amateur police. You don't get the training like we do in the Met.' Pete needled.

'Shut up, Pete. Just get on with it.'

Pete guffawed. 'Shut up and talk. That's a good one. Well, you thought you were clever with your pseudo-warrant card. But the receptionist saw me at breakfast and was surprised I was still at the hotel. She asked me if I'd seen you. Once I got a description of the so-called police officer, then I knew it was you.'

'That's why Linda had to go home on Sunday morning. Ahhh…. You were worried I'd let the cat out of the bag.' Jo pretended she was confident and smug.

'No cats, no bags, because if you mention my work meeting to anyone. And I mean anyone, I'll be letting the MOD or maybe the Brigadier of the Women's Royal Army Corps herself know.' He lowered his voice to a harsh whisper. 'That you two dykes are having it off together in one of Her Majesty's Senior Ranks' Messes.'

Terry stood up straighter and spoke. 'Thanks for the threat, Pete. But if it was a genuine work meeting, why're you threatening us? Tell the MOD or whoever you like, and we'll tell Linda. Now fuck off.'

'Be worse for you than me. I can always find another Linda.'

Jo got up from behind the desk, her fists at the ready and her jaw set. She checked herself, ensuring she wasn't the one escalating things. 'Why don't you just piss off out of everyone's lives, seeing as you can find another Linda?'

'Oh Jo, your sister would never leave me! Whereas you two,' he sneered, 'would be up shit creek. You'll never find another job like the ones you have now—even Woolworths wouldn't touch you with a barge pole. And I doubt Brian and Sylvia would have you back. Especially you, Terry, after all they've done for you. Paying them back like that—that's not right.' He shook his head, mocking them. 'And that means.' He adopted a false, sad voice. 'Diddums here would have to follow Terry to whatever shit heap she lands in. Because…,' Pete raised his voice. Adding in a confident tone, 'Mummy and Daddy won't have either of you back because you are both a fucking disgrace to the family.'

There was a knock at the door.

'Chaps, I need you to go.' Cook came in, pausing at the doorway as she observed the conflict on the faces of the three occupants. 'Sorry, I've come at an awkward time. But really, unless you're here on official business, I need you to leave. Terry, why don't you ask the RSM if Pete can join you for dinner? Be nice to have some male company.' This time, Cook winked at Pete.

'Thanks. We already asked him. He has to be at Wembley—don't you, Pete?'

'Well, I could stay for a quick bite.' Pete grinned.

Terry led Pete out of the office escorting him to the front door of the mess. 'You're not staying for dinner.'

'Bye then,' said Jo.

'Remember, girls.' Pete put his finger to his lips. 'Mum's the word, or your business will be all over Toy Town.'

Terry shoved Pete through the door she had opened. 'Fuck off, Pete, and don't let the door hit you on the way out.' Terry let the door go before turning to Jo. 'You okay? You look awful.'

'Yeah. Surprised, that's all. Let's go into dinner. I could do with an early night. It's been a shitty day.'

Jo and Terry ate their meal, listening to the idle chatter of their colleagues. When they finished their meals, Jo suggested they go to her room. They sat on the bed.

'What is it, Jo?'

'We've got a problem.'

Terry stared at Jo.

'I told Mum we saw Pete with his bit on the side.'

'Shit!'

'Quiet Terry. We don't need the whole neighbourhood to hear. Yeah, she asked me why I was crying on Friday night.'

'She knew you were crying. Not laughing?'

'Yeah, she and Dad heard us.'

'What? All the conversation?'

'No, that's why she asked me what I was crying about. So I didn't lie. I couldn't face another lie, so I told her about Pete.'

'Jo!'

'I know. I'm not proud of it. But what could I do? It was me or him.'

Terry got up and stood facing the wall while bracing against the wooden desk. She turned around.

'He won't say anything. I know he won't, even if Mum has it out with him, which I doubt. Right, well, sleep well if you can. As you said, it's been a shitty day.' Terry left for her room.

Jo sat back against the bedhead to calm the thoughts springing from the depths of her mind, spreading anxiety to her vital organs. She leaned over and opened the bedside locker drawer, pulling out the purple box containing the silver suffragette medal awarded for valour, nestled in green velvet. Smoothing it with her finger, she hoped the memories it evoked of her grandmother would soothe her.

'Now what, Nana? It's a mess,' she whispered. 'He's a bastard to our Linda. What do I do?'

She ran her finger back and forth over the silver bar, engraved 'Fed by

Force'.

'Whatever it takes. That's what you would say. I just hope I'm made of the same stuff Nana.'

## Chapter 24

*Day Four*

Everyone had returned to barracks after the Easter Holiday. Jo and Nick were preparing for Corporal Quade's investigation in the Interview Room. Sergeant Major Hart joined them sitting at the desk.

Nick placed the last of two chairs in front of the desk, slumped into his seat, got a pad of paper and a pen, and began doodling. 'What jolly japes have we got on today?' he said.

'Blimey Nick, you're a happy sod, aren't you?' said Jo.

'I had a great weekend, and now I have to deal with this shit. I dunno—this isn't proper policing, is it? I ask you?'

'So, you want to be a proper policeman, do you? Well, join The Met or something,' Hart retorted. 'Anything, I don't bloody well care but get yer act together and finish this job so we can all go home and do some proper policing, as you put it. We're all fed up with this crap, but it's what we get paid to do. So, let's get it done. Right now, we're dealing with something quite unusual. I've only seen this once before in my career. So, listen in and take notes, Nick, because you're beginning to brass me off.'

Nick sat up—a pen poised above his open notebook.

'Right,' Hart exhaled. 'Corporal Quade's father is a QC. And it seems he's been catching up on his bedtime reading. He's been quoting The Army Act and Queen's Regs at Major Marwood, and she's not happy.'

'And he's a Lord, something or other,' Jo stated.

Hart paused. 'So I gather. Right then, pay close attention. We don't want any fuck-ups. As you know, Corporal Quade is to be represented by Captain Trueman.'

'What I don't get is—why not a barrister? Or something like that. Daddy is a silk, after all,' Jo said with some sarcasm.

'It would be too much. Lord Quade discussed it with the OC. It seems everyone wants to play this down. His Lordship wants his daughter to have a long and happy career in Her Majesty's Forces.'

'And the OC wants to make Brigadier. So, his Lordship gets to pull a few strings for his daughter. Why isn't she an officer?' Nick chimed in.

'Oh, you are listening this morning, Nick,' Hart said. 'I don't know, maybe you can ask her? The interview is delayed until tomorrow morning. So, I want to see your prepared questions before we start.'

'Delayed? Why?' Nick asked.

'Captain Trueman needs more time to prepare.'

Nick and Jo nodded.

'Good! Work in here until you're done. Let's start at eight-thirty tomorrow morning sharp. Jo, I'll see you in the mess at lunchtime—that way, we won't be eating on our own.' Hart left the room, her heels clicking a steady march along the corridor until she reached the RSM's office.

'Morning, Kirsty,' Hart closed the door. 'Sitrep for you.'

'Sounds ominous.'

'I've just briefed my team. There will be no interviews today. Captain Trueman has asked for more time. My team are prepping.'

'Ah, I understand Corporal Quade has connections that are making the situation trickier than usual.'

'Father's a QC. Some Lord or something.' Hart said.

'Well, that'll do it. Bet the OC's not best pleased.'

'When she briefed me this morning, she seemed quite chuffed, especially as Quade had chosen Captain Trueman.'

'Ah, well, no love lost there,' RSM Gordon said.

'Something I should know?'

'Petty rivalry. Personally, I think it's mostly in the OC's head, but there you are.'

'Nothing important then. So, the interview will start tomorrow morning. Nick is in the Sapper's mess, and Jo is with me in your mess.'

'Didn't know you were staying over. That means we can have dinner together.' The RSM enthused. 'We could go into Finchley.'

'Me neither. I've got to go and get some clothes. And wait out on dinner. I've got Jo with me. Might look weird, you and me going out to dinner. Plus, I don't want to leave her on her own.'

'You don't need to worry. I believe a certain Sarn't Terry White, will take care of her.' Gordon gave a knowing grin.

Hart paused, then smiled as realisation dawned into a broad smile. 'Oh.'

Gordon nodded slowly.

'Right, I'm on my way to Rochester Row to pack. I'll see you later this evening.'

Jo and Nick spent the last hour of the morning before lunch prepping for the interview. Having prepared a few questions over the weekend, Jo decided to do some research and went to the Orderly room to find a copy of Debretts.

'And to what do I owe the pleasure?' Sergeant Treacher asked.

'Got a copy of Debretts?'

'We do. The OC has it right now. I suspect,' Treacher assumed an air of superiority. 'That you want it for the same reason the OC did?'

'Probably.'

'Mm-hm, I can save you the bother. Viscount Quade—also known as Alexander Blackstone-Quade. So, proper pukka nobility.'

'Thanks. See you at lunch.'

With the rest of the afternoon at her leisure, she went for a run—something she hadn't had time for since the investigation started. Setting out, she had no idea how far and where she would run. She decided to take a route along the perimeter roads of the barracks and through the married quarters. Adopting a steady pace, she ran through the green square that separated the Headquarters building from the cookhouse and out through the car park.

Her mind free to roam, she considered Quade and the interview tomorrow and how events can make sudden turns and changes with differing consequences. She turned back to the barracks, and as she approached the Officer's mess, she saw Treacher unlock the door to a flat adjacent to the officer's mess, carrying a plastic grocery bag branded Tescos. Terry had told her the OC had a separate flat with everything in it, though rumour had it she was not much of a cook, so she ate in the officer's mess. Jo slowed to a walk, leaned against a tree, ensuring she was out of sight, and waited. Within a few minutes, Treacher came out, locking the door and then giving it a shove before getting into her car, parked outside the flat. Jo watched before continuing her run.

Now, what would Ann Treacher be delivering? The bag was too heavy for just fags. Booze?

Jo sprinted back to the headquarters building, arriving simultaneously with Treacher.

'Busy?' Jo asked.

'Not particularly. Why do you ask?' Treacher answered. 'Just done the OC's shopping.'

'Do you always do her shopping, then?'

'Why do you ask?'

'No reason. Curious. Just me, being me.'

'A nosy policewoman,' Treacher spat in a low voice.

They walked into the Orderly room.

'Private Dawson, make me and the OC a coffee, will you?' She turned back to Jo. 'I just get the OC's fags 'n' stuff when she asks. It makes for a nice outing. Anyway, I'm busy. Anything else? Hop to, Dawson, the OC and me haven't got all day.'

Jo left the orderly room, deciding to pop back to her temporary office at the end of the corridor. On her way, she passed Dawson making coffee in the small office cum kitchen.

'Sarn't Treacher, have you doing this all the time?'

'Yeah, mostly. And then, she,' Dawson nodded in the direction of the Orderly Room. 'Gets all the credit.'

'Don't like her much?'

'Sarn't Treacher or the OC?'

'Either.'

Dawson thought for a moment. 'Neither. Want one? Might as well as I'm here.' She shrugged. 'I'll bring it to your office, shall I?'

'Yeah,' Jo smiled. 'That'd be nice. Thanks.'

Jo settled at the table. Dawson knocked on the door before entering and placing the mug of coffee on the desk.

'Thanks.'

Dawson hovered in front of the desk.

Jo looked up, cocking her head to one side, adopting an encouraging smile.

'You know Sarn't White, don't you?'

'Mm-hmm.'

'I suppose you must be all right then, if you know her.'

Jo laughed. 'Don't forget I'm SIB. I'm not supposed to be friendly. It's my job.'

Dawson chuckled. 'You're all right, yer know.' She walked to the door. 'Not just fags. Know what I mean?' Dawson tapped her nose with her forefinger before shutting the door behind her.

## Chapter 25

*Day Five*

Jo and Sergeant Major Hart ate their breakfast on a separate table from the other Senior Ranks of the mess, ostracised for the work the Ministry of Defence required them to complete. Jo contemplated what was ahead of her. How would an interrogation with a unit representative be different? Were her questions good enough to incriminate Corporal Quade? Anxiety quelled her appetite. Instead of her usual hearty breakfast, she sipped a cup of tea.

'All right, Jo?'

'Not really, ma'am. Will it be very different from the usual way we conduct interviews?'

'No. But you might think carefully before applying pressure on her. She has a witness to make sure that we play by the rules. Finish your brekkie, and I'll brief you and Nick in a few minutes. I took a gander at your questions—stick to the script, and everything will be fine.'

Jo walked without the usual spring in her step to the interrogation room. As a rule, she could compartmentalise the various aspects of her job so she could handle the most unpleasant situations and people, but with Quade, it was different. She wanted revenge, lesbian or no lesbian—there was no place for a bully in the Army, especially one who had more or less murdered her friend. And for that reason alone, she was keen to break Quade with questions that would force her to incriminate herself. However, despite what Hart said, Captain Trueman was an added complication to the process.

When Jo got to the interview room, Nick and Hart were huddled around the table.

'Ah, here you are, Jo' Hart pulled a chair out next to her for Jo. 'Sit down. Let me go over some guidelines with you. Captain Trueman will advise and take advice from Corporal Quade, so you might find yourselves waiting for answers to your questions. Make sure your question technique is not interpreted as coercive. And one more thing. If you can't get Corporal Quade to admit her sexuality through a confession, then you have absolutely nothing to go on. In that event, try for a name. Unlikely, but possible.'

'So, all the normal rules around questioning apply? Right? We must get them to be explicit about their sexual exploits—otherwise, they might be trying to get out of the Army for free.' Anxiety roiled Jo's stomach once more.

'That's it and think about asking open questions rather than piling on the pressure with leading questions. Don't worry—I'll be there. It'll be a good experience for you and Nick. Because this is rare, I'm going to be back up. Make sure everything is done right. When I brief the OC, I need to be sure that I have all the information to hand. I know she is concerned about this development.'

Trueman knocked on the door and walked in. The three Senior Ranks stood for the Commissioned Officer.

'Morning, Sarn't Major. Please sit down.' Trueman sat in one of the chairs facing the Queen's photograph at the back of the room as she placed two thick red books on the table. 'Brought them with me just in case.' She nodded at the Queen's Regulations and The Army Act 1955.

'Good thinking, ma'am. But I'm pretty sure you won't have to open them,' Hart chuckled.

'I hope so. I'm sure none of us is looking forward to this. Corporal Quade is in with her platoon sergeant. I'm ready. Let's get on with it. Sarn't Major, are you staying? I'd appreciate it if you did. I want to make sure no mistakes are made. We can't risk it with an important and litigious father. Not to mention, the OC is on the warpath.'

'Already decided, ma'am.'

Trueman smiled her relief.

Hart collected a chair from the stack in the corner of the room and placed her chair a little way from the table, in neutral territory. Nick shifted a small table in front of her. Hart sat down and put her copies of the Queen's Regs and the AA 1955 with a pad and pen on the table. Jo and Nick sat at the table opposite Trueman.

Quade knocked on the door and marched in. She came to a halt in front of Trueman and saluted.

'At ease, Corporal Quade. You may sit and remove your hat,' Trueman instructed.

Jo began the proceedings. 'Right, Corporal Quade, we have reason to believe you are a lesbian.'

Hart coughed. Jo and Nick looked at her.

'My apologies. I'm Sergeant Clark, SIB, London Provost Company, and this is Sergeant Acorn of the same. To my left is Sarn't Major Hart, a neutral observer in the proceedings. We will be taking notes throughout the course of the interview, which may be used as evidence. We note that you have elected Captain Trueman to represent you.'

'Before you start.' Trueman interrupted the proceedings. 'I have a letter here that Lord Quade has written on behalf of his daughter. I won't read it because it is quite long and full of legal terms. However, basically, he writes that his daughter is present for this interview in the spirit of cooperation and collaboration and that he is certain she is innocent of the suspicions you have of her. Furthermore, he hopes you will proceed in accordance with the aforementioned spirit.' Trueman placed the letter on the table. 'For your records.'

Jo checked with Hart that she should proceed. 'Thank you, Captain Trueman and Corporal Quade. We look forward to cooperating with you, too. Corporal Quade, do you have any questions for us before we begin?' Jo attempted a genuine smile.

Quade shook her head. Nick made a note before nodding to Jo.

'We have noted that Corporal Quade has answered in the negative. Corporal Quade, we have asked you here in connection with the suicide of Private Lowe. We believe her actions resulted from pressure from a group of lesbians that you are part of. What can you tell us about this matter?'

'You know more than me.' Quade stared at the shine on her drill shoes.

Nick leaned forward. 'How often have you been to the Camden Palace?'

Quade said nothing; her brown eyes stared straight ahead.

'Do I need to repeat the question?'

'No. I'm not answering it.'

'Corporal Quade,' said Jo, leaning forward on the desk. 'We're conducting this interview with you in the hope that you can help us. We want to know who bullied Private Lowe. It's a serious matter because she committed suicide. And I'm sure you would rather be seen as a cooperative rather than a hostile witness. I'll ask you again. Have you ever been to the Camden Palace?'

Quade leaned over to Trueman, cupping her hand to the officer's ear. Trueman nodded.

'No law against it, is there?' Quade answered.

'No. So, you have been there?' Nick pushed.

'Loadsa us go there.'

'Have you ever been on a Tuesday?'

Quade considered her answer. 'Might've.'

'So, you know that Tuesday is a women-only night.'

'It's also half-price drinks night, cheaper than the NAFFI.'

'You're not denying, then, that you chose to go to a lesbian dance night at the Camden Palace?'

'Not lesbian—women only. You get a lot of hen parties there, too. A group of us go occasionally and have a laugh at the bridal parties and dance. No crime in that. It's better than the NAFFI because we don't get the cat calls from drunken Sappers, and it makes a change.'

'Who do you go with?'

'The girls.'

'Could you give us their names?'

Jo sat, ready to record the information.

Quade looked at Jo, then at Nick.

'No. No Names.' Quade sat up and ran her hands through her blonde hair.

'That's not very cooperative. Especially considering that, as you say, it's not a crime to go to the Camden Palace.'

'Yes, well, I'm afraid I am unable to trust you. So, absolutely no—no names.'

Jo cocked her ear to Quade's answer. Had Quade's accent changed? Jo shifted in her chair, then leaned forward, signalling to Nick she would take over.

'I've been reliably informed that you are the ringleader of a lesbian gang here at Twelve Company. I've also observed first-hand that you have a group of women who hang around you like, like er, er harem.'

Quade scoffed. 'Very funny. I'm popular. What can I say?'

'Tell me, Corporal Quade, you being nobility, we're wondering why you aren't an officer.'

In the polished accent of the upper class, Quade leaned forward and retorted. 'I felt it was not for me. I've been told I'm a natural-born leader; frankly, one tires of it. So, I decided that a short time in the ranks might be of some value in my future.'

'Hmm, that contradicts what I've been told. I have it on record that you've signed up for twenty-two years.'

'Again, I'm not sure what this has to do with the investigation, but I signed up for three years and converted. I like the Army. It's better than volunteer work and following Mummy to endless lunches and dinners. At the same time, as they look to marry me off to some minor noble.'

Jo considered the information and pressed on with her original line of questioning. 'Got to be hard, though, slumming it in a four-man room? Especially after mummy and daddy's stately home.'

'I have my own room as a corporal. I've spent more time at boarding school than I ever did at home. I spent most of my holidays at school or on school trips. So, the Army is just an extension of boarding school. And I am inured to your taunts. You grow up away from home—you soon learn to stand on your own two feet and blend in.'

'Your parents didn't want you at home for the holidays, then?'

'That's none of your business.'

'And there was me feeling sorry for you.'

'Funny? Really? Shame.'

'What do you mean?'

'Well, all that expensive education wasted. Or.' Jo tapped her chin. 'Oh, I get it you want to piss mummy and daddy off. Bet daddy is seriously brassed off with you now—eh?'

'Sergeant, I'm not sure what this has to do with the investigation. You seem to have lost your focus.' Quade, smirking, leaned forward.

Jo felt the sting of the subtle reprimand and tried another tack. 'You're being posted soon, aren't you?'

Quade nodded.

'Where to?'

Quade fixed her eyes on Jo.

'We can check it ourselves, Corporal Quade, so you might as well answer. In the spirit of cooperation and all that.'

'Rheindalen.'

'Coincidentally, so was Private Lowe.'

Quade guffawed. 'This is the best you've got? Good lord, practically every Postie is posted there. It's where we go unless we get some glamorous post like Cyprus.'

'Would you make a note, Sarn't Acorn, to look up the name of every woman postal and courier operator due for posting in the next few weeks, alongside Corporal Quade here? We'll start there unless Corporal Quade wants to help us get there quicker?'

Jo waited, returning Quade's hostile gaze with a confident smile. 'No?' Jo turned to Nick. 'That's not very cooperative, is it?'

Nick picked up the questioning. 'We have reason to believe there is a group of lesbians harassing their colleagues, forcing them to go to the Camden Palace on a Tuesday. They ply them with alcohol, force them to dance with them, and, in due course, have a sexual relationship with them. What do you have to say?'

Quade clenched her jaw and gazed out of the window. Trueman whispered in Quade's ear. Quade ducked her head behind Trueman's and mumbled.

'Corporal Quade declines to answer your questions. And she says that unless you can show her the evidence behind your accusations, she wishes to be dismissed. Therefore, I have to ask, do you have evidence?'

'Yes, we do—tons of it,' Jo's exasperation was showing.

'May we see it?'

'We've shown it to her.'

'We'd like to see it again.'

'Alright, Sarn't Acorn, would you oblige us?' Jo rolled her eyes with impatience.

Nick opened a file and tipped a dozen or so photographs onto the table. 'All of these photos, ma'am, were confiscated from Corporal Quade's bed space.'

Quade spread the photographs across the desk as if to see them better, then slowly picked each one up, examining it and smiling for the benefit of her interrogators.

Irritated, Jo leaned forward and stopped Quade from picking up another. 'This one here, it's Corporal Watson, isn't it?'

'Dunno.'

'Really? I know it's Corporal Watson. And we have her confession that she is a lesbian. And you are in this photograph with her.'

'I know I was photographed with her. But we did not discuss her sexuality.'

Everyone in the room instinctively knew Quade had lied.

'Corporal Quade needs a break. Is that all right with you?' said Trueman.

'Of course, ma'am. We'll reconvene in half an hour,' Jo replied.

Trueman stood, followed by the other soldiers. 'Thank you. Corporal Quade, with me.'

Jo sat down and exhaled. Nick flopped back in his seat. Hart left the office, returning moments later with Dawson carrying a tray of coffees. 'Hello again, Sarn't.'

'Thanks,' said Jo.

'No more runs, then?' Dawson winked at Jo before shutting the door behind her.

'What's that about?' Nick asked.

'I dunno. Let's look at what we've got here.' Jo reviewed her notes. 'Absolutely bloody nothing!'

'Patience, Jo. You're both doing a first-class job. Keep at it. You have her rattled,' Hart advised.

Trueman knocked at the door and entered, carrying a cup of coffee. 'Mind if we start earlier? I think we can wrap this up quickly.'

'Ma'am,' said Hart.

Jo mouthed, 'What?' to her superior as she sat down.

Quade marched in and saluted the captain. Then, at the request of the officer, she sat her legs crossed at the ankle, and leaned back in her chair, projecting an air of confidence.

'I believe where we left off was Sarn't Clark and Corporal Quade were examining some photographs,' Trueman began the second interview.

'Ma'am,' acknowledged Jo.

'And I believe you said this was your evidence against Corporal Quade? Is there anything else?'

'No, ma'am.'

'I see. So, all of these pictures are taken in varying locations and with individuals from Corporal Quade's wide circle of friends. In themselves, they are not evidence, just pictures of people.'

Trueman gathered up the photos and pulled and pushed them into a rough pile before shoving them in Nick's direction and asking, 'Again? Is there any other evidence?'

Jo and Nick looked at each other.

'Hearsay, ma'am. Corporal Quade has a reputation. In fact, we've heard she's called The Stud. That's her nickname,' Nick replied solemnly.

Quade leaned forward. 'That's not true. And I believe hearsay is not evidence, just gossip.'

She sat back in her chair, arms folded across her chest, her dark eyes glowering at her two inquisitors.

Hart got out of her seat and put both hands on the table to speak to both sides. 'Well, if that's all we have, then you may go, Corporal.'

'Can I say something, ma'am,' Quade asked Trueman.

'Of course.'

'I think these witch-hunts are a waste of my time and yours, As well as a waste of taxpayer's money. You have nothing on my friends or me. And if I were you, I'd look a bit closer to home.' She winked and then adopted an affected cockney accent. 'Know what I mean?'

'Corporal Quade,' Trueman commanded. 'You are dismissed.' Trueman waited for Quade to leave the room. 'My apologies, Sarn't Major. I had no idea she was going to be unpleasant.'

'No worries, ma'am. That's nothing to some of the stuff we have to put up with.'

'I'm sure. I gather the problem is that you need the suspect to incriminate themselves by giving you the sordid details of any improper relationship. And I'm afraid Viscount Quade has worked that out and apprised Corporal Quade of that fact. I'm sorry, but you're wasting your time with her. She's bombproof. It's annoying because I know, and you know, that she is probably queer and a bully. Still, unless you have a witness or we can get some other corroborating evidence, we're sunk.'

## Chapter 26

After Quade's interview, Sergeant Major Hart preferred to clean up the interrogation room than brief the OC, Major Marwood. Quade's parting comment made her wonder who she meant. Was it her, Nick or Jo? It could be any one of them or all of them. It was unsettling. She knocked before entering the RSM's office and sat in the armchair without waiting to be asked.

The RSM got up and shut the door. 'You look tired. Coffee?'

Hart shook her head. 'I don't know where to start.'

Gordon tilted her head and smiled.

'Quade was a complete shit.'

'Mhmm.'

'Captain Trueman is sympathetic to the cause, but she knew Quade was bulletproof, in fact, said so. Pisses me off when those who mind their own business like Corporal Watson get discharged, and those you know are damn guilty get off because daddy is nobility.'

'Tough one.'

'You know, she even had the temerity to suggest that we look closer to home.'

'What do you think she meant by that?'

'Don't know. Could be me, Jo, or even Nick?'

'Not Nick.'

'Maybe, every now and then, I glimpse a different Nick. Anyway, I don't know what I'm going to tell the OC.'

'What've you got left to do?'

'Half a dozen or so interviews to go. If we're lucky, we might finish by Friday, depending. Frankly, it's been a disaster results-wise. The good ones have gone, and the shit is left behind to create more havoc. Mark, my words, Quade is going to come up again. And one of us will be interviewing her again, and daddy will get her off—again!' Anger and frustration fought for prominence in Hart's tone.

'I'd be careful of Quade. When I did some digging, I found out the women are scared of her. Her Employing Officer has spoken to her a couple of times. Apparently, she bullies the girls down the depot. Makes them do the jobs she doesn't want to. He doesn't like her. In fact, he says she has a bad effect on the morale when she is on shift. He's glad she's going to be someone else's problem. And, worse still, she keeps score and likes to take her revenge cold.'

'So, she did upset Private Lowe?'

'Maybe. Probably. It's just gossip. I haven't got to the bottom of it yet. But I will. My point is she's bullying you and your team. Subtle, I grant you. But bear in mind she's vengeful. Make sure your team take care of themselves. I'll find out what I can here. Maybe we can get her before you finish up.'

'Gosh, this is the nastiest witch-hunt I've ever dealt with. And that's saying something.' Hart got up. 'I'd better get it over with.' She exhaled noisily as she left the RSM's office. Her shoulders slumped—her heels clicked a slow tempo up the tiled corridor.

She knocked on the door and entered the OC's office, only to find it empty. Turning to leave, she bumped into Sergeant Treacher. 'Where's the OC?' Hart noticed Treacher was carrying a full, Tesco-branded plastic bag.

'Basic Fitness test, with Sarn't White. Can I help?'

'No, I had an appointment to see the OC this morning.'

'Yes, you did. She was expecting you earlier, and when you were a no-show, she bumped up her PT session with Sarn't White. She should be back after lunch.'

'Okay. Do you do the OC's shopping all the time?' Hart nodded at the bag.

'Blimey, Jo asked me the same question. Don't you people do favours for your bosses now and then? Probably not. You're so busy enforcing the rules.'

Hart waited. Her quizzical look knitted her brow, showing her impatience.

'You want an explanation?'

Hart arched her eyebrows.

'I don't know what it's got to do with you nosy monkeys.' Treacher waited for the insult to fall. Dissatisfied by Hart's lack of reaction, she finally gave up the information. 'If you must know, my brother has a corner shop in Finchley. He does cash 'n' carry. When he gets stuff in, I get the OC a little something at his discount. Keeps her sweet. I just happen to use Tesco's bags. Not that it's any of your business.'

During the lunch break, Treacher walked to the OC's flat. She rang the doorbell. She heard Marwood call out but couldn't understand what she said. Nevertheless, she stayed because she needed to be paid for this and the last two deliveries. A few moments later, Marwood opened the door.

'Obviously, you didn't hear me. I said leave the stuff outside.'

Marwood reached for the bag. Treacher put it behind her back. 'I need payment for this and the last two shops, ma'am. Twenty quid all told.'

'Twenty quid! In that case, I'll give it to you in the office later this afternoon.'

'If you don't mind, ma'am. I want to collect it now.'

Marwood hesitated. 'I'll have to get my handbag. Hang on here.'

'Ma'am, I think I'd better come in. I don't think you want to attract any attention.' Treacher looked over her shoulder, mindful of Jo and Hart's questions.

Marwood grimaced. 'Well, wait in the hallway, then.'

Treacher stepped inside. Marwood went through to the living room, and to protect her privacy, she shut the door behind her.

Treacher stared at the magnolia-coloured walls as she shifted her weight from one foot to the other. The OC seemed to be taking her time. She checked her watch, and if she didn't have the money soon, she would be late for a staff meeting. She weighed her options. On the one hand, to hassle the OC or, on the other, to leave without the money again. She was already down £20. The more she loitered and thought about it, the more indignant she felt at being made to wait like a servant or some lackey—she was better than that. She knocked on the living room door and walked through. A strong smell of tobacco permeated the room. 'Ma'am, I need to go. Can I have the money, please?'

'I've mislaid my handbag. I know it's here somewhere.' Marwood lifted some copies of old newspapers and magazines, forming an untidy heap on the dining table, and some shirts that needed ironing that lay limp over chair backs. 'Ah, here it is. Right.' She pulled her handbag from under the melee and rummaged in it. On finding her purse, she unzipped it before producing three five-pound notes. 'Looks like that's all I've got for now. I'll give you the other fiver tomorrow when I've been to the hole-in-the-wall.'

'Ma'am, I don't want to say this, but in the future, it has to be strictly cash on delivery. I have to pay my brother, and at the moment, I'm subbing you on my Sergeant's salary. Doesn't seem right.'

'I'm sorry, it's a tad awkward. I haven't been to the bank. That's all.'

Marwood paused. 'For goodness' sake, Sarn't, don't you trust me!' Marwood's irritation tainted her reply.

'Not that, ma'am, but you haven't paid me for the last two deliveries. Gets a bit awkward, my mess bill coming up and all that.'

'I'm paying you now, aren't I?'

Treacher winced. 'Well..., not everything you owe. I'm sorry, but this is too much. Let's call it quits.'

'No, wait! I'll pay you. You just need to hang on until tomorrow.'

'I don't think so, ma'am. I don't want to fall out with you or anything. So, let's leave it at this.'

Treacher turned to go. Marwood, lunging toward the Senior Rank, grabbed her upper arm, spinning her around so they were now face to face.

'Ma'am?'

'Look, I need this. So please—why don't I sort it out tomorrow and pay you in advance for future deliveries? What do you think?' Marwood smiled, encouraging Treacher to acquiesce.

Treacher thought for a moment. 'No, ma'am. I'd rather not. What started as a favour, once every few weeks, has become a twice-weekly chore. And, if it's all right with you, I'd like to end this now. No one will hear a word about it from me. I hope you will do the same?'

'Of course. That's your prerogative. No one will hear anything of it from me.'

## Chapter 27

After lunch, Sergeant Major Hart hesitated outside a green door with a brown nameplate. Cream letters showed the current occupier as Major L E Marwood WRAC. Officer Commanding. Hart exhaled, pulling her shoulders back before squaring her chin. She knocked loudly and entered.

'Ah, good afternoon. My apologies for not seeing you this morning. Please, take a seat, Sarn't Major. I hope you have some good news for me.'

Hart sat in one of the Army-issue low, easy chairs, crossing her legs but failing to find a comfortable position. The elasticated green nylon seat cover sagged to one side, exposing a tattered yellowy-brown foam cushion underneath. The magnolia ceiling, stained with tobacco smoke, matched the chair foam in its colour and disrepair. A large and impressive oak desk appeared to command the office. The desk, marred by chips at the corners and circular heat stains on its surface, betrayed its origins in that it was not oak but cheap stained wood, completing the shabby ensemble that reflected the lack of budget allocated to the MOD.

The OC sat at her desk, leaning forward with her hands clasped in front of her. 'Well?'

'Ma'am, we've conducted a full and frank interview with Corporal Quade. Present were myself….'

'Yes, yes, woman.' Marwood waved her hand at her informer. 'I know all that. Sarn'ts Clark and Acorn and Captain Trueman were there. Get on with it.'

'Well, as you know, ma'am, Corporal Quade's father is a solicitor, and he counselled her to have a unit rep. And as you know, Captain Trueman fulfilled that role.'

'Oh, don't tell me—Trueman got her off!' Marwood rolled her eyes.

'Actually, no, ma'am, she did her job. There just wasn't any evidence to convict her.'

'There was no evidence. Why?' Marwood demanded, leaning forward a further inch with the intention to intimidate.

Hart, undeterred, carried on in a steady tone. 'All we had were photographs, and the images can be interpreted as just friends having a good time.'

'But I thought you said they were in Brighton.'

‘I did, but being in Brighton is not an offence, nor is it evidentially indicative of being a lesbian. Obviously, Brighton is populated by heterosexuals as well.’

‘I know that!’ Marwood’s patience was diminishing. ‘So, what else do you have?’

‘Just tips. Which, as Corporal Quade pointed out correctly, is just hearsay.’

‘I see. So now Corporal Quade is our legal expert!’

Hart pulled her lips into a straight line and counted silently to ten as she clasped her hands, clenching and unclenching her fingers. ‘And you don’t have anything else?’

‘Ma’am, I don’t know whether you realise this, but unless we catch her in bed with someone or at a lesbian club, then we rely on a confession, and she must give details of at least one sexual act.’

‘I see. It’s all too bloody, sordid if you ask me. So that means Quade is free to return to work and continue operating her ring of queers?’

‘Yes, ma’am.’

‘Well, let’s hope the press doesn’t get hold of it. It would make a great story for the Sunday People, especially after that article on the Gay Glosters—the embarrassment. God, what a bloody mess.’ Marwood’s shoulders slumped forward. She inhaled from her ever-present cigarette, exhaling as she examined a scar in the desk’s veneer.

Hart got up.

‘Hold on a minute, Sarn’t Major.’ Marwood looked up. ‘Where do we go from here?’

‘Well, ma’am, we can finish the list of names we have. Though right now, not much is coming up apart from Corporal Watson, MOD.’

‘What about Corporal Minter and the whip?’ Marwood gave a leery smile.

‘Turns out Captain Trueman is right. She works at the local stables when she’s off duty. It seems she’s quite good with horses. The stables like her.’

Marwood shook her head and stubbed out a fag end. Automatically, she reached for another cigarette from a pack of Rothmans King Size and lit it with a monogrammed silver cigarette lighter. She took a long drag before tilting her chin to the ceiling and exhaling the smoke in a veil of frustration.

'Sorry—do you want one?' Marwood slid the pack across the desk.

'I don't, ma'am. Thank you.'

'So, nothing?'

'That's right.'

'Well, what about the others on the list? How many discharges?'

'One, ma'am.'

'One! Corporal Watson is your only one? The clerk to the Defence Minister! Probably the most intelligent woman in the unit—is the only one?'

'We couldn't make the evidence stick, ma'am. And they wouldn't confess. No names so far, either.'

'All this—all this chaos!' Marwood. A cigarette in one hand, she threw her arms into the air. 'For one woman! You should be ashamed of yourself.'

Marwood's tirade could be heard throughout the headquarters building. Soldiers visiting the Orderly Room across the corridor lingered, catching wind of the heated conversation through the closed door before remarking to each other on the information they gleaned.

Prompted by the hum of discussion, RSM Gordon poked her head out of her office door. 'Good afternoon, ladies. Go back to work or the block. Off you go now.' When she saw the last woman leave the headquarters building, Gordon strode the few paces to Marwood's office. She knocked on the officer's door. She knocked louder again, entered, and shut the door behind her. 'Ma'am, I thought you might like to know you can be heard in the Orderly Room and along the corridor.'

'Oh. Sorry, RSM.' Marwood got up and walked around her desk to perch on the front edge. Sarcasm filled her sentences. 'But have you heard? We have the almighty haul of one single, solitary discharge to show for all of this chaos.' Her tone changed to disappointment as she looked at her black patent leather court shoes. 'This isn't good.'

'No, ma'am, it isn't. But look on the bright side. We have the rest of the unit intact. Corporal Quade is being posted soon, and everything will settle back down fairly quickly once she's gone.'

Marwood looked through the RSM, jutting out her jaw in anger. 'The incompetence of this team is beyond belief!' Marwood stood up, inhaling and exhaling nicotine as she paced the room.

'Ma'am,' the RSM chided the OC while smiling at Hart. 'I'm sure Miss Hart here is aware of your disappointment. I'm sure she is disappointed too.'

Hart nodded for emphasis.

'There are still more interviews to follow over the next few days, aren't there? Miss Hart?' The RSM continued her placation of her OC.

'Yes, Miss Gordon. We have a couple more left.'

'Yes, well,' Marwood took another drag while scrutinising Hart. 'If they get wind of your incompetence, they're highly unlikely to confess now, are they?'

'Ma'am, if they can hear what you're saying, they definitely won't confess. Miss Hart, please leave us.' The RSM waited until they were alone. 'Ma'am, in a way, this is good news. We have just one. That's what it will look like to the authorities.'

'No, it won't! Don't you see I pulled all the resources? I allowed a witch-hunt to be conducted, and for what? It makes me look incompetent. The Brigadier disapproves of witch-hunts if they are without merit. And this.' Marwood waved her right arm about the room, a cigarette still in her fingers, dropping ash on the carpet. 'Has absolutely none! I look like a complete nincompoop.'

'I understand your predicament. But I think you can make it sound quite positive. I'll have a word with Miss Hart and see what she can do in the way of a good report that you can use.' The RSM turned to go. 'I'll get Sarn't Treacher, to get you some tea.'

'No! I don't want any tea from her.'

The RSM studied her OC. 'Ma'am.' The RSM paused with her hand on the doorknob. 'No problem, I'll have Private Dawson bring you a cuppa.'

## Chapter 28

*Day Six*

On Thursday morning, Major Marwood sat at the dining room table in her flat. She finished her cigarette, stubbing it in the already full glass ashtray, before downing the last dregs of coffee. One perk of having a flat was that she could make her own meals if she wished, though not being a cook—she took full advantage of the mess next door. She checked her appearance in the mirror at the front door. Her customary green eyeshadow made the bags under her eyes darker, and her hair, normally in a tight bun, was already fraying. She poked some whisps of hair back into place, knowing they would escape immediately. Closing her front door, she felt the sun on her face, relishing it after the past few days of rain and clouds. Maybe things might change direction with the weather, and in less than ten days, they would have another long weekend for May Day.

It was a break she could do with following the events of the past few days. She walked to the gym, careful to conserve her energy for her fitness test. She had to pass it today because if she didn't, she would be medically downgraded, setting off a chain of events that would damage her career. It would mean her place at staff college would be placed on hold, triggering a slowing of her career progression, notwithstanding the failure of the witch-hunt. She put the negative thoughts to the back of her mind and continued her steady walk to the gym, where Sergeant White was waiting for her with a clipboard and stopwatch.

'Morning, ma'am. Ready?' Terry grinned. 'Big day, so big effort!'

'Yes, yes, don't patronise me, Sarn't. I'm ready. Do your countdown.' Marwood's tone was patronising despite her rebuke of Terry for the same thing.

The two women set off at Terry's pace. The OC kept up, though she was unable to speak. She clenched her jaw and strode purposefully, matching every stride with the PTI. The one-and-a-half-mile circuit comprised a marginal incline in the first half-mile and a matching decline in the last half.

'Come on, ma'am. It's all downhill from now on. You're doing so well.'

Marwood spoke for the first time. 'Thank you, Sarn't. I don't need the encouragement. Save it for the troops. Just keep an eye on that stopwatch.' As she spoke, she inhaled the cool spring air. She coughed. She coughed again, hacking up the contents of her lungs while trying to keep pace.

'Ma'am, we can stop if you like. We can do it again another time.'

Marwood stopped walking to heave the phlegm from her lungs. She spat it out on the pavement. Terry revolted, looked away. Marwood strode forward. 'Come on, Sarn't, keep up.'

Terry jerked into action and caught up to the OC within a few paces. Marwood's breathing was uneven, causing her to gasp for breath.

'Slow, deep breaths in, ma'am, and then blow out the carbon dioxide. Breathe in, two, three, and out. That's it. Keep it going. Ma'am, you need to keep up now. Lengthen your stride. Eyes on the prize. We have about two hundred and fifty yards to go. Use your arms—come on, propel yourself forward.'

Marwood coughed and hacked, her breath rasping in her lungs, causing another bout of coughing. Temporarily disabled, she stopped and tried to speak.

'It's okay, ma'am. Deep breaths.'

Marwood waved her hands to indicate that deep breaths were the problem.

'Hands on hips, ma'am, lift your head and breathe.'

Marwood's chest heaved with the effort to inhale and then exhale, as Terry had advised. She worked hard to gain control of her breathing until relief came. Terry waited patiently by her side until Marwood adopted a slow walk for the last two hundred yards. 'I suppose I failed?'

'Mm.'

Marwood sighed her defeat.

'Not by much, ma'am. You'll do it next time for sure.'

'Do you know how irritating your enthusiasm can be? I'm not one of the other ranks. As an officer, I can motivate myself. It's just this damn cough. I've had it all winter. Okay, Sarn't—you can leave me here. I can make it to the mess by myself.'

'Tomorrow, ma'am?'

'Are you going to send this result in?'

'I need to, ma'am. London District needs the unit results today, or they'll chase me.'

'In that case, when can I retake it?'

'I'm not sure, ma'am. Whenever you're ready—I mean, don't stop trying.'

'When I'm ready.' Marwood considered her options. 'In that case, not tomorrow. After the bank holiday.'

Terry changed direction and jogged to the gym. Marwood walked to her flat to shower and change into barrack dress uniform.

An hour later, Marwood was in her office. Sergeant Treacher placed a cup of coffee on her desk. 'There you go, ma'am. Is there anything you need?'

'Do you know anything about this?' Marwood held a blank envelope by a corner between her forefinger and thumb.

'No, ma'am, did you ask for an envelope?'

'No. Inside was a note. Know anything about it?' Marwood cocked her head on one side, regarding Treacher, watching for a telltale sign.

'As I said, ma'am—no.'

'Then, will you have Miss Hart come to my office immediately?'

'Yes, ma'am.'

Treacher ambled up the corridor as she passed each platoon officer's door, checking they were at their desks. Finally, she reached the makeshift interrogation room at the end of the passage. She knocked before entering. Sergeant Major Hart, Nick and Jo were huddled around a table. 'Morning. Miss Hart, the OC, would like to see you if you don't mind.'

Treacher accompanied Hart to the OC's office. 'Good luck, she's not in a good mood.'

Hart hesitated before knocking. Then, with what she hoped showed confidence, knocked again before striding purposefully into the office. 'Good morning, Major Marwood. You asked to see me.'

'Yes, sit down. I think you should see this. The envelope was not sealed or addressed. I opened it before I realised what it was. When I did, I called you immediately.'

Hart took the sheet of A4 paper. The lined paper had newsprint glued to it, creating a brief note. Hart read the note out. 'Sergeant White is gay.' She turned the paper over. 'Of course, it's anonymous. When did you say you got it?'

'This morning, when I got to my office. It was lying right here.' The Major pointed to the spot on the desk. 'Naturally, I was curious, so I opened it. I was surprised the flap was open but was interested to know what was in it. Didn't think it would be—well, that!'

'Hoped it was money?' Hart chuckled.

'I'm sorry?' A tinge of annoyance edged into Marwood's question.

'Can I have the envelope?'

Marwood slid the envelope across the desk.

'I'll get forensics to look it over. But my thinking is that whoever has done this is probably clever enough to use gloves. So, I don't think we'll get much. Maybe some idea about the paper and that sort of thing.'

Marwood interrupted. 'Well, my fingerprints are all over it. I hope that's not going to be a problem.'

Hart scrutinised the irritated officer's face. 'Shouldn't think so, ma'am, we can eliminate yours easy enough. We'll have to take your fingerprints, but someone will come to your office to do that. So, it shouldn't put you out at all.'

'Well, that's a relief.' Marwood lit a cigarette, inhaled, and then exhaled a plume of smoke.

'Looks like someone has a grudge and is using us and, worse still, using you to get at Sarn't White.'

'I take your point. Have you dealt with this kind of thing before?'

'Yes, ma'am—once before. It's what we call a revenge tip. It's a nasty business. Sometimes the informant is right.' Hart paused. 'It's just plain nasty.' She studied the note again.

'Do you think there is something in it? She's a good PTI and very popular. I'd be sorry to lose her. I don't know if this is of any consequence, but Lance Corporal Dart follows her around like a puppy. Lover's tiff?' The OC tilted her head. Be nice if it was true.

'Maybe. Thank you, ma'am. I've made a note of that. I'll be in touch. Is there someone in the Orderly Room who does your mail?'

'I don't actually know—I presume Sarn't Treacher. Why? You think they might have something to do with it? I've already checked with Treacher. She says she has no knowledge of the note.'

'Didn't call us immediately, then?' Hart grinned and continued. 'It's one angle. Who has access to your office?'

'Captain Trueman, the RSM and Sarn't Treacher. They can come and go as they please. Occasionally, someone from the Orderly Room will deliver tea or coffee or one of Sarn't Treacher's errands—they wouldn't dare come in here without permission.'

'Ma'am, I appreciate your confidence. But if the person writes an anonymous note, I don't think they'll be seeking permission.' Hart smiled.

'Course. Absolutely. Right, well, if there isn't anything else? I'll leave you to it.'

'I'll need to interview HQ staff, see if anyone saw anything or anyone delivering the note. We'll try not to be a nuisance.'

'Well, that's another intrusion we can do without.' Marwood blew out a small cloud of smoke and waved it away with her other hand.

'I know, ma'am, but we need to find the perpetrator.'

'Of course.'

'Right, I'll be on my way then, ma'am.'

Hart scratched her head as she left the OC's office. She paused momentarily, undecided about where to go, then headed to the RSM's office. She gave a perfunctory knock, walked to the easy chair, and sat opposite the RSM. 'Kirsty, things are not good.'

'Mhmm. You look glum.'

'Read this.'

The RSM read the note held up by Hart. 'I see. You plan to interview her?'

'I've no choice. Looks like a revenge tip to me.'

'Indeed. When do you plan to talk to Terry?'

'I know the OC wants it sooner rather than later. But frankly, we need to plan this carefully. So, I will take my time and grin and bear the OC's wrath.' Hart got up. 'This investigation stinks. I've seen two developments that I rarely see and certainly not together.'

'Me neither. I'll see what I can find out.' Gordon picked up the phone and dialled the gym.

Hart joined her colleagues in the interview room.

'You all right, Sarn't Major?' Jo asked.

'Yes, fine. Listen, I need to go to Rochester Row in a minute. Something's come up, and I need forensics.'

'What?' Nick asked.

Hart placed the note between her colleagues on the desk, observing Jo's forced neutral reaction. 'Another weird development! And this means we won't be wrapping things up this week.'

'Fuck!' Nick got up and paced the room.

'Sorry—loo.' Jo left the room in a hurry.

Hart considered Jo's reaction before responding. 'Right, I suggest you both return to Rochester Row and prepare for tonight's Mess dinner. Tomorrow, type up the reports and put together a list of names of who might have some knowledge of this bloody note.'

'Yes, ma'am. We're up to date with the lesbian investigation reports.'

'Good, because next up are interviews to learn more about this note.'

'What about Jo?'

'What about Jo?'

'Well, you know?'

'Know what?'

'She's pretty thick with Sarn't White…'

'I'm aware of that, Nick. And I'll be taking the lead on this case from now on. Okay with you?' Hart showed her annoyance and turned to leave.

'Yes, ma'am! By the way, you might like to know that Lance Corporal Dart is pretty thick with Sarn't White.'

'You're the second person to tell me that today.' Hart's tone conveyed her irritation.

'Sorry, ma'am, didn't know you knew.'

'Thanks, Nick. You weren't to know. Just hate these last-minute things coming up. It's irritating.'

'Ma'am… Don't know if you know, but Corporal Dart. Well, she …, she was brought up in care. And I think maybe she has a crush. I don't think anything is going on between them.'

Hart turned to face Nick—her curiosity piqued. 'And you know all this because?'

'Because Jo knows Sarn't White. And I'm pretty sure that Jo would've said something.'

'Like what? Like Dart and White are a couple, or that Dart thinks she has a rival and would send an anonymous note?'

Nick shook his head.

'That's the problem with you, Nick. You only think about the obvious. It's the stuff that isn't obvious that you need to think about.'

'Yeah, but Jo wouldn't… she's too self-conscious. You know she wouldn't put herself in a position where she could be found out,' rambled Nick.

'For goodness' sake, Nick, loose lips!' Hart raised her voice. 'Think before you shit on someone's reputation.' Hart tutted, then with a tired tone, she continued. 'Nick, just take care of her because, although you're an annoying hairy-arsed little shit, she would take care of you.'

'I know, and I'm trying.' Nick's eyes showed he, too, was tired yet earnest.

'Don't try! Just do it!

## Chapter 29

Jo pushed the door to the ladies' toilets open. She braced herself against a basin and looked into the mirror. Her face was ashen. Brushing a wayward strand of hair out of her eyes, she leaned closer to the glass. 'What now? Can anything else go wrong?' she whispered to her image. Her stomach churned at the thought of Terry having to undergo the indignity of an interrogation. She knew Terry was strong, but would she hold up under the questioning? It wasn't fair for someone to do this to Terry when all Terry ever did was work hard.

Jo wanted to help Terry but had no idea how to without making it more difficult for them both. This was the dilemma of all dilemmas. She would have to play it by the book for both their sakes. Tears welled and then spilled down her cheeks. She fished for a handkerchief in her jacket pocket. Dabbing her face, her mind whirled around the consequences of an anonymous note. Who would have sent such a thing? It was both devious and dishonourable. Think Jo!

Her eyes dry, she squinted at herself while she considered all the awful possibilities that might lay ahead. What happened next was more important than who had sent the note—how could she contain the fallout? Think Jo!

Terry would be interviewed. There was no doubt about that. What if she was tasked with leading the interrogation? Jo looked at her reflection with a new determination. She'd do her job. If there were no evidence, she wouldn't look for any. Jo paced the length of the four cubicles in the toilet. But what if she wasn't the lead? What if it was Nick? Would he attempt to break Terry? If Terry gave in. Then, it would be her turn in the hot seat. She shook her head. She couldn't think about the shame. And who would interview her, Nick? Carol Hart? She would deny everything, even her love for Terry if it meant she could save Terry. She would have to practice her answers and her demeanour if she were going to be credible.

She swallowed the bile, threatening to erupt. What would she tell her family? Linda would be thrilled. Good God! There was so much at stake. A future shame filled Jo with heat and nausea. She made a dash to the nearest cubicle and lifted the seat before vomiting loudly into the pan. She heard the entrance door open, so she turned and shut the cubicle door, waiting for the sickness to subside, not wanting to be observed. She needed to be alone to think things through. Think how she would get her and Terry through this vicious mess.

'Jo?'

'Yeah?'

'Mind if I come in?' Nick pushed the door open to find Jo kneeling before the porcelain god.

'Get up.' Nick helped her to her feet. 'It's a bit cramped in here.' Nick led her to the row of washbasins. 'Wash your face and mouth out. I've got some chewing gum.' He waited while she dried her face on the roller towel.

'Always a weird smell with these towels. Never smell clean, do they?'

'Can't say I go around smelling them as a rule,' Nick chuckled as he offered her a stick of gum. 'Listen, I know what you're thinking.'

'Do you? I hope not.'

Jo gripped the edge of one basin with both hands, her knuckles whitening under the stress. Was this it? The moment she would confess her sexuality to Nick.

Nick leaned closer, looking into the mirror. He held Jo's stare. He placed an arm around her shoulder. 'I know.'

'Know what?' Jo jumped back with fear.

'About you and Terry.'

Jo spluttered, her shock and anxiety choking and killing words in her throat at the edges of her lips as her breaths rose and fell so shallow she could barely breathe. She had hoped no one knew—especially Nick, because if she had kept her sexuality hidden from him, she surely would've fooled everyone.

'It's okay. Breathe. I won't say a word. Come on, breathe, slowly, deep breaths.'

Jo followed Nick's commands. 'How do you know?'

Nick tapped his nose with his forefinger. 'I just do.'

'So… so, you are gay too?' she whispered.

He nodded and smiled before putting a finger to his lips.

'I thought so, but then, you'd throw me off the scent with your sexist banter.'

'Worked then?'

Jo giggled. Laughter was a welcome relief from fear.

'Sometimes, Jo, you try too hard.' Nick joined in Jo's laughter.

'I don't always.'

'Well, not today, obviously.' Nick laughed and then mimicked Jo vomiting.

Jo, with a wry smile, shook her head at his antics.

Nick stepped close to Jo and held her. 'Don't worry, Jo. I've got your back. We'll work it out.'

Jo pulled out of his embrace. 'But what if? Supposing you have to interview me? Or Terry?'

Nick replied instantly. 'It won't come to that. I'll make sure of it. Now, if you don't mind, ma'am, I'll be leaving this 'ere establishment. Not my sort of place.' He winked. 'Know what I mean?'

Jo giggled at his sarcasm and innuendo.

'See you tonight.' He opened the door to the main corridor. 'It'll be fine, really it will. Just hang in there.'

## Chapter 30

*Day Six evening, The London Provost Company.*

In her room, Jo got ready for the Mess Dinner. Tonight, the mess expected several senior members of the Metropolitan Police Force and some officers from Scotland Yard, with whom the unit had worked during the year. It was Jo's first Regimental Dinner since being promoted to Sergeant. She pulled out the Haute couture Mess Dress. It was the only long dress she had ever owned and the first she was about to wear. In fact, it was the only dress she possessed that had been made to measure. She checked the long green sash attached at the shoulder with three red stripes denoting her rank. She was pleased it didn't need ironing because she wasn't sure how to iron silk. Hanging the dress on the back of the wardrobe doors, she rummaged at the back of the cupboard for her patent leather court shoes. Dusty, from neglect, she gave them a quick spray of polish shined them with a yellow duster. Everything prepared, she took a shower in the shared ablutions. On her return, she dressed before putting on her makeup. Her mind had wandered to the anonymous note more than once in the shower, and when it snuck into her thinking, she edged it out by concentrating on her first mess dinner—it promised to be a night of many firsts and a grand occasion.

She peered into the mirror to apply mascara. As she looked into her own eyes, she flinched. Who was she? What did she stand for? And how was she going to handle the situation with Terry? She pushed the wand back into its holder and then exchanged it for pink lipstick. As a rule, she didn't wear pink, let alone lipstick, but tonight was important, and she wanted to be and do everything required for such an ostentatious event. Plus, she didn't want to attract attention to herself. Completing her makeup, she closed the bag and popped it into a drawer. Everything was tidy in her room, just as she had learned years ago in basic training. The surfaces were decorated with a few photographs, and Agatha Christie's novels were supported by two horse-head bookends in the middle of the desk. She stepped in front of the full-length mirror to the left of her desk. Checking her appearance from head to toe, she smoothed down the figure-hugging ivory brocade dress, feeling the roughness of tiny slubs of silver beneath her fingers. She was surprised at how much she liked it, and she felt feminine, probably for the first time in her life. A moment of pleasure was interrupted by an unsummoned image of her interrogating Terry. She shook her head before checking her watch. It was time to join the others for the dinner. Altering her gait to accommodate the tight-fitting dress and the high heels, she left her room and descended the stairs for the anteroom.

The bar was full of men in scarlet shell jackets, cut to just above the waist and tailored tight to flatter the wearer's shoulders. A white dress shirt, black tie, and a white waistcoat complemented the tunic. The navy trousers with broad scarlet stripes down the side seams fitted the male buttocks in such a way as to leave little to anyone's imagination and tapered to a highly polished George boot. Loud laughter and banter filled the room. Every man had a pint in his hand and joked with his comrades. Jo entered the room and for a moment, conversation hushed as most of the male members watched her walk to where Nick was standing with Staff Sergeant Armstrong. As she joined them, the hubbub returned to full volume.

'You brush up nice,' Nick said.

'Not so bad yourself,' Jo retorted. 'Mine's a half.'

Armstrong ordered her drink and passed it to her. 'How's it going, Jo?'

'Fine Staff.'

'Nick just told me Carol Hart is leading the investigation. Something to do with an anonymous note.'

Jo nodded. She had hoped the note would not spoil the evening, and there, not a half pint in, it was front and centre in her first conversation, the cause of speculation and nasty gossip. How was she going to handle it all? Jo took a sip of beer, avoiding Armstrong's questions with mumbled single-syllable replies. She was sure perspiration was appearing under her arms, which concerned her because there would be no concealing it in a short-sleeved dress.

'Jo, let's look at the seating plan.' Nick took Jo by the elbow, rescuing her from Armstrong's interrogation. He guided her to a seating plan mounted on a large board, running his finger along the lines of tables with seats assigned by rank and last name. 'Look, Jo, we're at the end of the long table. Top table mind. Thank God we're sitting next to each other. It won't be so bad. My first mess dinner, I was so bored. I got stuck next to some old woman, and all she did was ogle my backside.'

Jo laughed. 'Now you know how we women feel when men do it to us all the time. Mind you, Nick, you've got a nice bum.'

'Shut up, woman,' Nick chuckled and turned his back to her. 'Does my bum look big in this?'

'Stop it, you tart!'

'At last, she laughs.'

Jo cocked her head to one side.

'You hardly spoke on the journey back from Mill Hill. I know what's bothering you.'

'Don't, Nick. I don't want to think about it.'

Carol, escorted by a civilian in a dinner jacket, approached them. 'Evening, you two. Nice to see you. I'd like to introduce you to the Commissioner of Hendon Police College.'

The Commissioner smiled and made small talk before talking just to Nick. 'Tell me, what do you plan to do when you leave the Army? We'd be very interested in seeing you at selection. Drop me a line if you want to attend, and I'll ensure we interview you.'

'Thank you, sir.'

Carol raised her eyebrows at Jo. The old boys' network was alive and kicking right in front of them as if they weren't there.

The dinner gong sounded, and the band struck up the Regimental March, The Watchtower. Carol steered the Commissioner toward the dining room. Nick held out the crook of his arm to Jo. 'Madam, if you'd do me the honour.'

Jo giggled, though self-conscious, she took his arm and was grateful for his escort. They walked past other mess members standing at their seats on the far side of the room. The band blew the last notes of the march. The RSM asked the padre to say grace and the temporary congregation lowered their heads and said amen before taking their seats. Mess staff served the first course from silver platters as the band played arrangements of the top ten hits. Jo spoke to an older man on her left. A combination of his deafness and the fact they had nothing in common eventually led Jo to converse only with Nick. And as Nick had no one to his right, he was happy to oblige. Jo and Nick made sure they left the subject of Terry and the anonymous note out of the conversation.

'You know Jo—you could join the Met too. Maybe we could join together? Be better for both of us. The Army's so old-fashioned, and you never know with our experience we could rise up the ranks much faster than in the Army.'

'Yeah, but he's only interested in you, Nick. By the way, what is this we're eating?'

Nick pulled the menu sheet towards him. 'Breast of Quail in a lime sauce.'

'Ugh, it's a little bird.' Jo didn't even try the starter. Instead, she glanced at Carol, sitting at the centre of the top table with her assigned guest. 'She looks like she's having as much fun as we are.'

Nick looked along the table. 'No, we're having much more fun. Drink up, and I'll get us some more wine.'

'Not sure I like this wine—prefer beer.'

'You'll get used to it. You'll have to get used to it unless…'

'Unless?' Jo rolled her eyes. 'Oh wait, I know the answer to this one! I join the Met with you.'

'There you go. There's the first pro to leaving the Army. Might be better all 'round if you do.'

'Meaning?'

'Nothing.'

'I know what nothing means.'

The mess steward poured more wine for Jo and Nick while another steward served the main course, Steak Tournedos. Jo tucked in, making sure she got every bit of the sauce by mixing it with the creamy mashed potato. As they ate, Jo and Nick gossiped about their colleagues, commenting on who was brown-nosing, who was helpful, and who was difficult to work with. The dessert was crème brûlée with a caramelised topping that proved challenging and led to much laughter and merriment as the mess members experimented with how best to break the brittle topping. Jo and Nick had resorted to chipping at the hardened sugar with the handle end of their spoon before turning it around to scoop out the creamy custard filling. Once the dessert plates had been cleared away the mess stewards placed Port and Madeira decanters at various points along the middle of the table.

'Make sure you pass it to your left, Jo. You don't want a fine for sending it the wrong way. And don't take a sip until the Loyal Toast.'

Jo reached for the decanter and made sure to avoid a fine. When each diner had poured themselves a drink, the RSM stood with his glass raised.

Everyone responded, standing poised with their glass.

'Ladies and Gentlemen, The Queen.'

Glasses were raised, and the reply was made.

'The Queen.'

After the first sip of port, they sat. Mess stewards brought cigars and cigarettes for those who wanted to partake in the traditional after-dinner custom. A haze of tobacco smoke clouded the air as stout men in ill-fitting scarlet sat back and puffed on their cigars as if they were born to such luxuries. After a few words of introduction from the RSM, the Police Commissioner spoke.

Jo felt her mind wandering to the note and its consequences. First, she considered who might have sent it—had Pete meddled? The question was how seriously the authorities would take the message. Indeed, Terry had been scrupulous in how she behaved when they were together. They never took any risks. The threats in her head mounted as she considered her vulnerability. As she tried to dismiss those questions from her mind, the precarious nature of her career stormed into her consciousness. The real problem would be if she had to interview Terry. Could she do her job properly? Would Sarn't Major Hart see through her and be forced to take action? What if Terry was discharged? She was certain Terry would not give her away. Someone had exposed Terry? Could they do the same to her? She sipped her port, and soon, her glass was empty, for she had taken a sip with every frantic thought.

'Steady Jo, this is heady stuff.' Nick placed his hand on Jo's forearm.

'I like it. It's sweet. Is there any more?'

'You have to wait for it to come round. My advice is not to have another if you don't want a hangover tomorrow. Stick to the beer in the bar after. Trust me, I know.'

Nick passed the port to Jo. She poured another glass. He raised his eyebrows in disapproval. The Commissioner summed up his talk to applause. The band struck up Greensleeves, which prompted the diners to vacate the dining room for the anteroom. By the time Jo and Nick got to the bar, Staff was organising a game of mess rugby. He pulled Nick into one of the teams. Jackets were removed, and play commenced with a cushion instead of a ball. Jo watched, realising the game had few or no rules. Nick caught the cushion and began to run. Three men from the opposing team launched themselves at him. A few more men piled on top. Finally, the cushion popped out of the melee and was touched down in between the two easy chairs, which acted as goalposts. The game continued with some men leaving for refreshment or to avoid injury. Nick took his chance to rejoin Jo. After tucking in his shirt and fixing his black tie, he retrieved his jacket from the arm of a nearby sofa.

'Glad that's over. I hate that game. I think Staff Armstrong grabbed my goolies. Clearly, he's not fond of me.'

'Blimey! Are there any rules?'

Nick grinned. 'No. I think it's about settling old scores by kicking the shit out of someone you hate. And, of course, to score a goal. Come on, let's go to the bar before Staff ropes me in for High Cockalorum. That will definitely give me a bad back. Is my tie straight?'

Jo nodded, and Nick took her arm and led her into the bar. A few senior ranks clocked the pair arm in arm.

'Didn't know you had it in you, Nick,' one catcaller offered.

Another suggested. 'She's a class act, Nick. Too good for you, mate.'

'They think we're an item,' Jo whispered.

'I know. I want them to.'

'Why?' Jo's eyes were wide, her pupils dilated, and her comprehension impaired.

'Because...,' Nick paused. 'Someone needs to look after you, and I think it should be me.'

## Chapter 31

Unsure how to respond to Nick's suggestion, Jo fled the bar, leaving Nick behind, through the anteroom double doors to the stairway that led to the bedrooms. In her hurry, she tripped on her dress and lost a shoe. Cursing, she removed the remaining shoe and picked up the other. Hoisting her dress, she staggered up the stairs, recognising that she was feeling the effects of mixing her drinks and the quantity she had drunk. She gathered herself and her clothing at the top of the steps before hurrying to her room at the end of the corridor, occasionally using the wall to springboard her progress. Finally, she stumbled through her bedroom door, diving for the bed as she flung her shoes towards the desk. Burying her face into the pillow, she sobbed. Stress and sorrow ripped her apart at the seams, displaying the stuff she wasn't made of. She needed to break this dam of terror. Yet, it was important that her discombobulation was unwitnessed because showing one's emotions in public, even to one's closest friends, is a weakness in the military.

A polite knock at the door helped her recover herself.

'Go away.' She returned to the pillow. 'Not now, Nick.'

Nick opened the door a crack, slipping his slim frame through the narrow opening he had created before closing the door without a sound. 'Budge up.'

Jo, though reluctant, obliged. Nick sat on the bed so he could look at her face. He pulled a handkerchief from his pocket and gave it to her. 'Careful, your mascara will run. I hope it's waterproof.' He grinned.

Jo nodded, taking the handkerchief before wiping her eyes and blowing her nose. She was about to return it to him.

'I can wait 'till you wash it.' He pushed her hand away.

Jo chuckled.

'That's better. I know you don't want to do this, but you need to. Clean up your face.' He got up and crossed the room, retrieving her court shoes. 'Put your shoes on and come back down. Leaving before our guests and the RSM will get you extra duties and a fine. So, hurry up before they notice you're gone. And, believe me, they will notice very soon because you look stunning in that dress.'

Jo complied, and when she was ready, he linked his arm with hers to return to the anteroom. Carol walked up to Jo with two glasses of brandy. She offered one to Jo. Nick took the hint and found some friends at the bar.

'Come with me,' Carol ordered, leading Jo to a quiet corner of the anteroom. 'Sit. Now, what's all this about? Drink your brandy.' Carol sipped hers and waited patiently for Jo to marshal herself and her story.

'I'm worried about Terry.' Jo felt the warmth of the alcohol relax her.

'Mhmm. I can understand that. You're good mates.'

Jo nodded.

'Good mates, watch out for each other. Only natural. What I don't understand is why you had to leave in such a tearing hurry.'

'Nick said,' Jo stammered, 'Well, he said...'

'Go on.'

'He said I needed looking after.' She paused. 'And that he was the one to do it. It's all a bit too much.' Unsure, Jo gave Carol a wan smile and swirled the digestif inside the glass.

'And what's so bad about that? I asked him to keep an eye on you. We both know Terry's a good friend, and we guessed you would be upset about the developments in the case. So, as his superior, I asked him to look out for you. And I'm glad he's taken my advice.' Carol sat back in her chair, nursing her brandy.

'Oh,' Jo was unsure if she was pleased or disappointed. 'I thought… Actually, I don't know what I thought.'

'Oh, you thought he was asking you to marry him?' Carol guffawed. 'I've heard of some, shall we say, interesting proposals in my time, drunken ones, hasty ones, and to give a child a father but you and Nick! Give over!' Carol laughed. 'Though it's not as bad as it used to be now that the Army has finally moved with the times. At least now, if you marry, you can stay in 'till you have sprogs. Otherwise, if he were proposing, and you accepted, I'd be a man down, which would never do. Still, don't see you two marrying. Now I will give you the same advice as I did Nick. Look out for him, Jo. You need each other and make a good pair, and I need you both on my team.' Having dispensed wisdom and love, Carol left Jo alone. As Carol walked away, she called over her shoulder. 'And don't drink anything else this evening, and make sure you don't leave before the RSM.'

Jo sipped her drink—the brandy soothed her nerves. Before her attention had time to wander, Nick was at her side.

'Mind if I join you?' Nick sat down. 'Shouldn't be long now, then we can get to bed. The Commissioner has left. I give the RSM fifteen minutes, and he'll be going home. Thank God. It's after midnight, and they both should've done the decent thing and left at ten. The Commissioner always outstays his welcome.'

Jo listened to Nick's musings.

'Sorry, Nick, I know you were only trying to look out for me. I just freaked.'

'Mmm.'

'You know, I think if we could get Quade, this would all go away.'

'Obviously, you are very drunk because you don't remember that we could not get Quade to confess, no matter how hard we tried. And now there is an anonymous note containing a clear accusation, which we are obliged to investigate.'

'What if we could prove it was Quade?'

'It's not her, Jo. I don't know why I think that, but it isn't.'

'Could be. We just need to find the evidence.'

'What evidence? There is no evidence. Mark my words. Even though forensics will give it a good going over, there will be none.' He paused as he discerned Jo's intention. 'Listen, I'm going to put your crazy idea down to the fact that you are drunk. And I suggest you don't mention this terrible idea to anyone.' He leaned back to get a better look at her. 'I'm surprised at you. I never thought you'd stoop that low. Whatever you do, you need to get control of your emotions and deal only with the facts and not what might be. Otherwise, you're going to go mental. And God knows what else.' He got up. 'Come on, let's see if the RSM has left yet. I need to go to bed.'

Jo steadied herself on his arm. They joined the other tired and drunk mess members waiting to go home. The drunks hovered near the front door, dreading the reactions of their long-suffering wives who had been waiting for over an hour or more. Those who lived in the mess wanted to go to bed to sleep off their excesses. It had been a long night for everyone. Jo and Nick settled on a sofa near the anteroom doors.

The RSM left, and within a few indecent moments, the first brave men left. Some helped their friend stay upright as they escorted them to a polite wife, who was perhaps not so polite at home. In the morning, the senior rank would have a sore head from alcohol and his wife's scolding.

'At last! I'm going to bed,' Jo got up.

Nick offered his arm. 'Allow me.'

Nick helped her up the stairs and to her room. Closing the door behind them, he unzipped her dress. 'Need anything else?'

'No, thanks.' Jo turned to face him. 'And thank you.'

'Good night, Jo. It will seem better in the morning. I promise.' He slipped out of her room, ensuring no one saw his exit.

Jo got ready for bed. Her last action was to set her alarm clock to wake her at seven. She slipped beneath the duvet and was asleep in seconds.

In the early hours, she woke with a raging thirst, which she quenched from a tooth mug, glugging water as if she had had no liquid in days. Satisfied she had sufficient hydration, she returned to bed, adopting the fetal position, expecting sleep to bless her. Instead, remorse delivered a lightning strike to her nervous system, quickening her heart and plaguing her with images of the women she had interrogated and degraded. Her imagination raced to what was surely inevitable—the interview with Terry. It led to a dishonourable discharge for both of them. Her heart still racing, she envisioned the humiliation she would feel having to explain to her parents why she and Terry had returned home without a job or pension, no references, and no other employment prospects. Would her parents throw her out? Could she create another plausible explanation? She considered the lies she would need to tell to cover her tracks, the shame of lying to her parents about why she had left a promising career. She knew none of them would be credible. Where would she and Terry go? What would they do? Maybe she should join the Police Force as soon as possible to avoid the disgrace. Her final thought before falling asleep was a decision to join the Met.

## Chapter 32

*Day Seven Inglis Barracks.*

Lance Corporal Maxine Dart, Max to her friends, sat on the edge of her bed, one of four in the four-man room she had been allocated. She looked around her. The room was similar to where she had spent most of her life at the children's home in Hornchurch. The foot of every bed pointed into the middle of the room. And just like in the 'home', the walls were painted in establishment magnolia. There was one difference. In this room, each woman had a wardrobe and a large chest of drawers with a mirror on top, which she positioned to give herself maximum privacy. In contrast, the home she had been sent to because her teenage mother couldn't care for her, and here, was that she felt safe here, in this room at 12 Company, at least she did until now. Back then, when she was just nine, a so-called House Father would come during the night, reeking of booze, rousing her from feigned sleep, to take her to the 'sleep-over room'. Sometimes, his wife, the House Mother, would wake her and present her to 'Sir'.

She shook her head, erasing the unpleasant memories she rarely visited these days, returning to the present and bulling her drill shoes—the process was soothing and allowed her mind to drift. Max considered whether the Special Investigations Bureau had been able to discern any of the content of the letters she had attempted to burn. If they hadn't, she would stay Schtum, just as Sergeant White had advised. Max felt her stomach stir. If this went wrong—she tried not to think about the consequences. 'Focus on the now.' Another of White's sayings. Max added more Kiwi Black Parade gloss polish to her yellow duster, dabbing it into the tin lid containing water. Finally, she worked it into the leather of each shoe. The small circles, at first dull, polished the wax into a patent leather shine. She held up the shoe and saw her reflection in the toe cap before checking the heels and sides to ensure the shine was even all over. Satisfied, she placed them under her bed before visiting the ablutions to wash her hands.

'Hiya. Getting ready for your interview?' Private Dawson asked.

'Yeah, how do you know?'

'We know everything in the Orderly Room. Want some goss?' Dawson didn't wait for a reply. 'They're going to arrest Sarn't White.'

'What!' Max recoiled as if her face had been struck.

'Yeah.' Dawson relished the moment without realising its full effect on the recipient.

'They can't. She's done nothing wrong.'

'Someone dobbed her in.'

'You needn't look so smug.'

'Well, I'd be careful in there,' Dawson jerked her head toward the headquarters building. 'The OC wants them to step up the search. She's miffed there aren't more discharges.'

'How many have there been?'

'One.'

'I heard that.' Max turned off the tap.

'They can't be that shit hot then, can they?'

'Dunno. I'm not taking any chances. I'm playing it straight.'

Dawson looked at Max and guffawed. Max opened her mouth, surprised by the laughter. A beat, and then she joined Dawson in laughing at the unintended pun.

'Better go,' said Max, sobering up from the brief moment of humour.

'Good luck, Max.'

Max marched up the incline from the Junior Ranks' Accommodation to the HQ Building, pushing open the front door without breaking her pace and onward to the interrogation room. At the closed door, she took a breath and relaxed her body as if preparing for a sprint race, then straightened up as if she were on parade before knocking on the door. There was no reply. She tapped again, and with no order to enter, she opened the door sufficient to peer in. The room was empty. She checked her watch—that's right, ten o'clock was when she had been told to report for her interview. Flummoxed, she hesitated, deciding whether to leave and count herself lucky, at least for the moment, or to wait. She decided to give her interrogators the benefit of ten minutes. Standing at ease, her feet slightly apart and her hands behind her back, her thoughts idle, she inspected the shine on her shoes, wiggling her toes, feeling them slide about in the nylon tights—she hated tights, she could never go a day without getting a ladder or a hole in them, no matter how much care she took to remove them. Her reverie was interrupted by the arrival of the two detectives. She stood to attention.

'Stand easy, Corporal Dart. We'll be with you in a few,' Jo said.

Max smiled and relaxed. Surely, Sarn't White had told Sarn't Clark how she had taken the message in the gym and destroyed the photo of them together in Brighton. Max hoped her actions had bought her a few brownie points and maybe an easy interview.

Five minutes later, on command, she marched into the room and came smartly to attention in front of her interrogators.

'Take a seat, Corporal Dart. You may remove your hat.' Nick leaned over the table. Max sat upright, her arms straight and tense, with her knuckles on her knees.

'Relax, Maxine.'

'Max, my name's Max.'

Nick smiled before he went through the standard introductions, identifying himself and Jo.

Max interrupted him. 'I know who you are. We all know who you are. What do you want to know? Why am I here? Is it because of that bloody Staff Sergeant assaulting me?'

Jo and Nick exchanged quizzical glances.

'Ah, you don't know, do ya?'

'Know what?'

'Well, if you don't know. I'm not gonna tell ya.' Max leaned back in her chair, folded her arms, and adopted a smug grin.

Nick shot a glance at Jo. Jo nodded, indicating he should ignore Max's attempt to derail the interview.

'Corporal Dart, what can you tell us about these letters?' Nick pushed some A4 sheets of paper with fragments of scorched pink paper glued to them across the desk.

Max shrugged.

'You see here, Max,' he pointed. 'This here is a capital 'M' and a lowercase 'a'. And we think as you are the only person in that area of the barrack block to have a name beginning with an 'M' and an 'a', these belong to you.'

Max looked at the scraps of paper and screwed up her face.

'What do you think, Max?'

Max didn't answer.

'We found a photograph, too. Though this one has been torn in half, we can easily identify the people. And one of them is you, Max. Who is the other girl?'

Max looked at the photograph, pleased that her companion's face was desecrated, even if she hadn't totally destroyed the picture.

'Who is it, Max?' Nick waited for a reply. 'We can find out, you know, even if you don't tell us.'

Max fixed her eyes on the portrait of Queen Elizabeth on the wall behind her interrogators.

'Looking for inspiration, Max? You won't get it from the Queen because she dislikes lesbians. After all, she's head of the Armed Forces, and we all know the rules.'

Max shifted her gaze to the window. She let her mind wander to the last game of hockey she had played. White had told her she was great, and she had basked in the simple compliment uttered with encouragement and received as a lover's billet-doux.

Nick sat back in his chair and looked at Jo, jerking his head in Max's direction for Jo to take over. Jo stirred in her seat, leaning toward Max. 'Look, this isn't great for us either, you know. But you need to confess your relationship. This one and the others. We know you've had a lot of girlfriends.'

Max corrected her interrogators in her head. Just the one. But you know nothing. Keep Schtum.

'Okay.' Nick got up. 'Me and Sarn't Clark will leave you to think about your options. And about the relationship you have with Sarn't White. Because we know all about that.'

Max stiffened. Of course, you do. I saved your arse, Sarn't Clark, and you know it.

Jo and Nick walked casually out of the room.

Left alone, Max fiddled with the seams of her skirt, then pulled her woolly pulley down over her skirt. Her mind was tense, filled with a similar experience of waiting for something dreadful to happen. She reminded herself that what she was going through now was nothing. No one could touch her now. No one could order her to kneel on the hassock, on permanent loan from the chapel, and swallow. She inhaled and pulled her shoulders back. She could handle them, whatever they might throw at her. A confident smile edged out her fear.

Jo and Nick huddled in an empty office after getting a coffee from Dawson's cubby hole.

'Hangover?' Nick shut the door.

They sat down in the two easy chairs.

'No, well yes, but took two paracetamol, so no.'

'What was that in there? You were worse than a limp willy.'

'You'd know all about that,' Jo warned.

Nick blanched and blustered. 'Well, fuck Jo, I'm not the one raining on the parade out there. You're about as useful as a chocolate teapot! Where's the Jo, I know, that is as sharp as a tack, getting under the skin of Lord Quade's daughter?' He paused and saw panic enlarge Jo's pupils. He placed a hand on one of her shoulders. 'Relax, Jo, she's just another one. You can get her easily.'

'Maybe I don't want to,' Jo mumbled, half hoping Nick wouldn't be able to hear.

'Why?'

'She rescued me and Terry from a mess.'

'I see. So you feel you owe her?'

'Well, no, but yes. Well, no. Well, yes.'

Nick laughed. 'Jo, you handle the interrogation. Take it where you want and how you want. But make it look good—we don't need word to get out that we're a soft touch. I won't tell a soul.' He zipped his mouth and threw away an imaginary key.

Jo slapped his upper arm.

'Sometimes Nick, you are…'

'So gay?' he chuckled.

Jo relaxed and smiled. 'Yeah, and sensitive.'

'Told you!'

Jo kicked off the second half of the interrogation.

'So, Max, now you've had a chance to think about things, can you tell us who is with you in this photograph?' She held up the torn picture, not expecting or wanting an answer. 'No? Well, who is writing to you so passionately?'

Max sat, looking without seeing. How could they tell it was passionate? They're just scraps of burnt paper. They're bluffing—schtum!

Jo changed her line of questioning. If Max was as hard as Terry said she was, she bet Max could take it, and the questioning needed to be convincing—just enough.

'What about Sergeant White? You go everywhere together. Seems to me you're having a relationship.'

'No, Sarn't, you're wrong.'

Jo thought Max looked guilty, but then the possibility that Max really did have a crush on Terry occurred to her 'You like Sergeant White?' she chuckled.

'Yeah, but not like that.'

'No?' Jo teased.

'You see, Sarn't White has come up in our investigations. And your name has come up a couple of times, too. Funny that you should hang around a lot together, and both your names have come up together.'

Jo pretended to try again. She chuckled because she could now officially confirm to Terry that she had a young admirer. 'Come on, Max. You and Sarn't White have been seen together in the store cupboard. I mean, no one goes in there unless it's for equipment, and you didn't come out with any equipment. Did you?'

Max was seething with anger she couldn't conceal.

'So, you aren't lovers?'

'No!' They're laughing at me!

Nick leaned forward and interrupted Jo's line of questioning. 'Not lovers, but you'd like to be? Right?'

Jo and Nick observed the colour rise from Max's collarbone to her hairline.

'So let me suggest a scenario to you, Max,' said Nick. 'You like Sarn't White. You suggest that the two of you could be more than friends. Subtle like. She laughs at you. Once again, you're not taken seriously, just like when you were in the children's home and accused one of the carers of sexual assault.'

'How do you know about that?' Max blurted.

'Because we know everything about you. It's all part of running a witch-hunt. We do our homework. But you—you know we're looking for names that we're looking to discharge lesbians. Somehow, in your cockeyed brain, you think we could do some of your dirty work—get rid of people who've slighted you.'

'No!'

'Let me finish! Jealous, you write an anonymous note telling us Sarn't White is gay.' Nick sat back, clasping his hands behind his head, smiling at the suspect.

'No! I told you! I wouldn't! She's been good to me. I'd never…'

'Never what? Write a note? Ask her out?'

Schtum.

Jo regarded Nick, waiting for him to continue the conversation. She broke the long silence.

'Anything you want to tell us, Max? Know who might write an anonymous note?'

'No. I don't. I don't think there is anyone who doesn't respect or admire Sarn't White.'

'And you would come to Sarn't White's defence if they didn't,' Jo said. The smile in her eyes was meant to convey to Max that everything was okay—she was in safe hands and needed no longer worry.

Max sensed something had changed. The interview was less hostile and less invasive. Nick picked up the questioning, repeating the same questions without the same emphasis, the same innuendoes, describing sexual acts and augmenting them with filthy words, suggesting she was unworthy to serve her Queen and her Country but with less vigour. Whatever they asked, whatever they thought about her, they were wrong. She would always be loyal. She was always prepared to do her bit for her Queen and Country. She glanced at Queen Elizabeth II on the wall and sat to attention. Schtum, keep schtum.

'Right, Max, you obviously need time to think.' Nick got up and pushed his chair under the desk. 'Make it easy on yourself and confess. Because tomorrow it will be harder. And it will get harder every time we talk with you. The more we have you in here, the worse it gets. And we will keep you here until you tell us what we want to know. And we won't be nice and tell you when we want to see you. We'll just haul you in so everyone can see who and what you are. Or,' He paused for effect, resting his hands on the chair back. 'You can get it over with and tell us everything now. Then you can relax and get on with your life.'

Max knew there would be no relaxation in Civvy Street for her. She had spent sixteen years in a children's home, sexually assaulted by those who were supposed to care for her. She had no family—the Army was her family. She had nowhere to go because this was her only home, and if she confessed, there would be no job. She had to be loyal to White. She owed her everything—her chance to be a PTI, a chance to be something, to be seen as something more than a waster from a children's home.

'All right. You can go,' Nick said, his speech lazy and bored. 'Just remember, we'll come for you any time we like.'

Max stood, put on her beret, and stared at Jo.

'Off you go, Max, and if I were you, I'd stay out of the PT store cupboard. Know what I mean,' Jo added a wink for confirmation.

Max all but skipped out of the HQ building.

## Chapter 33

*Day Seven—afternoon*

Jo skipped lunch and returned to the Rochester Row Barrack's Main Office. She was the only one present because most of the staff had already left for the weekend. Jo settled at her desk to draft the report for Lance Corporal Dart. She wanted everything to be up to date before leaving. Her mind switched between Terry and the report. Mainly, she focussed on Terry. Would Terry be interviewed? What if Armstrong was her interrogator? Shit!

The questions all started at the same point and ended with the same grand finale of disaster, and it was crucifying her every hour she was awake and sometimes when she was asleep. She looked up to see Sergeant Major Hart slip into her office.

Jo considered discussing the anonymous note with her superior before deciding that she might give herself away. The door opened and Susan walked into the main office.

'Hello, Jo. Haven't seen you in a while. Still on the witch-hunt at Mill Hill?'

'Yeah. Off for the weekend?'

'Yes. Major Relish isn't around. Would you let him know I've left early?'

'Seems to be only me and Miss Hart in. If I see him, which I doubt. I'll tell him. Doing anything nice?'

'No. Mum and Dad can't get out much, so I take them around gardens. You?'

'Mum 'n' Dad's. Probably digging a pond.' Jo rolled her eyes.

'Have fun. See ya.' Susan trotted out of the building.

Curious, Jo tried Susan's office door. Her heart raced when she found it unlocked. She shut it again before checking whether Hart was still ensconced in her office. Confident she could enter Susan's office unobserved, she entered the room, closing the door behind her without a sound. She made straight for the Index Card system on the table, checking over her shoulder that her actions would not be witnessed. Jo ran over Susan's instructions in her head. Check the Index System first. If the name is in the index that says they are known to us, if they have a dot on the card, it means there's a corresponding Personnel File.

She scanned the small wooden drawers with paper name plates secured by metal frames, running her fingers over them until she arrived at 'C'. Opening the small drawer, she rummaged through the cards until she got to the start of 'Cl'. Carefully, she pulled each card forward, read the name and then moved on to the next one. Until she reached the section 'Co'. There was no sign of her name. Could it be that she had a card, but it had been filed incorrectly? She decided to be more diligent, starting again at the first card, checking each one and looking for her name. Working her way through at least fifty cards was taking time. Every so often, she would check the door and listen for a sound. At the final index card, she exhaled, not realising that she had held her breath as she had searched. Relieved that it was as she thought Susan was meticulous in all things. Encouraged, she located the drawer with the label 'WA-X'. She hesitated as she heard Hart move around in the main office. Jo moved out of sight. The window in the door was frosted, but she knew her shadow would be seen if anyone was curious. She was unsure what she should do if she found Terry's name filed with other suspects, but the need to know overcame her concern over what to do next or that she might be caught checking for files that she should hand off to Susan. If she was caught, suspicions might arise as to who she was and why she was violating the rules.

With some haste, she worked her way through the cards, pulling one card forward, then another until she reached names beginning with 'Wh'. She examined each five-by-nine-inch card before pulling it forward and reading the next one until she reached the end. At the last card, she leaned against the filing cabinet before turning and shutting the drawer. She scanned the room. All was as it should be—she had left no tell-tale signs. Inhaling a calming breath, she relaxed her shoulders and opened Susan's office door just enough to check on Hart. Satisfied Hart was occupied, she went back to complete one last task. She stood in front of the wooden block of secrets and opened the drawer labelled 'A-DR'. She hesitated when she heard Hart walk around in the Main Office. Perspiring, she hastily put together an explanation for her being in the catalogue room. Hart opened the door and peered around the frame.

'Ah, there you are, Jo! Doing some homework?'

'Yeah,' Jo tried to slow her speech, 'We had a hard time getting Dart to speak the other day. Nick told me the OC thinks Corporal Dart may have something to do with Terry, so I thought I'd do some research. Had to do it myself as Susan's left for the weekend.'

'Good thinking. When you've got a minute, pop into my office, will you?' Hart turned to walk off.

Jo released the air from her lungs, steadying herself on the wooden cabinet. In the next second, she knew she was not alone, realising that Hart was still in the room and now stood behind her.

'Did you check for your card?' Hart smiled empathically at Jo. 'I know I would. One never knows how or when one's name might come up. Anyway, finish up here, and I'll see you when you're ready. However, I do want to be on the road by three.' She walked out of Susan's office and shouted over her shoulder. 'I've got a home to go to!'

Jo pushed the drawer in without examining its contents and left the catalogue room for the Sergeant Major's office. 'Ma'am?'

'Come in and shut the door. I think everyone has left for the weekend, but just in case. Take a seat. Okay, I've had forensics check that note. The letters are all from one Newspaper—The Times.'

'Blimey, that's posh. Or—it could be someone who has something against Sarn't White, posing as an officer.'

'You have a point, but let's stick to the obvious for the moment. That narrows it down, I would think to an Officer or a Senior Rank. So, we have a choice of four officers and twenty Senior Ranks. I'll check with the RSM and the Chief Steward in the Officers' Mess what they do with their newspapers just in case an Other Rank decided to be clever.'

'Anything on the type of paper?'

'Not really. MOD issue stationery.'

'Mm-hmm. What're we going to do? I mean, do we have to interview Terry?'

'At the moment, I'm holding off on that. I've got RSM Gordon checking her contacts. Hopefully, we can resolve this letter mess without interviewing Terry. Like you, I've already checked for a card. She's not there, is she?'

'I didn't see one for her.'

'Right. Course not. Anything else, Jo? You know this is all highly unusual. We'll get to the bottom of it, but it could take time. I think we will be bothering the OC Twelve Company for a while. This malicious note needs sorting. So, you'll be back on interviews again next week. And I'll be briefing the delightful Major Marwood. There's something to look forward to,' Hart sighed.

'I just need to finish Corporal Dart's report, and then, if it's alright with you, ma'am, can I get off early?'

'Have a nice weekend. See you Monday. Shut the door, will you?'

Hart checked her office door was closed and waited for Jo to close the outer door to the main office before opening her desk drawer. She slid the card title W/Sgt T White 4062130 PTI to one side before opening the blue P File. Inside was a copy of every leave card White had signed for the last two years. She read the attached note.

Address given by W/Sgt Teresa White 4062130 matches address provided by W/Sgt Josephine Clark, 4062263 RMP.

The note was unsigned and, therefore, unattributed. Hart picked up the card and file, popped them in her briefcase, and headed for the car park.

## Chapter 34

*Day Seven. The Clark Family Home.*

Jo made it to Harold Hill within three hours, which was not bad in the bank holiday traffic. She collected her bag from the car's boot and wandered up the pathway.

Terry opened the kitchen door for her. 'Bet you didn't expect to see me quite so soon, did ya?'

Jo put down her bag and hugged Terry while Sylvia poured Jo a cup of tea. 'What's with all this hugging all of a sudden, you two? We're British. We don't do that sort of thing. It's not right.'

'Mum! People hug all the time,' Jo said.

'Very Continental, I must say,' Sylvia tutted and returned to the kitchen sink.

'How did you get here so soon?' Jo asked.

'She came home last night,' Sylvia said. 'Another weird thing. No warning, no nothing.'

'Didn't you want to see me then, Mum?' Terry joked.

'Course love, just surprised, that's all.'

Jo drank her tea, listening to her mother chatter about Linda and baby Karl. Terry signalled they should go upstairs.

Jo threw her bag on the bed. 'I need a proper hug.'

Terry stepped into Jo's arms. They kissed tenderly, tasting each other while breathing in their lovers' unique scent. After a few moments, Terry stepped out of Jo's arms. 'We need to talk, Jo. I'm home early. I got sent home by the RSM. Do you know what's going on? The RSM made me take an extra day. Said something to do with leave not used up. Which is weird because I'm pretty sure you and I have used all our leave.' Terry scratched her head.

'She didn't say anything else?'

Terry shook her head.

'Listen. Try not to panic now. There's been a development.'

'What kind of development? Is that why I'm on leave?' Terry's tone was rising.

'We got an anonymous tip-off yesterday.' Jo let the red flag settle before restarting. 'Naming you.'

'Why didn't you tell me?'

'I couldn't without arousing suspicion.'

'Fuck Jo.' Terry sat on the bed. 'Oh my God, what am I going to do?'

Jo sat next to Terry. 'I can see how this looks. But I checked the catalogue for your name, and there's nothing on you. Or me, for that matter.'

'What catalogue? Where?' Terry got up and paced the room.

'It's in the RMP offices. They log everything connected with lesbians. Every name, activity, etcetera, and they keep letters and photos.'

Terry turned to face Jo, clapping her hand over her mouth. 'Shit, they collect any scrap of evidence, or they think is evidence. God knows what's in there and who has said what to whom. That's terrible.'

'Sadly, it's called police work.'

'I'll be interrogated, won't I?' Terry's panic increased the pitch in her voice.

'Probably.'

Terry's shoulders slumped. Jo put a protective arm around her lover.

'It might be as early as Tuesday morning.'

'What am I going to do, Jo?' Terry's brown eyes grew wide and dark with fear.

'I dunno. But I'll have your back no matter what.'

Terry gave a weak nod.

Sylvia called up the stairs. 'You two ready for dinner?'

Jo and Terry went into the kitchen.

'Not in here, girls. Dining room.'

'Why?'

'Linda and baby Karl are coming over for dinner with us, and I'm fed up with the tight squeeze around the kitchen table, and it's time we used the dining room table for a change.'

'Gosh, Mum, you're getting all posh, what with buying proper baked bread from the bakery and now this. Linda staying over, is she? Pete on shift again?' Jo asked.

'No, they're not staying. Of course, he's on shift at some football match or other. Posh indeed!' Sylvia gave a self-conscious laugh. 'It was easier to feed you all in the kitchen when you were younger. Then it was just your dad and me, so didn't seem worth it. Now we're all back together, so.' She shrugged. 'It just makes sense. Now, before you go, you can take a couple of plates. Terry, this is yours, and this is Linda's. Jo, you take your dad's and yours.'

Jo and Terry bustled out of the kitchen, placing the plates in front of the designated recipient.

'Hello, Dad,' Jo pecked him on the cheek as she put his dinner in front of him.

'All right, Jo. Want to come to the pub later with us and meet the lads? They want to see you.'

'Yes,' Jo and Terry sang in unison.

Sylvia came to the table without her pinny carrying her own plate. The usual Clark family conversation filled the dining room before Linda took baby Karl home. Jo and Terry escorted their father to the pub, leaving Sylvia to enjoy a Babycham and put her feet up in front of the telly.

When the sun rose, Terry woke. She had hardly slept because a twin bed for two is not conducive to a comfortable night, but add two restless sleepers, and it becomes a nightmare. She waited patiently for Jo to open her eyes. Jo placed the crook of her arm over her face so her elbow hid her eyes from the dawning light.

'Tea?' Terry asked.

'Yeah, what time is it? I haven't slept all night.'

Six-thirty. No one else is up. I'll just make us a pot and bring it up.'

Five minutes later, Terry returned with two mugs of tea. 'I've been thinking. If they make you interview me, you could go easy on me. We could work it out that way.'

There's always someone with me. We work in twos.'

'So, who will be with you?'

'Probably Miss Hart and maybe Nick.'

'Oh.'

They sipped their tea in unison.

'I've been thinking,' Jo said. 'Maybe it's time to get out of the Army.'

'No, Jo! No way. You're not leaving because of me.'

'It makes sense. If they interview you, they will interview me. If we don't lose our jobs, then we will be in that bloody catalogue—for the whole of our careers. And that means it's just a matter of time before we get found out.'

'Not if we're careful.'

'No, I've had it with creeping about, as if I'm ashamed of who or what I am. I'm not doing it anymore. It's time to live my life. It's time to leave.'

'Jo, are you running away?'

'No. Why do you say that?'

'Because that's what you do. You run away when there's conflict.'

Jo thought back to the one-sided conversation she had with her grandmother about having the gumption to do the right thing.

'Terry, let's go to the Gateways Club in London. Let's go tonight!'

'Are you mental?'

'No. If I'm going to go down, then I want to go down fighting.'

'What if there's RMP there?'

'I'd know about it if there was a job on. And, if we meet others down the club, they are in the same position. So, they won't tell.'

'I dunno, Jo. That's too risky. Have you really thought this through?'

'Course.'

'Only when you are up against it and can't run, you tend to take very wild risks.'

'We'll be fine.' Jo slapped Terry's leg. 'Don't worry. What we really have to worry about is your interview. Maybe we should talk about that?'

'Maybe.' Terry paused. 'I thought I should just stay silent. Or maybe get Captain Trueman to be my rep? Like Quade did.'

Jo thought through the options. 'Don't drag Captain Trueman into this mess. We both know we're guilty. It's not fair to her.'

'Guilty!' Terry's anger brewed. 'I'm telling you, there is no such offence as being a lesbian. Legally, there is no law about women loving women.'

'Having sex! And shush. We don't want Mum 'n' Dad to hear.'

'Having sex then!' Terry repeated in a stage whisper before returning to her normal volume. 'The Army made it up. I assume because they needed to show it's a safe place for people's daughters to work. That's why we have bed checks until we're eighteen. The Army is our parent and guardian. They won't even let us live out of barracks without the Commanding officer's approval. It's archaic! Even Mum and Dad didn't check we were in bed by midnight.'

'That's because we were. We never went anywhere at night because

Dad said it was too dangerous.'

'Well, he isn't wrong. But my point is the whole thing against lesbians is a farce. Men are the ones the parents should worry about.'

'I know, I know you're right.'

'Yeah, I am.' Terry stood legs astride. 'But your lot never seem to investigate the creeps who slyly touch us up or suggest what they'd like to do to us or even assault us. If I'd had a quid for every perve who opens my office door without knocking while I'm changing, I'd be a rich woman.'

Jo sat with her eyes focused on the bedroom carpet. Her mind concentrated on going out, defying or daring God or the Gods or whoever sorted out one's fate. 'So, are you up for it?'

'Do you even know where it is?'

'I'll get a Time Out. The address will be in the gay section. So, we're on? Tonight? Best togs?'

Terry smiled. 'Seeing as there is no law against it.'

'Wanna say that in your interview?' Jo said, buoyed by her plan.

## Chapter 35

*Bank Holiday Saturday*

After dinner, Jo and Terry drove to Bramerton Street, a posh residential area of West London. Jo parked the car in the first available space before walking to the entrance. They hovered at the closed, solid green door, unsure whether to go in. They had heard things about this club, and most of it was intimidating. Not only that, but they had both watched the film The Killing of Sister George. The film and, in particular, the segment in the Gateways Club left them both fascinated and terrified.

Standing outside the green door Terry asked, 'Why're we here again? Oh, I know to go to The Gateways Club and prove something or other.' She raised her voice. 'What're you waiting for? Christmas!'

Jo walked away from the entrance, crossed the road, and returned to the car.

Terry followed her. 'Jo, you don't have to prove anything to me. I know you want to take matters into your own hands, but even I think this is a bit crazy. We're asking for it. I mean, what if the RMP has got surveillance here?'

The two women walked up the street and loitered outside a large townhouse.

'Let's go home.' Terry waited for Jo to unlock the car.

'No, wait, look.' Jo watched two women, one with short dark hair, dressed in black trousers and a navy blazer, the other, shorter, wearing a royal blue skirt and yellow skin-tight jumper with black knee-high boots. The woman in the blazer knocked on the door. It was opened, and the two women went in. The door was shut as soon as the couple was inside. Jo was now in two minds as to what she should do. She didn't want to appear weak. But what if someone from The Army was in there? What if she was propositioned? What if Terry was right there was surveillance that she didn't know about? Maybe they hadn't included her on the case because they knew about her and Terry. Perhaps they were choosing their moment to catch her? And if they were caught here, they would be banged to rights and dishonourably discharged within twenty-four hours. She noticed her heartbeat had increased in frequency, and the fierceness of its pounding was beginning to alarm her—she knew she had to make a decision ideally before paranoia set in.

Terry grabbed Jo's arm. 'Come on, go or don't, but make a bloody decision.' Terry walked to the entrance. Jo followed. They stood at the doorway.

'Well, knock then,' said Terry. 'Or don't. I don't mind either way. I'm not sure what you're trying to prove.'

'It's symbolic, Terry. Don't you see this is us saying, bring it on, we're going to be okay. And we're not afraid to be who we really are.'

Terry shrugged. 'If you say so. Let's get it over with then.'

Jo knocked on the door. A hefty, medium-height, butch-looking woman opened it. She looked them up and down before welcoming them in and closing the door behind them.

'Allo Ladies. Not seen you 'ere before. Army, are you?' The tall woman asked in a gruff voice that was deep but not sexy.

'What of it?' challenged Terry.

'Can tell by yer jeans. Only Army girls have white creases down the front.' She chuckled, her belly wobbled with her laughter. 'Well, welcome anyway. There's some of your sort here already. 'Ave fun.' She gestured they should walk down the stairs and opened the door to another client.

'She looks scary,' Terry said.

'She's supposed to. But she's not. Looks like she can handle herself, though.'

Jo took a few steps down and stopped to gawp. She watched the young DJ smile as she spun her magic, impressing her dark-haired, fresh-faced girlfriend. The DJ cued a single and then kissed her lover.

Terry pulled Jo down the last few stairs. 'Pint?'

'Please.' Jo's curiosity was pleasantly assuaged as she surveyed the clientele. They were mostly dressed casually in blue jeans, trainers and colourful tops. A few wore skirts. Some of the older women conformed to the stereotypes of butch and femme, but for the most part, they were dressed just like her and Terry. Terry returned carrying two pints, beer slopping over the sides.

'Generous pours and not too bad prices for London,' Terry gave Jo a glass before taking a sip of her beer.

'Terry,' Jo shouted above the music, drunk with freedom. 'Can you believe this? We're at the mecca of lesbian clubs in London. You and me!'

In the semi-darkened club, Jo stood with Terry, absorbing their surroundings. Jo kissed Terry. She drew back, and they grinned at each other. Terry gave Jo a lingering kiss just because she could. They shifted their glasses into different hands so they could stand with one arm around each other. It felt good to show their love without fear of repulsion or censure.

The DJ cued another single as the first few bars played. Chatter rippled through the crowd, followed by the scrapping of chairs, the emptying of tables, and the filling of the dance floor. The DJ waved her arms, encouraging her worshipers to sing louder. Headphones jammed on her head, the DJ bent low into the microphone and sang, 'I am what I am,' leading her congregation in their anthem. Jo and Terry placed their glasses on an empty table, along with a dozen others.

At first, their dancing was self-conscious and then Terry, a natural dancer, followed the other women's moves. Smiling, she encouraged Jo to join her. Soon, they were integrated with the clientele of The Gateways, swept up by the infectious beat of the music and the sentiment of the lyrics. The regulars sang all the words. Women, who were either new to the club or perhaps acknowledging their sexuality for the first time sang the chorus—many, uninhibited, punched their fists into the air. The atmosphere was a heady concoction of freedom, music and booze, which they could only enjoy until midnight and maybe the following weekend if they could afford it. The track faded into another single.

Breathless, Jo and Terry returned to the table where they had left their drinks. Eight or more women now occupied it, and Jo couldn't find their beers. 'Think they snaffled them,' said Jo, jerking her head at the group. 'Know better next time. Finish our drinks before we dance. This could get expensive, not mess prices.'

'I'll get a couple more. Be back in a jiffy.' Terry weaved through the crowd to the bar.

Jo watched two butch women talking in a corner, unable to withdraw her interest as one approached a slim young woman for a dance. Jo was surprised to see the much younger woman smile and coyly accept the older woman's request. Curious, she looked around the room for other trysts.

'What's caught your interest?' Terry offered Jo one of the pints.

'Put them down. We've gotta go. Now! On me!' Jo slammed her pint on the table, the beer slopping messily onto the table. She headed for the exit, slaloming between women, sliding her body between couples in conversation, groups sharing a joke, sometimes colliding with unyielding bodies, requiring an apology for her rude intrusion. Finally, she made it to the foot of the stairs.

'In a hurry?' said the butch at the doorway at the top. 'That's a shame.' She descended a few stairs slowly toward Jo.

Jo scanned the room for Terry, keeping an eye on the approaching butch while hiding behind a group of women.

'What're you running away from?'

'Not running.'

'If that's not running, hate to see you standing still?' The butch laughed. 'Anyway, need my help? We don't like trouble here. See that woman there? She's trouble. Pinches people's girlfriends. Thinks because she has money, she can do what she likes. Nasty piece of work. Had to see her out a couple of times. Handy with her fists—'specially when she's 'ad a few. Starts throwing her weight around. Women end up crying, and Muggins here has to go and sort her out. That who you're running away from?'

Jo nodded.

'I see. Good idea to stay away from her.'

Terry caught up with Jo faltering as she encountered the butch on the stairs above towering over them.

'It's all right, Terry. Everything's fine. But let's go.'

The butch stood to one side, holding open the door as Jo and Terry sprinted up the stairs and into the street. The green door shut behind them the minute the pair had exited.

'Car—fast!' Jo sprinted across the road. She started the car as soon as she got in, opening the door for Terry and not waiting for her to put on her seat belt. She slammed the gearbox into first and drove away, running through the gears to fourth within fifty yards.

'Slow down, Jo, you'll get us killed or a speeding ticket.'

Jo took the next turning, realising she was near Rochester Row and slowed to the required speed limit. 'We'll be home soon.'

'Good. What was that bouncer talking about?'

'Oh, she's there to sort out the troublemakers. She seemed kind of proud about it.'

'Is that the reason we left in a hurry?'

'No! I saw Quade!'

Terry gasped. 'Did she see you?'

'Don't think so.'

Terry looked at her watch. 'It's nearly midnight. We didn't miss much.'

'Is that all you can say?'

'What do you want me to say?'

'Don't you realise? I've got her!'

## Chapter 36

*Bank Holiday Sunday*

Just before lunch, Jo and Terry left Linda and their mother at home. They decided they needed to talk about recent events and agree on what they should do. They chose the saloon bar of The Nag's Head pub in Brentwood. Jo went to the bar to order drinks, and Terry found a table near the mature log fire.

'Linda's driving me mad.' Jo put the two pints and two bags of plain crisps on the table.

'Jo, I think we have more important things to discuss than Linda and Pete.'

Jo waited and sipped her pint. 'Like what?'

'Like, what if I get kicked out of the Army?'

Jo dismissed the thought rather than consider the options. 'You won't. Not now I've got Quade banged to rights.'

'I don't know how you can be so sure it will all end with Quade. And to date you have a bad track record with her and daddy.' Terry returned to her problem. 'That means there's still the chance I'm going to be interviewed. And what if they break me and link me to you? What then?'

'I know you, Terry, you won't break.'

'I've heard people do. What if they've got some kind of evidence on me?'

'They don't.'

'How do you know?'

'I'd've seen it.'

'Not if they are out to get you too.' Terry reasoned. 'Seriously, what happens if I get kicked out? What're we going to tell them? Where are we going to live? What're we going to do for a job? Have you thought about all these things? Because they could happen. We need to plan. Don't tell me you haven't thought about it. I know you, Jo. You think everything through when you're planning something.'

'Of course, I have. I can't think about anything else. But I don't know what to do. I think we have to wait until it happens and make the best of it.'

Terry sipped her pint. 'You worried about Linda?'

'Yes, and no. I mean, no, not really.'

'I'm pretty sure Linda knows. And because we don't say anything, she can blackmail us with Mum and Dad—especially you.'

'Why not you? Why're you different? You're in the same position.'

'Not quite. Linda isn't my sister. And, while Sylvia and Brian are better than my real parents, they're not my parents. They can choose not to have anything to do with me. You, you, they can disown, and Linda knows that.'

'Are you suggesting I tell them?'

'Not my parents. But if you want to stop Linda from blackmailing you, then yes. But more importantly, we both need to think about how we'd explain a dishonourable discharge to them and what our future might be after that.'

'It's all so complicated.' Jo held her head in her hands. She looked up at Terry. 'I don't think I can break their hearts. I can't, Terry.'

'If you don't tell them, you are letting other people control us and our future.'

'Aren't you doing that now? Telling me what to do.'

'Jo, I'm your partner. We should discuss and agree things. We should be united and take control, not have it dictated to us.'

Jo sipped her beer, looking around the pub for a distraction.

'Jo?'

'I don't know. It seems that whichever way you look at it, we're being told what to do by the Army, society, the church, and, and … well, everyone. As hard as I try, I can't seem to get control of my life all because I love a woman. All I want to do is have a good job and live with you. What's so bad about that?' Jo felt her emotions rising to her eyes and stopped. 'Don't answer. I don't want to talk about it anymore.'

They sat, drank their beer, and ate their crisps without speaking until they finished their pints.

'Come on, let's go home,' said Jo. 'And not a word, right?'

'But…'

'Because I really don't want to talk about it.'

## Chapter 37

*Day Eight*

Jo and Nick huddled in Pte Dawson's coffee cubby hole, drinking coffee. Jo's lack of conversation indicated her apprehension. Nick worked hard to distract her from her anxiety by talking about the latest football games and vilifying Margaret Thatcher, which usually sparked vitriolic conversation but at this moment failed to get any acknowledgement. Exasperated, he resorted to gossip. 'Staff is back today.'

'Shit!'

'Don't panic. Want to know why he had to take some leave?'

'Is this goss or legit?'

'Legit.'

'Okay,' Jo said doubtfully.

'You won't believe this, but Staff's son, you know, the PTI in the RAF, has been court-martialled and found guilty of homosexuality, conduct, etc.'

Jo's eyes widened.

'Yeah, I know, hard to believe. So, he might be easier to work with, you know, his son being gay and everything.'

'Morning, you two!' Sergeant Major Hart greeted them. 'You look guilty. What's happening?'

'Is it true, ma'am, that Staff is re-joining the team today?' Jo asked.

'It is. So, I'll start the interview and focus on the anonymous note. Once I have that out of the way, I'll leave you three to investigate the allegations against Sarn't White. I'll be around sorting stuff out.'

Staff Sergeant Armstrong bustled through the Main Building entrance to meet them. 'Morning, ma'am, Jo, Nick. I'm ready when you lot are.'

Hart strode to the far end of the corridor, her heels broadcasting her mood with every purposeful strike of two-inch heels on tile. She unlocked the investigation room. The team filed in and began stacking the spare chairs, grouping the tables to make an extended desk and placing four chairs around it. The finishing touches included clearing the scraps of paper from the desk and putting them in the wastebasket. Fully prepared, they sat down and waited.

Terry knocked on the door and entered. 'Alright, if I come in, Sarn't Major. The RSM told me you wanted to see me.'

'Yes, come in, Sergeant White, and sit down.'

Terry was dressed in the incongruous barrack dress uniform of a PTI, comprising blue tracksuit trousers, a white PT shirt, and a V-necked jumper. On her feet were her black drill shoes, and on her head was her green beret. She approached the table, removing her beret as she sat down.

Though Jo had practised staying calm, her breath was uneven. She worked hard to keep her face neutral, though she worried what might happen when Armstrong took over the investigation. She knew it would have gone well if it had been left to her and Nick. After all, there was no evidence to condemn Terry. But Staff, well, he was unpredictable even at the best of times. Maybe Nick was right, and Armstrong would be sympathetic now that his son had been outed.

'Right. Let us begin,' Hart visually checked that her team was ready.

'Sergeant White, my team and I have asked you here regarding an anonymous note alleging you are a lesbian.'

'I understand, ma'am.'

'I'm sure we can clear this matter up in due course. Do you know anyone who might want to harm you?'

'No.'

'Think, Sergeant White.'

'Ma'am, I can't think of anyone. I don't think it would be big-headed of me to say that mostly I get on okay with everyone.'

'So, no one then? Only we received an anonymous tip-off about you, and that usually means someone wants revenge.'

'May I see the note?'

Hart pushed it across the desk. Jo collected herself and pretended to be interested in the note. Terry slid the paper toward Jo, looking into her lover's eyes.

'You've no idea who wrote this?' Hart asked.

'No. Could be anyone.'

'Exactly. That's why I'm asking you to think about who might do this?'

Terry shrugged.

'Are you a lesbian?'

'Ma'am, I want to politely inform you that I shan't answer any more of your questions.'

'Sergeant White,' Jo pleaded, 'Answer the questions. A simple yes or no will suffice.'

Terry looked at her beret, rolled it into a sausage shape, unrolled it and repeated the movement several times.

Jo watched as her fears for her soul mate grew, but all she could do was observe.

'I can wait all day, Sarn't White,' Hart sighed.

Terry glanced up at the portrait of the Queen, pausing before answering. 'Then, ma'am, with all due respect, you'll have to wait all day and every day. But I need to umpire an inter-unit hockey match at three thirty.'

Hart got up. 'Staff, please take over. I'll be around if you need me.'

'Sarn't Major, can I have a word?' Jo got up and joined her boss in the corridor. She looked up and down the empty hallway, knowing every officer's and platoon sergeant's door was open. She whispered, 'There is one person who might do this. Terry won't say because it will probably cause a lot of trouble.'

'Jo?'

'Ma'am, Terry and I are being sort of blackmailed—by our brother-in-law.'

'Bloody Hell! This gets worse every time I turn around. Okay, I'll give that further consideration. However, we still have to interview her about the allegation in the note, and I want you to question her. We must be seen to have been thorough in this particular instance. Now, get back to your job. And Jo, it's vital that you keep your head for everyone's sake.'

Jo gave Hart a weak smile before returning to the morning's task. When she entered the room, it was silent.

'Good, you're back,' Armstrong stood and puffed out his chest before pulling out a chair for Jo to sit on.

'Staff, Sarn't Major, says I have to question Terry.'

'Okay, go ahead.'

Jo began her line of questioning. 'I understand you have a very close relationship with Lance Corporal Dart.'

Terry laughed. 'Is that your best? No, I don't. She wants to be a PTI, and I'm helping her prepare for her selection board. She helps me out at the gym because I'm short-handed. I need the help.'

'Where do you usually go for your holidays? And, before you answer, remember I have access to all your leave passes.'

'Home to my family.'

'And where's that?'

'As you have the leave passes, I am sure you can work it out, Sergeant Clark.' Terry's tone suggested they keep the appearance of adversaries rather than lovers.

Jo felt the stickiness of nervous perspiration underneath her breasts and armpits. She wanted to yell out that Terry was her sister, even though she knew it was, at best, a half-truth.

Armstrong interrupted. 'I give the orders around here, Sergeant White. The matter will be looked into. And should they prove suspicious, we will contact you again. Sarn't Clark, do you have any more questions?'

Jo looked at her pad and the long list of questions she had prepared for previous interviews. The problem was that those had some evidence, mostly half-cocked evidence, but even that provided some basis for questioning. With Terry, there was nothing, no photographs, no letters and no address book with other names to connect her to or follow up on—just an anonymous note. Terry's suggestion to check up on the leave passes bothered her. Her thoughts flew in and out of her brain, scarring her deeper with fear and dread. Her mind went back and forth between worrying whether Hart and Armstrong were sussing her out and what she could do to get Terry out of the room before they both lost their careers. A black terror rendered her dumb. She shrugged at Armstrong.

'Okay, I'll take it from here,' Armstrong said with uncharacteristic cheer and empathy, so much so that Nick stared at him. He caught Jo's eye and smiled a 'relax' it's going to be fine at her.

'I want you to think again, Sergeant White. Have you any enemies? Think because if you can, that might stop further investigation of you and your sexual behaviour.'

'No. I already answered that. I can't help you. I have no clue who might send such a note.'

'Okay, so with that in mind, let's move on to the allegation. Are you a lesbian?'

'I'm not answering any more of these absurd questions.' Terry stared at the Queen's portrait once more. 'I can't believe you're asking me questions about my sexuality based on an anonymous note. It's ridiculous.'

'Look, Sarn't White. It is better if you tell us. Because if not, it can get a tad awkward for everyone.'

Jo tilted her head to one side to study Armstrong.

'I'm going to step out for a minute. And if I were you, when I come back in, I'd be ready to share everything you know with us.' Armstrong left the room.

Jo and Terry looked at each other desperately, signalling all their emotions and encouragement to the other. Jo wanted to encourage Terry. To hold her tight, but the job forbade any interaction with a suspect except in the line of duty. Nick got up to look out the window, not wishing to eavesdrop on the silent conversation.

After a minute, Terry joined him. 'I need to stretch my legs.'

Nick nodded.

Two minutes later, Armstrong opened the door, pausing before shutting it. He walked to the chair Terry had left vacant. He moved it away from the desk into the centre of the room. 'Bit cramped, so close to the desk.'

Jo watched, remembering the last time Armstrong had done such a thing.

'Bit,' Terry agreed.

Armstrong's voice was calm and polite as he requested Terry retake her seat.

'Now, where were we? Ah yes. You're a lesbian. Would you like to tell us who you have sex with?'

'Nope and nope,' Terry leaned forward in her chair. 'You're making an assumption and then suggesting, based on that assumption, that I'm having sex with a woman.'

'Good looking gal like you. Got to be having sex!' scoffed Armstrong.

'None of your business, Staff. Whether I have sex or not and who with.'

'You frigid then?' His voice grew louder with the accusation.

'Nope.'

'You're a PTI. I bet you're fucking some bint. We know one of your many girlfriends is Lance Corporal Dart.'

Terry gave a belly laugh. 'You're kidding, aren't you?'

Armstrong got close to Terry's face. 'Struck a nerve, did I?' Armstrong strutted a circle around Terry. 'I have it on good authority that you're fucking Dart.' Armstrong removed his suit jacket and rolled up his shirt sleeves before leering into Terry's face again.

'What?' Terry reeled from his bad breath. 'Who said that?' She asked in an impatient and dismissive tone.

Nick and Jo shot each other a glance. Jo sensed that Terry's confidence and her answers intimidated and irritated Armstrong.

'Your OC, that's who. She says you and Dart are having a relationship,' Armstrong shouted.

'Well,' Terry said in a matter-of-fact tone. 'She's wrong.'

'Stand up, Sergeant.'

Terry stood. Jo braced herself, scared there would be a repeat of a previous interview. She signalled to Nick to be ready. He shuffled to the edge of his chair; his feet prepared to launch himself at Armstrong.

Terry stared at Armstrong as he struggled to find questions. He stuttered, failing to put a sentence together. Terry waited, watching Armstrong approach her, a sickly smile across his face.

'Think you're clever, don't you?' He taunted.

Terry looked through her interrogator, keeping her gaze on the Queen's portrait on the back wall.

'Answer me!'

'What do you want me to say, Staff? Looks to me like you're not having a good day. And I—.'

Armstrong grabbed Terry by the throat, knocking over the chair before dragging her to the nearest wall and pinning her against it with one hand while unzipping his flies with the other.

'What you need is a good fuck by a good man! That'll—.'

Jo and Nick sprang out of their chairs. Jo pulled at Armstrong's hands, enclosing Terry's throat. Terry thrust her arms up and between Armstrong's to break his hold on her. It weakened his grasp, but not enough. Nick placed Armstrong in an armlock around his neck and pulled him backwards while Jo worked at loosening Armstrong's grip. Between them, they broke his assault on Terry.

'Get off her Staff. Get off her!' shouted Nick, struggling to control Armstrong.

Terry rubbed her neck. Jo stared at Terry, desperate to take her hand and run to safety. Instead, she did her duty.

Nick kept Armstrong restrained, remonstrating with him.

'He's fucking bonkers! I'm filing a complaint of assault!' Terry yelled as best she could.

'You fucking dyke!' Armstrong lunged towards Terry. Nick caught Armstrong's arm and wrenched it up his back.

The commotion was heard along the corridor by Private Dawson. Who interrupted a meeting the RSM was having with Hart. Hart sprinted up the corridor, throwing open the door and stepping into the room in one swift movement, filling it with a commanding presence.

'Staff Armstrong, I'd like you to return to barracks. Sergeant White, you are dismissed. Sergeants Clark and Acorn remain here. I will need to take statements from you both.'

Nick released Armstrong, who strolled out of the room, adjusting his suit jacket and tie along with his dignity.

'I want to file a complaint of assault,' Terry said.

'All in good time, Sergeant White. First, I want to hear from my team about what went on here. I'll be in touch. Now, if you'd be kind enough.' Hart held the door open, closing it after Terry had left. She turned to Jo and Nick. 'Right! What the fuck went on here?'

'He just lost it,' said Jo. 'This time, instead of chucking furniture, he assaulted her. He just lost it! It took Nick and me to get him off her. He just went mad. I thought he was going to rape her!'

'Careful Jo. Okay, write up your statements. But listen, he is having a hard time. He just found out his son's at Colchester Glass House, doing two years for being gay.'

'Shit! It's true, then?' Jo looked at Nick.

Hart nodded.

'What does that mean for him now?' Jo asked.

'Probably no promotion. Guilty by association. And, certainly, no transfers because his vetting is compromised.'

'He'll never live it down,' Nick added. 'I mean, he is known for being the best at the witch-hunts. And now, his son, in the glasshouse. Blimey.'

'Hmm. Doesn't do to dwell on it. Get the statements done, and let's leave Sergeant White out of further interrogations for now,' Hart said. 'We can always get her back in if we need to. Though frankly, without evidence, it's a complete waste of time and money. I'm going to report to RSM Gordon. She needs to know what went on here.

## Chapter 38

Having been dismissed by Hart, Terry strode angrily to her office in the gymnasium. She had been assaulted, almost raped, and all Hart could do was say they would look into the matter! It beggars belief. She couldn't face lunch because she knew she would be the subject of gossip and conjecture. And it would be worse if news of Armstrong's assault on her leaked out. Some might not even speak to her in case it made them guilty by association. She kicked a stone from the pathway onto the grass in her angry stride before jogging to the gym entrance. Once in her office, she shut the door. In the mirror fixed to the back of it, she saw her reflection. She looked a little grey, almost sickly. She noticed sweat marks on her PT shirt under the armpits. That was odd because she was quivering with cold—no, she realised that shock was setting in. She sat down at her desk. All she wanted, all she needed was Jo. She needed Jo to hold her tight and tell her everything was okay. She felt vulnerable, and tears welled up and slid down her face. She looked at her watch as if it would tell her when Jo would come. But there was no knowing when Jo could get away without arousing suspicion.

Terry heard a polite and gentle knock at her office door. Max entered smiling and shut the door behind her, ensuring no one saw Terry crying. She placed an arm around Terry's shoulders. 'It's alright, Sarn't. A good cry is what you need.'

Terry wiped away her tears with a handkerchief Sylvia gave her. The memory of the gift and the feeling of safety it evoked triggered more tears. Max rubbed her back.

'Did you see Jo?'

'No. But Dawson told me what happened, so I came straight over to see if you needed me. Dawson said they were writing the incident reports in the interview room.'

'How do you know?'

'Dawson had to take them tea and coffee. She looked over their shoulders. Sarn't Major Hart is fuming. Dawson said the room was a mess, with chairs overturned and everything. A rumour is going around Staff Armstrong tried to rape you.'

Terry thought for a moment. 'Not sure he knew what he was doing. I seemed to make him angry. I know I was deliberately awkward, but his questions were just plain nasty. No one should have to answer questions about their sex life. It's a private matter between consenting adults. And if it isn't between consenting adults, it's illegal end of.' Terry wiped away the last tear, at least for now. Her vulnerability was replaced by anger and practicalities. 'We've an Inter unit hockey match in half an hour. Would you umpire with me?'

'Yes. Of course, That's partly why I came over. I thought you might not want to umpire and could do with some alone time.'

Terry got up and opened her desk drawer to retrieve her whistle. 'Duty calls. Plus I need something to take my mind off things.' She rubbed her throat.

'Bloody hell, that'll give everything away tomorrow morning. It'll be black 'n' blue, I shouldn't wonder.'

Terry examined her neck in the mirror. There were red finger marks, which Armstrong had scarred her with for the moment. They would fade hopefully with the memory of the incident.

Jo scribbled her report. Anger and sadness bubbled inside her like a poisonous gas, waiting for a match to light it and blow Armstrong to smithereens. She caught herself as she wrote the details of when Armstrong held Terry by the neck and worked to unzip his flies. She smiled at Nick, grateful for his intervention, and the realisation that he would always have her back.

'Nick, I'm nearly finished. I need to see Terry. Check she's okay. Alright, if I leave you on your own?'

'Course, you don't need me hanging around you two. If Sarn't Major returns, I'll let her know you wanted to check on the victim's welfare. Can't see her objecting to that.'

'Good God. I hadn't thought of her as a victim. I never think of her as a victim. She's the strong one. Well, usually.' Jo left Nick, finishing his report.

Taking the same route Terry had earlier, the ten-minute walk gave Jo time to reflect on what had happened on a personal level. She was no longer the on-duty policewoman. She was Terry's lover and protector. She knocked and opened Terry's office door.

Max acknowledged Jo before quietly slipping out of the office, shutting the door behind her, ready to umpire the inter unit hockey match.

Terry stood the moment Jo was inside the small office and buried her face into Jo's shoulder. Jo held her tight while she sobbed. Terry tried to explain how she felt between sobs and gasps for air.

'I'm the one who should be sorry, Terry. I knew he might do that. I've seen him do it before. I'm sorry I should've warned you. But I really didn't think he'd do it a second time.' She held Terry tighter to her, making a silent promise to protect her, that she would never have to go through any more violence—surely she'd gone through enough in her life. Terry's breath warmed the crook of Jo's shoulder, renewing her tenderness for her lover of over ten years. She kissed her head. Before remembering where she was, she panicked, pushing Terry from her. 'Don't want to get caught. Someone might come in.'

'I think they're all out. But point taken. I need to go home. I need to be somewhere where I feel safe. I'm sorry, Jo, I hope you don't think I'm being a wimp, but I feel shitty.'

Jo took hold of Terry's shoulders, wanting to take her in her arms and kiss her; instead, she chose the safest option for touching Terry. When would all this stupidity stop? When would everyone understand that they simply love each other? How can any love be wrong?

'Did you say a second time?'

Jo nodded.

'Bloody hell, he's the one who needs to be discharged. Not me.'

Jo, helpless because she knew Terry was right but suspected that, at the very worst, Armstrong would be busted down from Staff Sergeant to Sergeant, grunted her sympathy.

'I bet he gets away with it.'

Jo didn't know what to say. She agreed but knew they had no control over the situation. The Army would hush it up, and that would be the end of it. 'See if you can get some leave. I'm sure Captain Trueman will agree when she hears about the incident. I better get back. You'll be okay, won't you?'

'Bloody have to be, won't I.'

Jo opened the door. She was torn again between her duty to the Army and Terry. Being a lesbian was never easy, watching everything you said and did, but this, this was something neither of them had considered. If they wanted to keep their careers, there was no way they could react like a heterosexual couple would until they got home to Dell Close.

[illegible]

Joanna [illegible]

[illegible]

"Blood [illegible]"

[illegible] opened the door. [illegible]

## Chapter 39

After lunch, Jo sat in the interview room twiddling her thumbs. Now that Staff Sergeant Armstrong had been removed from the case, it was just her, Nick, and Sergeant Major Hart handling the interviews with the expectation that the whole matter would draw to a close by Friday. Jo had a new development, one she knew would be difficult to relate to Hart without incriminating herself, but one that would be the appropriate retribution for Lizzie's suicide. Her plan would switch the spotlight away from Terry and onto Quade, with the intention of finding her guilty. It would close everything down. After all, no one wanted a senior rank discharged, especially after six years of service. It had happened in the recent past. She knew of a Senior Rank who was discharged. The couple had broken the taboo that there should be no relationship between the ranks and the officers, especially if it were a gay relationship. Once discovered, it led to unequal justice because the senior rank was dishonourably discharged while the officer was allowed to resign.

Jo heard Hart's heels striking a steady tempo along the headquarters corridor. She got up in anticipation of her superior's arrival and mentally prepared her speech. The heels stopped. Jo guessed her boss was with the OC, which meant she would be alone for a while. Jo sauntered out of the interview room and down the corridor to the small kitchen.

'Thought I'd find you here. Any chance of one for me?'

Private Dawson smiled. 'Made you one already. I'll bring it in.'

Jo wandered back to her base. Minutes later, Dawson arrived with two mugs, shutting the door behind her.

'Mind if I sit down?' Dawson placed the cups on the table before pulling a chair closer to the desk opposite Jo.

Jo grinned. 'Thanks. To what do I owe the pleasure?'

'There's something you might like to know. But you didn't hear it from me—right?'

Jo nodded and sipped her coffee.

'It's to do with Sergeant White.' She paused. A frown crossed her youthful face. 'I don't want you to think I'm prying or anything, see. But it could be important.' Dawson scuffed her chair closer. 'Two things….' She looked over her shoulder before leaning forward and dropping her voice to a whisper. 'Leave passes and telephone call to Rochester Row.' She jerked her head up with relief.

'Can you be more specific?'

'Sergeant Treacher pulled all of Sergeant White's leave passes. Then she called her friend at Rochester Row Orderly Room and had copies of yours sent to her.' She leaned back in her chair and drew a deep breath.

'So, she knows we live at the same address?'

'No, Sarn't. She knows you go everywhere together.' Dawson nodded gravely, encouraging Jo to understand the importance of what she had relayed. 'So, I don't think the note is anonymous anymore—and one more thing. The day the anonymous note was discovered, I saw Corporal Quade loitering in the headquarters corridor, right near the OC's office. When she saw me, she defo looked guilty. And I know she didn't see her platoon sergeant or her officer because I was the only one in the building then. I like to get in early and get ahead. Keeps Sarn't Treacher off my back.'

'I see. Thank you, Private Dawson. If you see or hear anything more, let me know.'

Dawson stood up. 'Right, you are Sarn't. I'll keep 'em peeled and be sure to let you know.' She strode out of the room with a sense of purpose.

Jo heard her superior's heels echo in the hallway.

'Morning Jo.' Hart shut the door behind her. 'Just finished with the OC. I'm afraid we can't do too much with the anonymous note. The note was carefully put together. The perpetrator wore gloves and used glue that is in every office in the British Army. So, we have nowhere to go for now.'

'Ma'am, I've got some information of my own.'

'Go on.'

'First, I understand that Sarn't Treacher might be the sender of the anonymous note.'

'Interesting. Why do you think that?'

'She pulled all of Terry's leave passes since she's been at Twelve Company, and then she's pulled all of mine. She has a mate at Rochester Row. She's put two and two together and made five.'

'Five?'

'Because me and Terry, we're like sisters. My mum and dad took her in when we were about thirteen. It's a long story, but she and I have lived together—well—forever. We joined up together. Until the Army, we did everything together. She has to see her parents, who are mine too, and of course, we go home every holiday.'

Hart mentally recalled the file she had pulled on Terry.

'You guys never go anywhere other than 24 Dell Close.'

'That's right.' Jo lied. They had both taken a risk when they took a long weekend in Brighton, falsifying their leave address as their parental home.

'No Spain or France? Ever?'

'We don't like foreign food, ma'am. Plus, my dad has always got a project he wants help with.'

Hart knew the ruses and explanations—she had used some herself. 'All right, Jo, I'll take a look at Sergeant Treacher and see if she might be our sender. By the way, how do you know about the leave passes?'

'An informant, ma'am, who wishes to remain anonymous.'

'That's okay for now, but if we need the evidence, they will have to make themselves known. All right.' Hart inhaled. 'What's the other piece of info?'

'Ma'am, I have it on good authority that…'

'Another anonymous tip-off?' Hart exhaled, weary of the twists and turns events were taking. She forced a grin. 'Go on.'

'A friend of mine saw Corporal Quade down The Gateways at the weekend.'

'And this friend knows what Corporal Quade looks like, does she?'

'Yes, ma'am. She described her to me, and it's definitely Corporal Quade.'

'I see. How does your friend know to describe her to you?'

'She had the white lines down her jeans, apparently identifying Army girls, so the bouncer said.'

'The bouncer? Now, is it?' Hart smirked.

'Okay, you got me. She's the friend, but no names.'

'Right, anonymous.' Hart winked. 'And you thought? What? That we should do some surveillance on the club?'

'Yes, ma'am,' Jo was unable to hide her joy. 'And, my source tells me, Corporal Quade goes there most weekends. Throws her money about.'

'I know we all want her out. But, and it's a big but, doing surveillance on a civvy club needs permission from the Director of London District, and she's very careful about doing this sort of thing. She doesn't like bad press. And, if it goes pear-shaped, we could be in for a rough ride. We'd have to be careful. You better be right, Jo.'

'I am, ma'am. We need to get her out. Then we can close this whole thing down.'

'You're thinking that Terry won't be interviewed again? Sorry to disappoint you, but we might have to re-interview her because we must hunt down every lead. Sadly, it will go in her P file.'

Jo swallowed loudly. There had been no P file. She knew that because she had searched for it. Now, there was one?

'Even if there is no evidence?'

'That's how it works.'

Shit! Jo nodded.

'Right, I best make a phone call.' Hart placed her hand on the doorknob. 'You're free for now, Jo. Come back at two.'

Hart walked to the RSM's office, knocked on the open door, and entered. 'Sitrep,' she said as she closed the door behind her and sat down.

'Uh-huh,' RSM Gordon clasped her hands on her desk.

'Seems Sergeant Treacher has been doing her own investigation. Not sure why? The problem is that another anonymous informant is privy to the information. It rather complicates matters.'

'Why?'

'Because…,' Hart squirmed in her chair. 'I had purloined the file from the catalogue room.'

'What were you going to do with it?'

'Mislay it. Burry it deep somewhere in some files in my desk until I knew no one would miss it and then destroy it.'

'How?'

'Garden bonfire at home.'

'I see. Bit risky.'

'There'd be no evidence. I didn't sign the file out. And it would be in ashes. And if somebody does ask for it in the immediate future, Susan would say it was lost somehow.'

'I see. Is that it? Blame Susan?'

'No, of course not. But what I came in to ask is— uh, this is a bit tricky. I need your help on this.'

'Okay,' Gordon was guarded.

'I think we have a way of catching Quade.'

'Great, and?'

'We need to talk to Colonel Cato-West to get her permission to do surveillance. And, I thought, as you've worked with her, you might?'

'Okay, I'll put a call in. Obviously, you've got to make the request formally. But you just want to know she is open to it?'

'That's it. I don't want to make the request and have it denied. Gets awkward. Then the boss will want to know why, and then we're into all sorts of questions and some answers we don't want to give.'

'Your informant, Jo, by any chance?'

'Mm. She denied it, but I know it's her.'

'I see. Well, we need to avoid that and a bunch of other things. I'll get on it now.'

She picked up the phone. Within three rings, the call was answered, and she was transferred to Cato West.

'Ma'am, Miss Gordon speaking. I need a favour…'

## Chapter 40

Major Marwood played with the wooden name plate that adorned her desk, turning it repeatedly as she considered what Sergeant Treacher was proposing. She read and re-read the inscription. Major Marwood, WRAC. OC 12 Coy.

'So, ma'am, I'm suggesting that I'm given acting Staff Sergeant. It'll be a tad early, but not enough to create any suspicion on your part.'

'And, if I don't?'

'I think you know what happens.'

'I need time to think about it.'

'You have twenty-four hours, ma'am. That's all. No more stalling, and I want to see the correct forms to request it from Manning. And local acting won't cut it, because I need the pay.'

'I said, I need time to think about it.'

There was a knock at the door.

'You have a visitor. Shall I let them in?'

Marwood nodded and lit up a cigarette. Treacher opened the door for Sergeant Major Hart. As she passed her in the doorway, Treacher gave Hart a smug smile.

'Shut the door, will you, Miss Hart? I don't want any interruptions. What do you have for me?'

'Good morning, ma'am.'

'Yes, yes, get on with it, woman.'

'Ma'am, we're unable to trace the perpetrator of the anonymous letter.'

Marwood blew out a plume of smoke that hit the ceiling and dissipated. 'What about White?'

'Sarn't White, ma'am?'

'Yes, her!' the OC sneered.

'Ma'am, it seems the author had it all wrong. There is no evidence to back up their claims.'

'No evidence? Did you question her?'

'We questioned her for over an hour. She was mostly cooperative. But without documentary or photographic evidence to back up the claim, we have nothing.'

'So that's it! You know, and I know she's a lesbian.' Marwood stubbed the cigarette out and substituted it with another. She got up and paced the room.

'Ma'am, you may have your suspicions, but without a confession, we have nothing.'

'Confession? Confession?'

'Ma'am, the rule is that the suspect must give us details of a sexual act in order to avoid women leaving the Army…'

'Yes, I know that. It's ridiculous! She's as queer as a coot.'

'But she's not…the ringleader we're looking for.'

'Might as well be. Who is it, then? Don't suppose you've found out?'

'Ma'am, we believe it is Corporal Quade, and as you know we can't prosecute the case because of her father.'

'Yes, yes.' Marwood sat down at her desk, her face glum, her fingers rhythmically tapping ash from her cigarette, then inhaling the nicotine as deep as she could before pausing and beginning the ritual again.

'So, ma'am, my team will be wrapping up today. You can be assured that the names in the investigation will be logged in our catalogue for future reference. We just have the one discharge.'

'Bloody hell!' Marwood's head dropped before looking up at Hart. 'No Senior Ranks, I suppose. I bet you're all in cahoots with one another.'

'I don't know about that, ma'am. But no, no Senior Ranks. And no Officers.'

'Well, I don't expect officers to be queer. Do you? Altogether, a different type of woman.'

'No, ma'am, of course not, ma'am.'

'Shame about Corporal Watson. The defence minister called the DWRAC, insisting we review her case. Sadly, Sarn't Treacher had already discharged her. Shame, she was an intelligent soldier. Pity we couldn't get Minter.'

'No, ma'am, she's a horse rider—quite good as it goes.'

'Hmm, with a bit of luck, she'll get offered a job and leave.' Marwood inhaled deeply, filling her lungs to full capacity with nicotine. 'I did my best to rid the unit of a potential PR disaster. Huh! And what've I got to show for a career-limiting decision? Nothing, absolutely nothing.' Her voice began to crack. 'You may go, Miss Hart, and thank you for your efforts. Don't take this the wrong way, but I hope never to see you again.'

'Thank you, ma'am, and no offence taken. We will finish up here today. After that, everything should be back to normal. I shan't brief you again unless something comes up. I'll drop in to say my goodbyes when we finalise everything.'

## Chapter 41

*Day Nine. London Provost Company, Rochester Row, London.*

On Friday morning, Jo sat at her desk, stabbing typewriter keys, the wooden desk echoing the pounding of her frustration with this aspect of the job. She tore the beige form out of the typewriter and inspected it before submitting it in her 'out tray' for distribution to the OC. Major Relish had high standards, which he felt reflected on his unit, and Jo struggled to meet this one on a regular basis. She decided there was more Tippex than print, an exaggeration, but one that prompted her to place the document in the tray for burning and start again. She inserted a fresh charge sheet into the carriage and turned the knobs to level the paper. When the top edge surfaced, it was crooked. She tried again.

'Struggling?' Nick placed a mug of coffee on her desk.

'I hate bloody typing.'

Nick laughed. 'Yeah, I can see that. Move over and let me help. How many have you got to do?'

'This is the last one.'

'When're you leaving?'

'As soon as this is done, I'm off.'

'Doing anything nice?'

Jo looked around her. The office was empty except for them. 'Think I'm going to tell my parents, you know, this weekend.'

'Brave. Maybe foolish. Do you need to?'

'Sometimes I think I do, and other times not.'

'If in doubt, don't. He who hesitates is lost.'

'Steady, Nick, I'm not sure I can handle your support or Shakespeare at this time in the morning. Don't overdo it, now, will you?'

'Sorry. Listen, read me the report, and I'll type it.'

'Suspect, Woman Private Minter, 4506973, clerk, twelve company WRAC. Interrogated, the second of May nineteen eighty-four at ten thirty hours on suspicion of lesbianism.'

Nick stopped typing. 'Got the details. I know this one. I'll do it. No need to read on.' He cocked his head. 'What will you do if your parents aren't sympathetic?'

'Don't know.' Jo looked at the floor, realising that she had no way of knowing how it would go.

'And where does that leave, Terry?'

'I'm doing it for Terry.'

'Are you? Have you spoken with her?'

'A bit. She said she'll support me.'

'Support isn't doing it for her, Jo.' Nick was exasperated. 'Jo, you know your parents could tell the MOD.'

'Well, if they don't, I'm in danger of my brother-in-law doing it anyway, so I might as well tell them and control the situation.'

'I don't think you can control this—not once the cat's out of the bag. Think carefully, Jo. Your career, your home, your relationship with your parents—all gone in one sentence—one foolish moment, one you will regret the rest of your life.' Nick studied Jo's face, looking for her decision.

'You told your parents?' Jo asked.

'God, no! My old man would have a fit.'

'My sister Linda is already on to me. She keeps needling away at me. I'm afraid if Pete hasn't already said something, Linda will.'

'Let them. You can deny it. But you'll still have your job, home and career.'

'Is that what you're doing? Brushing it under the carpet?'

'I'm getting out.' Nick grinned, stood up and straightened his back. 'I'm joining the Met.' The triumph in his voice was unmistakable. 'I'll get a flat, and then I'll be okay. Have to be careful, but I can live my life the best way I can.'

Jo laughed. 'I think the Met is just as homophobic.'

'Maybe, but not as much as the Army, and I can live my private life privately, and I am only obliged to work my shifts. Either way, it's better than living with the stress of a perpetual lie. And your every move studied by your mates at work and in the mess. When I go home, I watch what I do because of my dad. The only time I get a bit of peace and quiet is when I'm with Julian.'

'Julian?' Jo rechecked the office was empty.

'My boyfriend. We've been steady for six months. He has a flat in Earls Court. I spend most weekends there now.'

'Blimey didn't know.'

'Lot, you don't know about me. Anyway, think on. I'll see you Monday. Have a nice one.'

'Thanks, Nick, for,' she hesitated, 'the chat and the typing. Have a good one.' She picked up her bag and headed to the car park to begin her journey home.

Jo pushed open the back door of 24 Dell Close, throwing her weekend bag in through the opening before stepping into the kitchen. She had expected her mother to be at the sink or the kitchen table, her pinny on and a teapot at the ready. Instead, Linda was sat at the table with a mug of tea.

'Hello, where's Mum?' asked Jo.

'Hairdressers.'

'Any tea in the pot?'

'No, I did a tea bag.'

'Mum won't like that.'

'Well, she ain't here, so I'm not worried.'

Jo filled the kettle and flicked the electric switch. 'You all right?'

'Yeah.'

'Where's Karl?'

'Pete's Mum's.'

'Sure, you're all right?'

'Yeah. What's it got to do with you?'

'Just asking. Making sure you're okay.'

'Well, don't. I'm fine.'

The kettle clicked off. Jo poured the hot water into the mug with a tea bag. Using a teaspoon, she bobbed the tea bag up and down in the cup before she squeezed it and threw it in the bin. She carried the mug to the kitchen table and sat down.

'Terry, not here yet?'

'Nope.'

'Just you, then?'

'Yep.'

Jo sipped her tea. Linda stared out the kitchen window.

'What time're you picking up Karl?'

'Depends.'

Jo picked up her mug and her weekend bag.

'I'm going upstairs, seeing as you're in such a chatty mood.'

Linda ignored her, so Jo walked up the stairs. Once in her room, she popped her Walkman on, and unpacked the few things from her bag. Lying on her bed, she thought about how to win Terry over to her decision to come out and then how to win her parents over once Terry was on her side. Various scenarios played through her mind, her parents throwing her out. Terry fighting her decision. Linda grinning because finally, the golden girl was not so golden. Emotionally exhausted, she dozed off until she heard the back door open.

Jo got up, attempted to hand iron the creases out of her jeans, and sauntered downstairs into the kitchen. 'Nice hair, Mum.'

'What time did you get home?'

'An hour ago,' Linda said.

'Terry coming home too?'

'Yeah, thought she'd be here by now.'

'Right Jo, peel some potatoes. Enough for five.'

'Five?'

'Yes, five!'

Jo knew, by her mother's tone of voice, not to question further. Linda grinned at Jo.

'Can't Linda do it?'

'No, she can't. She needs a rest.'

'Not preggers again, are you?' Jo asked.

'No, I'm not! And it's none of your business if I was.'

'Fallen out with Pete then?'

'None of your bloody business.' Linda stormed out of the kitchen.

'Now, see what you've done,' Sylvia chided.

'What? I only asked.'

'Well, don't.'

Jo peeled the potatoes and then the carrots. Sylvia placed them in large saucepans while Jo set the dining room table in the Living Room. Linda sat on the couch watching children's TV, deliberately ignoring Jo. Jo returned to the kitchen.

'Anything else, Mum?'

'No. Tea?' Sylvia placed two mugs on the table and poured from the brown teapot. 'Your dad'll be home later. Go to the pub with him, will you?

That way, me and Linda can have a proper chat.'

'What's going on?'

Sylvia exhaled. 'I dunno.' She shook her head.

'Why doesn't she leave Pete and just come home?'

'It's complicated. When you're married, you will understand. Are you courting yet?'

'No, Mum,' Jo scoffed.

'What about that nice Nick you work with? Hasn't he asked you out yet? I mean, both my girls are lookers.'

'No, Mum, it's complicated. You've got to be sure, you know, living in the mess together and everything. People watch your every move and take the mickey out of you.'

'You're way too sensitive, Jo Clark. Just like yer father.' Sylvia got up and washed her mug.

Terry pushed open the door. 'Hello, Mum. Been a terrible journey. Stop and go all the way.' Terry sighed and slumped into her seat. 'Any tea in that pot?'

Sylvia boiled the kettle.

'Linda's here,' Jo said.

'Again?' Terry whispered, 'Everything all right?'

'Mum wants us to go to the pub with Dad so they can talk.'

'Right.'

Sylvia placed the mug and teapot in front of Terry. 'Everything all right at work?'

'Yeah, fine. Why?' Terry lied.

'You look tired, love. Bit of home cooking and your own bed, and you'll be as right as rain. More than I can say for some.' Sylvia raised her eyebrows and nodded in the direction of Linda in the Living Room.

## Chapter 42

*Saturday, Clark Family Home.*

The smell of bacon filled the kitchen as the family gathered around the table to eat the enormous breakfast traditionally served by Sylvia on a holiday weekend. Family members ignored good manners in favour of a stretch or starve policy, which meant arms stretched over other arms, reaching for bacon, sausages, mushrooms, baked beans, and black pudding. Sylvia made room on the table for a plate of fried bread, starting a frenzy of activity as Brian stabbed a slice first, then Jo and Terry. Linda, watching her weight, chose another piece of toast.

'Who wants to join me? I'm going shopping in Romford. Probably do the market?' Sylvia moved an empty plate to the sink.

Brian rested his knife and fork and got up. 'Not me, Mother. I've got a pond to attend to. Terry, Jo going to help me?'

'I've got a migraine, Dad. I'm going to lie down,' Jo put a hand to her brow.

'Ah. Terry?'

'I need to go to Romford with Mum. I need some clothes.'

Brian closed the back door and headed for his shed.

'Coming, Linda?' Sylvia collected her handbag.

'I better stay here, Mum. Just in case.'

'In case of what? Pete comes to pick you up? Or Pete's mother drops Karl here?'

'Mum, you know what I'm like if I go shopping, I buy things, and Pete doesn't like it.'

'I'll buy you a new dress if that's what you want, love?'

'No, Mum, you know he gets jealous if anyone else buys me something. He says he should be the one to buy my clothes. Only he knows what suits me.'

'I'm going up, Mum. I need to get my head down.' Jo took a large glass of water with her.

Terry started washing up. 'Just you and me then, Mum.'

'Yeah, miserable lot. We'll go when we've washed up. Now, don't you go about mooching all day, Linda—do something. You've got time to yourself. Use it wisely, my girl. At the very least, make tea for your dad every hour. Keeps him happy.'

Half an hour later, Linda waved goodbye to her mother and Terry. She glanced out the kitchen window, noticing Brian still digging a hole to put his fibreglass pond shell in, which still hadn't been delivered. The house was silent, and with nothing to do but watch TV, she laid on the sofa for a rare nap.

Just before lunch, Jo, her migraine diminishing, went into the kitchen for a slice of bread and water. Someone had told her this would help her symptoms. Linda roused herself from her light sleep and joined Jo in the kitchen.

'Shall I put the kettle on?' Linda picked up the kettle and began to fill it from the tap.

'Go on then,' said Jo. 'Not supposed to have caffeine, but to tell you the truth, I always feel better after a cuppa.'

Linda laid out the fixings for two mugs of tea on the kitchen table and stood just as her mother did, leaning against the kitchen sink.

'Blimey Linda, you could be the dead spit of Mum like that. You look just like her.' Jo enjoyed the comparison and similarities.

Linda smiled. 'Do I?'

Jo nodded. 'Yep, you could be Mum. And you are as good as her, Lin.'

'Really—do you think so?' Linda's face lit up with a smile that radiated happiness.

'Pete doesn't know how lucky he is. Karl will when he grows up, just like we appreciate Mum and Dad. It's not 'til you get older, you understand what they did for us.'

'We are lucky. Pete's dad was a shit, by all accounts.'

'You thinking that's why he's like he is? Don't feel sorry for him, Lin.'

Linda warmed the teapot and put in the leaves before adding hot water. She brought the teapot to the table. 'How are you feeling?'

'Not too bad. I've got a pea rolling around in my brain, which is usually a sign it's on its way out.'

Linda screwed up her face in sympathy. 'Glad I don't get them.' She poured two mugs of tea.

Jo added milk and sugar to her cup and took a swig. 'Ah, nectar!'

Linda stirred in some milk and sat back from the table, both hands wrapped around her mug. A tear slipped down her cheek.

Jo placed her mug on the table and leaned forward, her forearms resting on the surface. 'What's the matter, Lin? Is it Pete?'

Linda shook her head.

'Karl?'

Linda didn't answer.

'Tell me, I haven't got a clue.'

'Just,' Linda gasped for breath, 'I feel safe here. I'm a rubbish mum to Karl. Pete says I'm always crying, and he's fed up with it.'

Jo shuffled her chair nearer her younger sister, placing a comforting arm around her sibling's shoulders. 'You don't have to go back.'

'That's what Mum said.'

'Well, there you are then. Stay here. I bet Mum and Dad will have you and Karl here in an instant.'

'Mum said I could have my old room back.'

'Come home, Lin. You'll be safe here. And more importantly, so will Karl.'

'I dunno.' Linda looked at the lino on the kitchen floor.

'All right for you and Terry, with your high-powered careers.'

Jo chuckled. 'It's not all jam, you know. Take this week, for instance. I had to interview some Lord's daughter for lesbianism.'

'How do you do that, Jo?' Linda stopped crying. Her curiosity pricked. She dabbed at her cheeks with her handkerchief before blowing her nose. 'Seriously, Jo, how can you?'

'What do you mean?'

'I'm not blind. You and Terry, you know,' she jerked her head up and to her right.

Jo observed her sister, watching for a clue that it was safe to confirm her sister's suspicions. 'What do you mean?'

'Jo.' This time, it was Linda's turn to comfort her sister by placing her hand on Jo's forearm. 'You two are obviously joined at the hip. By rights, both of you should be married—all those blokes and neither of you have had a boyfriend. You go everywhere together. You've always been as thick as thieves, you two. Why do you think I was jealous? I lost my older sister to her best friend. It was awful for me when Terry moved in.'

Jo opened her mouth, then shut it, tilting her head to one side. 'You…You resent Terry?'

'No, not exactly. But she was always your sister—your best friend. I was always left out. And then, you both go off and join the Army and leave me behind.'

Jo picked up her mug and sipped. Thoughts and emotions flirted with her lips but came to nothing as she realised the emotional toll her relationship with Terry had had on her sister. 'Terry's been interviewed by the SIB.'

'That's your lot, isn't it?'

Jo nodded.

'Did you, did you um…'

Jo nodded.

'No wonder you've got a migraine! Bloody hell, Jo, what're you going to do? Did she tell on you?'

'No, she didn't. She wouldn't. She just sat so confident.' Jo chuckled. 'Actually, she was so confident she pissed off Mark Armstrong. He nearly raped her. Nick and me had to pull him off her.'

'Blimey! She's tough—I'll give her that.'

'Yeah. I was shit. Nick did most of it. I felt so sick and so scared for her. It was awful. I kept thinking, what will Mum and Dad think if we're thrown out?'

'You've not been, though. Right?'

'No. Not yet anyway. But someone sent an anonymous note naming Terry.'

'When?'

'A couple of weeks ago.'

'Wow, and there's me thinking it's all beer and skittles for you two.'

'Hardly.'

'You know Mum and Dad might be shocked, but they wouldn't chuck you out or anything. That's the thing—they might be mad indoors, but none of us can do wrong to the rest of the world. I see it all the time. I know people talk about me and Pete. I see them talking behind their hands, staring at me or just plain avoiding me as if something I had was going to rub off on them. And Mum and Dad, they never say a thing. They hold their heads high and do what they can for me and Karl.'

Jo laughed. 'I know what you mean about something you've got might rub off on them. People worry about lesbians. They're worried that we'll corrupt their sisters or daughters.'

'They have a point, Jo.'

'No, Lin, they don't. You're either gay or you're not. You can't be straight and have a relationship with a woman. It just doesn't work that way.'

'How do you know, like, who is and who isn't?'

'You just know. Though its tough in the army, a lot of girls wear a black onyx signet ring on their little finger. It signals, well, usually, that they're one of us. I don't because I'd rather be private about things. My sex life is mine and nobody else's business.'

Linda laughed.

'What's so funny?'

'Blimey, what a pair we turned out to be, eh?'

'Yeah. You know, you don't have to stay with Pete. Terry and me, we'd support you. And you already know Mum and Dad will—just come back home.' Jo got up, taking her mug to the kitchen sink. 'Tell you what. Is Pete home now?'

'No.'

'Right, let's get yours and Karl's things, and from today, you are home and safe. I tell you, everyone will be pleased you're back under this roof. I know for a fact Dad will stop worrying. Come on, let's go now.'

Jo collected her car keys from the hook next to the back door.

## Chapter 43

Jo drove Linda from the Clark family home to Pete and Linda's house in a pensive silence.

'Turn down here, Jo.'

'You know I've never been to your house.'

'No, well, Pete only lets his mates come in.'

'Mum and Dad been here?'

'Once.'

'Once! That's it?'

'Yep. Mum has to wait outside. Park just here.' Linda tightened her limbs. 'Pete's car's here.'

'You can still do it, Linda. I'll come in and help.'

'No! That'll only make it worse. Thanks, Jo, but I'll have to stay now. I can't leave while he's here.'

'I can sort him out. We'll just tell him, and that's that. He can't make you stay.'

'Shut up! You don't know anything!' Linda registered the shock on Jo's face. 'Sorry. He just gets to me, that's all.'

'And…'

Linda held up a hand. 'I don't want to hear it. Thanks for the lift.' Linda got out of the car, gave a quick wave and dashed towards the front door. Just before she reached to put the key in the lock, Pete opened the door. He yanked Linda through the opening and slammed the door shut.

Jo looked at the street and observed net curtains twitching as she heard raised voices inside the house. She dithered between doing what Linda asked and what she thought was right. She opened the car door and put one foot on the road. Hearing a loud crash from inside the house, she withdrew her leg into the car. For a few minutes, she waited in case her sister emerged and needed rescuing. She started the engine and drove a few yards down the road. Panicked, she turned the car around and drew up outside the house once more, this time with the driver's side next to the pavement. The voices inside the house grew louder. A door slammed, then nothing. Jo wanted to knock on the door but feared she would make matters worse. She waited five minutes, and on hearing nothing more from the occupants, she drove away again into the countryside that joined Brentwood with Harold Hill. Driving on an autopilot, she thought about her sister; she couldn't leave her at Pete's mercy—she just couldn't. She turned the car around in the Nag's Head pub car park and headed back to her sister's house. As she turned into the road, she noticed a group of neighbours standing outside. She accelerated along the road, onto the pavement, and stomped on the brakes, bringing the car to a screeching halt outside. The neighbours stepped back.

'Anyone call the police?' Jo asked.

'No,' the neighbours chorused back.

'He is the police,' one woman shouted back.

For a moment, Jo thought about chastising them for their inaction and nosiness. She pulled out her warrant card. 'Military Police, step back! Please.'

The group shuffled backwards two or three paces. Jo pushed through them, jogged down the pathway, and banged on the door. 'Military Police! Open up!'

She rattled the windowpane in the middle of the door with her knuckles. 'Let her go, Pete. She needs to come home.'

Jo waited. Should she call for backup with the Met? No, that could be risky. She had interfered in a domestic dispute of non-military personnel. No, surely the Met would be okay with the fact it was her sister, and she was on scene.

'Linda, it's Jo. Grab your things and come home.' Jo shouted through the letterbox and then banged on the door with her fists before rattling a windowpane to the living room and then returning to look through the letterbox.

'You should break the door down,' suggested an onlooker. 'You don't know he could've killed her in there. You're taking your bleeding' time. Glad it ain't me.'

The crowd, growing in size, murmured their agreement.

Jo opened the letterbox again and shouted. 'Linda, it's me. Jo! Open the door.' She saw Linda hover in the hallway, Pete towering over her. 'One step at a time, Lin. You can do it.' Jo coached.

Pete stood in front of the letterbox, blocking Jo's view. 'Not so sharp now, eh, Sergeant Clark? She's staying here. Remember what I said? I know your dirty little secret.'

Jo spun round to see if the crowd had heard the exchange. She breathed a sigh of relief, realising that though they could hear Pete, they could not make out his words.

'Pete,' Jo said, 'Let her go, or I'll call the Met. If I have to do that, it won't go well for you.'

'Nor you Jo, because I'll tell them you're a lezzer. Linda! Tell her to mind her own business. You want to stay with me.'

A frail, frightened voice confirmed Pete's wishes.

'Let her go, Pete. This is your last warning!' Jo shouted back.

'Or what, Lezzer?'

'I'm going to ask one of the neighbours to call the police. I'll count to five.' Jo counted to four in a measured tone. Pete opened the front door on five, violently hurling Linda into the street so that she fell forward onto the cement pathway. She laid still.

'Take her. I don't want her or her shitty little kid. Take her! You'll be doing me a favour. She's a useless fuck of a wife and mother.' Pete slammed the door into its frame.

Jo knelt to help her sister, noticing blood pouring from a gash on her cheek. Her nose was crooked, probably broken, and her lip bled profusely. 'It's all right, Lin, I'm here.'

Tears flowed down Linda's face, snot was smeared on her cheeks, and some white powder clotted her hair. As she stood up, the blood streamed from her knees.

'I'll get you home, Lin, and we can fix you up there. Anything broken?'

'My nose really hurts, and I can't stop it from bleeding.'

Jo pulled out the large white handkerchief she had laundered and meant to return to Nick and gave it to her sister. Linda put it gently on her nose.

The front door opened again. Pete's angry energy burst through the opening before he threw a suitcase and some clothes at them. Leaving the door open, Jo waited for what was next—pulling Linda behind her up the garden path.

'And take this. I don't want to see you or your brat again.' He shoved the pushchair out of the door and over the step, sending it crashing into the bushes near the front door.

'Go to the car, Linda.' Jo ordered.

Linda hesitated.

'Now, Linda.'

Pete slammed the door for the final time.

Linda limped as fast as she could to Jo's car. Jo retrieved the pushchair from the bushes and wheeled it up the path. She loaded the stroller with the suitcase and clothes on the way, finally pushing through the crowd.

'He's a right bastard!' said a neighbour, to the agreement of the other onlookers.

Jo folded the pushchair and loaded it into the boot. She pushed the suitcase through the rear doors and onto the seat, throwing the clothes on top. Hurrying, Jo climbed into the car and drove away as fast as she had arrived. In the rearview mirror, she saw the crowd disperse to their homes.

'You okay? You're shaking. Not surprising. I'll get you home. You can have a bath and get cleaned up.'

'Karl,' Linda whispered.

'Where?'

'His Mum's. Gubbins Lane.'

Jo drove down the A12 at the speed limit, turning into Gubbins Lane and on past Harold Wood station.

'Here. Number 120.'

Jo parked outside and went to get out of the car. Linda caught Jo's arm.

'No, Jo, it has to be me. She has to see what her precious son has done to me. And she has to give me back my son.'

Jo watched, without taking a breath, as her sister limped up the white steps to the large house and knocked on a blue door. A middle-aged woman in a navy two-piece skirt suit opened the front door. A conversation with many gesticulations ensued. Jo, her patience wearing thin and her fear growing alongside it, got out of the car and walked to the front gate. Linda waved her away. Moments later, the woman handed Karl to Linda. Linda carried him to the car. Jo hovered over Linda like a guardian angel as she watched her sister secure her nephew in the seat. Twenty minutes later, they parked outside 24 Dell Close.

## Chapter 44

Dishevelled, Linda backed in through the Clark family's kitchen door, pulling the pushchair with her. She braced herself for everyone's reaction, expecting disapproval and hoping for love. She couldn't hide it any longer. She had married a wife-beater, and this time, Pete had done his worst. Her left eye was a vivid red, half closed, and her lip was bleeding. Her nose had finally stopped. Sylvia gasped the moment she saw her daughter. Terry bent her head, hiding a tear escaping from her right eye. Linda's gaze darted between her parents, a mixture of fear and despair. Her eyes begged for love and understanding. She tried to explain everything, but the words died in her throat.

'Pete,' she stammered.

Jo clumsily entered the kitchen behind Linda, dragging the suitcase and some clothes. Brian got out of his chair and wrapped a protective arm around his younger daughter, helping her to sit in the chair he had vacated. Jo steadied the suitcase against the kitchen wall and ran up the stairs to the bathroom to fetch the first aid kit. Sylvia put the kettle on while Terry played with Karl in his pushchair, trying hard not to show her emotions. Seconds later, Jo flew down the stairs and into the kitchen with the red box with the white cross on it.

Sylvia added some hot water to the Dettol, which she had poured into a small Tupperware bowl, and began cleaning her daughter's wounds while Brian made a rare pot of tea. 'What's this in your hair, love?' asked Sylvia.

'Vim.'

'Vim,' repeated Sylvia, unsure of how and why.

'He said I need to be scrubbed clean. He shook the container over me. Mum, I thought I was going to go blind. I shut my eyes…' Relieved, Linda finally let go of her emotions, her body shaking with violent sobs. Sylvia held her daughter tight against her breast.

Brian poured five mugs of tea, then stood behind them, his arms around them. 'Help yourselves, girls—milk and sugar on the table. Jo, get some brandy out of the cocktail cabinet. I think we could all do with a stiffener,' Brian said, his voice breaking with the sadness of his daughter's desperate situation.

Jo returned from the living room, placing glasses and brandy on the table. She poured two fingers into each glass before handing them around. Jo raised her glass. 'New beginnings.'

'New beginnings,' whispered Linda as she looked out of one eye. The other had now completely closed. Sylvia dabbed at the blood congealing around it with a cotton wool ball soaked in Dettol and warm water.

'Linda,' Jo said, 'What do you want to do?'

'Dad?' Linda exhaled with pain from her mother's care.

'Well,' Brian sighed, 'I don't think you can stay with him any longer. You've given it a good go. No one can say you didn't try. And, if you go back, I know your mother, and I would worry what might happen next and when.'

Sylvia picked up another cotton wool ball and placed it in the bowl of antiseptic. 'Your father's right. But it's your marriage and your life. We can only advise. Know this, Linda. This will always be your home, no matter what. And there is no shame in leaving a wife-beater. No shame at all.' Sylvia shook her head.

'Yeah. Everyone knows he's a shit. Copper or no Copper,' Jo said.

'Jo,' Linda said in a timid voice. 'I've had enough violence to last me for a lifetime. I don't need you adding to it. Mum, can I have a bath?'

Terry stood up and looked at Linda's nose. 'Linda, are you sure you don't want to go to hospital?'

'No, I want to stay here with you all.' She looked around at her family.

'Then I'm going to straighten your nose for you. It will hurt, and it might bleed. But if I don't, then…, let's just say you won't be as pretty. Are you ready?'

Linda nodded, closed her eyes, and tilted her head to Terry. Terry grasped Linda's nose and yanked it to the left. Linda howled, putting a hand to her face. Terry pulled Linda's hand away, checking she straightened Linda's nose.

'All good,' Terry wiped some blood off her hand.

'Mum, can I have a bath now?' Linda asked.

'Yes, love, you don't need to ask.' Sylvia helped her daughter up the stairs.

Jo shut the kitchen door and sat at the kitchen table. 'What're we gonna do, Dad?'

Brian and Jo exchanged a glance with Terry, considering the meaning of every word.

'I think,' he paused. 'We need to get her away from Pete for good,' he said firmly. 'She needs to be in a safe place, and so does Karl. It can't be right for the lad to witness this kind of violence.'

'Brian,' Terry said. 'We can't make that decision for her. If she's not on board, she could just as easily go back to him, and then it will be harder for her to leave him. The longer he controls her, breaking her confidence, the more difficult it will get. That's what my mum told me. So, we need to make sure when she's ready, we're ready.' 'Well, that's all well and good, but how do we do that?' Jo asked. I mean, she doesn't know whether she's coming or going right now. If you asked her today, she'd say she would leave him. But ask her tomorrow or next week, and she might change her mind.'

'I'll talk with your mother. We'll work something out.'

'Brian, I could talk to her. I could tell her about how my mum left us with my dad, only to come home and find him drunk and with my brother beaten to a pulp. You know the reason she stayed?'

Brian, struck by Terry calling him by his first name and then shocked at Terry recounting an experience she had never shared with them, spoke. 'Terry, you are my daughter, so always call me Dad. And, if you think it will help, talk to her. I need. No! She needs to know she and Karl will be safe here. That he can't touch her.'

'Why did your mum stay?' Jo asked.

'She said she stayed for us. Can you imagine? My brother and I half-starved. My brother beaten regularly to make him a man, or at least that's what my dad said. And me, neglected and whipped with the buckle end of his belt. She stayed for that!' Terry paused. 'I know the real reason, though. She had nowhere to go and no money, and what could she do when she had two kids? Whatever we do, Linda needs to know she will have money, a home, and she will be safe.'

And that she can start afresh,' Jo added.

'All in good time.' Brian patted Jo's thigh. 'First things first. I don't know about you girls, but I could use another brandy.'

Sylvia bathed Linda, starting with washing the Vim from her hair. Letting the blooded pink water mixed with the cleaner out through the plug hole. She placed a towel around her daughter before running fresh hot water.

Sylvia wanted to weep when she bathed her daughter's back. She knew she had to be strong, but she would never forget the deep red welts that covered most of Linda's back. Linda winced as her mother sponged the soap, cleaning the skin that had broken into open wounds.

Linda's breath became sharp as Sylvia tended to her.

'I'm sorry, love. I have to get it clean. We don't want an infection now, do we?'

Linda nodded.

Sylvia worked her way along her daughter's arms and then her legs. Pete had not neglected a single body part, inflicting his rage upon Linda's limbs, head, and torso.

'Mum? Where's Karl?'

'Downstairs with the rest of the family. Probably sleeping.'

'He hates Karl.'

'Mhmm.' Sylvia was desperate to point out how bad Pete was and that it was important that Linda left him. Everything to her was so obvious. She wanted to ask her daughter why she couldn't see what everyone else did, but her wisdom guided her to listen and not speak.

'What should I do, Mum?'

'Let's not think about that now. Come on, let's get you into bed. I'll send Jo up with some supper and some painkillers. Then, my girl, you need to sleep. We'll take care of Karl until you're ready and able to take care of him again. But for now, let us take care of you.' Sylvia let the second lot of bathwater out. Wrapping a fresh towel around Linda, Sylvia went into her bedroom and returned with a suitable nightie. 'Best I've got love. I know it's not your sort of thing. But it'll have to do until everything is sorted out. Now bed.'

Linda limped to her old bedroom. Pete had stomped on her right knee, and the swelling made walking difficult.

'Now, are you sure nothing's broken? We can take you to the hospital and get you checked out.'

'No, Mum.' Fear raised Linda's voice. 'They'll ask how I got this, and then I'll have to tell them and then Pete…'

Sylvia raised her hand and her voice. 'Bugger Pete! I'm only interested in my daughter. If you change your mind, we can go to the doctors'. Doctor Lakeland is sympathetic and diplomatic. She knows what goes on behind closed doors.' Sylvia pulled back the duvet for her daughter, and a ten-year-old

Linda slipped into her childhood bed. 'Right, I'll send Jo up. Then sleep, my girl.'

Sylvia entered the kitchen, and the family stood up as one.

'Mum?' Jo asked.

'There isn't a bone in that girl's body, that bugger hasn't beaten. I tell you, Brian, if I didn't think it would give him some kind of sadistic pleasure, I'd beat the living daylights out of him myself.'

Everyone was shocked at Sylvia's use of the word 'bugger'. She had always been particular about anyone swearing in the house. And at the same time, they knew she had to vent her anger somewhere safe.

'Tea or brandy?' Brian asked.

'Oh, tea,' Sylvia shook her head. 'Right now, she needs some food. I'd better cook her something. I said you'd take it up, Jo, with some painkillers.'

'I'll do it,' Terry got up. 'I'll do a cheese toasty. It's her favourite, and I'll talk to her.'

'Go gentle, Terry.' Sylvia thought for a moment. 'Just take her the cheese toasty. I don't think she's capable of listening or reasoning, let alone making a decision.' Sylvia rubbed her hands down her pinny. 'I know we all want her and Karl out of there and away from Pete, and we're anxious she decides as soon as. But we have to do it in Linda's time. And now is not the right time. She needs to rest and heal. When she wakes up tomorrow, she will hurt more emotionally and physically than today. And we all have to do our bit? Right?

## Chapter 45

*Sunday 6 May*

The Clark family, except for Linda, gathered around the kitchen table for breakfast and a family 'conflab'.

'Right, girls, your father and I talked last night. We must do our best to make sure Linda stays here.'

'She will need money and a room for her and Karl,' Terry said.

'We could move out of our room. It's bigger than hers, and we're hardly here,' Jo suggested.

'Yeah. Let's do that today,' agreed Terry.

Brian stood at the kitchen sink ready for action. 'Right, I'll help you girls get that all sorted. We'll have to move one of the beds into Linda's old room.

'No need, Dad. Not sure there's going to be that much room in there with two beds, anyway. One of us will sleep on the floor. It's only for one more night. Won't we, Terry?'

Terry nodded.

'Anyway, the quicker she settles here, the better.'

The family sipped their tea in unison.

'You sure?' Brian checked. 'I bet we can make it fit.'

'No, we're hardly here. At a push, one of us can sleep on the sofa if we have to. It'll do for now until Linda gets settled.'

'We could buy bunks, Mother?'

'We could.' Sylvia smiled. 'Karl would like that when he's older. But let's not rush into things. Linda needs to do this at her pace.'

Linda sidled in through the hallway door. 'Talking about me?'

'Yes, dear,' said Sylvia. 'If you'd like, Jo and Terry will move their stuff into your old room so you and Karl can have more space. At least if that's if you are planning to stay.'

The family held its breath.

'You'd do that for me and Karl?' Linda waited for Jo to change her mind.

'Of course we would. We want you and Karl to be safe,' Jo got up and offered Linda her seat.

Linda hugged Jo before sitting down. 'Thank you.'

'What's got into you girls with all this hugging thing?'

'Oh, Mum,' said Jo. 'People hug all the time.'

'Not where your dad and I come from, do we, Father?'

'No. But we must move with the times. We'll have to get modern Mother with a young boy in the house. Must say it will be good to have some backup!' Brian rubbed his hands together with a gleeful smile.

Terry shot Brian a warning glance. 'When do you want us to move our things into your room, Linda?'

'Can I have some breakfast and then do it?'

'What'll you have, love?' asked Sylvia.

'Bacon and eggs, Mum.'

'That's my girl—you need fattening up!' Sylvia lit the stove and got the frying pan ready. Brian left for the garden shed.

After lunch, Jo and Terry decided to take Karl to the park in Harold Wood. Jo parked near the tennis courts. Terry unloaded the pushchair and assembled it. Jo held a wriggling Karl and was glad to seat him in the stroller. Terry and Jo wheeled it along the pathway, passing the men playing cricket on freshly mown grass in the warm sunshine. Two umpires in white coats stood on the pitch, one by the wicket, the other in the field. Jo and Terry watched the bowler pound the turf to the wicket, swinging his arms in a windmill fashion before launching the red ball down the wicket to the readying batsman. Within seconds, a cry of 'Howzat' went up from the bowler and the fielding team. Jo and Terry walked toward the children's playground while the batsman returned to the pavilion.

'Do you think she'll stay?' Jo asked.

'Hope so. But as Dad says, 'there's nowt so queer as folk, except for thee and me'.'

'Talking of queer. I was planning on telling Mum and Dad about us this weekend.'

Terry stopped in her tracks, bringing Karl's stroller to a sudden halt. 'What?'

'I think it's best coming from us—don't you?'

'Yeah, but not now. Not this weekend.'

They neared the children's playground.

'Let's see if he likes the baby swings,' said Jo. She took him from the pushchair and popped his legs between the bars, pulling the bar across his body before gently pushing him into a rhythmic swing. Terry leaned against the metal poles of the swing frame. Karl thrilled and laughed at being swung.

'Why now?' asked Terry.

'Because I don't want the Army telling them. We might be out on our ears if things don't go well. And, frankly, I want a home to go to. Don't you?'

'Yeah, I would, but we can't tell them now, not with Linda.' Terry swung her body around the pole. 'Oh, look, monkey bars. I love monkey bars.' Terry dashed to the metal structure and began to swing from one bar to another with ease. Jo released Karl from his swing and put him back in the stroller before walking toward the monkey bars.

'Terry, we need to do this now. I don't know how this investigation into the anonymous note will go. Miss Hart might call you in again. And, who knows, there might be another note?'

'There won't be,' said Terry, hanging upside down, her knees gripping a bar.

'How can you be so sure?'

'Dunno, just know.'

'You know who sent the note?'

'No.'

'Well, how do you know there won't be another?'

'I don't, just don't think there will be.'

'Fuck Terry, you can't just shut your eyes to this.'

'Don't swear, Jo, not in front of Karl. Don't want him turning out like his father.'

'Talking of his father. Pete said he'd tell the MOD about us if Linda found out about him and his bit of fluff. And with Linda stopping at ours now, I wouldn't put it past him. So that's another reason we should tell them. By the way, I've already mentioned Pete to Miss Hart.'

Terry somersaulted off the monkey bars, landing with aplomb, facing Jo. 'Dix points,' said Terry, chuckling as she bent her knees, absorbing the impact of her landing. 'How did she react?'

'She said she'd look into it.'

'Seems like you've decided for us. You're going to tell them whatever I say.'

'Why are you so against it?'

'For one thing, they've got enough on their hands right now.'

Karl started grizzling.

'I think we should go home,' said Terry, taking over the stroller wheeling it to the car park. Jo walked beside her. 'Two, I don't think they'd let me stay with you at home.'

'We'll buy a house. We won't need to stay there.'

'Have you got a deposit?' Terry's arched eyebrows gave away her surprise.

'Some money, but you can get a hundred per cent mortgage linked to an endowment policy right now.'

Terry stopped. 'So, you've been making decisions for us without me.'

'No. Just thinking things through. We can get a mortgage. If not now, then soon. We have to save. RSM Gordon and Sarn't Major Hart, have one.'

'Yeah, but they're senior to us and about a hundred years old. Be reasonable. And what if we don't get a house, eh? We'll have told them, and then we can't be together, anyway.'

When Jo reached the car she unlocked the doors. Terry packed up the stroller and put it in the boot. Jo and Terry fought with Karl to get the right legs in the openings before strapping him into the booster seat.

'I think someone's tired,' Terry fastened the last strap.

'Yeah, tears before teatime. I know, Karl, I know. We'll get you home to mummy soon. Anyway, Mum wouldn't let Dad throw us out.' Jo started the car and headed toward Harold Hill.

'How do you know?'

'Because of what she said to Linda in the hairdressers. That children don't ask to come into this world and that good parents protect their children.'

'Yeah, well, they might just protect you from me. I'm pretty sure Brian won't be too happy.' Terry turned around to check on Karl. 'He's asleep. Must be the car engine. When are you going to tell them?'

'I thought tonight?'

'What about just before we leave on Monday afternoon?'

Jo thought for a moment. 'No, that's cowardly. It would be like telling and running.'

'Seems like a plan to me.'

'No, tonight, Terry.'

'What if it goes pear-shaped? I mean, Linda is always needling us?'

'She and I talked.' Jo pulled up alongside the kerb outside 24 Dell Close and turned off the ignition.

'And?' Terry prompted.

'She's okay with us. She was jealous of you, but she's okay with us. Really, she is.'

'Hmm. I can understand why. Well, we'll find out. But be prepared for some more screaming and crying this weekend. And be prepared to pack in a hurry if things go badly.'

## Chapter 46

After returning Karl to Linda, Jo and Terry went upstairs to freshen up before dinner.

'Bit cramped in here. Good job, Linda has our old room.' Jo sat on the bed.

'Yeah, about that—who is sleeping on the floor?'

'No one. Don't you see? We can sleep in the same bed, just like we always do. No one will know. And, if they catch us, we'll say that the floor got a bit hard, and we didn't want to wake anyone setting up a bed on the sofa.' Jo's smile was huge and self-satisfied.

'Right,' Terry's voice betrayed the fact she was unconvinced.

'I'm telling Mum and Dad at dinner.'

'Okay,' Terry sounded doubtful. 'I don't know how you can be so sure it will go well.'

The two women dressed in silence. Both their minds occupied by the events about to unfold.

'I don't want to ambush them. It needs to come naturally.'

'Okay. Can we eat first? I'm hungry. And I don't fancy leaving on an empty stomach,' Terry said.

'It's going to be fine.'

Terry nodded and opened the bedroom door. She touched Jo's upper arm. 'Whichever way it goes, we're together, right?'

It was Jo's turn to nod. 'No matter what.'

'Jo, no turning back. Remember, there's a chance they will ask me to leave.'

'Well, we'll see about that, won't we?'

Jo and Terry slid into their places at the kitchen table.

'Dining Table, you should know that by now.' Sylvia got the cutlery out of the drawer and gave it to Jo and Terry. 'And you can both help me by laying the table.'

Jo and Terry set the dining room table.

Linda was already seated at the table, having put on the tablecloth and table mats on the table. She was struggling to keep Karl from crying. 'Nice afternoon? In the park.'

'Mmm.' Jo murmured.

Linda studied her sister. 'Trouble?'

'Nope.'

Brian joined Linda at the table, rustling his newspaper. He turned to the back page to see how his beloved Manchester United had performed on Saturday.

Sylvia came in bringing a tray with plated meals of roast beef and all the trimmings.

'Oh great, Yorkshires! I'm starving.' Terry picked up her knife and fork.

Sylvia returned to the kitchen for the remaining two meals. 'When are you two not starving? Eat up, everyone. It's Sunday Roast—not like you lot to hesitate.' Sylvia smiled at her family, gathered under one roof, eating the meal she had prepared with love.

'We were waiting for you, Mum, seeing as we've gone all posh,' Jo said.

'It's not posh Jo, it's practical. Especially now we are five adults, and Karl needs to learn how to eat properly, doesn't he Linda?'

'Yes, Mum.'

As the family ate together, sounds of appreciation accompanied by words of gratitude were bestowed upon the cook. Jo was the first to place her knife and fork in the finished position. She fidgeted in her chair.

'What's with you?' Brian asked. 'You ate that quickly. Got ants in your pants? Something you need to tell us?'

'Linda,' Jo said. 'Can you take baby Karl out for a walk or something? I need to talk to Mum 'n' Dad.'

'Jo,' whispered Linda. 'I think you might need me.'

'Why would she need you? What've you done, Jo?' Sylvia asked.

'Nothing, Mum, I swear.'

'Well, you look guilty.'

'Not guilty, Mum. I've nothing to be guilty about.'

'Well, you look shifty then,' Sylvia disapproved.

Terry looked at Jo from underneath her eyebrows as she scrapped the last bit of gravy onto a roast potato. Brian placed his knife and fork at twelve o'clock.

'That was lovely, Mother. A cuppa will finish it just nicely.'

'I've got Jo and Terry's favourite for dessert.'

'What! Lemon meringue pie?' Brian grinned.

'I'll get it,' said Jo. 'Cream or ice cream?'

'Both!' shouted Linda.

Sylvia cut the pie into five equal pieces and one smaller piece for Karl. Plates were handed around the table, and Linda attempted to feed Karl, who thrust the spoon away from him.

'Doesn't like it, Mum. Probably the lemon.'

'Just give him ice cream then, love. Don't force it on him.'

'That was lovely, Mum. Thank you.' Jo paused. 'So, what I wanted to say—was.'

'Tea for everyone?' Terry got and collected the plates.

Everyone murmured their agreement.

'Well, get on with it. Can't be that big a thing,' Sylvia handed her plate to Terry.

'I'll wait for Terry to come back,' Jo said.

The family sat in silence, except for Karl, who cooed as he played with the ice cream, teasing his mother by offering her the spoon and then eating it himself, followed by a hearty chuckle.

Terry returned from the kitchen with a tray carrying mugs, a teapot, sugar and milk. She looked at Jo, who shook her head. Terry sighed as she sat down.

'Well, you obviously know all about this, Terry.' Sylvia's irritation was growing with the wait.

'There's no easy way to say this.' Jo looked at her father and then her mother. 'We're a couple, Mum, me and Terry.'

Brian stared at his elder daughter. 'A couple of what?' asked Brian.

'A couple, Dad—like you and Mum.'

'Is that right?' Brian said.

'Yes, Dad.' Jo watched sadness slowly crease her father's face. For a moment, she thought he was going to cry.

'Right, I'm off to the shed. See what you can find out, Mother.'

Jo watched her father leave the room, his head drooping as he walked.

'What do you mean, you're a couple?' Sylvia accused.

'I'm sorry, Mum. I know that's not what you wanted to hear.'

'No, Jo. It's not what I wanted to know.'

'But you must've known.' Jo's exasperation struck an unwelcome chord.

'It's one thing to know and another to be told and have it all confirmed. Now, I can't deny it without lying, can I? Sometimes, Josephine, you just don't think.' Sylvia got up. 'And your thoughtlessness has upset your father. A man who has loved you all his life and has given up things so you could all have new shoes or clothes when he went without. And that's how you repay him—us?'

Terry pushed back her chair and looked at the floor. 'I'm sorry, Mrs Clark.'

'No, wait, Mum, please sit down. I can explain.' Jo fidgeted in her chair.

Sylvia sat down. Linda attempted to pour another mug of tea from the pot. A trickle of thick brown liquid hardly filled the cup. 'I'll make another pot,' said Linda, leaving for the kitchen.

'Well, I suppose I have to ask.'

'What, Mum, anything?'

'How long've you two known?'

'I dunno, Mum, sort of forever, really.'

'Mhmm.' I guessed you were close. And I suppose deep down I always knew about you, Jo. A mother may not want to see things, but she knows.'

Linda returned with a fresh pot and poured everyone a refill and sat down. 'Dad's still in his shed.'

'S'pect he'll be in there 'til bedtime, love.' Sylvia placed a hand on her daughter's forearm, sipping her tea, a tear seeping into her right eye.

'Don't cry, Mum, it'll be all right.' Jo placed a hand on her mother's.

'It won't be all right, Jo. I don't know how you can think that. You'll never be able to get married, and I will never have your grandchildren. I don't think you know what that means to a mother.' Sylvia dabbed her eye dry. 'Well,' she smoothed her pinny, 'We all need to take care of your father. I'll talk to him, but tread carefully. Especially you, Jo. You're the apple of his eye, his little princess.'

'Princess!' Jo scoffed. 'He never said.'

'No, well, you know your father is a man of few words. But he's sensitive.'

'What? Dad? Never!'

'How little you know about your father. He may be a bluff

Yorkshireman, but he is as soft as butter underneath it all.'

Guilt struck Jo's heart—it didn't bleed—it haemorrhaged. Tears welled in her eyes. She pulled a handkerchief from her jeans pocket and blew her nose. Terry took hold of Jo's other hand and squeezed it.

'No matter what, Jo.'

Sylvia smiled. 'I hope you two girls know what you're doing. It's a hard life, and most lesbians end up suicidal or alcoholics. It will be hard to keep a job if people find out. You will have to live a life of lies, and that'll be hard.'

'Mum? Are you ashamed of me?'

Sylvia stood up and hugged her daughter. 'Never love. You're always my girl.' She placed an arm around Terry. 'You too, Terry. In fact, you're all my girls. Come here, Linda, and let's have a hug.'

'A hug, now is it, Mum?' Linda giggled. 'I thought only the continentals did that.'

Sylvia laughed. A loud slam of the back door to the kitchen ended the first few moments of ease with their new situation.

Brian came through the door—a small garden fork in his hand that he waved around as he talked. 'What I want to know is what brought this on?'

Jo looked up. 'What brought what on, Dad?'

'You telling us. You could've kept it between yourselves. We would've been better off not knowing.'

'Sit down, Dad.' Jo waited. 'The Army.'

'They found out about you two, then?'

'Don't know. There's been an anonymous tip-off. I'm fairly sure we're going to be investigated.'

'What the hell does that mean?'

'They just talk to us, that's all. See if they can prove we're gay.'

'Very far from gay, lass—you're bloody queer as far as I can see. And, for that matter, the Army thinks the same.'

'Dad, there's lots of women like us?'

'All of 'em?' Brian's eyes widened at the new fact.

'No, about the same as in civvy street.'

'Well, bloody hell! How many is that, then?'

'About ten per cent.'

'Fuck the bloody ten per cent. What's going to happen to you two?'

Brian's voice betrayed his panic.

'Nothing, Dad. Me and Terry are fine. But we wanted you to know before anything happened.'

'So, you're planning for the worst, then?' Brian paced the length of the living room, his fork shovelling fresh air. 'I don't know, Mother, we have a lesbian shacked up with a girl we brought into our house as a favour and a daughter whose husband beats and cheats on her. What kind of father does that make me? Where did I go wrong?' His voice cracked. Tears streamed down his face. He searched for a handkerchief in his trouser pocket and left the room. His footsteps pounded the stairs and along the landing to the master bedroom.

Jo wept silently. The chaos she had created by simply stating her sexuality had revealed her parents' love and fear for her. A profound appreciation for them swept through her.

'Shall I go after him?' Jo asked Sylvia.

'No love, leave him be.'

After a few moments of awkward conversation between the Clark women, Sylvia went upstairs to comfort her husband. He was sitting on the edge of the bed, dabbing his face with a large white handkerchief. The small fork cast aside. Sylvia sat beside him, placing a hand on his thigh. Minutes passed without sharing their thoughts, looking out the bay window, watching mothers pushing prams and couples out for an evening stroll or a short walk to the local pub.

'Where did we go wrong, Mother?'

'I don't think we went wrong. I think the world has changed,' Sylvia sighed.

'We can look after Linda, but our Jo. Well, that's a whole different kettle of fish. I mean, divorce has become more acceptable, but lesbians. Our daughter is a lesbian. How will I protect her from what people say and do to them?'

'What do you mean, Brian? I don't think people 'do' anything to lesbians, do they?'

'She could lose her job. And the church won't accept her.'

'We don't go to church. And Jo knows what she's doing. Do you think, for one minute, she's the only lesbian in The Army?'

'No, suppose not. But people will gossip and the shame.'

'Brian, people gossip already about our Linda and her excuse for a husband. We're still alive and kicking. If anything, we must ensure that Jo and Terry know they can always come back home and will be safe here, whatever happens to them.'

I'd rather she'd have been pregnant. I could stand that. This way, I've no grandkids from my eldest.'

'Well, we have Linda for that. Jo will do well. She's a chip off her father's block. Confident and very clever. She'll be fine. Now, don't worry. The most important thing is to support her and Terry. If we show our support, the neighbours will be less likely to give them a hard time.'

Brian nodded, then chuckled. 'So, do I have two daughters? Is one a son-in-law? Or what?'

'I think the correct term is partners. And I don't think it will do us any good speculating beyond that. We have always treated them as part of the family, and I don't see any need for that to change. Now, go and tell Jo it's all okay.'

Brian shoved his handkerchief back in his pocket, grinning at his wife before leaving the bedroom. Sylvia hovered at the top of the stairs, ready to eavesdrop as she watched Brian push open the living room door.

'Jo.' Brian sat down on the sofa next to his daughter. 'Dry your eyes. I was just shocked, that's all.'

'Dad. I'm sorry.'

He placed an arm around her shoulders. 'No, sorry needed. Was it something I did or said that made you queer?'

'Gosh, no, Dad!' Jo pulled away from her father to make better eye contact to reassure him before cuddling into him again.

'Good. And your mother and I have talked, and we're here for you both. If something terrible happens, I want to know about it, and it won't matter what it is. I'm here to protect you. Remember, your mother and I chose to have you, and we love you. Not that I'd rather you weren't queer an' all that.'

'Not queer, Dad,' Jo said gently. 'It's gay.'

'Nothing bloody gay about it. But if you insist.' Brian grinned. 'We all right then?'

'Yeah, course. One thing you should know.'

Brian braced himself for further revelations.

'You know you said, was there anything you or Mum had said or done that might've made me gay?'

'Yes,' Brian answered with caution.

'Well, Mum always said I would never find a man as good as my father.'

Brian looked at her quizzically.

'And she's right, Dad. No one can match you.' Jo kissed him on the cheek. 'Now, I think it'd be better if me and Terry go back to barracks. I've got a bit of a tough week ahead of me.'

'Not before you two girls help me with that bloody pond!'

## Chapter 47

*Bank Holiday Monday 7 May*

Terry snuggled into Jo as they lay in Linda's old twin bed. The couple relished that they could now enjoy a lie-in without worrying about who might catch them alone in what some might consider a compromising situation.

'It's very pink in here. Terry glanced around the room. 'Never really noticed before.'

'That's our Linda for you.'

A knock on the door made them sit up.

'Cuppa?' Linda carried in two mugs.

'Blimey, room service,' Jo smiled. 'What've we done to deserve that?'

'Nothing yet. Dad wants you up so you can dig the pond.'

Jo and Terry groaned.

'Mum says breakfast will be ready in five.'

Linda left the mugs on the bedside cabinet. Terry passed one to Jo.

'Well, that didn't go too badly. First morning and all that. Do you think Linda's staying?' Terry sipped her tea.

'Dunno. Maybe. Hope so. I'll go in the bathroom first. The smell of bacon is killing me.'

Jo, down first, went into the kitchen.

'Breakfast in here?' Jo asked Sylvia.

'Yes, your father's eaten. I'm doing brekkie in shifts this morning. Your dad wants to be finished by this afternoon before you girls leave. What time are you going back?'

'Dunno, when the ponds finished?'

'God knows when that'll be. He's been digging since Easter!'

Sylvia heard the front doorbell. 'That'll be his fibreglass thingy. I'll tell the man to send it round the back. Jo, go and tell your father.'

Jo stepped out into the spring morning sunshine.

'Dad… ponds here.'

Brian gave a little skip and hurried to the back gate and out to the delivery man. Terry came out of the back door.

'Ponds here,' Jo pointed to the roadway.

'I know. Should we go and help?'

Jo and Terry walked along the side of the house. The delivery man and her father were unloading a shaped fibreglass mould.

Jo laughed. 'Blimey, Dad, how big is it?'

'Twenty-six feet.'

'You'll never get it in, Dad.'

'Oh yes, I will. Now stop jawing and help.'

Terry and Jo added much-needed muscle to pull the pond liner from the lorry. Terry suggested placing it on the ground, each taking a portion of the irregularly shaped pond, which meant the weight was awkward and uneven. With much groaning, the group reached the back garden gate.

'Not going to get it through there, governor,' said the delivery man.

'Carry it over our heads,' Terry suggested.

'Need strong men for that,' advised the delivery man.

'You've not seen my daughters, have you? Right girls, show the man how it's done. Get on the other end, mate.'

Jo, Terry, and Brian heaved the pond above their heads. The delivery man reluctantly went along with the plan.

'Follow my lead,' Terry said. 'Now lift it higher—it's got to go over the gateposts. No, higher.'

Every arm strained, holding the awkward shape over their heads.

'Through,' Jo said.

'And down,' Terry placed her section on the ground.

'Gently,' Brian beamed with pleasure at the makings of his pond. 'Told you my daughters could do it.' Pride filled his voice and his smile.

'Yeah. They certainly helped. Right. Sign here, and I'll be off.'

Brian squiggled his signature and shut the back gate after the delivery man before sitting in his garden chair. 'I think tea is in order, girls—what do you think?'

Terry and Jo joined Sylvia and Linda in the kitchen.

'He wants tea,' Jo jerked her head at her father in the garden admiring his pond liner.

'He always wants tea,' said Sylvia. 'It's a wonder anything ever gets done 'round here.' She laughed, 'But it does. It does. Linda and I'll bring out the tea and biscuits for you. You better get digging. Otherwise, you'll never leave tonight.'

Jo and Terry returned to the garden. Brian gave his orders, and Jo and

Terry began to finish the hole Brian had been working on every weekend since Easter. Terry stopped after a couple of shovels.

'Jo, let's get the pond where it needs to be. Then, mark it out with a soil trail, then dig. Dad, help us move the pond to where you want it.'

The morning was spent measuring, re-measuring, digging, and some more digging until they finally had the right shape and depth.

'Sand's next,' Brian picked up his spade.

Brian shovelled the sand into the hole, and Terry, with Jo's help, smoothed it into the shape of the mould. After that, Sylvia and Linda were co-opted to lift the pond and place it into the ground under Brian's guidance.

Brian stood back to admire his new pond. 'Right water, that's what we need. Grab the hose, Jo, and let's get going. I have to put this special chemical in to make the water habitable for the plants and the fish.'

Jo followed her father's orders, leaving the hose in the pond to fill while they all stopped for lunch.

Once the pond was filled, Brian decided they should go to the aquatic shop a mile away and choose a fish and some plants. In two cars, the Clark family drove to a shop Brian had often been to, so he already knew the rocks, plants, and fish he wanted.

The Clark women, Linda pushing Karl in his stroller, perused the range of fish and plants. Everyone chose a fish, which the shop owner placed in a plastic bag. Sylvia carried the selected plants in a polystyrene tray. Brian put the fish in their plastic bags and placed them into a plastic tub he had prepared earlier. Jo and Terry loaded the rocks into the cars to distribute the weight evenly. Brian was more animated than anyone had ever seen him. When they got home, everyone helped unload the car. Brian was in his element, placing rocks and plants just so. Sylvia occasionally winked at the girls when she saw how happy he was.

'Right, now for the big test, do we have the right PH Levels for the fish? Fingers crossed, or they must wait in their bags 'til another day,' declared Brian, bending down and scooping some water into a test tube, then dipping a strip of paper into the tube. After removing the test strip, he checked the colour against a chart.

'Blast! It's one out. Can't do it, girls. Sorry. After all your hard work,' Brian sighed.

'Try it, Dad, don't think the fish will die,' Terry said.

'I dunno, lass. Lot of money wasted if they do.'

'Tell you what, Dad, I'll pay for another lot if they do. Come on. I want to see what all that hard work has been for.'

Brian hesitated.

Jo grabbed the plastic tub. 'Come on, Dad, do the honours.'

Brian needed little encouragement. He opened each bag one by one and watched as goldfish, guppies and ghost carp swum to the nearest rock or plant to hide. The family stood around the pond, disappointed.

'I know, feed them.' Terry's excitement was obvious.

Brian scattered some flakes of fish food on the surface of the water. Soon, the fish were feasting at the surface before darting to the safety of the rocks and plants.

'Well, girls, thank you for all your help. You know we should celebrate, wet the baby's head like.' Brian hurried into the kitchen and brought out some cans of lager.

'Right, let's celebrate. We have the first pond in the neighbourhood. That's something—right?'

The family raised their tins and swigged. As they enjoyed the impromptu celebration, Bob, the next-door neighbour, popped his head over the wooden fence. 'All right there, Brian? Got it done?'

'Aye, Aye, got it done.' Brian's grin of triumph told the whole story.

'All right, if me and Viv come over and have a look.'

'Yeah, sure. Want a beer?'.

'Thanks. We'll be right over.'

Moments later, Bob and Viv stood with Brian and the family, congratulating Brian on his new hobby.

'Well,' said Viv. 'When I saw the size of that pond, I thought to myself, they'll never get that done. And you two girls, well, you dug that hole like a coupla blokes. I dunno that Army training must be something.'

Brian stiffened, and his smile waned as he sipped. 'My girls are strong and aren't afraid of hard work.'

'So, Jo.' Viv began her enquiry. 'Haven't seen any boyfriends.' She gave a knowing look to Sylvia.

Jo was unsure how to respond.

'She's concentrating on getting another promotion,' Sylvia said.

'Oh. And I see, Linda, you're back home again.' There was no mistaking the viciousness in Viv's voice.

Brian stood beside Sylvia, placing his arms around his wife's shoulders. 'And you know what, Viv? We couldn't be happier. We have Linda back home with our grandson. And my two daughters will go back to their great careers later this evening. Right girls, best get in and get you packed. See you, Bob.'

Brian, having dismissed Bob, led the family back in through the kitchen door. Bob and Viv left their unfinished cans on a stone at the pond's edge and returned to their house. Brian made sure the back door was shut.

'What the effing hell! She's a nasty one, that Viv!' Brian shouted, shaking his head.

Sylvia placed a hand on her husband's shoulder. 'Never mind—it's all done and dusted now. She said what she came to say.'

'Dad, you, your pond and us will be the gossip until it's fish-wrap.' Linda hugged her father to calm him. 'And none of us care. We're Clarks, and family comes first.'

'That's true, Dad. One day, though, it won't matter. And she'll still be a lonely, bitter, barren woman. Who always thinks she knows best,' Jo said.

'Enough, Jo!' Sylvia changed her tone. 'I know Viv wanted kids—she just can't have them. And that's hard. But you're right. We always stick together through thick and thin. Not even if your Pete comes knocking on the door begging you to come home, Linda.'

'I'm never going back to him, Mum.'

'Thank God, Linda. I thought I would have to go and beat the bastard up myself,' Jo said.

Linda laughed. 'Well, that's a nice, responsible response, Jo. Can always guarantee you act before you think! But I shan't be requiring your services.'

'Promise me you'll never go back to him. Not under any circumstances.'

Linda hugged Jo. 'I promise. But only if you promise me that you two will always be there for me whatever happens.'

'No matter what,' Jo and Terry chorused.

'Right, best we get back before it gets too busy on the roads. Dad, keep us posted on the fish, won't you?' Jo asked.

'Aye, girls, I will, and if anyone gives you any trouble in that Army, you come straight home, do you hear me?'

'Yes, Dad,' Jo and Terry sang their response and rolled their eyes.

## Chapter 48

*Day Nine. 12 Company WRAC, Inglis Barracks, Mill Hill, London.*

Jo sat at the back of the interrogation room. The memory of the weekend made her smile. She had finally found the courage at twenty-five years of age to tell her parents she was gay. It had gone better than she had hoped. Why had she waited so long? Viv's sly comments, though unwelcome, helped the family stand united while coming to grips with the significant changes to the Clark family structure. Jo sighed her relief at Linda's decision to return home and keep Karl safe.

Nick came into the room. 'You look happy. Good weekend?'

'Yes 'n' no.'

Nick rolled his eyes. 'Do I need to know the details?'

'Nope.'

'Thank God.' Nick cocked his ear, then in a mocking tone. 'I hear our lady and mistress coming. Stand by your beds.'

Sergeant Major Hart's heels struck a 2/4 beat as she marched up the corridor. Jo and Nick stood up when she entered, exaggerating standing to attention and then with their stiffened bodies, knocking each other to the side before laughing.

'Very funny.' Hart closed the door. 'Obviously, you both had a great weekend. That's good because we have a job to plan this week.'

The two detectives sat around the table listening to Hart's briefing for the surveillance of Corporal Quade at The Gateways Club during the coming weekend.

'So, you will need to sign for an unmarked car. I don't care who drives—just don't prang it. The idea is to arrive before she does, watch, record and photograph her going into the club. And then again when she leaves. You do not and should not go into the club in any circumstances. We don't need a showdown, and you haven't got back up.'

Jo and Nick nodded.

'Easy does it and slowly, slowly catchee monkey. I'm looking forward to giving this young woman the boot.' Hart rubbed her hands together. 'And not a word to anyone. Loose lips sink ships; walls have ears and all that—right?'

'Yes, Sarn't Major,' chorused Jo and Nick.

'Okay, finish up the last interviews and the paperwork. I think we can leave Twelve Company today. And I know this sounds weird, but let's hope we're back next week. I'll let the OC know the good news that we're leaving. I'm not briefing her about the surveillance, just in case, and that means she thinks today will be our last day. See you at lunch, Jo?'

'Yes, ma'am.'

## Chapter 49

*Day Ten. The London Provost Company, Rochester Row Barracks, London.*

Jo went into the main office early. She had not enjoyed the banter of the all-male RMP senior ranks at breakfast. She realised that one of the silver linings of the cloud that hung over the investigation at 12 Company WRAC had been the all-female mess. The contrast between male and female messes could not have been sharper in Jo's mind. The London Provost Company's Senior Ranks Mess was all male except for herself and Carol Hart, and that meant the banter was usually full of sexual innuendo and always competitive. She never understood the need to make sure one's colleagues, with whom you needed to collaborate professionally, were verbally abused to the point of denigration. And, to achieve that, one insults the other based upon behavioural observations that are then lampooned with a smidgen of contempt, giving those who possess a sharper and perhaps nastier wit a positive advantage. Jo had noted that those with a quicker wit were usually not the most competent of soldiers. Whereas in the female mess, banter was almost non-existent because there was no need to demean your fellow soldier. In fact, no advantage was sought through conversation. Jo thought it collegial and relaxing, even if the talk of Bingo at the local church and fashion had bored her.

Jo picked up the first handwritten report she had to type from the top of her In-Tray. She placed it to her left and inserted the blank, beige-coloured form into the carriage before setting it. Something pricked her curiosity, leaving the blank report in the typewriter. Jo got up and walked to Susan's office. Before opening the door, she checked that no one had slipped into the office unnoticed, then knocked on the door. She had an excuse ready but didn't need it. She tip-toed to the block of small drawers containing the catalogue and, once again, checked for her details and then for Terry's—she found nothing.

A surge of inquisitiveness spurred her to research Corporal Dart. There was the card with the blue dot. She crossed the room and pulled out the P file. A single report, the one Nick had typed, was fastened inside it. With little to no more information than she had gleaned some weeks back, she considered who else's file she might peruse. Jo rechecked the office, and, secure in the knowledge that she was alone, she went to the drawer marked TA-TR. She located Sergeant Treacher's card and noted the blue dot. Crossing the office once again, she pulled out the corresponding P file. It was fat, containing numerous well-thumbed, tatty A4 pages, some typed and some handwritten.

Jo stood reading, absorbed by the mine of sordid information contained within. As she skimmed the pages, she made mental notes of key pieces of information. First, Treacher, when she had been a Private, was named as a possible lesbian. However, her Platoon Commander had put in a good word for, and the matter was now considered moot, mere lines on a page. But Susan had kept them, regardless of the fact that the case had been closed, and the closing paragraph said the document should have been destroyed in 1978, yet it was still there. Had Susan been lax? Or was there some other reason? Three years later, as a Corporal, Treacher was interviewed at 3 Company WRAC in Aldershot about a relationship thought to be with someone senior to Treacher, who remained unidentified. The matter was dismissed again, this time through the ministrations of her Second-in-command. Deep in thought, she was unaware that Susan had opened the door. Jo jumped when Susan greeted her.

'Morning Jo. How's things? Glad to be back? Can I help you with anything?'

'No, not right now. Maybe later.' Jo replaced the file. 'Thanks, Susan.'

'Close the door, will you, Jo? Got some sneaky, beaky stuff to do.'

Jo obliged. Susan retrieved Treacher's file, flicked through it, filing it correctly before crossing the room to her desk and making a call.

Jo knocked on Sergeant Major Hart's door. 'Good morning, ma'am. May I close the door?' Jo shut it without permission. 'I had a hunch, so I checked out a file.'

'And whose file would that be?'

'Sergeant Treacher's. She reported Terry's and mine's leave addresses because they were the same. Yet neither Terry nor I have a file.'

'Mhmm. Well, that would be because you haven't been interviewed or been named. I read that report. It was left for me to judge how we might use that information. As you know, Terry refused to help us, and so the information gave us nothing. However, a conversation between you and me clarified the matter when you explained how your family had adopted Terry.'

'No, not adopted exactly. My parents took her in,' Jo said. That would make what we have weird.

'I stand corrected.'

'But what I don't understand is…'

Hart raised her hand. 'Are you sure you want this conversation, Jo? Think carefully before you ask something you might later regret.'

Jo thought for a moment. Curiosity fought wisdom. She was sure something was amiss. She knew Hart knew something. Did she have their files? Why? What would she do with them?

Jo was about to speak.

'Careful. Think carefully, Jo.'

'Mmm. I was thinking?'

'Yes…'

'Does Sergeant Treacher know about Terry as my sister?'

'I don't think most people know. Why should they? You don't share a last name. Is it something you shared during basic training at Guildford or any other posting?'

'No.'

'So?'

'Well, I'm thinking, did Sergeant Treacher know you did nothing with the information she furnished?'

'I didn't do nothing, Jo. You gave me the information, remember? And I made a judgement call.'

'Yes, of course, ma'am. But if she didn't know you had looked into the matter and concluded there was nothing to follow up on, she could be behind the anonymous note. You know she was unsatisfied because you hadn't taken her seriously. It's a motive.' Jo sat back in her seat, relieved she had unburdened her thoughts to her superior.

Hart leaned back in her chair and rubbed her chin while looking at Jo.

'I've seen her read The Times in the mess,' added Jo.

'My instincts tell me that's not the case.'

'Why not?' Jo was indignant because she was sure she had found the culprit. 'She's been named several times and got off every single time. Whose arse has she crawled up now?'

'I hope you don't mean that literally.' Hart guffawed.

'I suppose I do,' Jo said, irritated her hypothesis was considered meritless. 'Have you ever seen her with Major Marwood? She's brown-nosing with her the whole time.'

'That's quite an accusation. If it were to get out that we considered Sarn't Treacher to be the author of the note, that would be bad. But if we were wrong, that would be worse still. And think of the implications if we were to name Major Marwood in all of this. Because I think you are suggesting that Sarn't Treacher is having a relationship with her OC.' Hart leaned as far forward across her desk as possible, encouraging Jo to meet her halfway. 'That would be career suicide. One doesn't accuse an officer of such an offence without having all the cards stacked in their favour. And Major Marwood is considered to have a bright future. Could even reach Brigadier if she passes Staff college, and she is expected to do so with flying colours.'

'But,' Jo said. 'I've caught her visiting the OC's flat not just once, but twice.'

'Shopping'

'That's a bloody lot of shopping. And she's right nasty when you challenge her.'

Hart sat back and rubbed her chin. 'I know. I did the same thing. She had a bit of a chip on her shoulder about it. So, let me get this straight. You think the OC and Sarn't Treacher, are having a relationship? And why would she write the anonymous note?'

'Simple,' said Jo. 'The OC must pass her fitness test to attend Staff College. And Terry told me she can't pass it. So…'

'So, you think Sergeant Treacher wrote the anonymous note on behalf of or to protect the OC?' Hart fiddled with her earlobe. 'Possible. Not impossible, either, but my guess is the OC doesn't know a thing about it. After all, she brought it to our attention.'

'Exactly! That's what I'm saying. Sarn't Treacher has a track record of having relationships with people senior to her for whatever reason, and she gets off. Maybe this time she's overstepped the mark?'

'Fair point. But the only way we prove it is if either Sarn't Treacher confesses or we interview the OC, and that's not going to happen unless I get further evidence that is unshakeable. Without that, any move would be career-limiting, and I don't want that at my age and with my seniority. I need to protect my pension. So, unless Jo, you can come up with more than a hunch, that's it. I'll see what I can dig up with Kirsty, but I don't think anything will surface.'

Jo got up to leave. 'I know, but I'm right. I know I am. Sarn't Treacher is mixed up in this somehow.'

## Chapter 50

*Saturday 12 May 1984*

At 20:00 hours, Jo and Nick dressed casually and went to the Motor Transport (MT) shed to sign out an unmarked car. The tubby MT Sergeant, clad in lightweight trousers and combat jacket, his blue beret squared on his head, inspected the car with Nick.

'Sign 'ere an' she's all yours. Don't fucking prang it!' The MT Sergeant warned.

'This is nice,' Nick ran his hand along the silver wing of the Ford Granada Ghia 3.0 V6. 'I'll drive.'

'I want to drive,' Jo said. 'You only want to drive so you can imagine you're in The Sweeney.'

'It's the same car.' Excitement lit up Nick's eyes.

'I know. Don't be getting any ideas.'

Nick unlocked the doors and climbed into the driver's seat. 'It's for the best. You never know—you might need to go in the club, so it's best if I stay in the driver's seat.'

Jo secured her seat belt. 'Orders are not to go into the club, remember? No backup.'

Nick caressed the steering wheel while inspecting the dashboard.

'Lots of room.' Jo stretched out her legs. 'Nice leather. Blimey Nick, we'll be in serious trouble if we scratch this.'

Nick drove slowly out of the barracks and edged into the Saturday night traffic. 'Never going to find out what she can do in this traffic. It's terrible.'

'If things don't clear up, we might miss Quade. What if she goes to another club?'

'Patience. We'll get her.'

'Yeah, but we won't know if she's in there already because we got there too late. The idea was to catch her going in.'

'If we don't see her, we don't see her. That's all there is to it,' Nick reasoned.

Jo shook her head. 'No, we need to get her. We only get one shot at this, and she needs to be discharged. She's the reason Lizzie is dead, and I owe

Lizzie. And I bet she wrote the note. '

'Blimey Jo, let the note go. Anyway, I thought you said it was Treacher. You keep changing your mind. You're beginning to sound desperate.'

'I am desperate. Nick, we've got one crack at this, and I must get her. I don't care how, as long as it sticks and it's legal. Anyway, you need to keep up—I've got working hypotheses, so of course, they keep changing. Anyway, why are we on our own on this stag?'

'Budget cuts and Sarn't Major doesn't like waiting around on cold nights. And I think she had some dinner or something to go to. Met police dinner, I think. At least we're doing proper police work.'

'Just because you're driving a fast car like the Old Bill doesn't mean you're doing real police work. You're still trying to catch lesbians.'

'True, but I'd like to get her as much as you. Not because she's gay, but because of what she did to Private Lowe.'

'Soft spot, Nick?' Jo teased. 'And there's me thinking you're a real hard nut.'

'Told you, I'm sensitive.'

Jo chuckled. 'So, you keep saying.'

Nick drove the car in the stop-and-go traffic. He turned on the radio, and they sang along to tunes they knew.

'Turn down here, Nick.'

'I know. Green door, right?'

'Yep. Park over there.'

'I know.'

'We need to do a radio check. What do you want your call sign to be?'

'Wilde.'

Jo laughed. 'Right then, I'll be….' She thought, 'I know Radclyffe.'

'What kind of name is that?'

'You never heard of The Well of Loneliness?'

'No.'

'It was the first ever lesbian book. Got banned, actually.'

'Wow! Lots of dirty talk?'

'No. Kind of sad, really.' Jo picked up her binoculars.

Nick checked the Polaroid camera by photographing Jo with her binoculars pressed to her face. The camera slowly churned out the print.

'There you are, Jo, proper Mona Lisa.'

'Shut up, you pillock. Look, it's twenty-one hundred hours,' Jo jotted the time in her notebook. 'Bet we've missed her.'

'Ever the pessimist.'

Jo watched through the binoculars, the metal pressing against the bridge of her nose. After fifteen minutes, Nick pulled out two Mars Bars from his pocket and offered one to Jo. Bored, they opened the chocolate and savoured the energy it gave them.

Half an hour passed.

'We're too late,' Jo said.

'No, we can wait for them to come out.'

'Yeah, but what if she's not in there? What if she's somewhere else? We only get one chance at this.'

'Patience, Jo.'

Nick launched himself onto Jo, pushing her down, pretending to kiss her, releasing her after two women, arm in arm, had passed them.

'Oh, very cliche! Didn't know you had it, you!' Jo smirked.

'I can be very masterful when I want to,' Nick lisped, tossing imaginary locks and pointing his nose in the air. Jo laughed, even though she'd seen that move before.

'So what's your thinking now, on the note?'

'Don't know,' Jo stopped and then continued. 'Actually, my brother-in-law could've done it.'

'Your brother-in-law?'

'Yeah, long story.' About ten minutes later, Jo finished her story. 'So then he came to the mess threatening us on Easter Monday.'

'Shit, Jo! Listen, I've been thinking, and I could help you throw them off the scent.'

'What! No!'

'You'd be doing us both a favour.'

'Hang on, someone's coming out.' Jo held the field glasses to her face. She sighed, checking her watch, noting the time: 22.00 hours. 'We've been here an hour. My bum's sore.'

'Jo, are you scared?'

'Of what?'

'You know, getting caught.'

'I'm not getting caught, Nick. Because there's nothing to catch me for.'

'Come on, Jo,' Nick implored. 'You're gay!'

Jo smiled, 'What's with you? Why so interested?'

'Because I was thinking we're both gay. You're a good policewoman. And I'd hate to see you get chucked out.'

'Gosh, so romantic, Nick.' She undid her seatbelt. 'I've had enough of this. I'm going in.'

Nick attempted to stop her but failed.

Jo, now out of the car and across the road, jogged to the green door. Her heart pounding, she knocked loudly. She hadn't considered her subsequent actions. She needed to escape Nick and find Quade. The butch woman opened the door.

''Allo again. Bit late for you, innit?'

'Yeah, I'm looking for someone. Remember the woman you told me was trouble? You know? Threw her money around.'

'Yeah, she's over in her usual place, at the end of the bar. 'Ang on a minute, she's not there. Wait there.' The butch took a pace and turned back to Jo. 'You police?'

Jo nodded.

'Thought so. Military police, though–right?'

'Yes.'

'Not sure I should help you. But I don't like her. She's trouble. Wait there, an' I'll check out the lavs.'

Three minutes later, panting, the butch ran back up the stairs to Jo.

'Not there. I asked around. She's gone to the Sols Arms. By the way, she's onto you. She went out the fire exit about half an hour ago.'

'Thanks.'

Jo sprinted across the road, flung open the passenger door and leapt into the seat. 'Sols Arms! Step on it!'

'Where's that?'

'Eversholt Street. Right near Euston station. Got half an hour before closing time. Go!'

Nick stepped onto the accelerator. The tyres squealed their enthusiasm. Jo turned on the blue lights. She sat leaning forward, her A-Z Map Book in hand, as she directed Nick.

'Next one! You missed it!' Jo looked behind her at the turning they should have taken before her neck was yanked into a different spatial dimension.

Nick expertly stomped on the brakes and reversed the car, swinging the nose in the right direction before accelerating down the street. Passers-by gaped at the silver streak thrusting its way through the traffic, up pavements, and around pedestrian refuge islands as Nick weaved in and out of the traffic until it was so jammed Nick was forced to wait. He tapped his fingers impatiently on the steering wheel, waiting for a gap in the stream of cars.

'Blues are on!' Jo reminded him.

Nick stamped on the accelerator pedal, the car turned sharp left, clipping a traffic island bollard, which attached itself to the rear bumper on the driver's side.

'Shit, Nick! Did you just prang the bloody car?'

Nick shrugged.

'Should be on the right. No Left! Park here.' Jo jumped out of the car. 'Wait for me here.' She ran through the doors labelled Function Room and up the stairs. When she reached the top, she approached a woman seated at a small table counting coins and notes into a black metal box.

'Sorry, we're closed. Can't let you in.'

Jo flashed her warrant card and pushed past her into the dark function room. It took seconds for her to adjust her eyesight as she scanned the room, looking for Quade. Jo weaved through the crowded dance floor. Couples swayed to the music of the last dance. Her presence caused couples to open their eyes and stop smooching as they warily watched Jo scrutinise every woman. Gradually, she made her way to the back of the room. The music stopped, and the lights came on. Jo's eyes darted back and forth over the women leaning against the back wall. I know she's here.

A short woman broke away from a small group of women in the far corner and approached her. 'Sarn't Clark, ain't it?'

'No.'

'Think so. RMP, no, wait a minute, SIB, you arrested Janice.'

'Not me, mate.'

'Yeah, it was. I'd know your bleedin' face anywhere.' The woman swung a drunken punch at Jo. She caught the woman's wrist in mid-flight and pulled it behind her back. 'Now, I have your attention. I know you are posted at Twelve Company. So listen, whatever your name is—'

'Chris, my name's Chris. And you, you're SIB.'

'Right, Chris, why don't you go back to your nice friends?'

Chris grimaced, bending backwards to ease the pain. 'And what if I don't?'

Jo spotted Quade departing the small group. Fuck! Chris had been a decoy. She threw Chris' wrist away in disgust, running the few feet between her and Quade, whose entourage closed around her and then moved as one to the exit. Jo stopped in her tracks. She should have stayed in the car with Nick. She pulled out her radio.

'Radcliffe to Wilde. Watch the function room exit. Over.'

'Roger. Out.'

Jo stood and surveyed the room. She was on her own. She took stock of the occupants. Some were leaving—a curious few lingered, and others were riled up and ready to come to Quade's defence. The trick now was to get to a place where she would be safe from assault and still be able to monitor Quade. She hurried to the exit. She could no longer see Quade. Instinctively, she knew Quade was walking down the stairs to the exit. She hoped Nick would be ready to make an arrest. She pushed past some women on the stairs who made their irritation with her clear. Ignoring them, she was soon at the door.

'Wilde to Radclyffe. Lost her. Over,' Nick started jogging towards The Tube.

Jo started running and caught him up. The pair sprinted down the road, turned right into Euston Station concord, through the doors and into the melee of Saturday night partiers. Nick located the platform entrance and indicated Jo should follow him. The down escalator was packed. The usual etiquette of standing to one side so that others could pass had been abandoned by the passengers—some so drunk their friends held them steady, others animated, recounting the night's events to each other. Jo passed a young woman alone and crying.

She pushed on past three drunk men. One of them, angered by her, pushed Jo down the escalator. Four women, two abreast on a step below, braced her fall. Regaining her balance, she muttered her apologies and stumbled through the crowd to the northbound platform. A wave of passengers exiting the train pushed her back. Scrambling, pushing, shoving, she fought her way through to the train doors and onto the carriage, unsure if Quade was on the train. She pulled out her Clansman radio once again.

'Hello Wilde, this is Radclyffe, over.'

Her radio buzzed and crackled. The train came to a halt at Camden Town.

'Where are you? Over.'

'I'm on a train to Mill Hill East. Over.'

'Roger. Same train, I think. I'm in the middle. Over.'

'Roger. Going to the front end. Out.'

Jo zig-zagged in and out of passengers in the carriage, steadying herself on the stanchions, straps and grab bars as she progressed to the front. Opening the car's interconnecting doors, she stepped into the next one and spotted Quade sitting in one of the side-by-side seats, her leg pressed against another young woman's. Jo slipped inside, leaning against the door, the handle digging into the small of her back. Anxious not to be seen, she shifted her weight forward while hiding behind two men engaged in an inebriated conversation that grew louder and attracted disapproving looks and hushed comments from their fellow passengers.

Keen to remain undetected, Jo slid behind the men into the corner where she could observe and remain unobtrusive. She watched Quade and her companion stare into each other's eyes. Quade whispered into her friend's ear, and they giggled, leaning into each other.

Nearing midnight, the train rattled through the underground tunnels, pausing every two minutes so passengers could disembark the night's last train. Station by station, the passengers became fewer. Jo stepped into the next carriage at Highgate, keeping her vigil through the dirty windows. Her radio crackled; startled, Jo stepped away from the window.

'Radcliffe receiving over.'

'Where are you? Over.'

'Second carriage. Eyes on the suspect. Over.'

'Radioed for backup. At your location in five. Out.'

Nick struggled with the handle of the interconnecting door. With one foot in one carriage and another in the same carriage as Jo, the train screamed to a halt. He lurched. His forward moment halted by his firm grasp of the handle as the train starting its journey jerked along the single track. Nick bounced through the carriage to Jo.

'This train terminates at Mill Hill East. When the doors open, we must arrest her before she leaves the station and into the high street,' said Jo.

'Roger that.'

The two police officers moved to the double doors nearest the next carriage. As they began slowly sliding open, Jo whipped through the narrow gap, sprinting to the exit of the next carriage.

Quade alighted from the train in conversation with her friend, oblivious to everything but her girlfriend. She saw Jo and froze for a moment before darting to her right. Jo had anticipated Quade's intentions and stepped into the would-be fugitive, grabbing her wrist and pulling it up behind her. The young woman accompanying Quade found herself in a similar position with Nick.

Jo handcuffed Quade as she delivered her rights in unison with Nick and his captive. They marched them into the ticket hall and down the steps into the high street, where a Military Police Corporal, his scarlet beret, under the streetlamp contrasting against the midnight sky, was waiting for them.

'Over here, Sarn't.' The young soldier led the way, unlocking a black Ford Escort estate with military number plates parked on double yellow lines yards from the station. Jo sat in the passenger seat. Nick sat in the back with the suspects.

'Where to Sarn't?'

'Up the road to the barracks go through the barrier to the WRAC guardroom. I'll stay there and take to the two suspects. Then take Sarn't Acorn, to Euston Station. He'll show you where. Right, let's move out.'

## Chapter 51

*Sunday 13 May, The London Provost Company, Rochester Row Barrack, London*

During the early hours of Sunday morning, the red-capped Corporal dropped Nick at the Ford Ghia.

'Nice car,' said the Corporal. 'Pranged it?'

Nick strolled around the car. The traffic island bollard was still attached to the bumper, but worse still, someone had keyed the vehicle with a single line from front to back on the passenger side. Dismayed, he dismissed the Corporal, detached the bollard and left it next to a wall out of harm's way. He opened the driver's door. His heart sank. Below the window, in wild and awkward letters, the word 'Monkey' had been scored deep into the silver paintwork, exposing the white undercoat.

'Fuck!'

Nick drove slowly back to Rochester Row. He and Jo were in trouble and were in for a serious carpeting. He parked the car outside the Motor Transport Depot. After locking it, he searched for someone to return the keys to. The burly Sergeant met him before he reached the office.

'You fucking pranged it!'

'How do you know?' Nick asked.

'Bad news travels fast. There'll likely be an inquiry as you've damaged Her Majesty's property.'

'Shit!'

'I've made a note of the damage. Heard you parked her outside some lesbian club. They don't like you, do they? Sign here.' The Sergeant chuckled.

Nick checked his watch and was relieved that breakfast was available. He hurried to the Senior Ranks Mess.

Jo, having returned to Rochester Row in the early hours, ate her breakfast alone, enjoying a few moments of peace after a busy night. No one else was up at this hour on a Sunday save for the Orderly Sergeant, who had already left to perform cookhouse duties. Nick joined her pulling out a chair next to her. He placed his breakfast order with the mess steward.

'What a night!' Nick grinned at Jo. 'We got our man.' He waited for Jo's response.

Jo smiled. 'Yep and I'm tired.'

'Bit touch 'n' go down the old underground.'

'As long as Quade goes down, I don't care.' Jo relished seeing Quade's face when she told her they had all the evidence they needed to discharge her.

Nick cut a piece of sausage and dipped it into the yolk of his egg. 'Probably going to be an inquiry. You know about the car.'

'Think so?' Jo said. 'Least of our worries. 'Spect the Sergeant Major will want a chat tomorrow. Best get your earmuffs on.'

Nick finished his cup of tea and pushed away his empty breakfast plate.

'We should get our stories straight.'

Jo shook her head.

'I'm going to my pit to push up some zeds. We can talk later.'

## Chapter 52

*Day Eleven. The London Provost Company, Rochester Row, London.*

Jo and Nick entered the main office at 08:30 hours to prepare the report on Corporal Quade's surveillance and arrest. Jo positioned the typewriter carriage and struck the first key with her index finger. Her train of thought was interrupted by Sergeant Major Hart flinging open the main door. Her heels clicked at a fast tempo as she strode to her office.

'Sergeants Acorn and Clark in my office.'

Jo and Nick hurried to join their boss in her office.

'Shut the door!'

The two senior ranks stood on the small rug opposite their boss, seated at her desk.

'Want to tell me about the surveillance?'

Nick looked at Jo.

'Get on with it.' Hart drummed her fingers on her desk.

'Well, ma'am, we picked up the car at about twenty-one hundred hours on Saturday evening.'

'Cut to the chase, Sarn't Clark.'

'After we parked, we waited about an hour. Due to problems with the traffic, we arrived later than planned. And so we didn't see when Quade went into the club.'

Hart nodded.

Encouraged, Jo continued slowly. 'So, I thought…well...I thought I should go in and see if she was in there. Nothing else, just take a look, like.'

'Can you remind me of your orders?'

'Don't go into the club, ma'am. Stay outside for surveillance only, ma'am.' Jo looked straight ahead, not wanting to catch her boss's eye.

'So, what part of staying outside did you not get?'

'Ma'am, we got her! That's what we wanted, wasn't it?'

'So, the end justifies the means?'

'Sort of, ma'am.'

'And what if this had ended up with one of you being injured, or worse? That's why my orders were to carry out surveillance only.'

'I know, ma'am, but we needed to get her.'

'I don't care. Orders are orders! You don't pick and choose which ones to follow.'

Jo hung her head before mumbling. 'Yes, ma'am.'

'So, Sergeant Acorn, tell me about the accident and the keying of the car.'

Nick had kept his eyes on the small area of carpet in front of Hart's desk while Hart had interrogated Jo. Now it was his turn to be carpeted, he stared at a patch of the wall behind Hart's head.

'In pursuit of the suspect, I had to take some risks. During the pursuit, I collected a traffic bollard. I parked the car outside the Sols Arm's pub. I had to leave the vehicle in situ so we could pursue the suspect on foot and into the underground. After successfully apprehending the suspect and her girlfriend, I retrieved the car, only to find that someone had keyed it with the word 'Monkey'. Unfortunately, I do not know the perpetrator, as the incident occurred in my absence.'

'You were the sole driver?'

'Yes, ma'am.'

'Well, they'll be an inquiry as you've damaged Her Majesty's property. Much will depend upon whether they consider the fact you disobeyed my orders led to the damage. Let's hope the inquiry understands why you disobeyed me and lets you off.'

'Yes, ma'am.' Nick bowed his head once more.

'Right, now I understand you have observed Quade at two clubs.'

'Not exactly, ma'am. I didn't see her in The Gateways Club but I do have a witness who I have yet to confirm will testify that Quade was at The Gateways Club. And Nick and I have our notes. I saw her in the club at The Sol's Arms, and we both gave chase and apprehended the suspect and another soldier, who is a Postal and Courier Operator at Mill Hill. So that will be two more to add to Major Marwood's short list of discharges.'

'Well, might be one more. I'm sure Lord Quade will have something to say about the matter. So, on that note, we will interview Quade and her accomplice. What's her name?'

'Private Balcombe, ma'am.'

'Well, we'll interview the two of them and get the confessions in order before doing the necessary. I'll meet you outside of our mess at two. Be ready to stay a couple of nights. This is our top priority. Especially if we are to justify the surveillance gone wrong and the damage to the car.'

## Chapter 53

*Day Eleven 12 Coy WRAC, Inglis Barracks, Mill Hill, London.*

At 14:00 hours, Sergeant Major Hart stood looking at the portrait of Queen Elizabeth the Second on the back wall of the oblong room. 'Wonder what she's witnessed in this room?'

'I was told it used to be an Orderly Room for one of the platoons, but then the unit got smaller with budget cuts and the heating so expensive they decided to decommission it. Now, she's just a witness to our interrogations. Can't be any too pleasant for her,' Jo said.

'No,' Hart replied, preoccupied with the impending interview of Corporal Quade.

'Does the OC know about our interviews?' Nick asked.

'Nope, better go and tell her.' Hart walked to the door. 'Wait 'til I get back, then I'll brief you both. Then we may start today or tomorrow. Depends.'

'On what?' Jo asked.

'What the OC has to say if anything. And if Lord Qaude has any input.' Hart shut the door behind her.

Jo and Nick unstacked two tables and placed them together. Then, one chair was placed on one side of the desk and three on the other so the interrogators would have their backs to the Queen's portrait.

'We need to focus on Private Balcombe,' Jo said. 'Get all the juicy stuff so we can pin down Quade.'

'You think this is going to be a piece of piss?'

'They're banged to rights. We saw them. We have a witness.'

'Yeah, but is she prepared to testify?'

'Haven't been able to see her yet. I called the club and got no answer. I'll have to try again at the weekend when they are open.'

'Just the weekend? Can't make much money.'

'Hmm, probably not. They used to be the only game in town. Now clubs like the Sols Arms are opening up all over London. Anyway, I'll call on Friday afternoon to see what's what.'

'We can try, but my betting is Major Marwood will have a view as to whether we can interview Quade again. Talking of which, I hear the clicking of the heels,' Nick cocked his head. 'Always a dead giveaway about her mood. And I'd say not happy.'

Hart opened the door, strode in, shut it, and seated herself at the table in what seemed to be a single, fluid and determined movement.

Jo and Nick waited.

'Right, well, the OC's a bit miffed we didn't mention the surveillance. She's pissed that we haven't mentioned we apprehended Quade and Balcombe until now. Seems she learned it from Captain Trueman. I think that pissed her off as well. Worse still, Lord Quade has been on the phone bending her ear.'

'So, what does that mean?' Jo tutted. 'I bet the OC's caved? He's not got her off again?'

'No. Listen up, Jo. Lord Quade wants his daughter to be represented by Captain Trueman again. And she wants time to prepare to give Quade her best support. Lord Quade is going to coach her on the phone this evening. So, that means we either start with Balcombe or wait and start with Quade when Captain Trueman's ready. Any suggestions?'

'Maybe we should do Balcombe and wait until I get our witness. I'm having trouble tracking her down. Club's closed until Friday.'

'Okay, let's do a prelim on Balcombe. After that, Jo, you get down that club, break down the door if you have to, and get that witness. Let's go nice and easy on Balcombe. That way, she'll tell her girlfriend it was a piece of cake. Then we can go in hard on Quade. Any other thoughts?'

Jo and Nick shook their heads.

'Right then, let's get her in.'

After the usual rigmarole, Balcombe sat in front of her three interrogators.

'Right, Private Balcombe. Now you know who we are. We have some questions for you.'

Balcombe glared at Hart.

Jo began the interview, opening her notebook. 'Private Balcombe, were you or were you not at The Gateways Club at 239 Kings Road, London, on Saturday, the eleventh of May?'

Jo waited for a reply. Balcombe didn't oblige.

'Come on. It's an easy one. You were either there or not.'

'Dunno.'

'Dunno what?'

'The address.'

'Okay, so were you at the club called the Gateways?'

'Dunno.'

'Okay, how about the Sols Arms near Euston Station the same night?'

Balcombe shrugged.

'You don't deny that we saw you get on an underground train at Euston and alighted at Mill Hill East around midnight the same night?'

'Nope, you arrested us, so no.'

'Why do you think we arrested you?'

'Dunno, still trying to find out. Coz it's not a crime riding on public transport.'

'Yeah, but you didn't just ride on public transport, did you?'

Balcombe's feet twisted together under her chair. 'Yeah.'

'Yeah, what? Where did you go?'

'Town.'

'To do what?'

'See friends?'

'Where did you meet them?'

'Dunno—couple of pubs.'

'Like The Gateways Club in Kings Road and the Sols Arms on Eversholt Street?'

'I dunno, I jus' followed the others. We're in a group, and I jus' went along with the group. They knew where they was going. I jus' went along for the ride.'

'So, if I say you were in The Sols Arms, you'd believe me?'

'Dunno, was I?'

Balcombe moved her feet from under her chair to look at the shine she had bulled on her shoes earlier.

Nick spotted Jo's growing impatience and picked up the questioning. 'Let me help you remember. You exited the Sols Arms, a pub near Euston Station, and got on a Northern Line Train heading to Mill Hill East. That's right, isn't it?'

'Yeah, so that's why I'm here. I got a train and got back after midnight. I'm eighteen, so I can stay out after midnight.'

'So, you admit to being at the Sols Arms?'

'It's a pub, ain't it? I said I went to a pub. What's the problem?'

'The problem,' Jo leaned forward. 'Is that the Sols Arms Pub has a lesbian night there on the second Saturday of every month? And I saw you there.'

'Does it? Wondered why there were so many women there. Just thought it was popular with us Army girls. Met some nice RAF girls there from Northolt, too.'

'So, you admit you were in a lesbian club in London?'

Balcombe, her legs crossed at the ankles uncrossed and recrossed them before shuffling her feet back under her chair, which forced her to lean forward slightly. 'I don't admit that. Because you're going to make out, I went knowingly to a lesbian club, and I'm telling you I didn't.'

Hart stood up. 'All right, Private Balcombe, that's all. We may call you in again.'

Balcombe stood, put on her beret and marched out of the room.

'Well, that went well,' said Jo with some sarcasm.

'Not great, but I think we can discharge her for being at the Sol's Arms, and if we can get the witness from The Gateways, that would put the tin lid on it. That result could be good for the inquiry about the car. Might even get you out of trouble, Nick. Jo, you need that witness statement from the bouncer at the Gateways Club. That's going to be more crucial than I thought. Let's call it a day. I'll see you in the mess, Jo. Tomorrow, Nick.'

## Chapter 54

*Day Twelve*

The following morning, Jo, Nick and Sergeant Major Hart were seated again at the table in the interrogation room. Captain Trueman knocked and entered, and the senior ranks stood up.

'Please sit down. As you know, I've consulted with Lord Quade. He is adamant that his daughter has not committed a crime. However, as I have relayed to Major Marwood, should his daughter admit to being a lesbian, she will not be dishonourably discharged. Instead, she will terminate her service. He is prepared to make the necessary payments to make that happen. So, we will see if she admits to it or not.'

'Have you counselled her, ma'am?'

'No, sorry, Sarn't Major, I haven't. She has refused to let me help her. I know she has spoken with her father, but how will this interview go…' Trueman shrugged. 'Well, who can say?'

'Right, ma'am, are you ready?'

'As I'll ever be.' Trueman took her assigned seat.

Nick went to the door and summoned Quade, who marched in and saluted the officer.

'You may be seated and remove your hat,' Trueman said.

The senior ranks sat at the table, took out their notebooks, and waited for Jo to start the interview.

'Good morning, Corporal Quade. I think you know everyone present, or would you like me to go over that again?'

Quade shook her head.

Encouraged by Quade's silence and mild demeanour, Jo began the interview.

'Corporal Quade, you are here to establish whether you are a lesbian, which is in contradiction to MOD policy. That is to say that homosexuals are not allowed to serve in Her Majesty's Armed Forces because it is likely to cause problems concerned with fraternisation between the ranks, favouritism and the increased likelihood of unwanted sexual acts among fellow soldiers and finally, the possibility of being a security risk, for example, blackmail. Now, we have reason to believe that you frequented a lesbian nightclub, The

Gateways, in The Kings Road on Saturday, the eleventh of May. Later that evening, you also visited another lesbian club called the Sols Arms. Can you confirm that you visited these establishments?'

'Ask me one on sport.' Quade cackled.

'This is not a game, Corporal Quade. We are conducting a legitimate enquiry to maintain good order and military discipline within this unit.'

'Hmm, if you say so. Not sure what being a lesbian has got to do with it.' This time, there was no pretence about Quade's education and class origins. She met Jo's questioning with an accent a cut above Jo's East London dialect.

'So you are admitting you are a lesbian?'

Quade looked away.

'Can we agree that I chased you down the stairs at The Sols Arms on the said Saturday?'

'Yes, you can. And, frankly, I consider it harassment, for which there is a policy that no one bothers about. The men get away with it, all the time.'

'Accusations of bullying are taken seriously—I can assure you.'

'Yeah? I'd say about as seriously as sexual assault is,' Quade scoffed.

The irony was not lost on Jo or Hart. Trueman shifted in her seat, crossed her arms and legs, and nodded for emphasis.

Nick was about to pick up the questioning when Jo signalled she was happy to continue.

'So, let me recap. You agree you went to The Gateways Club and the Sols Arms?'

'I agree that you saw me at The Sols Arms.'

'The fact that you were at The Sols Arms and were later seen with Private Balcombe suggests that you are a lesbian.'

'No, it doesn't. I went to the Sols Arms because I knew it would be a safe place for a woman to drink with female friends. I travelled back to barracks with my friends on the tube. That is all you saw. And none of this makes me a lesbian.'

'I saw you gazing into the eyes of Private Balcombe!'

'Did you? Are you sure? We were both under the influence, sharing jokes and taking the mickey out of our friends. If you think I was, what was it? Gazing into her eyes, I was not. I was simply sharing some private jokes. Once again, Sergeant Clark, no crime and not specifically lesbian behaviour.' Quade leaned into the back of her chair, sprawling her legs casually in front of her before crossing her arms and cocking her head. 'By the way, sorry about your car. I heard someone named it with a key. What was it now? Oh yes, I remember, 'Monkey'. How apt!' She smirked.

Nick leaned forward. 'You seem to know a lot about the car. Tell me, where did you see it?'

'I didn't see it. I heard about it on the grapevine.'

'Don't suppose you heard who did it?'

'No, sorry. But you know, even if I did, I wouldn't tell you.'

'Well, nice. Nice to know you're honest and upright, just like your father.'

'What?' Quade shifted in her seat.

'He said,' Jo took over the questioning. 'You are just like your father.'

'The compliments are really falling from your lips today.'

'No compliment,' said Nick. 'He's an arrogant know-it-all, just like you.'

'Nice try, Sergeant. I'm not going there.' Quade looked at her watch. She stood and addressed Trueman. 'Now I believe it's time for lunch, ma'am. Permission to leave?'

Trueman glanced at Hart, who gave her tacit agreement. Quade replaced her beret before saluting the officer and leaving the room.

Jo got up. 'We'll never get her at this rate.'

'No, I don't think we will,' Trueman put on her forage cap. 'She's toying with us. And if Corporal Quade gets to stay in the Army, God knows what she'll get up to. She is a malignant force, and she needs to go. Sarn't, do you have any other evidence?'

'Not yet, ma'am. I'm working on it.'

There was a knock on the door, and a breathless Private Dawson entered. 'Sorry to interrupt, ma'am, but there's an Archie someone on the phone for Sarn't Clark. She's on a pay phone and is running out of money!'

Jo hurried out of the room, running down the corridor to the Orderly Room to reach the phone. She grabbed it out of the Orderly Corporal's hand. 'Hello, Archie? It's Sergeant Clark. Where are you? Give me your number—I'll call you back.'

'At the club…'

The line gave the unwanted pips and then went dead.

'Shit!' Jo slammed the phone back on the handset and ran into the interview room.

'Ma'am, that was my witness. We got cut off. I can't wait for her to call back because she might not. I need to get to the club as fast as possible.'

Hart tossed Jo the keys to the Army car.

'Want me to come with you?' Nick asked.

'Best she goes on her own. Get back as soon as you can,' Hart said.

'Should we continue after lunch?' Trueman walked to the doorway.

'No, I don't think so, ma'am. We'll let you know when we want Corporal Quade back in.

## Chapter 55

*Day Twelve The Gateways Club, London*

Jo parked outside the club entrance on Bramerton Street. Having secured the car, she crossed the road and rang the doorbell on one side of the green door. She waited a few seconds and rang again.

'All right, all right, keep your 'air on!'

The door opened a crack, and Jo recognised Archie. Archie opened the door wider. 'Oh, it's you. Come in.'

Jo entered from the bright sunshine into the dim light of an empty club. Though she had been to the club twice before, once for fun and the other for work, she had not realised just how small it was. And even though it was Tuesday, and the club last opened at the weekend, stale cigarette smoke permeated the air. The bar was at one end of the space, taking almost the entire length of the back wall. Seated at the bar were two women, one an elegant woman with faded film star looks and a cigarette holder, the other a butch who spoke with a slight American accent.

'Welcome to The Gateways,' said the film star. 'I understand you are looking for information about one of my clientele. As a rule, I dislike interference from any establishment or those who wish to impose their politically correct ideas on me. I'm all about people feeling safe, secure, and having a good time. Politics and the law have no place here. So, you may be wondering why I'm happy to have Archie here speak with you.'

'Yes,' Jo said.

'It's simply a matter of business. But what you hear from us should not be repeated. The woman you seek is disruptive. We have had to ask her to leave on a couple of occasions, haven't we, Archie?'

Archie nodded.

'And if you can deal with her, I hope it will suit us both. I don't want to see her in here gain. She has money, but it's not worth it for the hassle she gives. We're happy to help officer. Do we call you officer?'

'Sergeant Clark is fine, Miss er Miss?'

'Gina. Everyone calls me Gina. Remember, no names, and I believe the saying goes, no pack drill,' she giggled before elegantly exhaling smoke.

'So you've seen her down here before?'

'Loads of times,' offered Archie.

'Good. And you've chucked her out. How many times?'

'Three,' replied Gina.

'And that was for?'

'Being drunk, fighting. Like I said to you, she likes to pinch other people's girlfriends,' Archie said.

'Who did the chucking out?'

'I always speak to my clients and read them the riot act very gently, but shall we say firmly? If that doesn't work and they don't settle down, Archie helps them outside,' Gina replied.

'Yeah, I done that three times with 'er. We don't need 'er back. Like I told you, she's trouble,' Archie said.

Jo couldn't help but notice the tattoos on Archie's arms. She'd never seen so many. And, though Archie was what many might describe as a butch lesbian cliche, a gentle giant dressed in men's clothes, she was clearly loyal to her bosses. Jo admired and respected her loyalty and the clarity she displayed around her sexuality, something she could never do. Tattoos were frowned upon in the service and perhaps even taboo. She had never seen a woman with tattoos before and was both fascinated and in awe of the butch with the gruff voice.

'Thank you. That's been most helpful. I wonder if you could provide me with a written statement. I've brought the paperwork with me.'

'I won't,' Gina, gifted Jo with a smile she would never forget. 'Archie will, won't you?'

'Yep.'

Gina and the American disappeared, leaving Jo, and Archie huddled at the bar.

'Look, I don't write so good. Can you write it?'

'No problem. Just tell me in your own words what you saw last Saturday night. Then tell me about the other incidences.'

'Righto. You know she's got a nasty mouth on 'er, and she can get a bit 'andy with 'er fists. I've had quite a bit of trouble with 'er. And we don't like trouble 'ere. We're all about having a good time, that's all. She's close to getting banned, and we don't usually do that.'

Jo slowly took Archie's dictation for the next hour and emerged into the sunlight with her trophy. Surely, at last, they had Quade banged to rights.

## Chapter 56

*Day Thirteen 12 Coy WRAC, Inglis Barracks, Mill Hill, London.*

At 08:30 hours, the three Royal Military Police senior ranks gathered around the two tables in the middle of the interview room. On the wall, in her portrait, Queen Elizabeth the Second smiled benevolently upon those who served her, grateful they had sworn their allegiance to her and their country.

'Ma'am, I have two sworn statements. The first is from Archie. Her real name is Catherine Archer, but she likes to go by the name of Archie. If you met her, you'd understand,' Jo said.

Sergeant Major Hart nodded.

'The second is from Gina Ware, the club's owner. She didn't want to give me one at first because she was very clear she doesn't like politics or the establishment interfering in people's lives, especially in the lives of her clientele. However, when she heard about Private Lowe and, given the trouble Quade has caused in her club, she understood why we needed a statement from her and Archie.'

'Brilliant! What's the plan?' Hart asked.

'Nick can soften her up with a few expected questions. Then I'll go in for the jugular. I'm sure we've got her this time—Lord Snooty or no Lord Snooty.'

'Have you informed Captain Trueman of the witness statements?'

'I haven't, ma'am. Don't want to give Quade the heads-up. She can get Daddy's advice after the interview.'

'Hmm, I think you should give them to the Two I C.'

'She's not defending her, ma'am. She's just a unit rep. She is there to see the suspect is treated in accordance with The Queen's Regs, that's all. Right?'

'Yes. But it would be courteous to do so.'

'Ma'am, I want to ambush Quade so bad it hurts. I want her out, for Lizzie's sake. And I'm not giving her any opportunity to wriggle out of this. The more I learn about her, the more I know she shouldn't be in the Army.' Jo stood, her head tilted to one side, waiting for further instructions from her boss. At last, she had the chance to avenge Lizzie's death. Quade would be there, right in front of her, at her mercy, and she would give none.

Hart sat, considering the options and the etiquette. 'It'd better happen, Jo.'

'Trust me, ma'am.' Jo sat in the middle with Nick to her right and Hart to the other side. Nick jiggled his knee up and down. Jo checked her notes repeatedly, ensuring she remembered the key facts. She needed to move the interview through to its end swiftly and efficiently, giving Quade no option but to accept defeat, and she would have her vengeance.

Trueman knocked and entered. The senior ranks stood to attention. 'Please sit down. I presume the reason we are here is that you have new evidence.'

Hart leaned forward and spoke in a low voice. 'Ma'am, we have two sworn witness statements. The evidence is pretty clear.'

'And the reason I haven't seen them?'

'Element of surprise, ma'am,' Jo said. 'And we don't have to share the evidence. This is an interview, not a court martial. This interview is to determine The Army's next course of action.'

'Steady Sarn't.' Hart cautioned. 'Ma'am, If we'd given them to you, you would be obliged to share them with her, not because you have to, but, I'm sure, out of a sense of duty, you would want to. So, we didn't want to put you in a difficult position.'

'Hmm, well, I'm in that position now. Better get on with it, then. And you'd better have your ducks in a row because if you haven't, I can bet your bottom dollar that we'll all be for the high jump.' Trueman sat down opposite the senior ranks.

At 09:00 hours, Corporal Quade knocked at the door, entered, marched in and came to a halt in front of her officer before saluting.

'Take a seat, Corporal Quade. You may remove your hat.'

Nick began the proceedings by reminding Quade who her interrogators were. The formalities completed, he began. 'Corporal Quade, first of all, I'd like to establish the context in which we find ourselves today at this interview. I'd appreciate a simple yes or no to my questions, as I am keen to ensure that you understand the facts about this case and your predicament. Do you understand?'

'Yes, Sergeant.'

'Good.' Nick paused and glanced at Trueman. 'The reason the SIB were called in to investigate whether lesbians were serving contrary to a MOD policy was prompted by the suicide of Private Lowe, 462359, on Sunday, the fifteenth of April. During our investigations, we learned that a female soldier had threatened Private Lowe for refusing to enter into a lesbian relationship.' Nick stopped and checked with Quade that she had followed his preamble.

Quade nodded.

'During our investigation, your name came up several times in connection with Private Lowe and several other women.'

'Yes. Yes,' Quade's attention span was waning. 'We've already been over this. You interviewed me, remember?' Quade's impatient tone was unmistakable. She calmed herself. 'I'm sorry. What was it you wanted to know? Exactly.' The upper-class accent and confidence surfaced once more. 'We've been over this. My father, Lord Quade, has discussed the matter with your higher-ups, and I believe the matter is closed. Now, unless you have something specific, you need to ask me,' Corporal Quade turned to her Two IC. 'Then I think I can be dismissed. Ma'am?'

'Wait out,' Trueman said.

Quade stopped preparing to leave and relaxed back in her chair, smiling.

Jo leaned forward. 'Have you ever frequented a lesbian nightclub, known as The Gateways, in The Kings Road, London?'

'No.'

'No? Are you sure?'

'Yes, of course, I'm sure.'

'Have you frequented the Sols Arms?'

'You know I have. Seriously, Sergeant, we've been over this already. And, as I said, drinking at a lesbian bar doesn't necessarily mean one is a lesbian.' Quade's tone changed to sarcasm. 'I'm pretty sure my memory serves me well. And that we had this discussion during my last so-called interview.'

'We did Corporal Quade. You're right. Once again, I'm just establishing context. Be kind enough to bear with us.' Jo realised she had changed her tone. It was as if she was speaking to an officer. She corrected her approach. 'Sorry about this, but I just want to be sure about something.' Jo tapped a pencil against the side of her head. Then she scrubbed out something on her notepad before looking up and smiling at Quade. 'Erm, right. You did confirm that you have never frequented The Gateways nightclub in London?'

Quade studied Jo.

'Did I say that?'

'You did say that. A few minutes ago.'

'Hmm, well, I might've been a bit hasty. I think I've been there once. It's not a crime.'

'No, you're right, Corporal Quade. It's not a crime. But if a pattern is established that you regularly frequent lesbian nightclubs, one might come to the conclusion, as you put it, that one is a lesbian. Don't you think?'

Quade pondered her options. 'I'd like to speak to my father.'

'This is not a court of law or a civilian police interview. You need to answer the questions, and we decide when you are released from his interview,' Hart reminded Quade.

Quade looked to Trueman for advice. 'Ma'am?'

Trueman leaned toward Quade. 'I'm afraid they're right. It's best if you cooperate.'

Quade sat back in her chair, folded her arms, and crossed her legs. 'Well, get on with it then!'

'Right,' Jo said. 'You've been to The Gateways Club. How many times?'

'Just the once.'

'Are you sure?'

'Course, I'm sure.'

'Can you remember when that was?'

'The night you saw me at the Sols Arms. That is the only time I've been to that club. We just thought it'd be a laugh. You know, being with all those butches and femmes and pitying their terrible dress sense.'

'So you were there the night of the twelfth of May?'

'I just said so.'

'And that is the only time?'

'Yes, for goodness' sake.'

'So, you lied to me about going to the Gateways?'

'Yes, big deal. And it's not much of a pattern because it was just one night. So…' Quade trailed off.

'As you know, we've been investigating any breaches of MOD policy. And, with that in mind, we conducted further investigations into your attendance at The Gateways.'

'Oh, come on! Not that again!'

'Do you know someone called Archie?'

Jo watched Quade sit up a little, trying not to show her concern. 'No.'

'What about a Gina Ware?'

'No, should I?'

'She's the owner of the Gateways.'

Quade stared at Jo. Jo watched as the significance of her questions perplexed Quade.

'I see. I can't say I know her.'

'Well, she knows you.'

Quade's eyes widened at the new information.

'And so does Archie or Catherine Archer. The bouncer at the Gateways.' Jo waited for Quade to recognise the significance of her statement.

'What of it?'

'They have both made a sworn witness statement about your behaviour in the club.'

Quade picked some imaginary lint from her barrack dress skirt. Her eyes narrowed as insolence flared in her face.

'It seems you have frequented club on several occasions.' Jo paused, then continued. 'And on at least three occasions, you were ejected from the club.' She paused again. 'I think we agreed earlier that a pattern of behaviour usually indicates future behaviour and lifestyle?'

'Not exactly. You said that.'

'Hmm, well, you've been to two lesbian clubs. You lied about one of them until we had evidence to prove you were there.'

'Of course, I lied,' Quade raised her voice. 'If I'd said I'd been there, you'd have discharged me for being a lesbian, which I deny.'

'I know you do. But the evidence is pointing more and more to the fact that you are a lesbian. And more to the point, you've been caught red-handed.'

'As you say, Sergeant, but it's circumstantial.'

'The thing is.' Jo smiled. 'You were kicked out of the club because, on each occasion, you were fighting and attempting to steal other people's girlfriends. And the owner was having none of it.'

'I was not fighting.'

'Course you were! The same as you've not been lying to us all the time.

Why don't you just give up? You're banged to rights!'

'I'm not. I'm not! I am not a lesbian! And you can't discharge me for that. You have no proof that I am a lesbian. I am not confessing to that, do you hear? Captain Trueman?' Quade stood up and walked toward the door.

Nick followed her, placing his hand on the doorknob.

'Please sit down, Corporal Quade. We're not finished yet,' Jo said.

Quade returned to her seat as if her shoes had lead soles and sat down. She focused on the floor.

'To put a lid on this, Corporal Quade, the reason Archie and Gina said you were fighting is because you attempted on at least three known occasions to steal someone's girlfriend. You see, that's a pattern, and if you weren't a lesbian, why would you want to cause trouble by stealing people's girlfriends?'

'They made it up. I need to talk to my father.'

'Do you have anything else you wish to add before the interview is concluded?'

'Yes. You,' Quade pointed at Jo. 'You are victimising me.'

'Victimising you?' Jo acted surprised.

'Because you think that I killed Lizzie.' Quade stared at Jo for a moment before looking away.

Jo could see Quade was having difficulty controlling her emotions, and she sensed an opportunity to close the case beyond any doubt.

In a calm voice, she spoke for Lizzie. 'You did kill her. At the very least, you had a hand in her death.' Jo's voice croaked with both anger and sadness at the memory of cutting down Lizzie's body. She collected her emotions and continued. 'You bullied her for refusing to be your girlfriend.' Jo's lungs gasped for breath.' And, I had to cut her down.' Jo jumped out of her chair and leaned over the table. 'You deceitful selfish bitch!'

Nick pulled Jo back into her seat.

The room was quiet. Tears streamed from Quade's eyes. She spoke with a surreal calm and quietness. 'You've got it all wrong. I loved her.' She looked at the Queen's portrait. 'She told me she didn't love me to spare my feelings. I know she loved me. But she couldn't tell her parents about us. She said she was ashamed. And I tried everything to get her back, to support her. And, yes, I know I was mean to her, but that was not why she hung herself—shame was. I loved her. I would've done anything to make her happy. These other girls? They were just to make her jealous and to make me feel good about myself.' Quade, broken by her loss, allowed herself to grieve. She slumped in her chair as her heartbreak wracked her body.

Jo was stunned. Her long-awaited victory dissipated. At a loss as to how she should proceed, she stared at Quade in disbelief, though she knew Quade had spoken the truth.

Blindsided, Trueman placed an arm around Quade's shoulders.

Nick broke the melancholic silence by offering Quade his handkerchief before continuing the proceedings. 'Now that we have presented the facts as we have them. And you have been unable to provide us with a satisfactory alternative set of facts. I'm obliged to inform you that you will probably be charged under Section 69 of the Army Act 1955, Conduct Prejudice to Military Discipline. And because you were ejected from a civilian club for fighting, you will also be charged under Section 66 of The Army Act 1955, Disgraceful Conduct. I'm sure your father is familiar with both sections and the supporting Chapters of The Queens Regulations, especially chapter three.'

Jo couldn't look at Quade. She knew Quade was right. Shame and parental rejection were a powerful motivator and played a significant part in Lizzie's death. She silently thanked her parents for accepting her sexuality and realised this was the difference between life and death for many lesbians.

Quade nodded, accepting Nick's summation before turning away from her interviewers and the officer.

'We will now hand you back to your unit. I believe Captain Trueman will prepare the charge sheets.'

'Then what happens?' Quade sniffed. She had been ambushed, and everyone knew it, but she held her head high.

'You will appear before your OC, who will hear the charges and evidence. It will be up to her what happens after that.'

'Yeah, but what usually happens?' Quade's cut glass accent faded with her confidence.

'Well, the evidence is overwhelming. You can choose between accepting the OC's punishment or going for Court Martial. I'm sure Captain Trueman would not recommend that to you.'

'What's she likely to do to me?'

'The OC? I would think,' Jo hesitated, her speech faltering, looking to Trueman for support. 'That she will discharge you. Maybe a fine? For the fighting. Not a very good advert for the WRAC, is it? And I believe that your father has offered to buy you out. So, before long, you will be back in civvy street.'

'Are we done, Sarn't Major?' Trueman stood.

'Yes, ma'am, I believe we are.'

'Corporal Quade, you are dismissed.'

Quade got up put on her beret and stood to attention. Tears fell from her cheeks onto the floor, nevertheless she saluted smartly before turning to her right and marching from the room.

'Well done, Jo. You did a nice job. Though it's a very sad state of affairs,' Hart said. 'Now, Captain Trueman, it's down to you. Need any help with the charges?'

'No, thank you, Sarn't Major. I've got this, and if I have an issue, I'll consult the RSM.'

'Quite, ma'am. Miss Gordon is a wise woman. Been round the block.'

'Right, 'I joined the Army because I wanted an exciting life. Thank you all for your contributions,' Trueman chuckled. 'Hopefully, I won't see you again. And thank you for your sterling work.' Trueman turned to leave. 'Bloody sad if you ask me.' She put on her hat and left the room.

The senior ranks waited for the door to close before congratulating each other on the successful conclusion to the investigation—they had got the target and two other discharges.

'Can't help thinking,' Jo said. 'If there had been no anti-lesbian policy, we wouldn't be in this situation.'

'You think Lizzie would still be alive?' Nick asked.

'Dunno. Maybe if her parents hadn't hated or disapproved of lesbians so much, Lizzie would've been okay. Can't say for sure. But if we didn't have an archaic MOD policy that's out of step with UK law, then we wouldn't have to interview people about their sex lives. What a waste of time and money, let alone good careers gone.'

No one countered her statement.

'Right, I will go and give the OC the news,' Hart walked to the door. 'I'm sure it will be short and sweet and all, 'about time you did your job, etcetera,' but it will feel good to be out of here. She will have a big scalp. Well done, I think.' Hart smiled her respect for her team, guessing everyone felt hollow inside, just like she did.

## Chapter 57

After lunch, Jo met Terry outside the gym for one final run before she returned to her unit. Jo was conflicted. She wanted to leave Twelve Company behind and all the misery she had endured. But that would mean she would only see Terry on weekends and holidays. The sun warmed her face, and she looked up to the heavens. I got her for you, Lizzy. I'm sorry I didn't know about you and Quade. If only you'd said. I would've helped you. Jo sighed a loud heavy-hearted sigh.

'How'd it go?' Terry joined Jo, enjoying the sunshine.

'Successful.' Jo's response was lacklustre.

'How? Did she confess?'

'Nope. Fighting down the Gateways. Daddy did a deal and got her off the lesbian thing.'

'Fuck!'

'Yep, we won't be going down there again in a hurry.'

'No fuck! She was fighting!' Terry was incredulous.

'Yeah.'

'Oh, disrepute then? Blimey, don't attract attention if you don't want to get caught. Is she stupid?'

'Nope.'

'Everything okay?'

'Nope.'

'What?'

'Turns out she was in love with Lizzie. And Lizzie couldn't face her parents because she felt ashamed. And Quade was jus' trying to win her back.' Jo's sadness was evident.

'Oh. She admitted to being a lesbian, then?'

In a resigned voice, Jo corrected Terry. 'She admitted to being in love with Lizzie. She was in love with her and she was trying to get her back.'

'Oh. That's sad.'

'Yeah.'

'So, what happens to her now?'

'In a couple a days, she'll be on orders before the OC and await the OC's decision.'

'She's going to kill her. She hates anything that's not feminine or brings the WRAC into disrepute.'

'Exactly. Sarn't Major Hart is breaking the good news to the OC this afternoon. Can't help feeling bad for Quade though.'

'No. I know.' Terry let a silent moment pass before attempting to rally Jo. 'Let's do our run. Take your mind off it. How far do you want to go?'

'Terry, I don't think I'll ever get over this. It's been awful and all because we can't be open about our sexuality. What a fucking waste!' Jo let her growing anger subside before adding. 'Coupla miles?'

Terry set the pace, and Jo jogged alongside her out of the barracks and down Bittacy Hill. 'When we get to the school, we'll turn around. So, finally, you'll be gone. And I won't see you every day, and I can't call you because we can't make it obvious or raise suspicions. Makes me sad.'

'Yep. Me too. Sad to go on one count and pleased on another. I like to think we found the right balance between throwing out the rubbish and keeping the best. But can't help that niggling feeling that if we were allowed to be who we are, none of this would've happened.'

'Any other regrets?'

'Corporal Watson would still be in.'

The women kept pace with each other. The steady pounding of their trainers on the pavement provided a kind of rhythmic comfort.

'Stretch out your legs, Jo. Try for a longer pace length.'

Terry concentrated on regulating her breathing, quickly pushing out the carbon dioxide and inhaling the oxygen slowly.

'Yeah, but think about it—we no longer have to hide in front of Mum and Dad. And we would've kept it a secret if the note hadn't happened. Worked out for the best, them being fine about it and everything. Turn now, Jo. There's a slight hill. Best to shorten your stride but keep the pace if you can.' Terry pulled out her stopwatch. 'If we keep this up, we should be dead on time. What're you working on next?'

'Don't know yet. I suspect we'll have lots of admin to do. I'll be kicking my heels at Rochester Row until the weekend for The Trooping of the Colour. Then we will be busy and, as Nick puts it, 'doing proper police work' alongside the Met. By the way, Nick told me yesterday he's joining the Met. He says he can't face any more witch-hunts.' Jo chuckled.

'Not surprised.'

Jo took a long sideways look at Terry. 'Why?'

'He's gay.'

Jo stopped. 'How did you know?'

'Keep up, Jo! Just by looking at him.' Terry sprinted ahead. 'Way too tidy, and his suits spell hip fashion. You don't see many senior ranks dressed like him.'

Jo caught up with Terry and ran alongside her, cogitating on Terry's hidden depths that kept her on her toes and in love with her. They turned into the barracks. Terry was heading for the gym, along the road which led past the two officers' messes and into the main barracks.

'Is that smoke?' Jo sniffed the air.

'Where're you going?'

'Just want to check something.'

They took the narrow side road that led to the WRAC Officer's mess. At the OC's flat, Jo stopped.

'I definitely smell smoke.' Jo approached the flat's front door and rang the bell three times. She stood back, appraising the situation, then bent down to look through the letterbox. 'Smoke! Stay here, just in case she comes out. I'm going to the guardroom to get the fire brigade.'

Jo sprinted back up the road towards the guardroom.

Terry banged on the front door. 'Major Marwood, Major Marwood.'

With no response, Terry instinctively ran to the bedroom window at the front of the flat and banged on the window. Afraid and frustrated, she returned to the front door. Terry took a few paces back, then sprinted toward the door, launching her body at it. Her slight frame bounced backwards and she fell in a heap. The door was firmly closed. Bruised, she got up, frantic to get the OC out of the flat. She looked at her surroundings before running to the flower bed and finding a decorative rock. Terry returned to the bedroom window, smashing the glass by the lock. She went to open the window, withdrew her hand, took off her PT shirt, wrapped it around her hand, and opened the window. Smoke billowed out. Terry tied the Aertex shirt the best she could around her nose and mouth before poking her head through the open window. She couldn't see any flames. Terry took off her shoe and brushed the glass from the inside sill. After retying her trainer, she hoisted herself onto the windowsill and slid her legs through the opening. The window was waist high, so she could keep her balance when her feet landed on the carpet inside the bedroom.

The smoke was dense but not so bad she couldn't make out a body on the single bed. Wherever the fire was, it was not in the bedroom. Fortunately, the OC had heeded MOD's advice and had shut the bedroom door. Terry opened the second window, praying she wouldn't ignite the fire, but the smoke would leave the room sufficiently so she could see what she was doing.

She turned back to the OC, who had not woken. Concerned that the smoke had overcome Marwood, Terry was anxious to get her out. Frightened by what might be beyond the door, she pulled the OC's slim frame into a fireman's lift and shuffled the three or four paces to the window. Terry dumped the Major's body, so half was hanging out of the window. Leaving her, she scrambled out the second window, turning to pull the OC to safety. The officer's limp body resisted her rescue.

In frustration, Terry started to cry and then swear. Regaining her focus, panting and desperate for help, her sweat creating grey streaks and black smears across her face, she looked about her for something that might aid her. There was nothing. Undaunted, she leaned into the smoke, grabbed the OC by the waistband of her skirt, and tried to hoist her over the window.

'Grab her left arm!'

Terry flinched, surprised at hearing Jo's voice.

'I'll get the right and pull on three,' said Jo, coughing as she breathed in the smoke. 'They've called the fire brigade.'

Together, the two women wrestled the dead weight over the ledge and out of the flat. The three women fell in a heap below the window ledge. Jo and Terry's legs and arms thrashed in the air while their lungs heaved, fighting for oxygen.

Relieved, Terry knew they had to get away from the flat. She tried to yell above the sound of sirens and flames. Her voice crackled with smoke as she coughed and wheezed commands to Jo. The next minute, someone tall and strong turned her body upside down. She saw the ground passing beneath her head at speed before being laid onto a stretcher, and an oxygen mask was thrust over her face. Frantically, she gestured and shouted.

'It's okay, mate,' said the ambulance man. 'We've got them both. They've already gone to hospital.'

He secured the rear doors, and the driver turned on the vehicle's blue lights and sirens and sped to Edgware Hospital.

Two days later, discharged from the hospital, Jo and Terry took a minicab back to the barracks. They were informed at the guardroom to report immediately to the RSM. Jo paid the driver while Terry waited. Each carried an overnight bag prepared by one of their colleagues while they were in hospital.

'Wonder what the RSM wants,' Terry said.

'Dunno. I thought we were supposed to be granted medical leave for a week.'

'Maybe to sign the leave passes?'

'Soon know,' Jo knocked on the RSM's door and responded to the request to enter.

The two women, dressed in jeans and a sweatshirt, stood to attention in front of the RSM's desk.

'Take a seat, ladies. You've earned it.' The RSM smiled and pointed to the two easy chairs in front of her desk.

Jo and Terry sat scrutinising the RSM's face for clues. To their right, Captain Trueman and Sergeant Major Hart leaned against the window ledge. A knock on the door announced the arrival of mugs of hot coffee.

'Hallo Sarn't you're real hero yer know.' Private Dawson left the tray on the RSM's desk. 'If 'ain't bin for you, she would've died. I also got a plate of biccies.' Dawson grinned before nodding in the direction of the OC's office.

'On your way, Private Dawson. Shut the door, please.' The RSM chuckled. 'Help yourselves. Right, before you take your leave, you need to know a few things.' The RSM paused to check that Jo and Terry understood the gravity of what she was about to say. 'First, well done getting the OC out of her flat and away from danger. You were all seconds away from the flat burning down around you. Secondly, and this, shall I say, is more delicate. It seems the OC had one too many and went for a nap, forgetting she had lit a cigarette, which she left in the ashtray on the arm of the sofa in the living room, and that was the cause of the fire. The OC is currently in the King Edward the Seventh Hospital for officers in London receiving treatment for alcohol addiction. Needless to say, we need to keep this quiet.'

Jo raised an eyebrow at Terry. 'Anything else we should know? I mean, why are you all here?'

Hart stood up. 'It seems the OC was the one who sent the anonymous note.'

Terry inhaled noisily. 'What?' she croaked. 'Why?'

'Major Marwood has resigned her commission. She confessed when she heard that Terry had rescued her from the fire. She has been relieved of her command pending treatment for alcohol addiction. Captain Trueman is now the Acting Officer Commanding Twelve Company.' Hart coughed. 'It seems Major Marwood had become desperate because she had failed her fitness test, the lesbian investigation had not gone well, and she knew her chances of attending staff college were fading fast. In an alcoholic moment, she resorted to creating the anonymous note.'

Trueman moved from the window to stand in front of them. 'Ladies, I hope we can be assured of your discretion in this matter. If you sign your leave passes, you are free for a week. Have fun, ladies. Don't do anything I wouldn't.' Trueman winked as she left the RSM's office.

The RSM slid two brown pieces of paper in front of them. Their home address had been completed identically on the forms and was there for all to see.

They quickly scribbled their signatures.

'Lovely. I'll see you next Monday, Terry,' The RSM smiled.

'And I'll see you, Jo, at Rochester Row, to do some proper policing,' Hart opened the door for them.

## Chapter 58

*Friday 18 May, The Clark Family Home.*

Jo and Terry reached 24 Dell Close at lunchtime. They had telephoned ahead to let the family know they would be home for a week on medical leave. Arriving almost simultaneously, parking their cars one behind the other, the two women with holdalls ambled up the cement pathway and entered the kitchen.

'Tea?' Sylvia smoothed down her pinny.

'Love a cuppa,' Jo kissed her mother on her cheek.

'Come here, my girl,' Sylvia pulled Jo into a hug. 'Now you, Terry, love. Your dad's in the shed. He took the day off because he knew his two heroines were coming home. We've been waiting all day. Why did it take so long to get here?'

'Paperwork, Mum,' Jo said.

Terry rolled her eyes and nodded.

The kettle clicked off, and the brown teapot, rarely empty, was filled once again. Linda came through the kitchen door carrying Karl.

'Hello, you two, say hello to your aunties, Karl.' Linda took Karl's hand and helped him wave at Jo and Terry. 'We'll go and tell Dad, Mum.'

'Alright, love. He doesn't have to rush in unless he wants tea.'

'Is the Pope Catholic?' Linda carried Karl to the garden shed.

Moments later, they returned with Brian.

'Hello, girls. Let me look at you. Well, all things considered, it looks like you got away with it.'

'That's an understatement,' Jo said.

'Nasty fire?'

'Not great, Dad. Mostly smoke, though.' Terry's voice crackled with the last vestiges of smoke.

'Aye, better smoke than flames. Officer all right, is she?'

'Yeah, fine, Dad. Still in hospital, though.'

'Smoke?'

Terry and Jo glanced at each other. 'As far as we know. Her being an Officer and all that, they don't tell us much.'

Brian scratched his head. 'Aye. Hope she recovers.'

The Clark family murmured their hopes for Marwood.

'Did you get your suspect, Jo?' Linda asked.

'Yep. She's been discharged.'

'For being gay?'

'Not exactly. Her dad had some agreement that his daughter could buy herself out.'

'Always the same,' Brian said. 'The rich always get away with things that we common people don't.'

Jo and Terry finished their tea.

'Why don't you girls put your stuff upstairs?' Sylvia suggested.

Jo and Terry picked up their bags and trudged up the stairs, followed by the rest of the family.

'Why're you all following us?' Jo turned to look at her family.

The group stood outside the bedroom door.

'Open the door, lass,' Brian urged.

Concerned, Jo cautiously opened the door and peered inside the bedroom before pushing the door open wider. Delighted, Jo turned to her parents. 'Thank you!'

'Oh my God, Jo!' Terry exclaimed. 'No pink!' She smiled at Linda. 'Sorry, Lin.'

'No, sorry needed.'

Excited, Brian babbled. 'It was your mum's idea.'

'And yours, too, Brian. Your father wasn't happy with the space you two had. He kept going in and out of the bedroom, trying to work out how to get you more space. He decided on bunk beds. You know he likes a bunk bed,' Sylvia winked.

'Then Mother suggested a double bed. And that was the solution. Linda, here, she chose the duvet cover and things like that, and your mother chose the paint colour. Do you like the green? I believe it's called Sage.'

'Love it, Dad. Very restful. Just what me and Terry could do with.' Jo patted her father's arm.

'Well, we'll leave you two to unpack. No jumping on the bed now.' Sylvia grinned.

'Mum, we're not seven!'

The family returned to the kitchen. Jo and Terry leapt on the bed and cuddled.

'Let's try it out,' Terry winked.

'Good god, no! They'll all be listening.'

'Be listening tonight, so why not now?'

'Something about your parents listening. And better in the dark. Then I can persuade myself they can't hear.'

Terry giggled. 'Cuddle up.'

Jo rolled into Terry. 'God, Terry, who'd have thought Mum and Dad would've bought us a double bed?'

'The times are changing. Good to be home. Good to be ourselves.' Terry cuddled Jo.

'Yeah. We'll be together, always, no matter what.'

'No matter what.'

THE END

## Glossary of Army Terms and Slang

*Regiments, Corps Acronyms*

WRAC—Women's Royal Army Corps formed in 1949 and disbanded in 1992.

Redcap —Royal Military Police (They wear red berets or caps)

APTC—Army Physical Training Corps

Ranks

*Non-Commissioned Ranks*

Other rank—a term for a non-commissioned soldier of any rank.

Pte—Private, the lowest rank.

LCpl—Lance Corporal,

Cpl—Corporal

Sgt-Sergeant

Sarn't—the way particular corps and regiments pronounce Sergeant

Staff—Staff Sergeant. A rank above Sergeant

WO2—Warrant Officer Class two, can be referred to as Q or Sarn't Major or Miss or Mr

WO1—Warrant officer Class 1 can be called Sarn't Major, RSM, Miss, or Mr.

*Commissioned Ranks*

2LT—Second Lieutenant (pronounced lef tenant)

Lt—Lieutenant

Capt—Captain

Maj —Major

Lt Col—Lieutenant Colonel

Col—Colonel

Brig—Brigadier

*Acronyms/ Slang/ Army Colloquial*

2IC—Second in Command

Beetle Crushers—slang for women's drill shoes.

BFT —Basic Fitness Test, a half mile to be run by women soldiers in 10 mins 45 secs. (Women over 40 had 12 minutes plus to complete it.)

Bull Night— the night when the WRAC clean their barracks rooms.

Bulled—the acting of shining boots or shoes to a mirror-like shine

Coy—Company

CO—Commanding Officer (usually a Lt Col)

Commissioned Officer—An officer who has completed an officers' course

Junior Rank—Private, Lance Corporal or Corporal

Medic—Someone who is a member of the Royal Army Medical Corps or, in the case of the WRAC, a woman soldier trained to be a medic

Monkey—derogatory term for the Royal Military Police

MT—Motor Transport, when the RMTC (Royal Military Transport Corps) works. They manage or drive all vehicles.

NATO Standard—a hot tea or coffee with milk and two spoons of white sugar

NAAFI—Navy, Army and Air Force Institutes. They run clubs for the Junior Ranks and supermarkets in barracks and garrisons

Non-Commissioned Officers—Corporals, Sergeants and Warrant Officers

OC—Officer Commanding usually of a company within a regiment or corps at a specific location

Orderly Room—Where Admin takes place. Sometimes known as the Admin Office.

PCDRE—Postal and Courier Depot, Royal Engineers. The depot was situated behind Inglis Barracks. Two regiments were resident at Inglis Barracks, 12 Coy WRAC and the Royal Engineers. They kept separate accommodations and Senior Ranks and Officer Messes.

POETS Day—Push off early tomorrow's Saturday.

PTI—Physical Training Instructor. Sgt and above are transferred from their original Regiment or Corps to the Army Physical Training Corps. Ranks below Sgt, remain as an AcI or Acting Physical Training Instructor- these are all corporals on completing the course at The Army School Of Physical Training in Aldershot. In 1984, the women, though trained at the Army School of Physical Training did not transfer to the Army Physical Training Corps, instead they remained in the WRAC.

Provost—Royal Military Police

QEMH Woolwich—Queen Elizabeth Military Hospital, based at Woolwich

RSM—Regimental Sergeant Major, usually a position held by a Warrant Office Class 1 See below.

Sapper—Nickname for a member of the Royal Engineers

SIB—Special Investigation Bureau, a branch of The Royal Military Police.

Senior Rank— refers to Sergeants and above, for example, Sergeant, Staff Sergeant and Warrant Officers.

Warrant Officer—WO2 (Class 2), usually a Sergeant Major and WO1 (Class 1),

Woolly-pulley—Barrack dress jumper (sweater for the USA)

If you would like to support this Indie Author please leave a review.

If you would like to know more about this book and the characters go to my website: Jmripley.com

www.ingramcontent.com/pod-product-compliance
Lightning Source LLC
LaVergne TN
LVHW040216110826
845146LV00005B/1308

* 9 7 9 8 9 9 1 6 6 3 8 0 9 *